"They're ships, sir . . . firing their weapons."

"At what? At each other?" Rogeiro said as he jumped up from his chair and raced up the curved starboard ramp to the raised section of the bridge.

"No, not at each other," Uteln said. "I don't see a target, though. They seem to be firing *into* the nebula."

"It's got to be the *Argus* in there," Sisko said. "Can you identify the ships that are firing?"

"Scanning them now," Uteln said. "They all have relatively small profiles. Their hull geometry is—" The tactical officer stopped in midsentence, then glanced up knowingly at the captain. "Their hull geometry is helical."

Sisko understood immediately what that meant. As far as he knew, only one class of starship employed a helix-shaped design. "Tzenkethi harriers."

STAR TREK
DEEP SPACE NINE®

SACRAMENTS OF FIRE

DAVID R. GEORGE III

Based upon *Star Trek*® and
Star Trek: The Next Generation®
created by Gene Roddenberry
and
Star Trek: Deep Space Nine
created by Rick Berman & Michael Piller

POCKET BOOKS
New York   London   Toronto   Sydney   New Delhi   Terev'oqu

Pocket Books
An Imprint of Simon & Schuster, Inc.
1230 Avenue of the Americas
New York, NY 10020

This book is a work of fiction. Any references to historical events, real people, or real places are used fictitiously. Other names, characters, places, and events are products of the author's imagination, and any resemblance to actual events or places or persons, living or dead, is entirely coincidental.

First Pocket Books paperback edition July 2015

POCKET and colophon are registered trademarks of Simon & Schuster, Inc.

For information about special discounts for bulk purchases, please contact Simon & Schuster Special Sales at 1-866-506-1949 or business@simonandschuster.com.

The Simon & Schuster Speakers Bureau can bring authors to your live event. For more information or to book an event, contact the Simon & Schuster Speakers Bureau at 1-866-248-3049 or visit our website at www.simonspeakers.com.

Manufactured in the United States of America

10 9 8 7 6 5 4 3 2 1

ISBN 978-1-4767-5633-2
ISBN 978-1-4767-5634-9 (ebook)

To Paul E. Roman,
a man who lived a quiet life of greatness,
an unparalleled friend and batterymate,
with whom I shared
many priceless and unforgettable moments.
I miss you.

HISTORIAN'S NOTE

The events of the primary story in this novel begin in September 2385, days after the assassination of Federation President Nanietta Bacco (*Star Trek: The Fall—Revelation and Dust*), and they continue into December of that year.

Deep away, in a distant ebon night,
Those who would slip the bounds of their darkness
Gather to consecrate an untried path,
To behold a fiery sacrament.

Seeking Truth, they journey toward the Children,
Carrying paradox along with them:
They thunder as they search for peace of mind,
Extinguishing verity as profane.

They unleash Fire, a penultimate act
That expands limits in one dimension
Just as it collapses in another,
Setting all for the final Ascendance.

—Akorem Laan
Revelation and Dust, "The Path to Ascendance"

Prologue

Ignition

Beneath a panoply of stars, the ritual unfolded, a sacrament defined by scripture and recorded by history, but absent from the universe for fifty millennia. Votiq stood at the center of the caldera, the disc of black volcanic glass extending in all directions until it met the rocky slope that led up to the crater rim. He watched with an amalgam of excitement and trepidation as knots of Archquesters slowly descended toward him, methodically arranging themselves in concentric rings. They all faced Votiq, starlight shining through the thin atmosphere of the desolate world and glistening on their silvery exoskeletons. Their fluted golden eyes reflected the capering flames at the heart of the gathering.

As the leaders of the Ascendants' Orders came together for the first time in uncounted generations, Votiq stepped away from the circle of fire he had ignited. The warmth on his flesh and the acrid scent of burning chemicals both faded with every stride he took. After ten paces, he joined the innermost ring of Archquesters, taking his place amid the eldest of his kind. On the cusp of finishing his fourth full century of life, he occupied the highest station among them, a cynosure by virtue of his having pursued the Quest for the longest time.

Over the prior thousand days, Grand Archquester Votiq had coordinated reports from various Orders that many knights interpreted as omens that they would soon locate the True, the

Unnameable. Questers and Archquesters alike believed that they stood on the brink of the Final Ascension, when they would at last find their gods, who would judge them, and burn them, and unite with the worthy among their ranks. Votiq hungered for those events, prayed daily for them, but the latest cycles of his life had allowed a nascent skepticism to fester within him. He had always lived with the conviction—with the white-hot *certainty*—that he would eventually achieve the objective of every knight to join with the Unnameable. Of late, though, his thoughts had lingered on the legions of Ascendants who had come and gone before him, each of whom had undoubtedly trusted that they would reach the Fortress of the True in their lifetime. Not only had the untold dead of ages past been denied that aspiration, but they had, during their far-reaching search, brought their entire race closer and closer to extinction.

In front of Votiq, the circle of fire at the center of the caldera flared repeatedly, as designed, the flames strengthening as more Archquesters arrived. According to the ancient texts, the Ascendants had not congregated around such a display since they had assembled to deliberate how to contend with the pestilence of the Eav'oq's heresy. That gathering resulted in the extermination of most of the blasphemers, but the unifying effect on the Orders had been transitory. The crusade against the Eav'oq brought an internecine conflict down upon the Ascendants. Knight turned against knight, allowing the remaining Eav'oq to make good their escape, and resulting in the destruction of the Ascendants' homeworld.

The Great Civil War had purified the Orders, purging them of those who would deviate from dogma. Afterward, the surviving Ascendants fled their devastated planet, their hegira turning them into nomads. They escalated their efforts to hunt down the sacrilegious while continuing their search for the True. While some knights traveled in clutches of two or three, and a few others in larger factions, most maintained a solitary existence. Every Quester related their locations, observations, and activities to the leaders of their Orders, who in turn kept the Grand Archquester appropriately informed. The general isolation of individual Ascendants made pairings rare, and as a consequence, their numbers had declined precipitously over time. Votiq did not know for how many more generations his people would endure, but it no longer seemed unthinkable to him that they could perish without ever reaching the Fortress of the True.

Votiq wondered if his people had grown too single-minded. He loathed considering such a possibility, even if turning the idea over only in his own mind. It made him feel . . . unclean. He had lived for so long, and had spent every moment on the Quest, seeking his gods and defending their sanctity along the way. The mere suggestion that he might be misguided—that they *all* might be misguided—troubled him greatly.

And yet, for century upon century, millennium upon millennium, the True had remained out of reach. The Ascendants scoured enormous volumes of space, researched innumerable interpretations of the holy writ, tracked down every potential sign, all to no avail. Votiq always reasoned that each step— and even every *mis*step—the knights took, that every distance they traveled, no matter how small, brought them closer to the Unnameable.

But what if I never reach the Fortress? he thought. *What if we never reach the Fortress? Have all our efforts been in vain?*

The questions chilled Votiq, and he feared the answers. He knew that he could not tolerate such heterodoxy, even in his own thoughts, and so he pushed back against his doubts. He told himself that, even as he yearned to attain the Final Ascension, his individual success did not matter. He reminded himself that his people *would* reach the Fortress because it had been foretold by prophecy. Whether or not he lived to stand with them before the True, whether or not he felt the cleansing flames of the Unnameable as he burned beneath their judgment, he had contributed mightily to the Ascendants' Quest. He had also helped to defend the sacred character of their gods whenever he had encountered the profane—aliens who dared to worship the True, as well as those who deified other beings.

The Dominion provided an example of the latter, with many member species of the interstellar empire according divinity to the shape-shifters who led it, and the Founders themselves venerating a creature they called the Progenitor. In the face of such heresy, Ascendants would execute any heathens they happened upon, seeking assistance from other knights—and even from entire Orders—when necessary. Encompassing considerable territory and comprising an extensive and varied population, the Dominion had long endured despite the numerous offensives the Ascendants had launched against it. Only recently had Aniq—a young knight who had yet to live out her first century—managed to loose a specialized attack that had crippled the Founders and left their empire rudderless.

Votiq knew that, ultimately, the Ascendants would defeat the Dominion entirely, just as it had so many other powers. In recent cycles, knights had eradicated the Reskott, the Andersvint-Notalla, and the Myshog, all of whom idolized their own pantheons of so-called gods. Such heresies did not equate with the desecration of aliens worshipping the True, as the Eav'oq had, but Votiq believed that the Ascendants could not permit such odious cults to stand.

But while all knights adhered to the principle that those who falsely revered the Unnameable must be destroyed, not all agreed in the merit of eliminating those who prayed to counterfeit deities. The variance marked just one point of contention in a mounting discord among the Orders. A growing minority of Ascendants catalogued recent events as signposts on the Path to the Final Ascension: the shifting of a region of the galaxy that had caused a realignment of stars, and the rumored return of the Eav'oq that had followed it; the vanquishing of the Founder "god"; and the discovery of another race who worshipped the True. Those who counted such occurrences as harbingers of the End Time had sought a congregation of Archquesters to clarify—and unify—their collective direction. For longer than they should have, they believed, the Ascendants had spread themselves too widely across space, searching in as many places as they could for auguries of the Unnameable, but mostly doing so individual knight by individual knight. As Votiq understood it, those who imagined the Final Ascension close at hand wished to argue that all of the Orders should come together and continue the Quest as a single united force.

For his part, Votiq opposed such a strategy. Whatever progress the Ascendants had made on their long journey had come from exploring as much territory as they reasonably could, and the Grand Archquester saw no reason to put the pace of future advancements at risk by changing course. Regardless, Votiq recognized that the incompatible interpretations of the alleged signs, as well as the desire to modify the practical details of the Quest, threatened a schism. They could not abide that, any more than they could allow the Eav'oq, if they truly had returned, to go unpunished. The Ascendants must move forward dedicated to one course. All of the Archquesters understood that, and for that reason, had agreed to the historic convocation—even if it led to another civil war and the elimination of one faction.

A two-toned signal rose in Votiq's mind like the memory of music once heard. The proximity alert indicated to him that the last of the Archquesters had arrived. He cast his gaze upward, around the rim of the crater, and confirmed that the drift of knights down into the caldera had ended. The time had come to initiate the process that, at worst, would put an end to the division of thought afflicting the ranks of the Ascendants, and at best, would represent the beginning of the final push to reach the Fortress of the True.

Votiq separated himself from the inner ring of Archquesters and paced toward the fire. His flesh warmed as he neared the circle of flames, and the harsh scent of burning chemicals intensified. The hard soles of his feet clacked along the glassy black surface.

When Votiq reached the fire, he raised his hand and waved it high, a gesture intended to convey to all the knights present the formal commencement of their congregation. It also served to deactivate the metal ring from which the flames emanated.

As the blaze flickered and died, it revealed within it a pyramidal shape. The object, intact and unharmed by the fire that had surrounded it, sat atop a cylindrical base. Its dark triangular faces did not reflect the starlight, but retained a lusterless quality, lending the Ark an impenetrable air.

Votiq lifted his other arm and gave voice to the words he had so often read throughout his life, but that he never believed he would be called upon to recite. "O Unnameable, O True," he cried out, his high-pitched, melodic words pealing out across the crater. "O great and holy gods, we, your devoted and genuine worshippers, beseech you to throw wide the portal of your Fortress and reveal yourselves to us." Votiq paused, expecting to hear the distant echo of his prayer. Instead, only a laden silence greeted him. In that moment, distress washed over him like an awful wave, threatening to drown him in layers of fear. It terrified him to think that the True would not answer his entreaty, and much as he did not want to admit it, it also terrified him to think that they *would*.

Before he lost the courage to continue, he appealed to the gods once more. "We implore you to reveal yourselves, O True, O Unnameable. We plead with you to bestow a sign of yourselves to the Archquesters who serve you, who work tirelessly to protect your purity and sacred nature against heretics and blasphemers, and who journey across aeons and vast distances in search of your Fortress. We beg you to make yourselves known to us here and now, and to sanctify this congregation of your faithful soldiers."

Votiq closed his mouth and waited, his arms still raised toward the star-bedecked night sky. The assemblage of knights seemed fraught with anticipation and anxiety, with hope and dread. The Grand Archquester detected not a single movement within the silent bands of Ascendants ringed about him.

Within the stillness, Votiq brought his palms together above his head, his long, dexterous digits pointing upward in a display of piety and supplication recognizable across many cultures. In his own thoughts, he repeated his prayers, willfully shunting aside the doubts that had come to plague him. Finally, he parted his hands and spread his arms wide.

As though mimicking the movement, two sides of the pyramid separated along their common edge. The Ark blossomed open like a flower, disclosing the blessèd secret held within it. A shape roughly hewn, as though crudely hacked from solid crystal, belled out at the top and bottom from a narrow middle.

Votiq beheld the Eye of Fire, as he always did, with reverence. For him, his elevation to Grand Archquester had endowed him with nothing more special than his curation of the hallowed object. While the Ascendants looked upon the sacred writings as indisputably true and divinely inspired, they embraced the Eye as something even holier: an indirect physical link to the Unnameable.

Ages ago, there had been nine of the mystical artifacts, and they had burned with the radiant glow of the True. Ancient annals chronicled the claims of some knights that they had felt the watchful gaze of the Unnameable through the Eyes, while a brace of venerable tales related how two Questers had once peered in the opposite direction, glimpsing the True and being driven mad by their aspect. More often, the historical accounts recorded instances of contact with an Eye imparting visions to a knight.

But all of that had happened before the Great Civil War left the Ascendants' home planet with irradiated soil, poisoned water, and ash-choked air. The decimation of their world also claimed all the Eyes of Fire but one, and left the last—the Eye of Prophecy and Change—with its inner light extinguished. It had stayed dark ever since.

Votiq dropped his hands and turned away from the Ark and its precious cargo. He faced the empty space he had occupied in the innermost ring of Archquesters. With the fire quenched, the eyes of his comrades took on a contemplative stillness. He peered left and right at the serious and expectant faces. Between the knights, he could see the next circle of those convened, and the next past that.

The Grand Archquester opened his mouth to speak, but then a green glow began to suffuse the exoskeletons of the knights. Votiq watched as astonished expressions bloomed on their faces. He quickly realized that the light emanated from behind him.

Votiq whirled to see a dazzling flash of white light engulf the Ark and the sacred artifact it contained. As he fell to his knees, he had just enough time to register the image of the Eye of Prophecy and Change radiating an intense green before everything in his field of vision vanished in the overwhelming burst of brilliance. He felt a momentary surge of heat as he raised his hands to protect his head, but even as he did so, the light faded, leaving the surroundings to appear as though they had been scrubbed of any color.

Directly before Votiq, somebody reached out and closed the Ark by hand. As the Grand Archquester lowered his arms, she turned to face him. Smaller than an Ascendant, she stood perhaps three-quarters his own height. Raised ridges ran across her bare, gray flesh in different places, almost like patches of scales. They ran in semicircles around her deep-set eyes, framed her forehead and her jaw, and swept prominently down along the sides of her neck to her shoulders. Unprotected by any natural armor, her body looked vulnerable, but her determined countenance imparted a different impression.

Into the silence, a voice intruded from off to one side, from the inner ring of Archquesters. "Who . . . are . . . you?"

Votiq already knew the answer, and it rekindled the passion in his soul. Any doubts he might have indulged melted away like ice beneath the warming rays of a sun. He felt privileged to be present for a moment long prophesied, a marker that heralded the End Time.

An instant later, the alien looked out over the congregation and confirmed it, speaking as though reciting directly from scripture: "I am the Fire."

ILIANA GHEMOR UTTERED the words as though she had been waiting to say them all her life. They did not tumble tentatively from her mouth and drop to the ground unnoticed, but roared out across the black landscape for all those present to hear. The tall, gleaming aliens amassed in circles about her—and one kneeling directly before her—reacted to her pronouncement as though she had physically struck them. They all stared at her, clearly anxious to hear what she would tell them next.

Ghemor let them wait. She felt no fear, and no uncertainty. She did not know what she would say or do in the ensuing moments, but she had complete confidence that she would choose her words and actions correctly. In longer than she could remember, strength coursed through her mind and body—*real* strength, *individual* strength, and not the kind approximated by wealth or technology, by intimidation or force, by the careful planning of strategy or the successful implementation of tactics. Ghemor felt strong in herself.

She gazed down at her body and saw that she had at last been freed from her final prison. Still, to be absolutely sure, she reached one hand to her face and felt the bridge of her nose, up to the curled depression in the center of her forehead, then along her jaw and around her eyes. Her Bajoran features had gone, replaced by those of her Cardassian heritage.

Not replaced by, Ghemor thought. *Restored to.*

For she had been born and raised a proud daughter of Cardassia. In Ghemor's youth, her mother, Kaleen, taught at Central University as a first-tier inquisitor, and her father, Tekeny, served as a legate for Central Command. She grew up in privilege, a wide-eyed and patriotic citizen of the storied Cardassian Union, who saw and experienced the best her people had to offer.

Ghemor had gravitated to the arts, eventually moving to Pra Menkar to continue her studies there. While away at school, a man named Corbin Entek approached her and attempted to recruit her into the Obsidian Order, the Union's elite intelligence agency. Flattered—and perhaps a bit frightened—by the overture, but uninterested in such work, she demurred. But when members of the Resistance killed Ataan Rhukal, her betrothed, during his military tour on Bajor, she reconsidered. Ultimately, she joined the Order, then volunteered for a deep-cover assignment to infiltrate the Bajoran underground. Mind-control experts buried Ghemor's own personal history beneath implanted memories of a life lived as a Bajoran, and surgeons altered her appearance so that she looked precisely like one of the members of the Resistance cell responsible for the death of her beloved. More than just the murder of her intended spouse, the Shakaar cell had perpetrated many other heinous acts of terrorism against the Cardassians, who stayed on Bajor seeking only to elevate the lives of the backward Bajorans. The Resistance had to be stopped, and to that end, Iliana Ghemor became Kira Nerys.

She had become Kira, but she had not been able to take her place—at least, not in the way she had envisioned. Before deploying to her mission, she ended up in the custody of Skrain Dukat, a *gul* in the Cardassian military who functioned as the prefect of Bajor. He secretly imprisoned her, keeping her locked away for more than five thousand days as his personal plaything, beating her and raping her according to his depraved whims.

Five thousand days, Ghemor thought, not without anger. She had been held in sexual slavery for virtually all of her time as an adult, and nearly half of her entire life. *And all because of Kira Nerys.* Had the terrorists not killed Ataan, or had Kira not so closely resembled Ghemor, Iliana would have remained on Cardassia, doubtless living a fulfilling existence as a wife, mother, and artist.

Ghemor raised her head and gazed skyward. A vast array of stars stared coldly back at her. She tried to pick out the pinpoint of light that had long ago burned warmly above the comfortable days of her childhood, but she did not recognize any constellations. She searched in vain for the Long and Lonely Sojourn, for the Flower of Knowledge, for the Bitter Children, but the patterns she could see looked completely unfamiliar to her.

No, not completely *unfamiliar,* she realized. She picked

out an alignment of five stars that Shing-kur had informed her about after their prison break, during their time on Harkoum. Like the lone spark in the wilderness that grows into an all-consuming inferno, the first inkling of a new course of action lit in Ghemor's mind.

In the six hundred days since the end of her captivity in the high-security prison on the Cardassian moon of Letau, she had devised several goals, along with plans to accomplish them. At the end of Cardassia's war with the Federation and its allies, an attack on Letau had left her detention cell damaged. She fled with four other prisoners, including Shing-kur, a Kressari woman who became her staunchest compatriot. Together, they plotted Ghemor's revenge on Kira Nerys—and not just on the Kira Nerys who had denied her a satisfying existence, but on *all* versions of Kira Nerys in *all* universes.

Ghemor had employed mind control to compel a Jem'Hadar soldier to attack Kira, although the subsequent implant of an artificial heart had prevented the Bajoran's death. Ghemor dispatched Kira's counterpart, known as the Intendant, in a parallel universe, before deciding that she would take a page out of Bajoran religious history and fulfill Trakor's First Prophecy, becoming the Emissary of the Prophets in that alternate reality.

Instead, Kira joined forces with Ghemor's own doppelgänger to thwart her efforts, and the three of them had ended up together inside the Bajoran wormhole. They all came face-to-face with the Prophets—or at least with the visages they chose to assume: Ghemor's mother and father; Kira's parents; Ataan, whom Ghemor had loved; Entek, who had brought her into the Obsidian Order and then trained her; Shakaar Edon and Dakahna Vas, two of Kira's coconspirators in her Resistance cell; and the vile, contemptible Dukat. The Prophets declared Ghemor the Fire, and Ghemor demanded of them that they give her back her life.

And the aliens who resided in the wormhole had done just that. They unspooled before her all the moments of her existence, laying bare the brutal, tortuous path she had traveled—

both as Iliana Ghemor and as Kira Nerys—to arrive at that place and time. They showed her all that she had been, all that she had done, all that she had *felt*. In the end, they also allowed her to glimpse the path forward.

Ghemor lowered her head from the endless firmament above and regarded the alien kneeling before her. "I am the Fire," she said again, in quieter—though no less commanding—tones. "Who are you?"

The kneeling alien looked at her with the sort of awe Ghemor had imagined the Bajorans in the alternate universe would when she emerged from the Celestial Temple as their Emissary. "I . . . *we* . . . are the Ascendants," he said, raising his arms wide, plainly to include all those present. He sounded as though he sang rather than spoke. "We here are the Archquesters, the leaders of the knights in our Orders."

The leaders, Ghemor thought, pleased that the few hundred aliens arrayed about her did not constitute their entire force. "Rise," she told the genuflecting Archquester. She watched him do as she'd ordered. At his full height, he towered over her. It looked as though he wore a close-fitting environmental suit, almost like a silvery liquid coating. But because Ghemor saw no helmet or mask, and no obvious place where one could attach, she guessed that the aliens—the *Ascendants*—possessed a naturally occurring armor shell. They also had large golden eyes, with radial striations around their outer edges.

Ghemor stepped forward and peered upward at the Ascendant. "Who are *you*?"

"I am Votiq," he said. "I am the Grand Archquester."

"And why are you here?"

"We have come together to debate events that some see as signs of the End Time," Votiq said. "At least, that is what we thought. It now becomes clear that we are actually here to greet you, as presaged by scripture, and to follow the Fire on the Path to the Final Ascension."

In just the few words he spoke, Votiq revealed his religious zealotry. Ghemor readily heard the emphasis and importance he gave to phrases like *End Time*, *the Fire*, and *Final Ascension*. She also understood that he believed—and perhaps that all the Ascendants there believed—that she had come to lead them. Ghemor believed that, too. The wormhole aliens had declared her the Fire, and then had sent her to a race apparently awaiting the Fire—a race whose leaders stood together with an Orb of the Prophets in their midst. All of that seemed less like the result of chance and more like the mark of a direct connection.

"What is the Final Ascension?" Ghemor asked. Votiq inclined his head slightly to one side—almost like a pet trying to understand the words of its master, Ghemor thought. She knew that she should proceed with caution in seeking out the information she needed. "What do *you* know about the Final Ascension?" she amended, implying her own knowledge on the subject.

"It will occur after we locate the Fortress of the True," Votiq said. "The Ascendants who reach our divine destination will stand before the Unnameable. The gods will judge us, and burn us, and join with those of us they find worthy."

His words veritably dripped with his belief. *The Fortress of the True. The Unnameable.* Ghemor wondered if those terms equated with the Celestial Temple and the Prophets. She didn't know, but the pieces all seemed to fit. She also knew that it didn't matter. The Celestial Temple might be the Fortress of the True, but if not, then it could certainly stand in credibly for it.

Ghemor stepped back from Votiq and reached around for the pyramid-shaped container holding the Orb of the Prophets. She lifted it, hoping it would not weigh too much for her to bear, but it actually felt lighter than she'd expected, as though it held nothing within it. She squatted and set it down on the sleek black ground, then climbed atop the empty plinth.

Ghemor turned in place, looking out at the rings of Ascendants. Even simply standing there, they appeared an impressive force. She couldn't know for sure at that point, but she would find out. She hoped that the Prophets would not have sent her there if not to fulfill her destiny, and having a formidable army of religious crusaders following her might well allow that to happen.

"I have come here from the Fortress of the True," she called out. "I have come to lead you there."

A great trill rose up around Ghemor as many of the Ascendants broke their silence. She watched them closely, searching for any signs of opposition. She saw none. Some Archquesters bowed in her direction and some dropped to their knees, prostrating themselves before her. She knew that they would follow her. At her behest, they would summon the rest of the Ascendants, and once their armada had formed its ranks, Ghemor would lead them not just to the Celestial Temple, but through it, and into the Alpha Quadrant, where she would employ them as the blunt instrument of her vengeance. They would attack Deep Space 9, where she would finally conquer the author of her tragic life. Iliana Ghemor would see the space station in flames, and Kira Nerys along with it.

She threw her fists into the air above her head. *"I am the Fire!"*

I

Smoke

Captain Ro Laren stood in the four-pad transporter room adjoining the Hub, the disc-shaped command complex that crowned Deep Space 9. She stared at the stranger who had just materialized there. Ro's chief engineer, Miles O'Brien, hadn't beamed the man onto DS9, though, but had transported aboard an hourglass-shaped object that glowed green and looked like an Orb of the Prophets. It exited from the wormhole moments earlier, and sensors detected a life-form within it. Once brought aboard, it vanished in a brilliant flash of white light, leaving a Bajoran man standing in its place. "Who are you?" Ro asked.

"My name," the man said, "is Altek Dans."

The name meant nothing to Ro. She glanced to one side, to her security chief, Lieutenant Commander Jefferson Blackmer. He carried a phaser in one hand, a precaution the captain had ordered before allowing the Orb on board. Ro nodded her head toward the room's lone freestanding console, where O'Brien had stationed himself to operate the transporter. Following the captain's unspoken command, Blackmer quickly crossed the compartment. After handing his weapon off to the chief engineer, he took a position beside him and began working a secondary panel on the console.

As she heard the feedback chirps of the security chief's efforts, Ro introduced herself to the stranger, giving her rank and name. She saw no hint of recognition in the man's expression. When he did not respond to her, she scrutinized him. The ridges at the top of his nose identified him as Bajoran, but such characteristics could be faked, and so she would have him examined in Sector General for confirmation. Perhaps a head taller than Ro, he had dark hair, straight and cut short, and dark eyes. A bronze complexion showcased his chiseled features, while several days' growth of beard did nearly as much to hide them. He wore grimy, disheveled clothes—heavy black pants and a black, long-sleeved sweater—and well-worn hiking boots. Dirt covered his hands and smudged his face. More than anything, he looked as though he had lived at least the prior few days outdoors.

"Are you sky?" the man asked abruptly. He spoke Bajoran, but with a peculiar patois that Ro couldn't place. It raised her suspicions, thinking that perhaps he had learned the language offworld.

Offworld, like on Ab-Tzenketh, Ro thought, not without bitterness. Five days earlier, at a ceremony intended to inaugurate the new starbase and to help sow peace in the region, the captain and most of her crew had witnessed the ruthless assassination of Federation President Nanietta Bacco. Initially, a Bajoran national—Enkar Sirsy, chief of staff for the first minister—had been implicated in the monstrous crime, but just the day before, additional evidence had cleared her and pointed instead to Tzenkethi involvement.

"Am I . . . *sky*, did you ask?" The question made no sense, and Ro wondered if she'd correctly understood the oddly accented words.

The man looked away from her and around the transporter room. He wore a mien of confusion, perhaps even of disorientation, and he began to exhibit signs of agitation. When he eventually peered back at the captain, he blurted, "I'm not ice." The avowal seemed as absurd to Ro as his question.

Suddenly, the man started forward, toward the two steps that led down from the front of the raised platform. Ro quickly raised her hand, palm out. "I wouldn't," she said sharply, and the man stopped at once. "We've erected a level-one containment field around the transporter."

"I don't . . . I don't know what that means," the man said.

"It means that there's a force field surrounding the platform you're standing on," Ro said.

The man shook his head as though confused. "Where am I?" he asked. "How did you bring me here?"

Before Ro could reply, Blackmer spoke up from the console. "Captain, I can't find any record, in any of our databases, of an Altek Dans."

"Well, Mister 'Altek'?" Ro said. "Would you care to tell us your real name, as well as where you're from and what you're doing here?" The captain could not help thinking that the wormhole connected to the Gamma Quadrant—home to the Dominion, an interstellar power that had waged a long and brutal war against the Federation and other Alpha Quadrant nations. Occurring so soon after the assassination, and only a day before Deep Space 9's ten thousand civilian residents would begin to arrive, the unexpected appearance of an unknown individual on the starbase gave Ro serious concerns.

"I've told you my name," the man said. "I'm from Joradell, and I have no idea how or why you've brought me here—or even where *here* is."

"Is Joradell a planet in the Gamma Quadrant?" Ro asked. "Is it part of the Dominion?" The investigation into the murder of President Bacco had not uncovered any connection with the Founders, but the captain wouldn't exclude any possibilities, especially regarding present or historic enemies of the Federation.

"Joradell isn't a planet," the man said. "It's an Aleiran city on Bajor."

"I was born and raised on Bajor, and I've never heard of any such city," Ro said. "Why don't you drop the pretense and—"

"Captain!" Blackmer called out, racing back up beside her. Ro saw that he had taken his phaser back from O'Brien. "Automatic sensors didn't issue any alerts, but I performed a manual scan. It revealed that the man is carrying a projectile weapon."

The information distressed Ro. President Bacco had been killed with such a weapon. "Chief," she asked O'Brien, "can you disarm him?"

"Isolating the weapon now," the engineer said, his thick fingers marching across the transporter console.

"Beam it into the bunker," Ro ordered. Officially designated the Explosive Device Containment Chamber, the compartment, located in an outer section at the base of Deep Space 9's main sphere, provided a secure environment into which potentially dangerous objects could be placed. Physically reinforced bulkheads and triply redundant containment fields separated the chamber from the rest of the starbase, and a sophisticated transporter system could automatically redirect the force of any detonations out into the vacuum of space.

"Aye, sir," O'Brien said. As he operated his controls, Ro heard a muffled, high-pitched hum. The man, obviously hearing it too, seemed to concentrate for a few moments on the sound, then quickly reached to the back of his hip—to where, Ro assumed, he carried his weapon. His hand came away empty.

Ro paced forward until she stood just in front of the steps leading up to the transporter platform. On her face, she could feel the tingle of the charged air between her and the unseen containment field. "Mister Altek, or whatever your actual name is, I am placing you under arrest for illegally bringing a weapon onto this starbase. You will be detained pending our investigation and the filing of formal charges against you."

"Starbase?" the man said. "I don't . . . I didn't—"

"Chief," Ro said, "transport our guest to the stockade."

"Aye." In just seconds, strands of white light formed above the platform, joined an instant later by equally bright motes. As they expanded to envelop the man, his face grew panicked. After a moment, he faded from view.

Ro turned to face her security chief. "I want him under constant surveillance."

"I understand, Captain."

The entire incident troubled Ro, but something more specific gnawed at her. "Why didn't the firearm show up on automated scans?" she wanted to know. After a projectile weapon had been employed in the assassination of the Federation president, the captain, in consultation with Blackmer, had decided to order the sensor protocols within the starbase modified to include monitoring for such arms, despite their antiquation and rare usage.

"I need to verify this," the security chief said, "but I believe it's because our visitor's weapon was far more primitive than . . ." He didn't finish his statement, but he didn't need to; Ro understood that he meant to compare the firearm just brought aboard to the one that had ended President Bacco's life.

The captain nodded. "Have your security team conduct an examination of the weapon, and then work with Nog to adjust the internal sensors accordingly." Lieutenant Commander Nog functioned as both DS9's chief of operations and its assistant chief engineer. "I want to know when a weapon of any kind is brought aboard this base."

"Aye, sir."

"In the meantime, execute a deeper search for information about our visitor, and then interrogate him," Ro said. "I want to know who he is, and how and why he traveled out of the wormhole in an Orb."

"So do I," Blackmer agreed, his seriousness of purpose evident in the set of his jaw.

"Chief," Ro said, addressing O'Brien. "Inspect the weapon in the bunker. Let's make sure it's not more than it appears to be. Also, try to determine its point of origin."

O'Brien acknowledged his orders, and Ro headed out of the transporter room, her two officers falling in behind her. She commanded a shining new state-of-the-art starbase, constructed by the Core of Engineers and outfitted by Tactical in such a way as to render it as impregnable as Starfleet technology allowed, and yet Ro felt less secure at that moment than she had on the old station—despite the fact that rogue elements of the Typhon Pact had, just two years previously, reduced the original Deep Space 9 to dust.

COLONEL CENN DESCA, DS9's first officer and its official liaison to the Bajoran government, stood up from his exec's chair as the captain exited the transporter room with Chief O'Brien and Lieutenant Commander Blackmer. He expected Vedek Kira to follow behind them, but the doors closed once the three officers entered the Hub. The two men headed for their dedicated workstations, which perched on the raised, outer level of the control center. All of the Hub's primary consoles faced inward and overlooked the Well, the lower, inner section that housed the situation table. As O'Brien sat down at the primary engineering panel and Blackmer took his position at security, Ro addressed the command crew.

"The Orb did carry a passenger," she announced, "but it wasn't Kira Nerys."

As the captain described what had occurred in the transporter room and spoke about the Bajoran man who had appeared there, Cenn listened, but he also tried to organize his thoughts, which all at once began to spin. Cenn felt as though he'd taken a fist in his gut. The emotion didn't compare to the despair he'd suffered when the Celestial Temple had originally collapsed and trapped Vedek Kira within it, but the moment still struck him like a loss.

If the Prophets chose to send somebody back to Bajor, he asked himself, *why wouldn't They have decided on Nerys?* When the Celestial Temple had gyred back open that day for the first time in two years—rewarding Cenn's faith that it eventually would—he had almost been unable to control his elation. When an Orb of the Prophets then appeared exiting it, and sensors revealed that it contained a life-form within, he knew as surely as he had ever known anything that Kira had returned. While many people believed that she had died inside the wormhole when a starship battle within had caused it to fall in on itself, the Vedek Assembly considered her missing and presumed to be in the hands of the Prophets. Cenn could not have agreed more with the position of the vedeks.

But then where is she? he thought, frustrated. Cenn had served under Kira during her two-plus years as commander of Deep Space 9. After she resigned her commission and left the station to become an acolyte in the Bajoran religion, they stayed in touch with each other. While Cenn traveled to Bajor to visit family and friends as often as his duty permitted, Kira only rarely made trips to DS9, but their bond nevertheless grew during that period. They shared a great deal through their common faith. Cenn had been raised by devout parents who had, early in his life, imparted to him the gift of devotion to the Prophets, and he had never strayed from that piety. Kira had likewise grown up as a faithful adherent of the Bajoran religion, but it had taken her joining the clergy to prompt the friendship between her and Cenn to fully flourish. Over time, they bonded strongly over their many theological discussions, examining their beliefs and posing deep questions to themselves and to each other.

Cenn missed those times, and he missed Nerys. He could tell himself that he wanted her to come back to Bajor for her own sake, but how could her existence improve from walking with the Prophets? No, Cenn had to admit that he hoped for Kira's return out of his own self-interest. That seemed like a poor reason for him to question the ways of the Prophets, and he chastised himself for it.

The captain finished her briefing about the unknown man the Orb had deposited on the starbase. She crossed the width of the Hub's outer ring, to where Lieutenant Ren Kalanent Viss and Ensign Vendora deGrom worked at adjoining consoles. Until recently, deGrom's dockmaster station had been configured at a secondary position on the outer bulkhead of the control center, but because of Deep Space 9's fully operational status, the impending influx of ten thousand new residents, and an expected increase in maintenance and shipping traffic, the sciences panel had been swapped out for it.

"Kalanent, contact Admiral Akaar's office," Ro said to Viss at communications. "I need to speak with him, in real time, as soon as he's available. Report to follow." In the aftermath of the assassination, Starfleet's resources had been reorganized to permit undelayed communication between Deep Space 9, in the Bajoran system, and Starfleet Command, on Earth.

"Right away, Captain," Viss said. Her words always sounded slightly off to Cenn, the heavy translation required of her underwater speech rendered somewhat mechanical by the helmet of her aquatic-environment suit.

As the Alonis woman operated her console, Ro made her way around the Hub, past one of the four sets of turbolift doors that served the control center. When she passed the command and exec's chairs to her left, she said, "You're with me, Desca." Then, back over her shoulder, she added, "John, you're in command." The starbase's primary science officer, Lieutenant Commander John Candlewood, rose from his peripheral station.

Cenn followed the captain into her office. Inside, Ro moved behind her desk, which sat in the center of a long bulkhead to the left. Cenn took one of the two chairs opposite her.

"What's your view of all this, Desca?" Ro asked. A large circular sculpture, composed primarily of curved metal rods, hung on the bulkhead behind her. Cenn had been told that the artist intended the piece as a modern, planar interpretation of Deep Space 9 itself, but he'd never really been able to see it.

"Honestly, I thought the Orb was carrying Vedek Kira," he said. "But we can't always see or understand the paths the Prophets lay out for us."

"That's just it," Ro said, shaking her head slowly. "I'm not convinced this has anything to do with the Prophets."

Cenn felt his brow crease involuntarily, and he forced himself to flatten his expression. "Begging the captain's pardon, but I'm not sure why you think that," he said. "The wormhole just opened up after being gone for two years—two years during which Federation scientists couldn't find any readings at all that it even still existed. And when it finally reappeared today, it expelled an Orb. How can any of that not have to do with the Prophets?"

"I don't know," Ro said. "It's just a feeling I have."

Cenn certainly appreciated the value of intuition, even in the face of contradictory evidence, but the idea that the Prophets hadn't been involved in the renewal of the Celestial Temple, or in the subsequent discharge of the Orb, seemed unlikely in the extreme. "Sir, I know that you're a nonbeliever. Could that possibly be shading your thinking in this case?"

"Oh, Desca," Ro said, pushing herself up from her chair. "I'm not really interested in labels. Why do I need to classify how I think and what I feel?" She paced away from the desk toward the far side of her office.

Cenn had heard such arguments many times before, often from people who had previously professed or even demonstrated their disbelief. He always found it sad, as well as strangely ironic. Such individuals denied the divinity of the Prophets, but they had so little conviction in their own disbelief that they scorned any attempt to brand them as atheists. He would never tell Ro Laren, but he felt genuinely sorry for her. Not only did she deny herself the joy and comfort that would come from putting her faith in the Prophets, but in at least one important way, she lacked faith in herself.

The captain stopped at the outer bulkhead, in front of the rounded rectangular port there, which looked straight out into space, but also provided a view from on high of DS9's sphere and the *x*-ring that circled it at its equator. Ro brought her hands up to her hips and peered outward. She didn't say anything for a moment, and Cenn worried that he had offended her by questioning her thought processes. He considered apologizing, but then, still facing the port, the captain said, "It's not that I'm a nonbeliever, and it's not that I'm a believer." She rounded on her heel and walked back over to Cenn. "I don't dispute that there are beings who reside within the wormhole, or that they have some ability to manipulate it. We know that the Orbs exist and can have effects on people, and it's undeniable that the Prophets have had an influence on, and maybe even have interfered with, Bajoran society."

Cenn bristled internally at Ro's words, but he consciously maintained an even façade. "I would use the word *guide* rather than *interfere*, Captain, but everything you're saying is true," he told her. "To my way of thinking, though, your statements minimize the importance of the Prophets to the Bajoran people."

"I'm sorry, Desca," Ro said, propping herself against the corner of the desk. "I didn't mean to offend you. I don't underestimate the impact that the Prophets have had on Bajor, both directly and indirectly. I just don't know that alien beings who insert themselves, uninvited, into the affairs of another species deserve to be accorded the mantle of divinity."

"Well, first of all, I'd argue that many Bajorans, including me, have not only invited the Prophets into our lives, but would welcome Them even if we hadn't," Cenn said. "And second, I've heard the contention many times about the Prophets being merely an alien race. It's a particularly popular claim among the Starfleet personnel who've been stationed at Bajor and Deep Space Nine since the end of the Occupation." He shrugged. "It doesn't offend me. I just think it's an uninformed opinion, or a shortsighted one. I've not only seen the Orbs, I've experienced them. I've read prophecies that were recorded long ago by scribes who have been dead for centuries, or even millennia, and that have been borne out in my lifetime. I've seen the arrival of the Emissary, and I've witnessed the majesty of the Celestial Temple."

"I know that," Ro said quietly.

"You might try to characterize all of that as simply the actions of advanced alien beings," Cenn said, "but it's not as though the Prophets manufactured the Orbs in an assembly plant, or constructed the wormhole out of thermocrete and duranium, or inspired the penning of prophecies *after* they had already come true. What They've been to the Bajoran people and what They've done—" Cenn held his open hands up, as though encompassing the vast history of the Prophets. "—is absolutely nothing short of divine."

The captain actually managed a smile. "Your passion is compelling."

"I infer that as a compliment."

"I meant it that way," Ro said. "I'm envious of your certainty, and of what your beliefs obviously bring you." She shoved off from the edge of her desk and moved back behind it. "But I haven't made myself clear," she said as she sat back down. "What

I believe or don't believe with regards to the Prophets is immaterial in this case. I'm not saying that They couldn't have reopened the wormhole, or ejected an Orb from it with a passenger aboard. But President Bacco was killed here only five days ago with a projectile weapon, and the first person we arrested for the crime was a Bajoran woman. Now, we have a Bajoran man mysteriously appear on the starbase—a man we can find no record of in any of our databases—and he's carrying a similar type of firearm."

"I don't see the connection," Cenn said. "The evidence Doctor Bashir found yesterday exonerated Enkar Sirsy. We know that it wasn't Bajorans who plotted to kill the president, but Tzenkethi."

"That's the way the situation looks right now, but we're not that sure of our facts," Ro said. "Just because Enkar was cleared and the Tzenkethi implicated, that doesn't eliminate the possibility of Bajoran complicity."

"And you're concerned about a potential link between this Altek Dans and the assassination," Cenn said, more statement than question.

Ro nodded. "Something doesn't feel right about him."

"I trust your instincts about people, Captain," Cenn said, "but are you suggesting that the Prophets sent this man here as part of the plot to murder President Bacco?" He couldn't believe that he needed to ask such a question. As much as he endeavored to remain outwardly calm in matters relating to his faith, he couldn't keep notes of shock and disapprobation from coloring his tone.

"No, no, not at all," Ro said quickly. "But the wormhole doesn't open only into the Alpha Quadrant."

Cenn tried to follow the captain's train of thought. "Are you implying Dominion involvement? That they . . . what? Created a false version of an Orb and found a means of conveying somebody aboard it?"

"If Altek Dans is actually a Founder . . ." Ro's voice trailed off. She remained quiet for a moment, then said, "It doesn't make sense, does it?"

"I don't think so," Cenn agreed. "I mean, it's certainly straightforward enough to determine whether or not Altek Dans is a Changeling, but we've had no trouble from the Dominion since the end of the war. It seems improbable for them to have had a hand in reopening the wormhole and creating a false Orb, all for the purpose of placing one of their people on the new starbase." Something else occurred to Cenn. "Regardless, how could the Founders have played any role in the assassination when, until today, the wormhole had been closed for two years? The Dominion is seventy thousand light-years away, and they don't have slipstream drive, so they couldn't have traveled here."

"You're right," Ro said. "But there's still something about that man that troubles me—something even more than his sudden appearance from the wormhole, or the lack of any information about him, or the firearm he carried. He seems . . . different. Even the words he used, the accent he spoke with, didn't seem quite right."

Cenn recalled another incident related to the Celestial Temple from a dozen or so years earlier, although it hadn't involved an Orb. "Do you know about Akorem Laan?" he asked the captain.

"The name sounds familiar," Ro said. "Was he a famous writer?"

"A poet," Cenn clarified. "Actually, he's considered one of the great classical Bajoran poets. He lived two centuries ago, but one day, he sailed out of the wormhole in his lightship and docked at Deep Space Nine."

"What?" Ro asked. "Why don't I know about this?"

"It happened before either of us served here," Cenn said. He did a quick calculation in his head. "It was thirteen years ago."

The captain looked off to one side, as though gazing into her own past. "Thirteen years ago, I was living on Galion," she said.

Cenn knew that, at that time, the planet Galion had fallen within the Demilitarized Zone established by a treaty between the Federation and the Cardassians. If he recalled correctly, many of the Maquis leadership—and apparently Ro Laren—

had settled there. He also remembered that, during the Dominion War, Jem'Hadar forces had wiped out most of Galion's population. All of which suggested why Ro might not have learned about the lightship that had traveled out of both the wormhole and Bajor's past.

"Akorem's ship had been caught and damaged in an ion storm two hundred years ago, and he'd suffered a serious injury," Cenn explained. "He thought that he would die, but then his vessel fell into the Celestial Temple. The Prophets healed his wounds and returned him to the Bajoran system, but two centuries after he'd been lost."

Cenn saw recognition on the captain's face. "This was the man who thought that *he* was the Emissary, not Captain Sisko," she said.

"That's right," Cenn said. "He believed that the Prophets sent him forward in time not only to function as Their Emissary, but also to reinstitute the *D'jarras*." The Bajoran caste system had been abandoned during the Occupation and never reinstituted. "Captain Sisko stepped aside as Emissary for Akorem, but when Bajor tried to return to the D'jarras—my family was supposed to farm—it quickly became apparent that it wouldn't work. Captain Sisko and Akorem traveled back into the wormhole together. The Prophets confirmed that They had chosen the captain as Their Emissary, and that They'd sent the poet as a means of reassuring the captain of that position."

"What about Akorem?"

"According to Captain Sisko, the Prophets returned him to his own era," Cenn said, "though without any memories of the time he'd spent in the Celestial Temple or in the future."

"Are you saying that the situation with Altek Dans reminds you of what happened with Akorem?" Ro wanted to know.

"It does," Cenn said. "People knew Akorem because of his legacy, and because he lived just two centuries ago. But what if Altek Dans isn't a name out of the history books? Or what if he comes from much further back in the past?" The idea thrilled Cenn. "Depending on when and where he originated, he could provide a trove of information about unknown Bajoran history."

"Perhaps," Ro said. "But we also have to ask why the wormhole aliens would have sent him here."

"It is difficult to know the minds of the Prophets," Cenn said. "I would simply counsel you that it is enough to trust Them."

Cenn could see the difficulty the captain—a nonbeliever, despite her protestations otherwise—would have with such a perspective. "Desca, the Bajoran man carried a weapon similar to the one used to kill President Bacco."

"How similar?"

"Similar enough to get Jeff's attention, and my own," Ro said. "It's a projectile weapon."

Cenn understood why the captain would be slow to accept Altek's possession of such a firearm as a coincidence. Before long, she would be charged with the responsibility for nearly thirteen thousand lives—ten thousand civilian residents and twenty-five hundred crew members. Not only that, but the president of the Federation had been assassinated on a starbase under Captain Ro's command.

"If Altek is from Bajor's past," Cenn said quietly, "then it might make sense that he'd be carrying that type of weapon."

"It might," Ro said, though she sounded less than convinced. "It is imperative that we find out before we have to release him."

"How are you holding him now?" Cenn asked.

"I took him into custody for illegally bringing a weapon onto the starbase," Ro said. "It's the thinnest of pretexts, considering that he didn't actually board Deep Space Nine of his own volition."

"Which means that, since we can't actually charge him with a crime, we can't hold him for more than three days." Federation law prescribed such procedures quite clearly.

"No, we can't," Ro said. "Desca, I want you to coordinate with Jeff on this. He'll interrogate—"

The tones of the ship's comm system interrupted the captain. *"Viss to Captain Ro,"* said the voice of DS9's communications officer.

"Ro here. Go ahead."

"Captain, Admiral Akaar will be available to speak with you in forty minutes," Viss said.

"Very good," Ro acknowledged. "Confirm the meeting and open a comm channel at the appropriate time."

"Yes, Captain."

"Ro out." To Cenn, she said, "Jeff will interrogate the man, as well as oversee a thorough search of all available records to see if we can confirm or establish his true identity. I know you have significant knowledge about Bajor's historical past, so do what you can to help."

"Yes, sir." Understanding that the discussion had come to an end, Cenn stood up from his chair. As he started toward the door, the captain called after him.

"Desca, be broad in interpreting whatever information you find," she said. "If there's even the slightest possibility that this man poses a threat to this starbase or the people on it, I can't let him go."

Commander Gregory Desjardins of the Judge Advocate General's office would have something to say about that, Cenn knew, but he took the captain's point. "I'll do my best," he told her. Then he continued on through the doors and back out into the Hub.

2

Odo wore his quasi-Bajoran guise as he padded purposefully through the dimly lighted corridor, following the Starfleet security officer through the starship's simulated evening environment. The humanoid form he'd first created decades prior, and that he'd honed over time, felt both foreign and familiar to him. Since departing Deep Space 9 nearly ten years earlier and heading for the Dominion, he had spent than half his time in some other shape, or in no shape at all. But he had shifted to his approximate Bajoran appearance on a daily basis for such a long period—during his many years aboard Terok Nor and DS9—that it had eventually become almost effortless for him to assume and maintain.

Too effortless, according to Laas, Odo thought. A fellow member of the Hundred, Laas relished his shape-shifting abilities, rarely holding one form for very long or repeating it too often. He also preferred not to take on humanoid contours unless absolutely necessary. Many of the Founders felt the same way, favoring their base, amorphous state over any other, principally so that they could unite with each other in the Great Link.

The Great Link. Just thinking about the communal nature of his people evoked a complex mix of emotions within Odo. For most of his conscious existence, he had set himself the mission of finding them, and when he finally had, their distrustful, insular attitudes and their violent, controlling ways had been difficult for him to accept. Through the inexpressible joys and wonders of linking with them, of becoming one with them, he came to better understand them, and to yearn almost desperately for the time when he could join them for good.

Even through the Dominion War, Odo's dream of reuniting with his people had endured, despite that he'd chosen to oppose them in the conflict. It satisfied him not only that he assisted in stopping them from completely laying waste to the Alpha Quadrant, but also that he helped to cure them of the terrible disease that threatened to end their existence entirely. For a time, he also harbored the fantasy that he would be able to improve their relationships in the universe beyond themselves, but he didn't realize until too late that such a transformation would have to begin within them.

The Starfleet lieutenant guiding Odo through the starship approached the end of the corridor, where a set of doors parted and slid open before them. Odo entered the turbolift after the officer, who ordered the cab to take them to Deck 9. The lift immediately began to ascend. Without thinking about it, Odo adjusted the fluidic dispersion throughout his body to compensate for the effects of acceleration.

After the end of the Dominion War, it had been wrenching for Odo to leave Kira Nerys, but his choice to return to the Founders had been the only one he could reasonably make. He loved Nerys, but he believed that his people needed him, and he knew without doubt that he needed them. Although he left Deep Space 9 with heavy emotions, he did so in expectation of a fuller life ahead of him.

When Odo had reunited with the Founders, he'd learned a great deal more about them, and also about himself. Even as he basked in the abiding sense of community and the incomparable feeling of completeness that the Great Link provided, he discovered himself wanting more. It seemed gluttonous, hungering for something beyond the fulfillment of his deepest, lifelong wishes, but the existence he had lived among "solids" had helped to define him as much as the truth of his Changeling character. For the Cardassians, for the Bajorans, and for the Federation, he had functioned as an officer of the law, but he had done so in order to serve a greater purpose—justice—and the desire to continue filling that purpose remained within him.

The turbolift eased to a stop, and the lieutenant exited the cab into another corridor. Odo followed along after him. He mused to himself that he didn't require an escort, but he also understood the need for security, especially after the recent tragic events aboard Deep Space 9. Odo had heard a report earlier that day that the Bajoran woman accused of President Bacco's murder had been absolved, and so he wondered who, if anybody, would face justice for the crime.

Back in the Dominion, Odo's ideas of justice had extended to the everyday lives of its citizens. Under the rule of the Founders, the empire's constituent members amounted to little more than slaves. In some cases, as with Rindamil III and Overne III, the Changeling leaders seized worlds and populations to serve the needs of the Dominion. The Rindamil provided food to sustain important members of the empire, such as the Overne, who manufactured starships and weaponry. In other cases, the Founders bred species to satisfy particular needs. They had genetically engineered the Vorta from lesser, ape-like creatures, elevating their abilities so that they could manage many of the day-to-day affairs of the Dominion. That included overseeing the Jem'Hadar, the powerful, determined race that the Founders had made dependent on an enzyme called ketracel-white, and then sharpened to operate as the empire's frontline soldiers. Both species had also been implanted with the compulsion to worship the Changelings as gods.

Even before leaving DS9 and rejoining the Great Link, Odo had observed the narrow, empty lives led by the Vorta and the Jem'Hadar. Still, he had seen potential in them. When an infant Jem'Hadar ended up on the station amid a horde of salvage, Odo essentially tried to raise it, to nurture it, to demonstrate that an individual Jem'Hadar could reach beyond its manipulated genetic blueprint. He failed in the attempt, but years later, when a Vorta clone sought asylum in the Federation because he opposed the Dominion War, Odo felt vindicated in his belief that even members of such programmed species could still achieve more than they had been designed to do.

When he had arrived in the Dominion after the war, Odo had sent a single Jem'Hadar—an elder named Taran'atar aberrantly not dependent on ketracel-white—to act as a cultural observer on Deep Space 9. His intent had been threefold: to sow greater peace and understanding between the Federation and the Dominion, to wean people in the Alpha Quadrant from their distrust and fear of the Jem'Hadar, and to advance Taran'atar's personal development. Odo hoped that witnessing the everyday existence of others, as well as living in a different environment, one in which he was not relegated to the role of expendable soldier, would help him expand his worldview and perhaps even generate within Taran'atar new interests, or even aspirations.

Back in the Dominion, Odo had selected Rotan'talag, another Jem'Hadar free of ketracel-white, one much younger than Taran'atar. He also chose a Vorta, the latest of the Weyoun clones. Odo worked with those two individuals more than any others, attempting to guide them to something more than the protection and management of the empire. By degrees, he tried to expose them to new experiences, to new ways of thinking, to new ways of *feeling.*

And I failed miserably, Odo thought. *I was a fool to think that I could have any real impact on the Jem'Hadar and the Vorta.* Just as the fledgling Jem'Hadar on DS9 all those years before had quickly gravitated to the nature bred into him, so too did Rotan'talag and Weyoun frequently revert to form. At times, Odo thought his influence might be fostering progress, but at others, he perceived some sort of course-correcting mechanism within each of them that did not allow them to stray too far from the original purpose for which the Founders had created them.

But what about Taran'atar? he asked himself, not for the first time. Odo could not deny that something fundamental had changed within the Jem'Hadar. By all accounts, he had endured a great deal during his tenure on Deep Space 9 and in the Alpha Quadrant. According to reports he received from Kira Nerys, Taran'atar struggled with the freedoms granted him, both by Odo and by the crew of the station. He evidently fought a battle within himself, his genetic encoding at odds with the mission Odo had set him. On top of that, a mad Cardassian woman, a failed Obsidian Order operative, managed to brainwash Taran'atar to do her bidding, although he eventually escaped her clutches. He also visited the imprisoned Founder leader, held as a war criminal by the Federation, where she told the Jem'Hadar more about his gods than he could possibly accept.

In the end, the sum total of all those experiences had set Taran'atar on his own path. He violated his fealty to the Founders by defying Odo's orders, absconding from Deep Space 9, but not returning to the Dominion. Instead, he created a new function for himself—a function that, although it made use of his military skills, nevertheless fell outside his genetic programming. He apparently behaved in those last few hundred days as his own being, as somebody who not only controlled his own destiny, but knew that he did.

Because of that, his final act demonstrated just how far he

had come. The report of his death disappointed Odo, but the reason behind Taran'atar's demise, the how and why of it, gave Odo cause for hope. It heartened him, and made him believe that he should continue his work with Rotan'talag and Weyoun.

But Odo hadn't seen either of them for two years, since he'd ended up in the Alpha Quadrant with his route back to the Dominion—the Bajoran wormhole—collapsed behind him. *Except that's not the only way I could have returned to the Gamma Quadrant,* he told himself. The Federation had offered to employ one of Starfleet's new slipstream-equipped starships to deliver him back to the Dominion, a distance of seventy thousand light-years, in a matter of days.

But Odo had demurred. He chose to relinquish, at least temporarily, his responsibilities to Rotan'talag and Weyoun and the rest of the Dominion—including Laas and the few remaining Founders—and stay in the Alpha Quadrant. His decision weighed on him, but it also seemed right.

Focused on his thoughts, Odo almost walked into the security officer when he stopped before a door on the left-hand side of the corridor. The lieutenant reached up and tapped a small signal pad set into the bulkhead. A moment later, the door panels split and glided open to reveal Captain Sisko. Dressed not in his Starfleet uniform but in civilian clothes, he wore dark slacks and a patterned, brightly colored tunic.

"Odo, welcome aboard," he said. Then, to the security officer, "Thank you, Mister Stannis."

The lieutenant acknowledged the order and set himself at attention beside the door. Sisko invited Odo in and stepped aside as the Changeling entered the large cabin. Directly ahead, along the outer bulkhead, stretched a series of tall ports, below which sat a sofa and several overstuffed chairs arrayed around a low table. Single-paneled doors on both sides of the compartment obviously led to sleeping quarters, one for the captain and his wife, and the other for their young daughter. A blank glowpane hung on one of the doors. A desk sat against the inner bulkhead to the right, and a dining table filled the near corner to the left. Odo saw two used place settings on the table. The rich scent of cooking filled the air.

"I hope I'm not intruding," Odo said, gesturing toward the table.

"Not at all," Sisko said. "I was just finishing dinner with Rebecca when you contacted me." The captain did not mention his wife, Kasidy Yates, and Odo didn't ask, but he knew that she had taken on new responsibilities aboard the *Galaxy*-class *Robinson*.

"I did not mean to interrupt."

"And you haven't," Sisko insisted. "As I said, we were just finishing when you asked to see me." He motioned toward the sitting area. "Why don't we have a seat and you can tell me what you wanted to discuss." Sisko sat down on the sofa, and Odo chose one of the chairs. Behind the captain, the imposing main sphere of the new Deep Space 9 filled several of the ports.

"Thank you, Captain. I—"

The sound of a door easing open interrupted Odo, and he looked around to see Sisko's daughter entering through one of the side doors—the one on which hung an empty glowpane. "Hi, Mister Odo," she said, bounding into the compartment, wearing a red jumper over a white blouse. She looked like an amalgam, in miniature, of her parents. Like her mother's, Rebecca's dark hair reached down to her shoulders and framed her face, which featured Yates' slim nose and high cheekbones, and Sisko's rich, dark skin tone and arresting eyes. Though no expert in such matters, Odo thought her small for her age. She had been born on Bajor nine years ago that month, but she probably had yet to reach a hundred and twenty-five centimeters.

"Hello, Rebecca," Odo said.

"I thought I told you that Mister Odo and I needed some privacy to talk," Sisko said, though his words lacked any harshness.

"I know," Rebecca said, coming to a stop beside Odo. "I just wanted to ask a question and then I'll go back to my room." Without waiting for permission from her father, she said, "Mister Odo, what have you turned into lately?"

"Rebecca," the captain snapped. "I think that may be a rude question." During the seven years he had served with Sisko aboard DS9, Odo had made no secret of his desire to maintain his privacy, particularly with respect to his shape-shifting nature. "Mister Odo may not want to discuss such matters."

"Why not?" The girl looked at her father with a confused expression. Then, of Odo, she asked, "You like changing into other things, don't you?"

"It's all right, Captain," Odo said. "Yes, I do enjoy taking on different forms." He actually liked Rebecca. Although he often found it hard to understand the motivations of children, he appreciated their directness. While he had heard similar questions from children during his years on DS9, they typically asked out of a sense of wonder or momentary curiosity. Rebecca seemed different. Her questions carried a weight with them, as though she did not seek the answer simply to one question, but strived to put the knowledge she learned into a broader context. Her intellect seemed advanced for her young age.

"So what have you been lately?" she persisted.

"Over the last few days, while I've been on Deep Space Nine, I have only made myself into this humanoid form," Odo said, putting a splayed hand to his chest.

Rebecca scowled slightly, as though the answer did not satisfy her. "What about before that? What was the last other thing you became?"

Odo thought back. A week earlier, he had been contacted on Bajor by Captain Sisko, who delivered an invitation from the Federation president for a meeting before the new DS9's dedication ceremony. Prior to that, Odo had spent two months traveling alone throughout Alpha Quadrant space, searching for any signs either of the Hundred or of the Founders, just as he had done on a regular basis during the two years since he'd arrived from the Dominion.

The Hundred had been a group of unformed Changelings shipped out into the galaxy by the Founders. For a long time, his people had led Odo to believe that they had sent out the

Hundred for them to learn about the galaxy and then return that knowledge to the Link, but that had been a deception. The Hundred had been dispatched into space, alone and unaware, not to gather knowledge, but to act as living beacons for the Founders' god. They believed that a massive, powerful shape-shifting entity they called the Progenitor had created the entirety of the universe, and then, in the final stages of that creation, had infused an unchanging population of solids with its own essence, thereby creating the Great Link. As far as Odo knew, only seven of the Hundred had ever been accounted for: himself; an unformed one who had been brought to DS9, but who died shortly thereafter, though it had integrated its morphogenic matrix into Odo; Laas; two others located by Laas and brought back to join the Link; the ashy remains of a sixth; and a Changeling who called herself Moon. Sixteen months after his arrival in the Alpha Quadrant, Odo found Moon, who in the first moments of their meeting seemed to him like a kindred spirit. The joy of his discovery did not last, though, for Moon had been mortally wounded by the time he found her; within days, she died.

And even the two who returned with Laas are gone now too, Odo thought. *Not dead, but gone.* The Hundred had been sent out to lure back the Progenitor, and that plan had succeeded. The Founder god returned to a remote region of Dominion space, on the edge of the Omarion Nebula, but Odo soon discovered that the planet-sized shape-shifter had been destroyed by a race of religious zealots called the Ascendants.

The emotional impact on the Founders had been tremendous and swift. Some perished in the aftermath, although Odo never knew if they died as a direct result of the psychological toll of the Progenitor's demise, or by their own hand. The rest of the Great Link fell into terrible despair. Directionless and devoid of hope, they fled, not just from the world on which they made their home, but from each other. In their grief, they sought isolation, and the Great Link dissolved.

Since then, a small number of Founders had come back to the Dominion, but the vast majority remained absent. From a practical standpoint, Odo and Laas became the empire's rulers—although Laas mostly refused to interact with solids, choosing instead to continue searching for other members of the Hundred. Odo did periodically call on him for assistance, though, and Laas almost always acceded to those requests.

But Odo had been gone from the Dominion for two years, and so he didn't know what had become of it. He hoped that whatever progress he'd made with the Vorta and the Jem'Hadar in general, and with Weyoun and Rotan'talag in particular, had continued. Perhaps necessity and the lack of visible gods had at last allowed them to look beyond the concept of worship.

"Odo?" Sisko said, and the Changeling realized that the captain had spoken his name several times.

"I'm sorry," he said. "I was just trying to remember the last nonhumanoid forms I became."

"What were they?" Rebecca asked again, clearly determined to get her question answered.

Odo thought about his last arrival at the Vanadwan Monastery, where he stayed while on Bajor. "I became a Tarkalean hawk," he told Rebecca. "When I came back from my travels in space and descended into the Bajoran atmosphere, I took the form of a Tarkalean hawk."

"A hawk is a big bird," Rebecca said confidently. "And . . . *Tarkalean*? Does that mean it's a bird from the planet . . . Tarkalea?"

"That's right, honey," Sisko said.

"Okay," Rebecca said. "Wait a second." She raced back across the cabin to her door and plucked the glowpane from where it hung. She walked back across the compartment and asked her father how to spell *Tarkalean*. As he told her, she wrote on the glowpane with her finger. When she finished, she looked at Odo. "Okay. What else? You couldn't have been a hawk out in space."

"Rebecca Jae Sisko," the captain said, a measure of sternness entering his voice. "Mister Odo came here to talk to me, not to be interrogated."

"It's all right, Captain, I don't mind," Odo said. Actually, as anxious as he was to speak with Sisko, he did not expect the meeting to end with fruitful results, and so he welcomed the distraction. "You're right, I wasn't a hawk while I was in space. In fact, I didn't become a hawk until I reached the lowest part of Bajor's atmosphere. Before that, I was a parachute."

Rebecca's eyes widened. "You weren't a person or an animal? You were a . . . a *thing*?"

"I took the *form* of a thing, yes," Odo explained. "But even so, I was still myself. I could still think, and I made sure that I could still sense things."

"How do you do that?"

"Rebecca," Sisko chided his daughter.

"Okay, okay," she said quickly. "So what else?"

"Before I became a parachute, I made myself into an atmospheric reentry vehicle," Odo said. "A metal cone with a blunt nose, with wings extended out and bent upward at right angles."

"I'm not sure what that means," Rebecca said. "Or what it looks like."

"Here," Sisko said, rising from the sofa and walking over to his daughter. He took the glowpane from her, tapped at it to bring up a blank screen, and quickly sketched a drawing with his index finger. "Is that about right?" he asked Odo, holding up the image.

"Yes, that's very close."

"And you were made out of metal when you were like this?" Rebecca asked.

"I was."

"Wow." She glanced up at her father, then back to Odo. Very quietly, she asked, "What else?"

"Now, I think that's enough," Sisko said. "I told you that Mister Odo came here to talk to me. Besides, don't you have homework to do?"

"I already did it before Mommy went to her meeting."

"All right," Sisko said. "Then why don't you go into your room and read? I'll be in when we're done."

"Okay," Rebecca said, emphasizing both syllables in the word with nods of her head. "Thank you, Mister Odo."

"You're welcome." Without another word or a look back, Rebecca crossed the compartment and went to her room. Once the door had closed, Sisko sat back down on the sofa.

"Sorry," he said. "She's always been inquisitive like that. Wants to know everything."

"Aren't most children like that?"

"I suppose so," Sisko said. "I mean, Jake certainly asked his share of questions, but it's different with Rebecca. I'm not quite sure how to put it, but it's as though she's looking not just for answers to the questions she asks, but for other information as well. It seems to matter to her how somebody responds to her, and what words they choose, and maybe even what they don't say." He stared into the middle distance for a moment, as though thinking about his daughter's behavior confounded him in some way. Then he shook his head quickly and addressed Odo once more. "Anyway, thank you for indulging Rebecca. Now, what is it you wanted to see me about?"

"The conversation I had with President Bacco." Six days earlier, Odo had accepted the Federation president's invitation to meet with her aboard Deep Space 9. She also asked Sisko to attend, which he did. In that meeting, Bacco reiterated the Federation's open-ended offer to ferry him back to the Dominion aboard one of Starfleet's slipstream-enabled starships. Odo politely declined.

At that point, the president had revealed what seemed her true justification for calling the meeting. She reported that a Starfleet vessel conducting a scientific mission encountered a substance in an asteroid belt that they could not immediately explain. Further examination suggested that the substance might actually be alive, and possibly a shape-shifter. According to the president, its matrix did not exactly match Odo's, but it came close.

"You're here to ask about what the *Nova* crew found," Sisko said.

"Not to ask about it, no," Odo said. "As you know, I accepted President Bacco's offer to inspect the substance, to try to communicate with it, in the event that it turns out to be a life-form."

"Yes, and I'm glad you did," Sisko said. "I have an idea of what you endured when Doctor Mora began examining you, and it's not something I'd want another being to undergo." Decades prior, after finding Odo floating, unformed, in the Denorios Belt, the Cardassians had tasked Bajoran scientist Doctor Mora Pol with studying what they dubbed an "unknown sample." For Odo, the experience had not been a pleasant one.

"Which is one of the reasons I accepted the offer," he said. "But I also understood that President Bacco asked me to participate because there are still those in the Federation government who, even ten years after the war, still harbor fear and distrust of the Founders. I was asked to attempt communication at least in part to ensure that the Alpha Quadrant didn't face another threat."

"Perhaps," Sisko said. "I also took the president at her word when she spoke of wanting to avoid inadvertently causing another being unnecessary pain."

"I believed her as well, but it is the scientists I am concerned about," Odo said. "President Bacco told me that a Starfleet vessel would arrive at Deep Space Nine to take me to the facility where the substance is being kept. It's been six days, and that hasn't happened yet."

"It's been six days, yes," Sisko said, "but surely you can appreciate that the Federation is in the middle of a crisis at the moment. Starfleet vessels all over the quadrant have been reassigned or frozen in place as a result of the assassination. The *Robinson* was supposed to depart on an extended exploratory mission, but that's been placed on indefinite hold. I'm afraid it's likely to be days, perhaps even weeks or longer, before a vessel will be made available to transport you to the facility."

"I had assumed as much," Odo said. "But I am concerned about the scientists holding the substance . . . about what they might do if I don't get there soon." Ever the realist, Odo didn't necessarily believe that he would find the substance to be one of the Founders, though he did hold out hope that it might be one of the Hundred.

"According to the president, they're only observing it," Sisko noted.

"For now," Odo said, unable to keep cynicism from seeping into his tone. "But as you just indicated, the Federation is in the middle of a crisis. What happens when one of the scientists decides they can't take a chance that the substance *is* a shape-shifter, maybe even a Founder? What will they do to confirm its nature? And if it does turn out to be a shape-shifter of any kind, how far will they go to make certain that it doesn't become a threat?"

Sisko shook his head. "Odo, I'm painfully aware of the brutality with which a certain segment of the Federation treated the Founders during the war, and I can personally attest to the fears and even the paranoia people felt at the time. But the Dominion War ended nearly a decade ago. Things are different now."

"Are they?" Odo asked. "We've had peace, but not amity. The Dominion has isolated itself from the Federation and the rest of the Alpha Quadrant. I'm not sure that people here have let go of their fears. I tried, but . . ." He thought of Taran'atar, but the mission Odo had sent him on, as essentially a cultural envoy, had not proceeded as he'd hoped.

"The Jem'Hadar?" Sisko asked, obviously understanding what Odo meant.

"Yes," he said. "I really wanted him to find a place on the station. I wanted him to be something other than just a soldier, and I wanted Nerys and everyone else to see that we could all peacefully coexist."

"I know it didn't entirely turn out that way," Sisko said, "but many people consider him a hero for what he did."

"From what I understand, many more consider him a villain," Odo said. "And that's my point: fear can drive judgments, and those judgments can drive actions."

"In my experience, scientists aren't generally like that," Sisko said.

"*People* are like that, Captain."

Sisko lifted a hand, then dropped it to his knee in a sign of resignation. "Some people, yes. But what is it you think I can do for you?"

"I was hoping that you could help me reach the facility."

"Odo, I just told you that the *Robinson* has been ordered to remain at Deep Space Nine."

"Captain, I don't need your ship, or *any* ship, to travel in space," Odo reminded him. "I only need to know where I'm going."

"I'm afraid I don't know where Starfleet is keeping the substance."

"No," Odo said, "but you can find out."

"Odo, it's a *secure* facility," the captain said. "Part of that security comes from the secrecy of its location. Even if I could find out which facility we're talking about, I'm not sure that I could find out where it is, or that I could tell you."

Odo said nothing.

Sisko stood up and paced away. When he turned back to face Odo, he seemed conflicted. "I really wish I could help you," the captain said, "but even if I could, it wouldn't be safe for you to even approach such a facility, much less try to gain entry."

"I can be . . . stealthy."

Sisko folded his arms across his chest and looked away. He stood that way for a few moments, and Odo thought that the captain might help him after all. But then Sisko shook his head. "No," he said. "I'm sorry, Odo, but I can't even consider it—not with your safety at stake."

Odo rose from the chair. He had known Sisko long enough to recognize when he had reached a decision. "It's not *my* safety I'm concerned about, Captain."

"I know that," Sisko told him. "I really believe that everything will be all right—that the scientists won't harm the shapeshifter, if that's what the substance turns out to be."

"I hope that you're right, Captain," Odo said, "but my own experiences tell me something very different." He didn't wait for Sisko to respond, but crossed the cabin and exited into the corridor, where Lieutenant Stannis waited to escort him off the ship.

3

Vedek Kira Nerys existed in a realm she could not character-ize. Time did not seem to elapse—or perhaps it all elapsed at once: past, present, and future blending together the way colors did, into a perfect white. She waited to discover what new path the Prophets had laid out for her. Somehow, she knew that she was leaving the Celestial Temple.

All of a sudden, a flash of white light surrounded her for an instant, then released her. She saw coils of green luminescence twisting around her, and then those too faded. She looked around. She seemed to be on a transporter platform of some sort, in what appeared to be a cargo bay. She didn't recognize—

Kira's gaze came to rest on a figure standing across the compartment from her. She blinked, thinking that she might have mistaken his identity, but when her eyelids rose, he still stood there—he stood there alive, even though he had died years earlier. *But it's him*, Kira thought. Not a double, not a mirror-universe version, not a reanimated corpse, not an illusion or phantasm of any kind. She knew it was him.

"Taran'atar," she said.

The Jem'Hadar stalked toward her, his stare intense. He held an energy weapon in one hand, trained in her direction. He had threatened her before—had threatened her, and more. While in thrall to the crazed Iliana Ghemor—or had it been the Intendant?—he had plunged a pronged weapon deep into Kira's chest. As a result, an artificial heart beat within her.

Taran'atar stopped in front of the transporter platform, his weapon still pointed at her. She said his name again and took a step forward—and suddenly fatigue consumed her. Her knees trembled briefly, then folded beneath her. Kira dropped.

A hand thrust itself toward her, a powerful grip taking hold of Kira's upper arm. Taran'atar steadied her, then eased her down to the platform. "Captain Kira," he said in thick, resonant tones.

Kira lifted her gaze to see a face she had come to know well, with its rough gray-green hide, pronounced features, and the bony structures, almost like teeth, running along the jawline and up the back sides of his head. *You died,* Kira thought. *I watched you die—when? How long ago?*

"Are you hurt?" Taran'atar asked. He holstered his weapon.

"I . . ." She had difficulty finding the energy to speak. Her thoughts swam, and she mentally reached for something, anything, that would orient her. *When did Taran'atar die?* she asked herself again, stubbornly clinging to what she thought of as reality. She had been lost in the wormhole—in the *Celestial Temple*—but he had been lost long before that. *Almost six years,* she calculated. *But then how—?*

Taran'atar released his grasp on her arm and stood up. While he moved to a nearby bulkhead and toggled a switch, she slipped the rest of the way down to the floor. She lay on her side, completely enervated. "Taran'atar to Glessin."

The Cardassian surname sliced through the fog of Kira's thoughts. The idea of a Jem'Hadar working with a Cardassian conjured bloody images of the Dominion War. *A war that ended nearly eight years ago,* Kira thought. *What's happening? Have I imagined my entire life since the war? Is it still going on?*

"This is Glessin," said a disembodied voice that sounded less than intimidating. *"What is it?"*

"We've transported aboard a Bajoran woman," Taran'atar said. "She seems disoriented and may have suffered a head injury."

"Are you in sickbay?" Glessin asked.

"No, we're still in Two Bay."

"All right," Glessin said. *"I'll be right there."*

Kira didn't like the idea of a Cardassian doctor examining her, much less treating her, but then she caught herself. *The Occupation is long over,* she declared in her head. *The Domin-*

ion War is over. When she tried, she could recall everything since then: her taking command of Deep Space 9, the return of the Emissary, Bajor joining the Federation, the Ascendants, the death of Taran'atar, her decision to forsake Starfleet for the clergy. *I remember having an Orb experience, stealing a runabout, and entering the wormhole,* she thought, the images vivid in her mind's eye. *I saw a battle between Captain Sisko's ship—the* Robinson—*and a Romulan warbird.*

No, not the Robinson, Kira thought, combing her memory for details. *It was the* Defiant *vying with the warbird, but the Emissary was still on board.* She vividly remembered directing her purloined runabout onto a collision course with the Romulan starship. She had helped *Defiant* and its crew escape, and then—

Kira closed her eyes and visualized all that she had been through. Within the Celestial Temple, she witnessed the first meeting between Benjamin Sisko and the Prophets, during which it surprised her to hear, more than once, of her gods' concerns that corporeal beings would destroy Them. And then . . . and then . . .

And then Kira had not been Kira. She lived days, weeks, months somewhere—some*when*—in Bajor's past. In the identity of Keev Anora, she worked as part of a movement to free slaves from servitude, and in so doing, to unknowingly help rebuild the Celestial Temple. As Keev, Kira also fell in love with a freedom fighter named Altek Dans.

She opened her eyes, half expecting that she would find herself aboard the runabout she'd stolen—*Rubicon*—or in a bio-bed in *Defiant*'s infirmary. Instead, she saw Taran'atar regarding her, if not with a look of concern, then at least with a posture that suggested his interest in her well-being. *Is this real?* she asked herself. *Is this part of an Orb experience? Are all or some of my memories false?* Kira clearly recalled consulting the Orb of Destiny before appropriating *Rubicon* and heading it into the wormhole. She wondered if everything that followed her opening the ark had been a vision imparted to her by the Prophets, or simply a dream, or even a delusion.

But that doesn't make sense, she realized. By the time she approached the Orb, Taran'atar had been long dead. Kira had no real sense of how long she had spent in the Celestial Temple, but considering the abilities of the Prophets, she recognized that events that seemed to last months to her might easily have taken place in only a day—or even less—in real time.

Regardless, no period of time—no matter how brief, no matter how long—would have allowed for the resurrection of Taran'atar. As she considered that, Kira found that she could not keep her eyes open. Her mind began to drift as sleep— or unconsciousness—began to pull her into its folds. Just before slumber took her, she reached the only conclusion she could: she must have emerged from the Celestial Temple not in the moments immediately after she entered it, or even days, months, or years later, but sometime in the past.

TARAN'ATAR STUDIED KIRA NERYS as she lay on the transporter stage. He had recognized her as soon as the glowing green hyperboloid had vanished, leaving her in its place. At the same time, he thought of Iliana Ghemor, who had employed a subliminal waveform to transfer his innate obedience from the Founders to her. And then there had been Kira's counterpart in the parallel universe, and Ghemor's as well.

But he knew Kira. He had spent enough time with her on Deep Space 9, and then with the others who shared her visage, to know. It required a moment for him to be sure, but when he drew close, he saw it in her expression, in the way that she knew him.

Taran'atar noticed more than her identity, though. Kira did not wear her Starfleet uniform, but civilian attire: a yellow-green vest atop a maroon shirt, and brown pants. Dirt smeared her clothing, her hands, her face. Exhaustion wrapped her like a cloak, and confusion dimmed her normally bright eyes.

He watched her as she lost consciousness, and he wondered what had happened to her. Her presence so deep inside the Gamma Quadrant surprised him, as did her traveling alone, aboard an object that looked like one of the sacred relics of her people. When last he'd seen her, more than two hundred fifty days previously, after he'd been freed from the forced servitude of Iliana Ghemor, Kira had given him the choice of remaining on Deep Space 9 or leaving the station on an old, decommissioned Bajoran scoutship, to go wherever he chose to go, to do whatever he chose to do.

Except that I didn't really have a choice, Taran'atar thought. *Jem'Hadar never do.*

Odo had sent him to the Alpha Quadrant as an observer, and to follow Kira's orders as he would have any of the Founder's. But what sounded like the simplest of commands hid an obvious complexity: Jem'Hadar did not observe, other than in their role as soldiers. In so many ways, he failed in his attempts to do as Odo had bade him, but worse, his weakness allowed Iliana Ghemor to take control of him in the most obscene way, substituting herself for the Founders in Taran'atar's mind.

Taran'atar had served Ghemor well, and in so doing, had betrayed Odo and the rest of the Founders. That he eventually freed himself, and then allowed the Deep Space 9 crew to take him into custody and bring him back to the station, did not matter. His failures did not vanish in the performance of other deeds.

And so the choice Kira had set him had been no choice at all. His actions merited punishment. Kira refused to see that, but the Founders would not.

Taran'atar had boarded the weaponless scoutship and headed it into the Anomaly. Once back in the Gamma Quadrant, he set course for the Dominion, where he anticipated a swift death. His crimes had become legion, from biological breakdowns—his aging body's lack of dependence on ketracel-white had been joined by the occasional need to eat, sleep, and dream—to mental damage—the realignment of his allegiance by Ghemor—to his questioning the sanity of the Founder leader and his attempted murder of Kira Nerys. Not only did he deserve to have his life ended, he welcomed it. The very essence of his being told him that he would rather die as a Jem'Hadar than continue to live as an aberration, and as a failure.

But Taran'atar had never reached the Dominion.

One of the doors to Two Bay swung open with the creak of unlubicrated metal on metal. Allo Glessin, formerly a medic in the Cardassian Guard, served in the same capacity aboard the ship. He crossed the bay quickly, the rap of his heels against the deck echoing in the large, nearly empty space. He carried a medkit with him.

"What's her story?" Glessin asked as he mounted the transporter stage and kneeled beside Kira. Without waiting for a reply, he opened the kit and extracted a scanner and readout tablet. Taran'atar watched him, alert for any indication of the prejudice he had witnessed between the two races, in both directions. He detected none.

"I do not know her 'story,'" Taran'atar said as Glessin began waving the scanner above Kira's body. "She is from the Alpha Quadrant, but I do not know how she came to be here."

"How do you know she's from the Alpha Quadrant?" Glessin asked.

"Because I saw her living there," Taran'atar said, choosing to wait until he spoke with the captain before he said more. "I did not knowingly beam her aboard. Standard sensor sweeps detected an object out in space, ahead of the ship. It radiated energy, but it scanned neither as a vessel nor as a weapon. Captain Dezavrim chose to bring it aboard for closer examination."

As he studied the readout, Glessin said, "It didn't scan as a weapon, but I notice that Dez sent you down here by yourself to retrieve it."

"My function is security," Taran'atar reminded him.

"And you certainly do it well," Glessin said. Though the medic did not smile or change his tone, Taran'atar recognized the comment as arch. He saw no reason to respond to it.

Glessin finished his scans and stood back up. "What is her condition?" Taran'atar asked.

"She's not in bad shape," the medic said. "I can't find any indication of a head injury or any other significant damage to her body. I do read some scrapes and some bruising here and there, but nothing out of the ordinary. She has heavy concentrations of lactate in her muscles, and an increased heart rate, suggesting that she has been physically active recently. She's also suffering from mild dehydration. The status of her neurotransmitters indicates that she is also mentally fatigued. She's fallen into a deep sleep, and that's probably the best thing for her."

"You do not intend to treat her?" Taran'atar asked.

"Oh, we'll move her to sickbay, get her rehydrated, and deal with her minor skin injuries," Glessin said. "There's really nothing more that's indicated, other than to keep her under observation."

"I will notify the captain."

Glessin peered past Taran'atar, over toward the transporter control panel. "You can beam her directly to sickbay."

Taran'atar looked at Kira. "No," he said, even before he knew he would speak. He startled himself by refusing the medic's advice. He did not immediately understand why he had done so, but as he studied Kira's sleeping form, he perceived something about her that he really hadn't during the time he'd known her: vulnerability. Taran'atar had never judged the captain as a match for himself in battle, but the demonstration of her capabilities had still impressed him.

Lying alone and asleep on the transporter platform, with no apparent weapon or even the authority of her Starfleet uniform, Kira appeared utterly defenseless. Taran'atar had abandoned his assignment to Deep Space 9, he'd forsaken Odo's orders to obey the captain, but until she recovered and demonstrated her fitness, he would not leave her side. Instead, he settled onto his haunches, maneuvered one hand beneath Kira's back and the other under her knees.

He stood up with the captain in his arms. "Let's go," he told Glessin. Taran'atar carried Kira all the way to sickbay.

SHE WOKE to an unfamiliar face leaning over her.

"Welcome aboard, Captain," the man said in a deep voice, his tone more self-assured than hospitable. Humanoid, he had a muscular physique, gray skin, and light eyes. Not only did he not look familiar to her, but she didn't think she'd ever seen a member of his species.

Kira felt a strong sense of dislocation. She did not recognize the overhead she saw past the man, and when she glanced quickly around the small compartment, it all looked alien to her. She didn't know where she was or how she'd gotten there.

The man must have seen her confusion, because he said, "I'm Captain Zin Dezavrim. You're in the Gamma Quadrant, aboard the independent courier *Even Odds*."

Still feeling foggy, Kira looked down and saw that she lay on a bio-bed, a thin sheet covering her legs. She pushed herself up and back, propping herself against the pillows at the head of the diagnostic pallet. She opened her mouth to ask how she had gotten aboard the ship when movement past Dezavrim caught her eye. Two other people approached her: a Cardassian man . . . and Taran'atar.

A flood of images gushed through Kira's mind. She saw the Jem'Hadar elder standing at the head of the conference table in the wardroom on DS9, where Starfleet, Klingon, and Romulan officers stared at him with more than a little apprehension. She saw Taran'atar at attention and stationary in Ops, satisfying Odo's orders to act as a cultural observer with as much literalism as might be expected from an individual bred specifically for military action. She saw him shimmering into existence before her, weapon in hand, hurling an uneven blade deep into her chest, destroying her heart. She saw him in a holding cell, steadfastly maintaining his silence rather than defend himself. And she saw him as she had for the last time, just before the fabric of space had been torn apart and she had watched him die.

"We encountered an object in space," Taran'atar said as he and the Cardassian stepped up beside the alien captain. "An energy source too bright to visually identify." Dezavrim looked for a moment at the Jem'Hadar, and Kira thought she spotted annoyance fleeting across the captain's eyes, as though it displeased him that Taran'atar had offered such information. It made her immediately suspicious of Dezavrim, doubly so when he quickly covered his reaction by picking up the thread of the conversation himself.

"It didn't appear dangerous, so we beamed it aboard to examine it," he said.

"It resembled one of your religious artifacts," Taran'atar said. That time, Dezavrim's face did not react, but Kira nevertheless detected tension in his studied stillness.

"An Orb of the Prophets," Kira said. Another rush of memories burst upon her, but not of Taran'atar—of her own life. She pictured herself easing onto her knees in the Inner Sanctuary of the Vanadwan Monastery, opening the ark containing the Orb of Destiny, and letting its lambent form envelop her with its ethereal glow. Near Aljuli, at Bajoran Space Central, stealing a runabout from Chief O'Brien. In the wormhole, joining the battle between *Defiant* and a Romulan warbird. The Emissary meeting the Prophets for the first time.

But other images confused her. A woman known as Kay Eaton, who looked uncannily like Kira, chasing through the paved canyons of a vast, dirty city, calling after a man named Benny. Another woman, Keev Anora, also a double for Kira, reconstructing an underground passage. *Was that me?* she asked herself even as the memories began to fade, like the dissolution of dreams upon waking. *Was any of that real?*

"I have to tell you, we were all surprised to find the artifact carried a passenger," Dezavrim said. It seemed apparent to Kira that he preferred to seek information rather than give it.

"I was in the wormhole," she said. "I think I was trapped there for a period, and then I was propelled from it, obviously by way of an Orb." She remembered the conclusion she'd drawn just before losing consciousness. For the moment, she chose not to reveal her belief that, when she had exited the Celestial Temple, she had traveled backward in time.

Dezavrim nodded his head, but Kira thought it did not signal any sort of understanding so much as an effort to keep her talking. "Do you mean that you didn't exit the Anomaly—the *wormhole*, that is—of your own volition?"

"No, I didn't." Kira saw no reason to protect such information, but she resolved to be careful in speaking with Dezavrim.

"But then who sent you from the wormhole?" he wanted to know.

"The Prophets," Kira said. She knew that she had interacted with the Prophets in some way while she'd been in the Celestial Temple, even if her recollected details of that contact had softened around the edges.

"The Prophets," Taran'atar said with undisguised contempt. "Your 'gods.'"

"Taran'atar, please," said the Cardassian. "There's no need to affront our guest."

For the first time, Kira made eye contact with the Cardassian. At least on a first impression, he appeared free of any artifice. *Unusually so,* she thought, and then reproved herself for it. She had stopped treating all Cardassians as a monolithic population of evil oppressors long ago.

Except I don't really know when long ago *was,* she thought. *If I left the Celestial Temple sometime in the past, maybe the Occupation is still going on.* The idea horrified her.

"I'm Allo Glessin," the Cardassian introduced himself, then leaned in closer to her and whispered, "I'm not one of the bad ones." Kira felt her features redden as she wondered whether her mental generalization of Cardassians had shown. As though in response, Glessin stood back up and said, "I never served on Bajor or in support of the Occupation." Kira took note that he did not use the term *Years of Deliverance,* a euphemism employed by some Cardassians for their brutal military takeover of Bajor. "I also deserted before the war, so it's unlikely that I've killed any of your friends or family members." Kira reflected that she had rarely met a Cardassian whose sense of humor she shared.

"Allo does himself a disservice," Dezavrim said. "He kills people no more than I do." The captain gave Kira no outward reason to disbelieve the simple claim, but she did, and felt quite sure that Dezavrim had blood on his hands.

But then, so do I. Context was critical, and Kira did not

have enough information to accurately judge either Dezavrim or Glessin.

"Not only does Glessin not kill people," the captain continued, "he makes them well. He's the medic aboard ship. He tended to you when you were brought on board."

"How long . . . ?" Kira asked.

"In Bajoran time, you've been asleep for about eleven hours," Glessin said. "You had some minor injuries, abrasions and contusions, as well as minor dehydration, all of which I treated. Mostly, I think you were just suffering from exhaustion."

Kira nodded. "So I've been asleep for eleven hours," she said, "and you've all been standing here, waiting for me to wake up?"

Dezavrim barked out a laugh. "No, Captain," he said. "We may consider you precious cargo, but Allo and I have other responsibilities. We came down when your readings indicated you would soon awaken."

Two details struck Kira. First, although it hadn't fully registered the first time he'd done it, Dezavrim had just called her *Captain* again. While even in the Gamma Quadrant he might have known about her by reputation, Taran'atar had surely identified her for him. But Kira had held the rank of captain for only a relatively short period in her life. It had been only a little more than a year between when she'd transitioned from the rank of colonel—after Bajor had entered the Federation and Starfleet had absorbed a substantial segment of the Militia— until Taran'atar's death. Based on that, she could easily deduce the timeframe in which she found herself.

The second realization that drew Kira's attention was that when she'd asked if they'd all been there, waiting for her to awaken, Dezavrim had replied that he and Glessin had other work to do, but he had failed to account for Taran'atar. She looked directly at the Jem'Hadar. "Were you here?"

"Yes," Taran'atar said. "I have been here since we retrieved you."

"Why?" Kira asked, genuinely curious. While Dezavrim

did not inspire any sort of trust, she didn't feel as though he considered her a prisoner, or a threat to his ship and crew. His description of her as "precious cargo" had not sounded inimical, but reassuring.

"Actually, Captain," Dezavrim said, "we were wondering why you were traveling alone in the Gamma Quadrant, so far from the Anomaly and Deep Space Nine."

"You're familiar with Deep Space Nine," Kira said.

"We're aware of it," Dezavrim said. "Although we travel exclusively in the Gamma Quadrant, we stay apprised of events on the other side of the Anomaly. We also obviously have some crew originally from that part of the galaxy."

Kira nodded, then continued. "I told you all I know: that I was caught in the wormhole and then somehow discharged from it," she said. "Obviously on an Orb, since that's how you found me."

"Are you aware of what happened to the artifact?" Dezavrim asked. The nonchalance with which he posed the question seemed to Kira like a cover for his considered interest.

"I didn't even know I was on an Orb," she said. "I have only your word about that."

"Not mine," Dezavrim said. "Taran'atar's."

"I was alone in Two Bay when I transported the artifact aboard," the Jem'Hadar explained. "It disappeared almost at once and left you behind."

"I can't tell you how that happened because I don't know," Kira said. "But I've witnessed an Orb carrying a passenger. I was aboard Deep Space Nine when an Orb emerged from the wormhole. We beamed it aboard the station, and it deposited one of our officers onto the transporter platform. She'd last been seen entering the wormhole. When she appeared, the Orb vanished. We never saw it again."

"I see," Dezavrim said. "Well, that's good. We were concerned that we'd found an important Bajoran religious icon and then somehow lost it. It's good to hear that's not the case." He injected his voice with relief, but Kira believed she also heard disappointment. She thought that if Dezavrim had gained possession of an Orb of the Prophets, he would've been happy to present it to the Bajoran people—for a price. It reminded her all too well of when Grand Nagus Zek had extorted a fortune from her people in exchange for the Orb of Wisdom. If Dezavrim—

Dezavrim. The name suddenly sounded familiar to Kira. "What did you say the name of your ship is?" she asked.

The captain smiled, and for once, his expression looked genuine. "The *Even Odds*, an independent courier."

"The *Even Odds*. Captain Dezavrim." Kira realized that she knew the captain—or she at least knew *of* him—but the name of the ship resonated. *How could I have missed that?* She quickly scanned her memory and finally succeeded in plucking out the information she sought, in the form of a nickname. "Dez?"

"That's right," he said. "We found Jake Sisko last year."

Last year. That confirmed the deduction she'd made about the timeframe. "You brought Jake to the Idran system, almost all the way back to the wormhole," she said. "And Opaka and Wex, too." Wex had been the assumed identity under which Odo had made his way back, briefly, to the Alpha Quadrant.

"Yes," Dezavrim said. "I hope Jake spoke well of the *Even*'s crew. We enjoyed having him with us. We even invited him to stay."

"So he told me," Kira said. "And yes, he had very good things to say about the people aboard the *Even Odds*." In the rousing story Jake had told her about his experiences in the Gamma Quadrant, she could not mistake the strong bonds he had formed with Dezavrim's crew—and with Dez himself. By the end of his tale, though, Jake exposed his own disillusionment—mild, but real—with the *Even Odds* captain. He didn't speak in detail about that aspect of his adventure, but Kira inferred that the younger Sisko had discovered firsthand that not everybody he would come to love shared his values.

Kira looked down at herself and saw that she still wore the same shirt and vest she had donned that morning. *However long ago that was,* she thought. No matter how much or how little time she'd spent within the Celestial Temple, it did not mitigate the problems in thinking about a morning that had occurred seemingly in her past, but that wouldn't dawn for another six or so years.

Dirt covered her clothes, and for an instant, she envisioned herself lying supine on the ground amid a landscape of lustrous fractures, then, in another environment, bolting frantically through a narrow cave. The images faded before she could concentrate any of her attention on them, but she supposed it served as an explanation—if real—of how her clothing had become so sullied. She noticed the clean skin of her hands and assumed that somebody aboard *Even Odds* had washed her exposed flesh. *Probably Glessin,* she thought, unless he had a nurse or other assistant.

"Would it be possible for you to supply me with something clean to wear, Captain?" Kira asked Dezavrim.

"Please call me Dez," he said. "Some of the crew have already set aside a selection of clothes for you." He motioned to a corner, where a chair held a small stack of folded apparel.

"Thank you."

"I'm guessing you must be hungry," Glessin offered.

Kira hadn't thought at all about food in the few minutes she'd been awake, but as soon as the medic mentioned it, she felt the emptiness of her stomach. "I'm very hungry."

"We'll step out so that you can change your clothes," Dezavrim said. "Once you're ready, we'll escort you to the mess hall."

"Thank you again," Kira said. She pulled the sheet aside and swung herself up to a sitting position on the edge of the bio-bed. "Would it be all right if I took just a few minutes to talk to Taran'atar?" she asked. "We haven't seen each other in a while." She hoped her request wouldn't sound suspicious to Dezavrim. She didn't know how long Taran'atar had been aboard, or how much trust he had gained with the captain, but he seemed like a member of the crew—which astonished her. As much as she and Ro and the others had sought to make him feel comfortable—and even useful—aboard DS9, he'd never fit in. When he had taken that old, decommissioned Bajoran scoutship and departed the station for the last time—before his eventual final return to the Alpha Quadrant—Kira had been sure that he would head directly for the Dominion.

To Dezavrim's credit, he did not hesitate. "Of course, Captain," he said. "We'll see you in the mess hall when you get there." He and Glessin withdrew, the door skimming closed behind them.

Kira waited a moment, then hopped from the bio-bed and regarded Taran'atar. "It's good to see you," she said.

"Why are you here?" he asked without preamble. "Are you pursuing me?"

The accusation startled Kira. "No," she said. "I didn't come here intentionally, and even if I had, I didn't know you were aboard this vessel." She considered telling him that she had traveled back in time, but her years serving under Captain Sisko and her tenure in Starfleet had taught her the importance of the Temporal Prime Directive. She needed to find a way back to her own time as quickly as possible, while ensuring that she did nothing to affect the integrity of the timeline. *Which is convenient for me, since I have no desire to inform Taran'atar just how and when he's going to die.*

"Now that you are aware I'm aboard the *Even Odds*," the Jem'Hadar asked, "what do you intend to do?"

"At the moment, only to change my clothes and enjoy a meal." Kira tried to recall the last conversation she'd had with the Jem'Hadar before he'd left Deep Space 9 for good. "When I gave you the option to remain on the station, or to leave on the scoutship to go wherever you decided to go and do whatever you decided to do, I meant it. I wanted you to have the freedom to choose, and the freedom to live out your life as you saw fit."

Taran'atar looked contemplative, but he said nothing. After a few seconds, Kira crossed in front of him to the corner of the compartment, where she rummaged through the clothing left for her. To her surprise, she found several garments that, while she might have been able to make them fit, would have been more appropriate for wear on Wrigley's Pleasure Planet than aboard a space vessel, even an independent courier. *Except that, according to Jake, the* Even Odds *crew weren't couriers as much as they were fortune hunters—and perhaps, from another perspective, thieves.*

Kira eventually selected a pair of black pants and a dark-green shirt, along with some socks and undergarments. The shirt actually looked a bit big for her, but it bested her other options. She would just have to gather the material and tuck it into the pants.

When she looked back over at Taran'atar, he said, "I did not wish to offend you when I scoffed at the Prophets."

Kira tossed the clothing she'd collected onto the bio-bed. "You didn't offend me," she said. "My faith is internal to me. It can't be bolstered or undermined by the opinions of others." Kira also understood the personal crisis Taran'atar had experienced when he'd visited the Founder leader in prison and she'd announced to him that the Founders were not actually deities.

"I once believed that my own faith could never be shaken," he said. "But I have renounced my 'gods.' I have learned that the universe is knit together by ambition and lies, and that what I accepted as the truth for all of my life is not so. I no longer follow false gods, or *any* gods. I no longer *believe* in gods."

Although she worked hard not to show it, because she knew that he would object, Kira felt sorry for Taran'atar. She had always known that the belief of the Jem'Hadar species in the divinity of the Founders had been genetically encoded, rather than the result of some great truth. She knew some people argued that, because of their role in engineering the Jem'Hadar, the Founders actually could be considered gods to them. Kira did not subscribe to such opinions. Godhood was not relative.

"What *do* you believe in?" Kira finally asked him.

"I believe only in seeking to fulfill my purpose," Taran'atar said. "I am a soldier. It is why I first boarded the *Even Odds*, and it is the reason I stay. Victory is life."

Kira did not point out that Taran'atar's so-called purpose had been intentionally inserted into his genetic structure by a race who did so for their own protection, and who considered him and all his people expendable. Odo had hoped to expand Taran'atar's worldview, and Kira had done all that she could do to ensure his freedom. He *had* made a choice for himself—he hadn't returned to the Dominion—but she didn't know if that equated to him being free.

She did know one thing with certainty, though. Taran'atar avowed, as all Jem'Hadar did, that victory is life. In his case, his final victory would end in the destruction of *Even Odds*, and in his own death.

4

The Hub hummed with activity. *Dalin* Zivan Slaine crewed the tactical station and, for the first time all day, she sat back and took a breath. She glanced around at the crew—Colonel Cenn and Captain Ro in the exec and command chairs, respectively; Ensign Vendora deGrom at the dockmaster's station and Lieutenant Ren Kalanent Viss at communications; and Lieutenant Commander Nog at operations and Chief O'Brien at engineering. She then looked up at the ring of viewscreens hanging at the center of the control complex, above the situation table, and felt relieved to see only a few small vessels, most of them mercifully outbound from Deep Space 9. Long into their second consecutive shift, the command crew continued to coordinate the influx to the starbase of its ten thousand new civilian residents, a process that would continue the next day. Captain Ro had assigned almost all of her senior staff to a double shift in the Hub, saying that she wanted her most experienced officers on duty, both to maintain continuity throughout the arrivals process, and to leave no opportunity for error or vulnerability during a shift change.

Even if the captain hadn't ordered double shifts in the Hub, Slaine knew, it wouldn't have mattered. Simply as a matter of practicality, nearly the *entire* crew had been on duty during the alpha and beta shifts that day in order to make the relocation of the new residents to the starbase proceed as smoothly and painlessly as possible. Though a number of problems had arisen, the crew had handled all of them well, preventing any major issues from developing.

"It's been quite a full day, hasn't it?" said Ventor Bixx, who worked to Slaine's left, at the adjoining security console. The Bolian lieutenant had stood in most of the day for Jefferson Blackmer. As DS9's chief of security, Blackmer typically operated out of the Hub during his shift, but the captain had tasked him with investigating and interrogating the mysterious Bajoran who'd appeared on the starbase the day before via an Orb of the Prophets. The security chief had visited the Hub a number of times throughout the day, both to check in with Bixx, and to provide Ro with a status on Altek Dans.

"It's been such a busy day," Slaine told Bixx, "that I think I might just spend all of gamma shift at Quark's." Slaine—a Cardassian officer whose rank of dalin roughly equated to that of a Starfleet lieutenant commander—had served under Captain Ro for more than two years, first aboard the old station, then at the ground-based Bajoran Space Central, and finally on the new starbase. In that time, she had developed an appreciation for the loquacious barman's various establishments, the latest of which he grandiloquently called his Public House, Café, Gaming Emporium, Holosuite Arcade, and Ferengi Embassy to Bajor.

"Not me," Bixx said at once, his eyes widening. "Until the new residents get accustomed to the place, I think I'll avoid the Plaza as much as possible."

"You're right: it's bound to be overcrowded down there for at least a few weeks," Slaine said.

"The park, too," Bixx noted.

"I guess I'll just have to head for my quarters, prop up my feet, and open a bottle of *kanar*." Bixx wrinkled his bifurcated nose in disgust, which produced the peculiar effect of making it appear as though he had a Federation Standard letter *T* stamped into the center of his blue face. "Have you ever even tried kanar?"

"I have," Bixx said. "It's thick and syrupy and . . . it's just not for me."

Slaine shook her head in disapproval. "Somebody foisted the cheap stuff on you," she said. "You need to try an older vintage. Kanar doesn't even begin to thin out for the first quarter-century, and it takes at least another decade for the subtlety of the flavors to emerge."

"I think I'll stick to *wyscot*."

"Wyscot?" Slaine said, unable to prevent herself from rolling her eyes. She had sampled the Bolian liqueur on a number of occasions, and found it ineffectual. "I get the same experience drinking a glass of wyscot as I would from displaying an image of a glass of wyscot on a padd and then licking the screen."

Before Bixx could offer a riposte, a proximity alert issued a soft tone and displayed an amber light on Slaine's panel. She quickly checked the readout and saw that a vessel had just crossed the outermost sensor net surrounding DS9. Bulky and slow-moving, it possessed the basic characteristics of a freighter. Under normal circumstances, Slaine wouldn't have found that unusual, but with swarms of civilian transports making their way to and from the starbase that day and next, all cargo traffic and non-emergency starship maintenance had been scheduled for when the station had resumed normal operations.

She looked across the Well toward deGrom, whose station sat on the Hub directly opposite her own. "Dockmaster, other than the transports, do we have any ships with an inbound itinerary for tonight?"

"Negative," deGrom replied at once. "We pushed everything back to expedite the ingress of the civilian population." Despite her definitive response, the ensign tapped at her controls. A moment later, she confirmed her initial assessment. "The next ship on the schedule, other than the transports, is an Alastron cargo vessel called the *Renel'tsah*, due in tomorrow at twenty-one-thirty hours."

"Do your scans show an incoming ship?" the captain asked Slaine from the command chair.

"Yes, on our outer perimeter, something that reads like a freighter." Slaine initiated a detailed scan, then searched for its navigational beacon. "The ship identifies itself as an independent merchantman, the *Oxis Dey*."

"Vendora?" Ro asked, looking to the dockmaster.

The ensign worked her panel, then said, "I've got it. The *Oxis Dey* is registered as an independent merchantman. The current timetable has it arriving tomorrow at twenty-two-ten hours. Records show it typically works the Galador Corridor: Klaestron, Farius, Kotaki, Kressari."

"Not this time," Slaine reported. "Its beacon shows it coming from the Rexton Colony, by way of Nivoch." She then stated the obvious, just to be sure that the captain and everybody else in the Hub understood the implication: "That route would have taken them along the edge of the Badlands." The dangerous region of space posed many hazards to navigation and sensors, including numerous gravitational anomalies and frequent, massive plasma storms. Consequently, smugglers and other criminals notoriously utilized it for cover when fleeing authority.

"Not just along the Badlands," said Nog from the operations console. "The course between Rexton and Nivoch would bring the ship close to the Tzenkethi Coalition." At the main engineering station beside Nog, Chief O'Brien nodded his head in agreement.

Ro stood up from the command chair and started around the Hub toward the tactical console. "Give me a detailed scan, Zivan."

"Already under way, Captain." Slaine knew that merchant vessels—particularly those carrying only cargo—made adjustments to their schedules all the time, for any number of legitimate reasons. Though ships more often ran late than early, neither circumstance typically would have been cause for concern. But after what had taken place on the starbase six days earlier, the crew was exercising an overabundance of caution. Anything unexpected necessarily raised suspicions, but when Enkar Sirsy had been cleared of the assassination, Ro had informed her senior staff that the most recent evidence to arise implicated the Tzenkethi. That made *Oxis Dey*'s route to DS9 all the more suspicious.

The captain stopped beside the tactical console as detailed sensor data propagated across its screens. Slaine reported the merchantman's capacity and its actual tonnage. "I'm reading standard midrange warp engines, minimal weapons . . . the shields look like they've been upgraded, but only marginally."

"Nothing unusual?" Ro asked.

"Not so far."

"Keep checking." The captain headed down the steps to Slaine's right, into the Well. She peered up toward the communications console as she crossed past the sit table. "Kalanent, hail the freighter."

"Opening hailing frequencies," Viss replied through the translator in her aquatic-environment suit. "You have a channel, Captain."

"Deep Space Nine to *Oxis Dey*," Ro said. "This is Captain Ro Laren."

A surge of interference rasped through the Hub, but then a male voice spoke clearly. *"Deep Space Nine, this is* Oxis Dey. *I'm Tellion, master of this vessel."* Even through the universal translator, Slaine recognized the man's accent as that of the Rynosh, a nonaligned species known to have dealings with the Tzenkethi.

"Master Tellion, your ship isn't due at our starbase for another twenty-eight hours," Ro said. Slaine noticed that the captain spoke with a level tone, simply stating a fact rather than issuing a challenge. "We've got a lot of traffic right now and only a few free docking bays, so we were wondering why you've arrived so far ahead of schedule."

"We've experienced some good fortune for a change, Captain," Tellion said. *"We managed to get an expedited run through customs at Nivoch, and then we had favorable conditions all along the Badlands, which, I'm sure I don't have to tell you, doesn't happen all that often."*

"No, it doesn't," Ro agreed amiably. "Not even for Starfleet vessels."

As Tellion responded with general sounds of agreement, Slaine detected an unusual disparity in one of the numbers that ran across her panel. She quickly isolated and confirmed it, then searched for similar occurrences in the data. She found two other abnormalities.

"Captain," she said quietly.

"Stand by, Master Tellion," Ro said, still conversational, "while we see if we can find a suitable docking bay for you." She held up an open hand, then closed it into a fist.

"Channel on standby," Viss said.

"What have you got, Zivan?" Ro asked.

"Almost everything about the *Oxis Dey* reads as expected," Slaine said, "but my scans have detected three 'dead' zones on the hull, areas that the sensors can't penetrate."

"Do you have any suspicions?" Ro asked.

"Nothing specific, no," Slaine said. "In fact, there's probably a reasonable explanation, but . . ." She didn't need to finish to make her point. Although Slaine could see the crew every day trying to move on from what had happened, she knew that the ghost of Nanietta Bacco would hang over them for some time.

"Let's see what that explanation might be," Ro said. Then, of the dockmaster, she asked, "Vendora, what do we know about the crew of the *Oxis Dey*?"

"There should be six aboard, including the master, all of them Rynosh," deGrom said. "Tellion is the registered owner and pilot."

"I do read six life signs," Slaine said. "All Rynosh."

Ro nodded. "Open the channel."

"Channel open," Viss said.

"Master Tellion, I'm sorry for the delay," Ro said. "My tactical officer has noticed that there are three areas of your vessel that have been made impenetrable to our sensors. I hope you can understand why that would give me cause for concern."

"I can assure you that there's nothing mysterious about it, Captain," Tellion said. *"We're delivering delicate foodstuffs that*

wouldn't withstand the radiation along the Badlands without the additional shielding."

"Understandable," Ro said. "All right, stand by." She signaled toward the communications console, and Viss once more paused the open channel. "Zivan, what do you think?"

"It sounds like a perfectly sensible explanation," Slaine said. She hesitated, unsure if she should give voice to her nebulous concerns, and then decided to continue. "It also seems convenient. Maybe we should board the ship and inspect it before permitting it to dock."

Ro seemed to consider this, then asked her first officer, "What do you think, Desca?"

"I think we need to protect the people aboard this starbase," he said from the exec's chair. "That means we need to be overly cautious when it's warranted, but Deep Space Nine's going to see a lot of traffic, far more than the old station ever did. We're not going to be able to board and scrutinize every ship and its cargo before they dock here."

"You're right, of course," Ro said, and she sighed heavily. "Well, at least the *Oxis Dey* is early and won't fall behind its schedule if we slow it down a bit," Ro said. "Desca, contact Wheeler and have him take the *Defiant* over. Let's establish for everybody out there that, if they give us any reason for concern, they might have to stare down phaser-cannon emitters and quantum-torpedo launchers."

"Yes, Captain."

"He should be thorough," Ro said, "but unless they give him a reason otherwise, I want him to treat Master Tellion and his crew with the utmost respect." It seemed clear to Slaine that, in the wake of the assassination, the captain wanted to enact strong procedures for protecting the starbase and its residents from potential dangers, but that she was also mindful of keeping DS9 from gaining a reputation as a difficult or unfriendly place.

"Understood," Cenn said, and he worked the panel in front of the exec's chair.

"Kalanent, reopen the channel," Ro said.

"Channel open," Viss said.

"Master Tellion, please accept my regrets," the captain said, "but I'm requesting that you allow an inspection of your vessel before docking." The crew had no legal authority to board ships until they moored at DS9.

Tellion did not immediately reply, and his silence increased the tension Slaine felt. Finally, he said, *"Is that absolutely necessary, Captain? We don't often run ahead of schedule, and I'm keen to take advantage of the extra time we've gained for ourselves."*

"I understand," Ro said, "but in the light of recent circumstances aboard this starbase, I'm going to have to insist. I pledge to you that my crew will proceed as quickly and respectfully as possible." As she spoke, Ro climbed the steps out of the Well to Slaine's right, until she stood once more by the tactical console.

Another few seconds of silence followed, but then the owner and pilot of *Oxis Dey* relented. *"Very well, Captain,"* he said. *"I do urge you to be quick about it."*

"Thank you, Master Tellion," Ro said. "I appreciate your cooperation. Please bring your vessel to a complete stop and hold your position. My second officer, Lieutenant Commander Stinson, will approach you shortly aboard the *Defiant*."

"I just hope that the holosuites at Quark's are as good as I've heard," Tellion said. Considering that the starbase had only transitioned to full operational status six days prior, Slaine wondered what sort of marketing campaign Quark must have launched to reach the Rynosh crew of a freighter that usually worked the Galador Corridor.

"If you can make it past his *dabo* wheels and *dom-jot* tables, I'm sure you'll find them worth a visit," Ro said. "Deep Space Nine out." Viss closed the channel with a touch.

Slaine watched her readouts, then told the captain, "They're decelerating."

"There's probably nothing to this," Ro said.

"No, probably not," Slaine agreed.

Ro shook her head, then spoke quietly, so that only Slaine—

and perhaps Lieutenant Bixx beside her—could hear. "I don't enjoy this feeling of paranoia."

"You're just discharging your duty in a way befitting the situation," Slaine said. She fully understood what the captain felt, because the same emotions roiled within the tactical officer. "I don't think we need to worry," she added. "Deep Space Nine is well secured."

"I know," Ro said. "But that's what I thought a week ago." Without waiting for a response, the captain walked back toward the command chair, leaving Slaine alone to deal with her own doubts.

5

Sisko waited for the image of the Starfleet commander in chief to appear on the companel set into the wall. The advent of procedures and technology that effectively allowed for real-time communications across great distances had proven a boon in times of crisis, but since the terrible events on Deep Space 9, Captain Benjamin Sisko had spoken directly with Admiral Akaar far more often than he had liked. Sisko held no particular animus for the admiral, despite his deserved reputation as a stern and unforgiving taskmaster. In the captain's own dealings with the c-in-c, Akaar had been forceful but fair, demanding but supportive.

At that moment, though, Sisko simply didn't want to hear what he felt certain the admiral would have to say, in one form or another. Prior to the murder of President Bacco, the *Robinson* crew had been scheduled to depart on an extended exploratory mission out beyond the Bajoran system. Afterward, that plan had been temporarily placed on hold. With the subsequent revelation that the Tzenkethi—and, by extension, the Typhon Pact—might have been party to the assassination, Sisko feared that Starfleet's designs to return to the grand days of galactic exploration and the expansion of knowledge would be delayed indefinitely, or even scrapped entirely.

Sisko had just returned to his family's quarters after conducting an inspection that evening of main engineering—he endeavored to make good use of the ship's downtime at DS9— and he hadn't yet changed out of his uniform. The door barely closed behind him when Lieutenant Radickey contacted him from the bridge, informing him of an incoming transmission from Starfleet Command. With Kasidy nestled on the sofa in the living area with a novel and a glass of wine—Rebecca had already gone off to bed—Sisko withdrew to their bedroom.

Sitting at the companel set into the bulkhead, Sisko saw the Starfleet Command emblem wink off the screen, replaced an instant later by the wizened, white-haired, but still vital aspect of Leonard James Akaar. The admiral sat at the desk in his office, on the highest level of Starfleet Headquarters in San Francisco. Sisko could see the Golden Gate Bridge illuminated through the window behind him

"Captain, what is the current status of the Robinson?*"* In Sisko's experience, the admiral seldom troubled himself with pleasantries.

"All systems are operational," Sisko said. "The crew are anxious to begin our explorations." The captain didn't think that Akaar had asked about *Robinson*'s readiness so that Starfleet could send the ship on its way into unexplored space, but he chose for the moment to cling to that hope.

"I'm afraid that the Robinson's *assignment has changed,"* Akaar said, immediately ending Sisko's fantasy. *"You're needed as part of a show of force along the Federation border closest to the Tzenkethi Coalition."*

"Admiral . . ." Sisko began, but then he wondered what possible appeal he could make to compel Akaar to rescind his order. The captain knew that no such argument existed, but he still felt the need to speak his mind. "Admiral, I'm eager for the *Robinson* to begin the mission that's been planned for it, but I have far greater concerns than that about what you're ordering. It could be dangerous to send even one starship toward the Coalition's border, let alone enough of them to constitute a 'show of force.' If the Tzenkethi did conspire to assassinate the president, then armed conflict with them is likely the next step, but if they didn't, a sudden military buildup by the Federation could just as easily precipitate open hostilities. We could end up in a shooting war that has absolutely no justification."

"The evidence strongly suggests that the Tzenkethi were involved," Akaar said, but he delivered the words without much conviction—as though relaying somebody else's opinion, rather than stating his own. That the admiral even deigned to address Sisko's criticism seemed out of character.

"If the Tzenkethi were involved," Sisko said, "there will be plenty of time to engage them in battle, but it's crucial that we don't do anything to trigger a war that doesn't need to be fought." As much as the idea horrified him, the captain understood that the Federation would have to prepare for another confrontation with the Coalition, at least until the Tzenkethi's role in President Bacco's death could be confirmed or refuted. "Starfleet can send matériel to the Helaspont Sector, but keep it away from the border. We have a starbase there that's perfectly capable of monitoring the movements of the Tzenkethi."

"I . . . I don't disagree with you, Captain." It might have been the first time that Sisko had ever seen the admiral hesitate. Akaar leaned back in his chair, as though trying to distance himself from the conversation—or perhaps from the order he'd given. He folded his muscular arms across his chest, his massive Capellan form still powerful even two decades past his hundredth birthday.

"If you don't disagree, Admiral—" Sisko began, but Akaar wouldn't let him finish.

"Whether I disagree or not is immaterial," he said. *"Starfleet is under a great deal of pressure to respond to what's happened."*

"I can appreciate that, sir, but it has to be a measured response," Sisko said. "If the Tzenkethi aren't guilty, then escalating tensions with them until we go to war would not only be wrong, it would distract us from learning who actually perpetrated this horrible crime."

"For many people, Captain, there is no question that the Tzen-

kethi are guilty." The admiral sounded resigned to accepting that there were those who would draw such a conclusion without sufficient justification, and that revealed to Sisko the source of the greatest pressure on Akaar and Starfleet. The possibility of Tzenkethi involvement in the assassination had not yet been released to the public, and so neither the Federation citizenry nor the press could be compelling the admiral to send starships to the Helaspont Sector. If the Federation Council was attempting to strong-arm Akaar, he simply would not allow their judgment in matters of ship deployment to be substituted for that of Starfleet Command, and the same was true of the cabinet. That left only one possibility, only one place that could be leaning on the admiral: the office of the president pro tem, Ishan Anjar.

Although Ishan hailed from Bajor, Sisko had never met the man. The captain had heard rumors about him, though, including that Ishan had maneuvered his predecessor, Krim Aldos, out of his position on the Federation Council so that he could succeed him. If true, then it seemed reasonable to Sisko that such an individual, so invested in the acquisition of power, might want to demonstrate his strength and resolve as soon as he took office—especially if he sought to hold on to his new position beyond sixty days, when a special election would see the next president elected. A display of force against the perpetually belligerent Tzenkethi, and even war with them—regardless of their culpability in the assassination—could go a long way in establishing Ishan's bona fides as a leader.

"Respectfully, Admiral, shouldn't we wait for the investigation to be completed before setting the Federation at the cusp of war?" Sisko asked. The single piece of evidence pointing to the Coalition—Tzenkethi cellular material found on a technological device implanted in Enkar Sirsy—had been processed through the judge advocate general's office on Deep Space 9 and dispatched to a secure Starfleet scientific facility for further examination.

"We should *wait for the investigation to conclude,"* Akaar said, *"but we're not going to."* He tapped at a control on his desk.

"I've just transmitted to the Robinson *a set of coordinates and a navigational plot. Take your ship to the specified destination at once, and begin your patrol route along the far border in the Helaspont Sector. Make reports to Captain French, the commanding officer of Helaspont Station, twice daily, or more often, as circumstances dictate."*

"Yes, sir." Sisko knew he could say nothing more. He expected Akaar to end the transmission, but instead, the admiral looked away from the monitor, as though considering the situation.

At last, Akaar looked back and said, *"Captain, my official orders to you are to patrol a specific section of the Federation border in the Helaspont Sector. I also urge you to proceed as cautiously as possible under the circumstances, and to take no action against any Coalition forces unless absolutely necessary."* He paused again, then leaned in toward the monitor and lowered his voice. *"The evidence presently appears to implicate the Tzenkethi, Captain, but something about that doesn't feel quite right to me."*

Sisko concurred. He had his own dark history with the Tzenkethi, going all the way back to the Federation's last war with the Coalition. Sisko did not trust them any further than he could throw a planet, but their alleged involvement in the assassination depended on their being sloppy, and that did not sound like the Tzenkethi. Sisko believed that, had the Coalition chosen to murder President Bacco and incriminate Enkar Sirsy for the crime, Enkar would still be in jail, awaiting her trial, conviction, and sentencing.

"Sir—" Sisko said, intending to voice his agreement with the admiral and articulate his own thoughts about the Tzenkethi, but Akaar again cut him short.

"Have you anything more to report about the situation at Deep Space Nine, Captain?"

Sisko thought to mention that approximately six of the starbase's ten thousand new residents had arrived that day, but that information fell under the purview of Captain Ro. "No, sir."

"Good," the admiral said. *"You have your orders. Akaar out."*

The Starfleet Command logo appeared briefly, and then the companel screen went blank.

That quickly, the *Robinson* crew's mission profile had transformed from exploration to defense. Although he had anticipated the change, it did not sit well with Sisko. With no choice in the matter, he contacted Captain Ro aboard DS9 to inform her of his ship's imminent departure. He then spoke with the duty officer on the bridge, Lieutenant Scalin Resk, and ordered him to prepare *Robinson* for its journey.

Once he'd completed those tasks, Sisko headed out into the living area. Kasidy still sat on the sofa, her legs tucked beneath her as she read the novel on her personal access display device. She looked comfortable—and more than a little sexy—in a silk lavender chemise. She glanced up with anticipation when he entered, but her expectant expression fell almost at once.

"You're still in your uniform," she said. "I take it that's not a good sign for the rest of our evening."

"Unfortunately not," Sisko said. "I've got to go up to the bridge."

"Is everything all right?" Kasidy asked. She set her padd down beside her wineglass and dropped her feet to the floor. "You don't look pleased."

"I'm not," Sisko admitted. "I have to make an announcement to the crew."

"We're not going on our mission," Kasidy said. She did not sound surprised.

"No," Sisko said. "Instead, we're going to the Helaspont Sector to patrol the border and make a show of force to the Tzenkethi."

"Oh." Kasidy stood up, crossed the room, and put her arms around her husband's waist. "I know you must be disappointed."

"I am," Sisko said, feeling his frustrations rising. "But I'm not *only* disappointed. I'm also angry."

"At who? The Tzenkethi?"

"Maybe, if they did this," Sisko said. "But it's not just that.

It's the entire situation." He backed out of his wife's embrace and paced across their quarters. "I didn't rejoin Starfleet so that I could run patrols and go into battle."

"Actually, Ben, you did."

Sisko whirled back toward his wife. "What?"

"You went back to Starfleet during the Borg crisis," Kasidy reminded him. "You felt you needed to help protect the Federation."

Sisko remembered well his decision to resume starship duty more than five years after he'd previously worn the uniform, and more than four after his return from the Celestial Temple. "Yes, you're right, but I wasn't talking about that," he said. "I meant after the Borg Invasion, when I decided to stay in Starfleet."

"Well, you might not have stayed so that you could go into battle," Kasidy said, "but you didn't do it in order to explore the galaxy either. You were trying to save me and Rebecca from the dangers predicted by Bajoran prophecy."

The calmness with which Kasidy spoke of their ordeal reminded him of how far the two of them had come. Sisko had left her—and Rebecca—in the belief that he would have endangered their lives by staying. Since then, they had traveled a long and difficult road to restore their relationship, a journey for which Kasidy deserved a great deal of the credit. "Yes, you're right about that, too," Sisko said. "But then I took the *Robinson* on that six-month journey into the Gamma Quadrant." He walked back over to his wife and reached up with one hand to her bare upper arm. "That experience changed me," he said. "At least, it changed what I wanted out of my time in Starfleet. Before that, I never had an extended opportunity to blaze new territory, to make first contacts, to discover the unknown. It reinvigorated me." He could hear the passion with which he spoke.

"I know how much it meant to you," Kasidy said, putting her arms on his shoulders.

"It wasn't just what kept me wanting to stay in Starfleet," he told her, "but what allowed me to really envision bringing you and Rebecca along with me."

"How you felt about that experience also helped me to see the three of us living aboard a starship," Kasidy said.

Sisko leaned in and kissed his wife. She had endured so much—largely because of him—and yet she had proven herself strong and resilient and so loving. He considered himself a very fortunate man.

But now all of that's going to be put at risk. For the second time, Sisko stepped away from Kasidy. "That exploratory mission lasted only six months, more than *two years* ago," he said. "Since then, the *Robinson* has been relegated to patrol duty at Bajor. We've been waiting for this mission for so long—the entire crew has—and now it's gone."

"Maybe not gone, Ben. Maybe just postponed." She followed him across the room and put a hand on his back. "But really, your time in Starfleet has been good for us. Yes, you were confined to patrolling the Bajoran system for two years, but that allowed you and Rebecca and me the time we needed to learn to live as a family again, and then to transition to taking up residence on the *Robinson*."

Sisko nodded his agreement, but said nothing. Kasidy took him by the arms and gently turned him to face her. "Ben, I understand that the loss of the exploratory mission is only a small part of what's bothering you," she said quietly. "You're going to order this ship toward Tzenkethi space, and so you're worried about Rebecca and me."

"I know we talked about the dangers of living aboard a starship, but . . . it somehow never felt this real."

Kasidy actually smiled. "It's felt this real for me," she said. "Watching you travel through the wormhole and into the Gamma Quadrant . . . taking *Defiant* into battle again and again during the Dominion War . . . watching you return to Starfleet so that you could take on the Borg. Believe me, it felt *very* real."

"Then why are you smiling?"

"Because, right here, right now, none of that matters," Kasidy said. "What matters is that you and Rebecca and I are together. Look, I have no desire for our family to be in harm's way, but these are the choices we've made, and I don't regret them. We'll see this through together."

Sisko swept Kasidy into his arms and hugged her tightly to him. He loved her so much—so much that he wouldn't remind her that, twenty years prior, he had lived aboard a starship with his first wife and their son, and that, during the battle with the Borg at Wolf 359, he and Jake had lost Jennifer. He couldn't tell her that, and he shouldn't think about it himself.

Instead, he simply said, "I love you, Kasidy."

"I love you, Ben."

They kissed again, softly and slowly, and when they parted, the feel of Kasidy's lips lingered on his. Sisko gazed deeply into her eyes and saw everything he'd ever wanted contained there. He resolved never to waist a moment with his wife.

"Uh, pardon me, Captain, but . . . don't you have a ship to command?" Kasidy said.

"Yes, I guess I do, Admiral Yates." Sisko kissed her once more. "I'll be back as soon as I can."

"I'll be waiting."

Sisko started toward the door. He would go to the bridge, oversee the ship's departure from Deep Space 9, then set it on course for the crew's new assignment. He hoped for the best in the Helaspont Sector, but having had firsthand experience with the Tzenkethi in the past, he feared the worst.

6

Raiq lay back in the narrow main cabin of her blade-like vessel, her arms extended over her head, pushed into the regulator slots. She often dozed while taking her nourishment from the automated system, its pads lightly vibrating against the soft inner elbow joints of her exoskeleton as it delivered nutrients to her body, but she did not sleep that night. Anticipation like none she had ever known kept her awake, and so she made the canopy of her vessel transparent and watched as other ships arrived.

Thus had it been, for days upon days, the Ascendants assembling on the desolate world, and thus would it be, for days yet to come. It had begun with a call to action, a collective plea to the Grand Archquester, Votiq, who had disseminated the request for the leaders of the Orders to gather and deliberate about the signs so many had reported encountering in recent cycles. It had continued when such a congregation had come to pass, and had brought about the unexpected and hallowed appearance of the Fire. It would conclude with a new beginning—with the *last* beginning. Once all of the knights had convened—Questers with Archquesters—the Fire would lead them on the Path to the Final Ascension.

As two more vessels soared past overhead, Raiq sought to maintain her equilibrium. For nearly a century and a quarter, she had spent her life pursuing the goal of every Ascendant, but for each advance she had made on her voyage, for each heretic she had eradicated, the Unnameable had remained out of reach, the Fortress of the True unfound. Such constituted the burden of generation upon generation of Ascendants.

Still, Raiq had never lost faith in her purpose. Cycle upon cycle, she persevered in believing that, while she would die on the Quest, just as she had been born on it, her striving would ultimately assist those who would come after her in reaching the sacrosanct destination. She would be lying to herself if she denied that she sometimes imagined numbering among those who would reach the Fortress and burn beneath the judgment of the True, but she always treated such thoughts as the natural musings of a votary. Impossible though it seemed, the arrival of the Fire, prophesied in the holy texts, promised to make her dreams into a reality.

Another ship appeared above Raiq's, descending toward the surface of the barren world that now hosted more than half of the extant Ascendants. She had never seen a vessel of its design before—a sleek collection of triangular structures that looked menacing—but through the ages, as their population had diminished, her people had come to rely on technology rather than numbers to eliminate those who would blaspheme the True with their false worship. Over the decades, Raiq had augmented her own ship with upgrades to its propulsion, weapons, and other systems.

An auditory pulse tolled in the cabin, signaling the completion of the regulator's operation. Raiq withdrew her arms from the slots. She again considered attempting to sleep, but feeling the way she did, she doubted that rest would come easily.

Raiq inclined her chair and shifted it toward one of the forward consoles. She activated her ship's sensors and scanned the surrounding region. Scores more vessels had landed since the last time she'd checked, and with them, hundreds more Ascendants. Most Questers typically traveled alone, but some had clearly aggregated aboard larger ships, at least for their journey to reach the Fire.

While it would yet take days for the remainder of her people to arrive, the goal for which Raiq had worked her entire life seemed impossibly close at hand. She could not stop thinking about setting out on the Path behind the Fire. The prospect filled her with expectation and eagerness and—

Dread, she realized. While she coveted the opportunity to enter the Fortress of the True, to be looked upon and judged by her gods, and finally to join with them, some part of Raiq feared the end of her lifelong journey. The emotion surprised her, but it also made sense. Did not the replacement of something known for something unknown often cause anxiety?

Except that the unknown did not distress Raiq. She faced it continually on the Quest, and met each new circumstance directly and with fervor. She relished breaching every unfamiliar corner of the galaxy, cataloguing every foreign civilization, cleansing the universe of every strange life-form who would dare to worship the True.

No, Raiq did not fear the unknown. She feared disappointment. Hidden deep beneath the shell of utter confidence and absolute certainty she wore, the prospect that the True could pronounce her unworthy sometimes troubled her. In difficult times, in moments of weakness, the specter of being cast out from the Fortress fell like a shadow upon her soul.

The possibility existed, Raiq knew, though she could not envision living her life any differently than she had. Devout, she read the ancient texts regularly, and rigorously followed their pronouncements. If the facts of her existence displeased the True, she did not know what actions she could have changed.

Opaka Sulan.

The name rose in Raiq's mind like a rebuke. She had met the shaman not that long ago, when Raiq had taken ill, the victim of a minor injury she had suffered through her own misstep. Ignoring the wound when it happened, she visited an alien colony in order to evaluate it. The settlement, a quarter of a million strong, proved wholly secular and in no need of extermination, but a pestilence swept through the populace during Raiq's time there. Too late, after she'd departed, she discovered that their contagion had infected her through her wound. Raiq crashed on another planet, where Opaka Sulan and her wards nursed her back to health.

I should have cut them all down where they stood. But Raiq spared them, allowing the lifedebt she owed Opaka Sulan to mitigate that she venerated false gods she called the Prophets. Because of the circumstances, and because the alien leader and her followers claimed not to worship the True, canon permitted Raiq to let them live.

She had not been as kind to the residents of the colony whose plague had nearly cost Raiq her life. She returned to smite them, only to discover that the disease had already done most of the work for her. Raiq eliminated the few survivors, her vengeance more like a gift to a populace that had already lost almost everything.

But Opaka Sulan . . .

Word had recently gone out among the Archquesters that a new breed of heretics had appeared in the galaxy who openly worshipped the True. In retrospect, Raiq believed that Opaka Sulan had lied to her, that she had concealed her sacrilege, that she actually belonged to that new band of heretics. If so, then Raiq had failed in her responsibilities to the True, and thus could be judged unworthy . . .

After her lifetime of service to the Unnameable, it should not have been possible that she could disappoint her gods. No matter whatever mistakes she had made, Raiq had dedicated her existence to locating the Fortress and extinguishing those who would blaspheme by falsely revering the True. She deserved to burn beneath their gaze and be found worthy.

But then a terrible possibility, unthinkable until that moment, occurred to Raiq: what if her gods disappointed her?

Raiq slammed one hand down on the console before her and thrust her other into the hatch release. She clutched the mechanism, pulled and twisted it, until the canopy rotated upward. The air within her vessel rushed out to mix with the thinner atmosphere surrounding the planet.

Raiq threw herself from her ship, landing hard on the ground beneath. She dropped down to steady herself with one hand and managed to keep her balance. She stood up, slapped the flat of her hand onto the control panel on the hull of her vessel, then watched as the canopy spun closed.

All around, Ascendant ships dotted the flat landscape. Many resembled Raiq's own, with its long, narrow hull and tall cross section, the single-passenger design in use by the knights for generations. Other, newer classes of Ascendant vessels also proliferated, along with some notably older. She also saw a number of alien craft, ships obviously appropriated by various knights for their use on the Quest.

Raiq began to walk, her stride long and steady, though she had no particular destination. She desired only to outdistance her own heterodox thoughts. She weaved through the massed ships, changing direction whenever she saw another Ascendant directly ahead. She wanted neither conversation nor thought, only mindless activity.

Raiq walked for some time, her focus on the path ahead and the sound of her feet marching in the dirt. From time to time, she heard the melodious sound of Ascendant voices, their tones partially sapped by the reedy air. Another vessel passed overhead on its way to land, and then two more. Raiq paid them no attention, but when a fourth appeared in the sky above, the noise of its flight louder than the others, she glanced upward. What she saw banished the troublesome echoes from the corners of her mind.

Like Raiq's own vessel, the ship possessed a knife-edged profile, but it belonged to an older class. It towed another structure behind it, off into the distance. On the ground, Raiq followed. She could not mistake the nature of the haul, and she wished to see it up close.

As the ship started to descend, Raiq broke into a run. She arrived moments after it alit beside the distinctive crimson vessel of the Grand Archquester. Votiq stood alongside the Fire as both studied the new offering for the True.

Behind the ship, the massive torpedo hovered above the ground, borne aloft by antigravs. Twice as long as the vessel towing it, the once-sleek missile had plainly been augmented. Matching the projectile in neither color nor design, two tubular rings circled its cylindrical body, one near the nose cone and one amidships. Between the rings stretched three long conduits. However powerful the original weapon might have been, the modifications to it—the work, Raiq had no doubt, of Ascendant hands—lent it a more fearsome air.

While a young Quester leaped down from the ship, Raiq stepped up beside Votiq and the Fire. The Grand Archquester greeted her, but the woman who would lead them to the Fortress of the True said nothing. That the Ascendants' guide along the Path to the Final Ascension had appeared in the form of an alien did not trouble Raiq. She did not pretend that she could know the minds of the Unnameable—at least not yet. For now, their ways remained mysterious to her.

The Fire, Raiq saw, had been supplied with an Ascendant environmental suit. The glossy black armor, malleable prior to activation, had been fitted to her slender form and wide, reptilian neck. She wore no helmet. When Raiq peered into her eyes, she saw what seemed an infinite depth, and she had to look away.

The young Quester strode directly up to Votiq, who welcomed her by name. "Aniq," the Grand Archquester said, "you bring tribute."

"Tribute," Aniq said, facing the Fire and bowing her head, "and a tool."

"Tell me," said the Fire, her voice strong and commanding.

"I have acquired a powerful explosive device," Aniq said, "which I have modified with transformative fuel."

"For use in annihilating whatever heretics we encounter as we near the Fortress," Votiq said, his tone approving. "A final paean to the Unnameable before we stand beneath their judgment. Well done."

"Thank you, Grand Archquester," Aniq said, "but I see another possible use for this metaweapon: to initiate the Final Conflagration."

Raiq smiled approvingly. It felt to her as if all the pieces spread throughout the holy writ had come together to form a new page—a *last* page—recording the details of what would come next. It had long been a source of debate as to whether the True would commence the Final Conflagration—the prophesied burning of space and time in which worthy Ascendants would join with their gods—or the Ascendants themselves would have to do it. It pleased Raiq to know that, if required, the knights could unleash the flames that would send them on their way to purification.

"Yes," said the Fire. She paced forward, and Aniq had to quickly scramble out of her way. She approached the destructive device and drew her gaze slowly upon it, from nose to tail, eyeing it appreciatively. "Yes," she said again. "This will do nicely."

7

Ro walked along the main deck of the Plaza, along its outer edge. Above her, the curved transparent bulkhead that girded Deep Space 9's sphere at its equator arced from atop the third level and then back to encompass the residential deck below. Night had fallen on the station, and the holographically projected daytime sky had given way to the actual starscape.

From her vantage, Ro could see down past the meandering walking paths in the green grass of the residential deck and out into space, to DS9's horizontal *x*-ring. Both of the Starfleet vessels docked there for the dedication ceremony, and in the days afterward, had finally departed; Captain Dax had taken *Aventine* to enforce a blockade of Andor, while Captain Sisko had directed *Robinson* to the Helaspont Sector in order to forestall a potential Tzenkethi threat. Numerous other ships remained moored along the *x*-ring, mostly transports that had arrived during a second solid day of receiving new civilian residents to the starbase. The independent merchantman *Oxis Dey*, which had briefly caused some concerns when it had arrived early at DS9, had proven nothing more than its master had claimed it to be, and the ship had come and gone without incident.

As Ro made her way around the Plaza, she reveled at the crowds filling it, at the buzz of voices speaking in assorted languages, at the aromas emanating from the various eateries, at the eclectic mix of species represented. Though Bajorans and humans predominated, the captain passed people who were Efrosian, Boslic, Arbazan, Caitian, Benzite, and Frunalian. Among the throngs, she spotted the transparent skull of a big-brained Gallamite, and the bright yellow wings of a shockingly tall Aurelian. For the first time in two years, the Bajoran system had a space station that looked and sounded like the crossroads of the quadrant.

And it's starting to feel like home, Ro thought. Even after everything that had happened, she could not escape the sense that she belonged there. The thought made her smile. It also pleased her to see a number of her crew; they'd worked especially hard over the prior two days, working double shifts as they brought in the civilian population. Coupled with all of the events before that, they certainly deserved some rest and recreation.

While patrons flocked to virtually every establishment on the Plaza, some places appeared even busier than others. Ro doubted she could have squeezed into Starlight Gems & Jewelry, Alidosa's Fine Art, or the Sports & Recreation Reservation Office even if she'd been an Ithenite. Loud, rhythmic music and flashing varicolored lights bathed a packed dance floor at Vestel's Deep Space Night Club, and although the captain couldn't see beyond the entryway of Worlds Apart, the host at the restaurant turned prospective diners away at the door.

Although Ro hadn't eaten at Worlds Apart yet—it had only opened the previous night—she loved the idea of the place: each night, using projections of holographic recordings, the head chef set the restaurant in a different locale, tailoring the menu accordingly. DS9's primary counselor, Phillipa Matthias, had raved about both the culinary offerings and the romantic décor; during her dinner there with her husband, the place had been situated on the edge of a cliff, overlooking the spectacular Borvalo Falls on Bajor. A small, tasteful sign below the name of the restaurant identified the second night's backdrop as Titan. According to Phillipa, the dining room would be on a frozen lake beneath the prominent rings of Saturn—presumably without the usually opaque nitrogen atmosphere and the death-inducing cold.

As Ro continued around the Plaza, she heard a particularly raucous clamor up ahead. When she reached the source, it didn't surprise her to find Quark's brimming with customers. Past the wide entrance in the half wall that separated his establishment from the broad Plaza walkway, every table sat filled, including those Ro could see at the front of the second and third levels. Likewise, people congregated around all of the gaming surfaces: poker, dabo, and dom-jot. Ro also felt sure that, beyond the polished silver bar at the back of the main room, patrons also filled the three levels of holosuites.

Wearing a well-cut jacket with more colors than a spectrum, Quark mixed drinks at the bar. With the skill and confidence that came from long experience, he smoothly moved left and right, pulling bottles and glasses from the shelves with impressive speed. He appeared to be holding conversations with several customers, and Ro knew from personal observation that his Ferengi ears missed nothing.

Ro could not prevent herself from smiling again. She knew

the night's commercial success would delight Quark, and that delighted her. For all his capitalistic zeal, the Ferengi had shown her great kindness and caring in the time they'd known each other—and perhaps never more so than in those first few hours and days after the assassination. Their relationship—closer than a simple friendship, but something short of a long-term commitment—had actually lasted, off and on, for years. Owing to their responsibilities, both professional and personal, they sometimes went lengthy periods when they did not spend time together, but Ro always believed that she could count on him.

After watching Quark for a few moments—*Ferengi Businessman in His Natural Habitat,* she thought—the captain completed her circuit of the Plaza by passing Café Parisienne, Bella's Confections, and the Replimat, all of them just as busy as the other establishments. She then turned coreward and entered one of the four large atria serving the deck. People congregated even there, consulting the interactive holographic directory of the starbase, enjoying the artwork adorning the bulkheads, or just sitting on the benches lining the area.

Checking the chronometer on the directory, Ro saw that she had timed her stroll around the Plaza perfectly. She approached a turbolift, which opened before her, and rode the cab down to the deck below the equator of the starbase, which housed Sector General. The captain did not head for DS9's massive hospital complex, though, but for the offices of the judge advocate general for Bajor Sector. The JAG functioned as an independent legal authority within Starfleet, outside the starbase's chain of command.

Ro entered the outer office of the suite assigned to Commander Gregory Desjardins and his staff. To her surprise, the commander sat at the desk there, a padd in hand, reading. "Oh," Ro said. "I didn't expect to see you out here. I thought I'd be greeted by one of your assistants."

Desjardins tapped his padd as he stood up, and the device's screen went blank. "I try to keep the staff on daytime hours as much as possible," he said. "Since I wouldn't be meeting you until gamma shift, I sent everybody home." He offered the statement with no hint of complaint, but Ro wondered if she should infer one. Although she'd met with Desjardins when he'd opened the JAG office on the starbase fifteen days earlier, and spoken with him via comm a couple of times after that, she didn't really know him. Prior to his arrival, Starfleet had maintained the JAG office for Bajor Sector on Empyrion VI, under different leadership.

"I doubt your staff all headed to their quarters," Ro joked, hoping to take some measure of the commander through his response to humor. "Have you seen how busy it is on the Plaza? Or are officers in the JAG corps not permitted to indulge publicly?"

"We can indulge publicly all we want to," Desjardins said with a grin, "just as long as we do so *legally.*"

Ro chuckled. "Of course."

Desjardins circled around the desk and gestured toward an open corridor across from the main entry. "Why don't we go into my office?" He spoke Federation Standard with an inflection that marked him as a human raised in the Alpha Centauri system. Though significantly taller than Ro, he was not a large man and did not have an imposing presence. His dark hair had begun to gray along the temples, but his unlined face confirmed his mid-forties age.

Ro followed Desjardins down the corridor, which curved slightly as they made their way to its end. The commander stopped at the last door on the right, which opened after he submitted to a retina scan. He stepped aside to allow the captain to enter first.

The office impressed Ro as stylish and Old Earth. Large hardcover tomes filled deck-to-overhead shelves on the lateral bulkheads. On either side of the door hung two framed pen-and-ink prints, one of a classical building that a plaque beneath identified as Université Panthéon-Assas, and the other of the main building at Starfleet Academy. Several diplomas were displayed beside the pictures. A circular table stood in one of the near corners, atop which spread several padds and an open book. A companel sat in the other corner.

Desjardins passed Ro and made his way to his large wooden

desk, which sat below a wide port that rivaled the one in the captain's own office. It offered an expansive view of the *x*-ring from below. "Quite a vista," Ro said.

"I like to think of it as emblematic of the JAG office's position as the foundation of Starfleet," Desjardins said.

"Really?" the captain asked, skeptical.

"No, not really," Desjardins said. "But it is a nice view." He motioned to the chairs in front of his desk, and after Ro sat down, he sat beside her, rather than across from her. "So, Captain, I assume you're here to talk about Altek Dans."

"Am I that obvious?"

"Not you, no, but the situation is," Desjardins said. "What is it I can do for you?"

"After what's happened—including the arrest of Enkar Sirsy, a Bajoran national—I'm concerned about the sudden appearance of a Bajoran man whom we can't identify, and who won't tell us where he came from or why he's here."

"My understanding is that he emerged from the wormhole. Is that right?"

"It is, but I'm not really sure what that tells us," Ro said. "It doesn't necessarily mean that the aliens in the wormhole have plucked him from somewhere else in time and sent him here."

"Perhaps not," Desjardins said, "but isn't that a possibility? I mean, hasn't that happened before?"

"It has," Ro said, "but it didn't involve somebody coming out of the wormhole in an Orb."

Desjardins furrowed his brow. "Is that an important distinction?" he asked.

"I don't know, and that's the problem," Ro said. "And even if the wormhole aliens did send him here from the past, that doesn't tell us *why* they did so. My security chief has interviewed Altek several times over the last two days, but we're unable to corroborate either his identity or his story. He purports to be a doctor in a city called Joradell, on Bajor, which nobody's ever heard of, and he insists that he poses no threat to anyone, even though he possessed a primitive projectile weapon when we brought him aboard. He otherwise claims ignorance about his situation." Ro paused and shook her head in frustration. "Commander Blackmer believes that Altek is hiding something about his purpose, as well as protecting one or more accomplices."

"Stating that somebody has an accomplice necessarily implies that they've committed, attempted to commit, or conspired to commit a crime," Desjardins noted. "What crime are you talking about?"

Ro breathed in and out heavily, frustrated. "I understand your point."

"I'm curious: how has Altek's attitude been?"

"According to Commander Blackmer, he's been more or less even-tempered," Ro said, "though he has shown some signs of anxiety."

"I can imagine that being falsely imprisoned could be stressful," Desjardins said pointedly, though he did not linger over the potential criticism. "Has he consented to a medical exam?"

"He did," Ro said, "but because we do consider it a possibility that he's come from the past, I asked Doctor Boudreaux to conduct his examination in the stockade instead of Sector General, as simply as he could, and without the use of technological equipment. He supplemented that by using remote sensors."

"And is he a Bajoran?"

"As best we can tell, yes," Ro said.

Desjardins shrugged. "Maybe Altek Dans is what he says he is. Maybe he is a doctor from Bajor, and maybe he has no idea how or why he got here."

"Maybe," Ro allowed. "But the president of the Federation was just assassinated here. I need to be absolutely sure about this man before I release him."

"I understand your concerns, Captain," Desjardins said, "but I'm not sure how I can help you."

"I want to keep Altek in custody while we continue to investigate him," Ro said. "Until we can confirm who he is and why he's here."

Desjardins nodded slowly. "And he arrived here two days ago?"

"I know, I know," Ro said in a rush. "I can't legally keep him in custody for more than three days."

"No," Desjardins agreed. "Not without charging him with a crime."

"How about criminal trespass and illegally smuggling a deadly weapon onto a starbase?" Ro asked, only half-joking.

"Did Altek intentionally board the starbase without authorization?" Desjardins asked.

"When the wormhole opened and sensors detected the Orb emerging from it, we transported it aboard," Ro explained. "As soon as it materialized, it deposited Altek on the transporter platform and disappeared."

"Then perhaps you should consider yourself fortunate that Mister Altek hasn't brought charges against you for kidnapping and false imprisonment."

"That's not funny," Ro said.

"No, it's not," Desjardins said. "You, of course, have latitude when it comes to discharging your duty in protecting Deep Space Nine and Bajor, but there is a line, Captain."

"Believe me," Ro told him a little more vociferously than she intended, "I'm quite aware of all the lines Starfleet draws. Do I have *any* leeway here?"

Desjardins turned his head and gazed through the port for a few moments, as though searching for an answer out in space. Finally, he said, "Under different circumstances—"

"Such as?" Ro asked at once, interrupting the commander.

"Well, if you required information about Altek from a distant location, you could legally detain him for the time it takes a subspace transmission to travel back and forth between the two points, plus one day," Desjardins said. "But where would you send such a message? To the aliens in the wormhole? Regardless of whether they responded, that wouldn't extend the time you could legally detain Altek."

"It's possible that he didn't come directly from the wormhole," Ro argued. "He could have come from a world in the Gamma Quadrant . . . maybe even from the Dominion."

"You'd need some evidence to support such a claim, Captain."

"You know that we don't have anything like that," Ro said. She thought about simply charging Altek with some arbitrary violation of the law, but even if she could manage to get past an arraignment, she worried about the morality of such an action. While not as quick to defy orders or break rules as she once was, Ro wasn't above doing so in support of doing what was right. But the captain understood the justification for not detaining people without reasonable cause, and the uncertainty she felt about Altek fell far short of her ability to rationalize violating that principle. "I just need more time," she said, frustrated.

"There is one other possibility," Desjardins said. "Altek might not have boarded Deep Space Nine illegally, but he did enter the Bajoran system without warning, without permission, without documentation, and with a weapon. Bajoran authorities could charge him with those violations. Would that provide you the time you require?"

"Maybe," Ro said, folding her arms as she considered the possible course of action. "Maybe, though I don't really know how much time we're going to need—or if any amount of time will be enough to satisfy us about Altek." She knew that she didn't have many choices, though, and Desjardins's suggestion seemed a viable option. Ro stood up. "Thank you for seeing me and talking this through, Commander."

"That's one of the reasons I'm here, Captain," Desjardins said, rising to his feet as well. As Ro started for the door, he asked, "What are you going to do?"

"I'm going to take your advice," Ro said. "I'm going to contact Bajor and speak to the minister of justice."

8

Nog lay in bed, staring at the overhead. Sleep had not come easily to him during the past week, ever since—

"Ever since," he said aloud, not wanting to say or think more than that. Except that he couldn't stop thinking about what had happened on the starbase, and what it would ultimately mean for the Federation and the rest of the Alpha Quadrant. If Doctor Bashir and Lieutenant Commander Blackmer proved right in their belief that the Tzenkethi had taken part in the assassination, then war with the Coalition, and maybe even with the entire Typhon Pact, would become a real possibility.

Since the terrible events at the dedication ceremony, Nog had thrown himself into his work as a means of distracting himself. Even before the previous two days and the crew's efforts to bring aboard the new civilian population, he had routinely worked double shifts. Nog had also spent time talking to Lieutenant Valeska Knezo, one of the starbase's counselors, and he supposed that had helped to some degree, but he still felt low. He considered contacting Jake Sisko on Earth to talk with him, but he didn't want to intrude in such a negative way on his old friend's studies or the life he shared with his wife.

"Computer, what time is it?"

"The time is zero-two-thirteen hours," came the immediate response, in the ubiquitous female voice Starfleet utilized throughout its starships, starbases, and other facilities.

In the darkness, Nog shook his head, frustrated by his inability to sleep—or really to do much of anything besides work. Earlier that evening, after beta shift, he had actually forced himself to visit the Plaza. He thought he might benefit from being around people in a social setting. He went to his Uncle Quark's place, where he found several of his crewmates among the multitudes of newly arrived civilians, but he quickly discovered that he could find no enthusiasm for socializing with his friends—people who, even if they didn't mention it or show it, suffered in the same way that he did.

More than anything, Nog wanted to spend some time with Vic Fontaine. Since the destruction of the original Deep Space 9, the holographic character and his program had remained active, but inaccessible. Nog's uncle saved Vic by placing his holoprogram in a simulation tester prior to abandoning the station, but he then had to leave the singer in the device for the two years it took to construct the new DS9. The business Quark established on Bajor at first lacked holosuites, and when he finally did have some installed, the older models he purchased did not have the capacity to host Vic's complex matrix. The facilities on the new starbase did, but interface issues had so far prevented the program from a successful transfer out of the simulator. Quark had repeatedly requested assistance from DS9's engineers—including Nog—but the crew had been too busy with the transition of the starbase to full operational status to work on the issue. Vic's program continued to execute in the tester, where it advanced in real time, but without any interaction with flesh-and-blood people.

If the program hasn't failed, Nog thought morosely, *and if Vic's matrix hasn't degraded.* In the best-case scenario, the life of Vic Fontaine had proceeded without any external input, but any manner of software or hardware failure could have effectively ended that life. Even if the program could be made to run again, Vic Fontaine might appear as an empty shell, with all of the memories and personality traits formed out of his experiences on the old Deep Space 9 lost forever. In truth, Nog had no idea what he would find once Vic's program was returned to a holosuite.

"But I'm going to find out," he decided. A rush of intensity overcame him that seemed equal parts enthusiasm at the prospect of seeing his old friend, and refusal to deal with his troubled emotions. He didn't care. He threw off the bedclothes, jumped to his feet, and started to dress.

NOG KNEELED ON THE DECK of the holosuite, the simulation tester beside him. An optical data network cable ran from where he had removed an access panel on the bulkhead to the portable device—a gray metal cube, mounted on one corner atop a black base, with indicator lights, as well as input slots for four isolinear optical rods, one of which was filled. He leaned forward and pressed his face up close to the circuitry inside the bulkhead. He studied the architecture of the interface, then read through the numbers on the screen of his engineering tricorder. He saw nothing that didn't add up—no out-of-bounds tolerances, no potential for feedback, no failed or failing components.

"This should work," Nog told himself. The confusion he heard in his own voice accurately reflected his frame of mind.

Nog had arrived at his uncle's bar around zero-two-thirty. By that time, the crowds of customers he'd seen earlier had begun to thin. Nog offered to work on uploading Vic Fontaine's program. Despite having three unoccupied holosuites at the time, Quark objected, demanding that he come back at zero-four-hundred, arguing that, despite the lateness of the hour, he still hoped some other paying customers might want holo-experiences that night.

Nog had argued right back, even going so far as to quote the 108th Rule of Acquisition: *Hope doesn't keep the lights on.* He also threatened not to return at all, on that night or any other. Quark relented.

That had been ninety minutes earlier—ninety minutes in which Nog had made absolutely no progress. Before he started, he noticed that the maintenance logs indicated that somebody had been working on the problem. Nog wondered who on his uncle's staff might be capable of doing so, but he couldn't come up with a name. It concerned him, though, because somebody who didn't really know what they were doing could actually end up permanently damaging Vic's matrix before they managed to upload it. He would have to warn Quark about that.

Nog had begun his own efforts by attempting to upload Bashir 62—Vic's program—into the holosuite buffers. He did not succeed. He expected that, since it had been tried several times before, but he wanted to monitor the upload malfunction in order to understand exactly where the process broke down. Once that became clear, he believed he would be able to isolate the problem and devise either a repair or a workaround.

Instead, his observations had led him to the failure occurring in a component functioning well within its specifications. Nog replaced it anyway, only to have his next attempted upload fail as well. When he checked, the engineer found the disconnect in a simple interface that, according to the laws of physics, could not have crashed. Again, Nog switched out the two components that together formed the seemingly defective interface. His third upload succeeded no more than the first two had, and produced yet another diagnosis of where the process failed.

Frustrated, Nog had gone to the bar and retrieved one of the holoprograms Quark offered to customers, intending to download it to the simulation tester and then try to upload it to the holosuite so that he could see if it succeeded or failed. If it succeeded, he could compare the specifics of its upload to the failure of Vic's program. If it failed . . . if it failed, he would know that the problem lay specifically with the tester.

Nog had held up the isolinear optical rod of his uncle's holoprogram—the very first *Vulcan Love Slave,* as it turned out—over the input slot on the simulator, prepared to find out the worst . . . prepared to learn that he'd forever lost the Vic Fontaine he'd known. At the last instant, he stopped, unwilling to risk loading additional software to the tester for fear of disrupting Vic's matrix. Instead, he replaced all of the original components in the holosuite interface and readied himself to begin the process all over again.

As Nog studied the hardware architecture once more, a soft chime rang at the door.

"Go away, Uncle," he called. "I'm not done yet." Nog waited, expecting Quark either to start pounding on the door or just to open it and come inside. For a moment, nothing happened, and Nog went back to his work.

Then the chime sounded again.

Nog leaped up and reached for the door control, then realized that Quark might want back the holoprogram he'd taken. He quickly grabbed up the isolinear rod from where it lay beside the tester, then went back to the door and opened it. "Here's *Vulcan Love Slave* back—"

A young Bajoran woman stood in the corridor. A young *beautiful* Bajoran woman. She stood maybe a dozen centimeters taller than Nog, with flaming red hair, sparkling blue-green eyes, and curves that the black cocktail dress she wore did nothing to hide. Nog hadn't noticed her in the bar earlier, but he could only imagine that she must be one of his uncle's dabo girls—although he didn't know how he could have been in the same room with her and not noticed.

"Hi," she said.

"Hi," Nog replied, though the single syllable somehow came out in a garble.

The woman glanced down at the isolinear rod in Nog's hand. He'd held it out when he'd thought the door would open to reveal his uncle, but then he'd frozen in place. "I'm not here for *Vulcan Love Slave*," the woman said.

Nog felt a burning sensation crawl up his ears as embarrassment gripped him. He pulled his hand back and put it behind him, as though he could magically erase what the woman had heard and seen. Realizing the foolishness of what he'd done, he held up the isolinear rod again. "This isn't mine," he said. "It's my uncle's. I wasn't playing the program, I was using it to try to figure out why another program won't load." Nog pointed to the simulator, as though that would explain away why he clutched a copy of an erotic holoprogram in his hand, and then he noticed that the woman carried a silver tray. It held a glass and three small plates. "Are those baked blood fleas?" he asked. The sight of the Ferengi delicacy made him immediately hungry.

"Baked blood fleas," the woman said, pointing to the dish, and then, indicating the other two plates, "*lokar* beans, and tube grubs. Plus a glass of *eelwasser*."

"Wow," Nog said. "I guess my uncle must really want this program back online." Nog waved the isolinear rod in front of him, then remembered that it was *Vulcan Love Slave*, and tossed it to the deck.

"Quark didn't send me up here," the woman said. "I knew you were working. It's late, and you've been up here for a while, so I thought you might want some refreshments." She offered him the tray.

"Thank you," Nog said, touched by such a gesture from somebody he didn't even know—a *beautiful* somebody.

The woman smiled brightly. "You're welcome," she said. "My name is Lani, by the way. Ulu Lani."

"I'm Nog."

Lani smiled again. "I know." When she turned to leave, Nog heard Jake Sisko's voice whisper in his ear.

Stop her!

"Lani," he blurted, and when she looked back over at him, he felt something like an electric charge surge through his lobes. "Would you . . . would you like to join me in these refreshments?"

"I'd better not," she said. "I still have inventory to do."

"Oh . . . right . . . of course," Nog stammered, embarrassed again. "Maybe some other time," he added, knowing that no such time would come.

"Sure," Lani said. "Maybe when you succeed in uploading Vic's program."

"You know about Vic?" Nog asked, surprised.

"Your father mentions him a lot," Lani said. "And Doctor Bashir told me all about him. It's the doctor's program, right?"

"It is," Nog replied, suddenly understanding Lani's interest—not in him, but in Julian. Nog should have been used to it by that point. The good doctor had certainly enjoyed spending time with his share of beautiful women through the years, and it clearly didn't trouble Lani that he was currently involved with Sarina Douglas.

Lani pointed to the open access panel in the bulkhead. "Good luck."

"Thanks," Nog said as she headed out into the corridor. "And thank you for the snack." The door slid shut behind her.

Nog put the tray down on the deck, then sat down beside it and leaned back against the bulkhead. He sipped at the eelwasser and popped a few tube grubs into his mouth. As bad as he'd been feeling about recent events, he still found a way to feel sorry for himself. He just didn't understand women.

"Why Julian?" he asked the empty holosuite. It made no sense to Nog. Julian and Sarina had been together for something like two years. At the same time, Lani's visit to the holosuite did make sense, at least according to the 33rd Rule: *It never hurts to suck up to the boss.* Obviously, that included Lani using Nog to curry favor with Quark. It hurt his feelings.

Alone in the blank canvas of a holosuite, Nog shook his head and scratched at the back of his ear. He would have a little more eelwasser and a few more grubs, along with some of the fleas and the beans, and then he would get back to work. At that moment, he knew one thing above all others: he wanted to talk with his old friend Vic.

AN HOUR LATER, Nog stood back from the holosuite interface, cautiously optimistic.

When he'd begun working again, he'd executed another upload, which had produced another failure. Amazingly, though, it failed in a different way than it initially had, despite using the holosuite's original components. He therefore tried again, and met with the same results—that is, it failed in yet another distinct way.

Nog had wanted to reject his findings. Electrons and photons, conductors and insulators, the laws of physics all behaved consistently. The logic was unassailable: the operation of a device or the execution of a program should, under the same conditions, work identically each and every time.

Which means that either Vic's program is changing, or the conditions of the upload are, Nog had realized. *Or both.* It seemed an easy matter to point to the software as the source of change—since the program continued to run, Vic continued to live and grow—but Nog didn't believe he would find the source of the problem there. Rather, he thought about constants that didn't always behave like constants, but like variables. Two quantities came to mind: the power level, and the resolution of the holographic display.

Deep Space 9's reactors distributed power throughout the

starbase at an effectively constant rate, but microfluctuations could occur. On a brand-new facility only recently upgraded to full operation, such fluctuations would not be unusual. That could, in turn, impact the program's resolution, causing it to run outside practicable limits. In such cases, it could trigger an upload failure.

Nog regarded the open access panel, his gaze following the ODN cable that snaked out of the bulkhead and into the simulation tester. He had made numerous adjustments to the holosuite system, seeking to create workarounds that would either stabilize or account for any flux in both power and resolution. Nervous about experiencing another failure, but unwilling to surrender, Nog once again activated the upload.

Nothing happened. The upload didn't fail, but neither did the holosuite activate. The compartment remained completely bare.

And then Nog heard something: a slow tapping noise. *Not tapping,* he thought. The individual sounds had a weight to them. *Footsteps,* he realized. *Slow, unsteady footsteps.* At first, they seemed to spring from somewhere in front of Nog, but then they shifted, and they came from behind him.

Nog spun around to see a slim band of darkness in the middle of the holosuite, perhaps a meter wide and twice as long. The footsteps continued. "Vic?" he called out. "Vic, are you there? It's Nog."

The footsteps halted. Nog raced over to the projection and entered it. He could see nothing around him, other than the holosuite beyond the darkness.

"Computer," he said, "eliminate all light in the holosuite other than what's being projected from program Bashir Sixty-two."

The system issued a multi-toned trill, and then the holosuite went dark. Nog stood motionless, waiting for his eyes to adjust, listening intently. For a few moments, he heard nothing, but then a shuffling noise came from the darkness to his left. When he spun toward it, he saw shapes in the shadows—shapes that he recognized: two chairs on one side of a circular table, and past them, the edge of a one-armed bandit.

It's a casino, Nog thought excitedly. *Vic's casino.*

"Vic!" Nog called out again. "Vic, it's me, Nog. Are you—"

A flat tone filled the holosuite, and the shadows just visible in the darkness disappeared as everything went completely black. "Computer," Nog said, "lights up one-quarter." The holosuite brightened, but not blindingly so. The dark strip projected in the center of the compartment had vanished.

Nog sighed in frustration, but he actually felt buoyed that he had made any progress at all. He believed that some part of Vic's casino had been projected in the holosuite. He didn't understand why it had been dark—the casino never closed—but that didn't matter to him. Nog had found at least a partial solution to the upload problem, and he felt confident that, with more work, he could solve it completely and bring Vic back.

"Computer, what time is it?" he asked.

"The time is zero-five-eleven hours."

Nog groaned. For the first time in a while, he felt energized, but he also knew that he wouldn't make it through his shift in the Hub if he didn't get at least a couple hours of sleep. He quickly disconnected the simulation tester from the holosuite and replaced the access plate. He ordered the computer to save a record of the modifications he'd made, and then he reinitialized the interface.

Nog knew that he would have to fight his uncle for time in a holosuite. Quark wouldn't want him to monopolize any of his facilities when a customer might pay for their use—and if that night had been any indication, the new civilian residents would keep his Uncle Quark's establishment busy for the foreseeable future. Regardless, Nog vowed to himself to return the next night to continue his work, even if it meant having to keep late hours again. He would come back the next night, and the night after, and the night after that, until finally he had extracted Vic and his world out of the simulation tester.

At that moment, Nog had no way of knowing that, by the next night, he would be far from Deep Space 9, on his way to track President Bacco's killers.

9

Aboard *Even Odds*, Kira woke to the sound of feet scrabbling back and forth in the corridor outside her cabin door. Immediately upon waking, she did not recognize her location, but after a moment's thought, it all came rushing back to her. She retained all sorts of images in her mind, from Bajor to Deep Space 9 to the Celestial Temple, from Orb experiences to interactions with the Prophets to the lives of other women—both real and imagined—who wore her face. She had spent the previous day primarily resting aboard *Even Odds*—which hadn't been easy, given what Kira knew of the ship's eventual fate. After several hearty meals, an evening of solitary concentration and reflection, and a night of uninterrupted sleep, she felt good, and more than that, she had been able to separate out her actual, physical participation in events from incidents that had taken place solely in her mind.

Kira leaned over and reached to the foot of the sleeping platform to collect her clothing. After dinner the previous night, Captain Dezavrim—Dez, as he preferred to be called—had brought her a small bag of toiletries, along with her clothes, which he'd had cleaned. She glanced through the cabin's lone porthole to see that the ship traveled at warp, which she had already surmised from the general rumble pervading the deck.

As Kira rose, the inner edge of the sleeping platform rattled against the bulkhead. The footfalls outside the door ceased. She stopped as well and waited. After a few seconds, the awkward pacing began again. Kira ignored it, crossed the small, squarish compartment—it contained only a pair of sleeping platforms and a computer interface—and entered the refresher.

After she finished her morning ablutions and dressed, she offered a brief prayer to the Prophets, then walked back into the cabin. She straightened the bedclothes on her sleeping platform before sitting down to think about what next she needed to do. Outside, the clumsy footsteps continued.

After Taran'atar had attacked Kira aboard Deep Space 9 all those years ago, as she had lain on the verge of death while Doctor Bashir and his staff worked to save her, and stabilize her, and replace her ruined heart, she had experienced a vision of the Celestial Temple, and more. She saw herself as the head of an army, pursued by a merciless enemy and inexplicably shut out from her people's own fortress. In and around that dream, she came to know her place as the Hand of the Prophets, an instrument meant to guide the malleable future into the proper shape.

In the aftermath of that experience, doing what she thought needed to be done, she had pursued both Taran'atar and the crazed Iliana Ghemor. In the end, Kira physically ended up in the Celestial Temple, but not by herself; Ghemor and the Cardassian's sane, alternate-universe counterpart accompanied her. The Prophets opened up Ghemor's life for examination, and that life—devastated, broken, pitiable—played out for the trio to witness. The Prophets labeled Ghemor the Fire, and then They extinguished her—or, at least, Kira thought They had at the time. They dubbed her counterpart the Voice and sent her forth from the Celestial Temple to serve as Their Emissary in the alternate universe.

And They reaffirmed Kira Nerys as the Hand. They delivered her back to Deep Space 9, to her newly repaired body, with its replacement heart. It would be nearly another year before Iliana Ghemor and the Ascendants, as prophesied to her, descended on Bajor. Iliana Ghemor, the Ascendants . . . and Taran'atar.

That was almost six years ago, Kira thought. *In the line of my life, that was six years ago.* But time had ceased to be linear for her, and those events suddenly lay in the future. When she'd been alone in sickbay with Taran'atar, prior to having her first meal aboard *Even Odds,* she had asked him the current date on Bajor, which he'd calculated for her. She then lied and averred that she'd entered the Celestial Temple just before that time, but it told her what she needed to know: that the Ascendants' attack on Bajor, and Taran'atar's death, would occur in less than a hundred days.

And what am I supposed to do? Kira wanted to know—*needed* to know. The visions she'd endured after Taran'atar's attack on her had left her believing that she would play a substantial role in protecting Bajor from the Ascendants, and in uniting the forces that would stop them. Instead, she had done very little. The Ascendants had been stopped, but at a price.

Is that why I'm here in the past? she asked herself. *To lower that price? To take the proper action now and make up for not doing so then?* That sounded like it might be right, despite contradicting Starfleet's Temporal Prime Directive. *Maybe this time, I can save the Bajorans who died. Maybe I can save Taran'atar.*

Kira would have to think about that. The Jem'Hadar considered Taran'atar, at twenty-three, an elder among them. It didn't really make sense to risk so much to save him, since he would likely die from natural causes before too long anyway. Still, it would be worth it to consider saving the Bajorans who had perished. She would also have to ascertain *Even Odds'* position in the Gamma Quadrant, as well as its course. Depending on their proximity to the wormhole, she might have to act quickly.

Somebody knocked lightly on the door. "Hello, Captain?" said a male voice Kira did not recognize from the prior day. "Captain Kira? Can you hear me?"

In addition to Captain Dezavrim and the medic, Allo Glessin, she had met several other crew members: a mated Wadi couple, Itriuma and Fajgin, served the ship as art researchers and appraisers; a pair of Ferengi brothers, Feg and Triv, managed—naturally—finances; and a man named Pri'ak, who belonged to an unfamiliar species called the Merdosians, worked as an engineer. Pri'ak had an especially compact body, short and thickset, hinting that he might come from a high-gravity world. He also had transparent teeth, a consequence, he said, of an old Merdosian superstition asserting that the tongue of a liar would change colors. Despite the fallacy of the myth, it had become essentially a tradition for all of Pri'ak's people to implant clear teeth in their children.

"Captain Kira?" the voice outside the door said again, growing in volume and insistence. "Are you in there? Are you all right? Do you need some help?"

Though she could not remember all the names Jake had told her, Kira recalled several of the *Even Odds* crew he had described to her. He depicted one in particular as overly friendly and exceedingly talkative, who happened to look like a *tokka*—what Jake said humans called a dog. Between the skittering back-and-forth steps outside the cabin door and the tireless chatter, she could not visualize a more likely appearance for her visitor.

"Are you having problems, Captain?" the voice asked. "Is there something you need? Can I help in any way?"

Even as question followed question, Kira stood up, walked over to the door, and tapped its control. It withdrew into the bulkhead to reveal a being that, while not exactly the image of a tokka, certainly bore a resemblance: he walked on four legs, had a slim tail, a canine-shaped head with a narrow muzzle, and fur all over his body. The similarities ended there, though; colored the rich green of vegetation, the being had no long tongue flapping inside his mouth, no visible ears, long-fingered hands instead of paws, and a series of slender, flexible spines along his back—not to mention that he could speak. He wore nothing but a plain collar.

"I'm Kira Nerys, and I'm perfectly fine, thank you."

The being appeared to scowl at her, but when he rose up easily onto his two hind legs, he greeted her enthusiastically. "I would know who you are even if you didn't tell me," he said. "Even if Dez didn't tell me. Jake described you to me. Jake Sisko. He spent quite a while with us on the *Even Odds*." The tokka-like being offered up the information with a measure of pride.

"He told me about his time aboard," Kira said, finding the being's garrulous energy infectious. While she doubted that he truly would have known her based on any portrayal Jake had given—since those days, she had grown her hair much longer, down past her shoulders—she appreciated his friendliness. "Jake described you very well to me," she told him, "but I'm afraid I don't remember your name."

"Pifko Gaber," he said excitedly, as though bestowing some sort of honor upon himself. "You can call me Pifko, that's really my name. Or just Pif. That's what most everybody calls me."

"All right, then," Kira said. "How can I help you, Pif?"

"Help——?" Pif said, confused by the question. "Oh, no, I'm not here to ask for your help. I came to escort you to the dining hall for breakfast. Dez thought you might want to meet the rest of the crew."

"I do," Kira said, "although I'm not sure I'll meet anybody as interesting as you." Pif actually wagged his tail, and Kira had to resist reaching forward and petting him on the head.

"Come on, then," Pif said. "This way." He dropped back down onto all four of his legs and bolted down the corridor. He disappeared around a corner, only to duck his head back around as he waited for Kira to catch up. They continued on like that— with Pif racing ahead and then impatiently waiting for Kira to join him—all the way to the dining hall.

AT BREAKFAST, KIRA THOUGHT that Pif took great pleasure introducing her to the *Even Odds* crew, including, in some cases, those she'd already met. According to Pif, a plump humanoid man named Aslylgof contributed to the ship his expertise on weapons both modern and historical; he called himself a Rentician, had no ears, no eyelids, and exposed kneecaps and elbows, along with a full, gray-streaked beard and an air of arrogance about him. Juno Mellias, a Stakoran woman Pif identified as an archeologist and an expert in gems and jewelry, welcomed Kira with a smile. Another woman, a Karemman named Atterace Prees, held the position of chief engineer, assisted—or perhaps guided—by Srral, a fluidic, artificial lifeform that lived within the technological systems of *Even Odds*. Pif presented Srral to Kira by speaking with it via the ship's internal comm system, then removing an access plate from a bulkhead; Kira peered inside to see a silver, metallic substance that moved among the exposed circuitry almost like Odo when he shape-shifted from one form to another. Neane Tee, a four-armed Hissidolan woman, served as a general researcher of exceptional ability, at least by Pif's account.

For the most part, everybody offered Kira a warm welcome, although her brief conversation with Srral felt a bit like talking to a computer. Facity Sleedow marked the only exception. The final member of the crew and the ship's exec and comm officer, she arrived late to breakfast and barely acknowledged Kira when Pif jumped up from his meal to make the introductions. Of all those aboard *Even Odds* whom Jake had described to her, she had recalled Dez, Pif, and Srral most vividly, but many of the others at least sounded familiar to her when she met them. Sleedow did not, and Kira thought she knew why: Jake had never mentioned her, or if he'd said her name, he'd offered no details about her.

A tall, bosomy Wadi woman, Sleedow confidently and unapologetically exuded sexuality. As soon as Kira saw her, it became instantly clear from whose wardrobe the provocative clothing she'd been offered had come. Jake hadn't spoken about Sleedow, Kira figured, because to do so would have divulged more about him than about her.

After breakfast, most of the crew withdrew from the dining hall, presumably to tend to whatever duties the ship required of them. When Kira stood up as well, Dez, sitting across from her, remained seated and asked her if she would stay for a few moments. Beside him, Sleedow got up, exchanged a charged glance with Dez, and went over to the replicator to recycle her tray and dishware. "I'll be on the bridge," she said flatly. She exited without looking back, leaving Kira in the dining hall with only Dez and Taran'atar. The Jem'Hadar stood off to the side, at attention, as though standing guard. She had seen him in such a pose many times back when he'd first arrived on DS9.

"Please have a seat," Dez said, and Kira sat back down. "And please forgive Facity. She thinks the *Even Odds* already has one captain too many." The reference to Kira's rank reminded her of her implied lie; while she hadn't referred to herself as a captain, she also hadn't corrected anybody who referred to her by the rank.

"Do you two not get along?" Kira asked, and she immediately regretted the question. For one thing, it suddenly seemed absolutely obvious to her that Dez's relationship with Sleedow went deeper than that of just shipmates. For another, she gathered that Sleedow's concerns meant that she believed Kira would be staying aboard, at least for a while, which gave Kira pause.

"Oh, we get along well together," Dez said, his tone casual but telling. "Just some times better than others."

"Does she think that I want to join your crew?" Kira asked.

"Facity knows I want to discuss the possibility with you, yes," Dez said.

"Captain—"

He held up a hand to stop her. "Dez," he said, in a reaction that seemed more habit than anything else. "Before you turn me down, please listen to what I have to say."

Kira had no intention of becoming a member of the *Even Odds* crew, nor did she plan to remain aboard for very long. She wanted only to figure out what she needed to know about the ship and its crew, and then return to the Alpha Quadrant so that she could prepare for whatever action she would have to take. Listening to Dez—and anybody else in the crew—might bring her information that would help her puzzle out all of that. "All right," Kira said.

"First of all, please understand that I don't know what your situation is," Dez said. "We found you far from the Anomaly, wearing not a Starfleet uniform but civilian clothes. Now, maybe you haven't left your position on Deep Space Nine. Maybe you were on some sort of undercover mission, or even on holiday, when you got trapped in the Anomaly." Dez shrugged. "Maybe you committed a crime and were being chased. I don't know, and I'm not asking."

Although he hadn't asked, Kira noted that he had paid close attention to her reaction to each possibility he mentioned. She did her best to reveal nothing.

"Regardless of your situation," he went on, "I want you to know that there's a place for you here, and an opportunity that you might never have considered." He paused as though expecting Kira to comment or ask questions, but when she stayed quiet, he continued. "I'm sure Jake must've told you about what we do on the *Even*. We call it the 'retrieval' business, but that can be a bit of a euphemism. Some people have other names for it. Mostly, we track down items of value that have been lost or stolen— works of art, historical artifacts, precious gems, and such—and we . . . *re*appropriate them . . . back to the proper owners."

Kira wondered how often, and in what circumstances, those "proper owners" turned out to be the complement of the *Even Odds*. Although Jake had clearly come to care about Dez during their time together, the nature of his profession had also troubled the young man. Kira understood why, but she chose to let Dez finish making his pitch, wanting to learn as much as she could about his ship, since the explosion that would eventually tear it apart had never been fully explained.

"We're really good at what we do," Dez said. "It can be both exciting and lucrative, and I think you would be a valuable asset to add to the crew."

"Based on what?" Kira asked, curious, though she suspected she knew why Dez wanted to offer her a position on *Even Odds*. Despite being a resident of the Alpha Quadrant, she had spent a great deal of time exploring on the other side of the wormhole, and interacting with numerous species there. She imagined that her knowledge of the region could prove helpful to Dezavrim and his crew. Still, Kira wanted to hear what he had to say.

"Based on the fact that you've been a Federation captain," Dez said. "I haven't had direct dealings with Starfleet, but I've heard quite a lot about it, and I certainly know about organizations like it. I also know that you were in the Bajoran Militia, and that, during the Cardassian occupation of your homeworld, you were a terrorist."

Kira raised her eyebrows, not at the last label Dez had used to describe her, but at how much he appeared to know. She doubted Jake had said much on the subject of the Occupation and her role in it. The information conceivably could have come from Taran'atar, but even that seemed doubtful to her. She suspected that Dez and his crew made it a habit to learn as much as they could about prominent individuals in what amounted to their interstellar neighborhood. A search of *Even Odds*, she thought, would likely turn up more than a few acquired databases. "We preferred the term 'freedom fighters,'" Kira said, seeking to cover her surprise, "and we called ourselves the Resistance."

"My point is that you have a wealth of experience, from guerilla tactics to military training and procedures, from space exploration to first contact missions. You're a proven leader, and obviously good at what you do."

"Why is that obvious?"

"Because of what we've heard from various sources . . . because of what Jake told us . . . because of what Taran'atar has told us . . ." He looked over at the Jem'Hadar, who still stood motionless, like a sentry on duty. ". . . but primarily because, after the life you've led and all that you've been through, you're still alive."

"Survival *can be* a skill," Kira agreed, but rather than thinking about her own existence, she thought about that of her people. She began to wonder again if she had been sent by the Prophets into the past to alter events. *Maybe the timeline unfolded in a way that it shouldn't have,* she thought. *Maybe the Prophets sent me here, to this time and place, to ensure that the Even Odds never makes it to the wormhole.*

Or maybe I'm supposed to make sure that it does.

Kira's mind reeled at the opposing possibilities. For all she knew, while she had commanded Deep Space 9, a future version of herself had shaped the events through which she had then lived. Maybe she needed to maintain the integrity of the timeline after all.

She didn't know. Kira felt sure that she should do something, but that she didn't have enough information to decide what that should be. *But maybe I can get more information.*

"If I stayed," Kira asked, channeling her inner Ferengi, "what would be in it for me?"

"As I mentioned, our business can be profitable, on both an

emotional and commercial level," Dez said. "We also have an exceptional crew in terms of their skills and the way they mesh together."

"I'm not sure Ms. Sleedow has any interest in 'meshing' with me," Kira said.

"Don't mind Facity," Dez told her, waving his hand in a dismissive fashion. "She has an issue with authority. So do I. So do a lot of us on board, actually. Maybe that's why we're all here, and maybe that's why we get along so well. But I can promise you that, if you do join us, Facity won't be a problem. In fact, it wouldn't surprise me if the two of you teamed up and took charge of the *Even Odds*."

"And wouldn't that be a problem for you?" Kira asked, already knowing the answer, no matter how Dez responded. People of his ilk could not be pushed into relinquishing command.

"I'd have no problem at all," he said. "It might even be nice to let somebody else make the decisions for a change." Kira didn't believe that, but it also didn't matter. If she remained aboard *Even Odds*, it wouldn't be so that she could take command, but so that she could fulfill her role as the Hand of the Prophets—if only she could pinpoint just what that meant.

"What about this ship?" Kira asked. In the end, nobody had known precisely what had taken place aboard *Even Odds* prior to its destruction. While Jake had mentioned something about an other-dimensional deck on the ship, Starfleet's experts had ultimately concluded that unexplained subspace waves had triggered an isolytic subspace weapon. It might help Kira determine a course of action if she could discover what had caused the destruction in the Bajoran system.

"The *Even Odds* is . . . an interesting vessel," Dez said, in a way that implied he understated the case. "I've had it for more than a decade, but it's at least two centuries old."

"Two centuries?" Kira said. Few ships, even those privately held, remained in service for such a long period. "Who constructed it?"

"Who didn't?" Dez replied with a chuckle. "The *Even Odds*

has undergone at least a dozen major refits. Since I've had the ship, we've added a sizable section along the starboard stern, including a large cargo bay, a new transporter, and several corridors."

In her brief time aboard, Kira had noticed the disparate architecture in the sections through which she'd walked. None of it resembled that of any ships she'd traveled on, in either the Alpha or Gamma Quadrant. She said as much.

"You might recognize two parts of the *Even*," Dez told her. "The section I added we salvaged from a crashed Cardassian vessel. Another was taken from a Jem'Hadar attack ship."

"So does that make you allies of the Dominion, or adversaries?" Kira asked.

"Neither, I hope," Dez said. "We do our best to go about our business unnoticed. Sometimes it's not possible, but we do what we can to avoid drawing attention to ourselves."

"What about armaments?" Kira asked, hoping that she would not betray the reasons for her curiosity. "When you do draw attention, how do you protect yourselves?"

"With the strongest shields we can find," Dez said. "Our armaments are minimal. We stay alive mostly by avoiding trouble, and when we can't, we take a beating and run like hell."

"Some might call that craven."

"Better a craven survivor than a courageous corpse," Dez said. "We do try to keep somebody aboard to function as our security. These days, Taran'atar holds that position for us." He again glanced over at the Jem'Hadar, who hadn't moved during the course of the conversation, or even given any indication that he was listening to them.

"I wondered about that," Kira said. When she had given Taran'atar the choice of remaining on Deep Space 9 or leaving aboard an old Bajoran scoutship, he had elected to depart the station. Kira believed that he would immediately return to the Dominion to face punishment for what he perceived as his failures during his time in the Alpha Quadrant, but if he had, he obviously hadn't stayed. "How long has he been aboard, and how did you coax him to become a member of your crew?"

Before Dez could respond, Taran'atar walked over to stand beside the table. "I am a member of this crew not because I have been coaxed," he said, "but because it is how I fulfill my function."

Kira understood that he referred to his preprogrammed nature as a soldier. It underscored the difficulties Odo faced in attempting to offer genetically engineered species like the Jem'Hadar and the Vorta more opportunities and different ways of life. In many respects, it reminded Kira of a saying Captain Sisko had once used: you can't free a fish from water.

Then again, she thought, *the Alonis managed the feat.* The aquatic species utilized formfitting, water-filled environmental suits and antigrav chairs to travel beyond their homeworld and interact with other species. Not quite the same thing as the challenges the Jem'Hadar confronted in moving past their embedded militarism, but perhaps nonetheless a hopeful example.

"I understand your decision," Kira told Taran'atar, "but how did you arrive on the *Even Odds* in the first place?"

When Taran'atar did not immediately answer, Dez looked up at him. "Why don't you tell Captain Kira the story of how you joined us?"

And he did.

THE SHRILL PEAL of the engines saturated the main cabin of the old Bajoran scoutship, the threat of an overload racing toward inevitability. The faster-than-light drive, designed for a maximum velocity of warp five, pushed the small vessel through space just past warp eight. Taran'atar didn't know whether the ship's structural integrity or its engines would fail first, only that given enough time, each of them would. If he survived the disintegration of the hull and the explosive decompression that followed, he might remain conscious for a few seconds before cardio-respiratory collapse led to asphyxia. He considered putting on an environmental suit—he found four of them stowed for emergency evacuations—but he saw little point. He thought it more likely that the warp drive would explode before the ship broke apart, which would reduce him to atoms no matter how he protected himself.

Taran'atar sat down at the main console as the decommissioned Bajoran vessel navigated through the Gamma Quadrant, no longer on course for the Dominion. An unfamiliar pattern of stars showed through the forward port, but the Jem'Hadar did not see it. Instead, before he started back to work, he took a moment to think about what he had earlier heard over the scoutship's communications system: an audio signal that had originated several parsecs away.

It had required multiple attempts to tune and filter the message before it had resolved into words that Taran'atar could fully distinguish. Distorted by his digital manipulation and limited by both the weakness of the signal and the Bajoran vessel's outmoded equipment, it sounded reedy and thin. *"This is the independent courier* Even Odds, *calling anyone within range of this transmission. Our ship is under attack. Repeat, we are under attack. Please, if anyone is receiving this, we request immediate assistance."* The message repeated, obviously broadcast on an automated loop.

Taran'atar had listened to the distress call, iteration after iteration, but he'd otherwise taken no action. He maintained his course for the Dominion, and as he moved farther and farther from the source of the message, the signal began to break up. Eventually, it faded completely into the static and hiss of background radiation.

At first, Taran'atar had done nothing but deactivate the comm system. He continued on a straight-line trajectory toward Dominion space, traveling at warp five in relative silence, the white noise of the scoutship's engines a steady thrum in the main cabin. Alone, with no one issuing him orders or offering him options, he contemplated the distress call.

Less than ten minutes later, Taran'atar had made a decision. He took control of the vessel's helm and brought the ship about. He consulted the comm system for directional data, then set out to locate the source of the signal.

As Taran'atar had headed toward the ship under attack, the signal it transmitted grew stronger, at a rate faster than he'd expected. The Jem'Hadar checked the readings and determined that, even as the Bajoran scoutship drew nearer to the source of the distress call, *Even Odds* traveled at high speed in roughly the opposite direction, narrowing the distance between the two as its crew undoubtedly attempted to outrun its attackers. Even so, traveling at warp five, it would take days for Taran'atar to reach the assaulted vessel.

The Jem'Hadar had then made another decision. A choice of tactics rather than of personal direction, it came far more easily to him than the first had. He clambered belowdecks, into the engine compartment, where he worked to modify the scoutship's drive system. In little more than an hour, he increased the introduction of deuterium into the dilithium chamber, expanded the electromagnetic fields surrounding the crystals, and he uncapped the flow of warp plasma through the injectors, at the same time bypassing all of the emergency shutdown regulators. The engines would run hot and fast, but only for so long. If they held, and if the hull remained intact, they would get him to his goal in a matter of hours rather than days. Taran'atar estimated a fifty percent chance that he would reach *Even Odds* before the scoutship blew itself apart for one reason or the other. That probability satisfied him.

As the engines shrieked around him in the main cabin, Taran'atar understood that, in juxtaposition with the rest of his life, his decision to respond to the distress call made no sense. The existence of every Jem'Hadar came complete not with mere strictures, but with well-defined physiological imperatives. Taran'atar swore an oath to safeguard the Founders, but more than that, his mind and body drove him to protect those who created him. He believed his life forfeit at the beginning of every such battle, and that he could reclaim it only as a function of his effectiveness in defending the security of his gods.

Except that I have no gods.

The thought caused a profound ache within Taran'atar, as

though some part of his being had been hollowed out. He suffered solitude in a way that he never had, his purpose in serving something greater than himself relegated to a memory seemingly so remote that it might never have been at all. If he cut power to the scoutship's engines and allowed the vessel to drift, he would not have felt more aimless than he did at that moment.

Taran'atar did not entirely comprehend what had happened to him, otherwise he would have sought in some way to reverse everything that had brought him to that point. Many details had contributed to his newfound atheism. Certainly the declaration by the Founder leader—that the Changelings were not gods, that they revered their own creator, a massive shape-shifting prime mover who had given them life—had stoked the fire of his doubts, but that had also been but one flame in what had ultimately grown into an inferno.

The initial spark of uncertainty had accompanied his aberration. Unlike his fellow Jem'Hadar, Taran'atar had never been dependent on ketracel-white. Though he had hidden that fact for most of his existence, poisonous questions had risen in the back of his mind. How could the Founders have created him—or any Jem'Hadar—with such a flaw? Shouldn't such an error have been impossible for gods to make? Taran'atar could've blamed the Vorta who had run the hatchery where he'd incubated, but shouldn't the Founders have known about his deviation? Shouldn't they have done something about it?

Eventually, Odo had discovered his condition, and he'd subsequently ordered Taran'atar to Deep Space 9, not as a soldier, but as an observer. The Jem'Hadar could have understood the assignment as a punishment, but the Founder insisted that he intended something different from that. Taran'atar followed his instructions, but he never truly grasped his mission. Regardless, he tried to succeed, tried to watch and learn, but his failures compounded one atop another. His last had been allowing the co-opting of his allegiance, his will not strong enough to prevent the redirection of his fidelity away from the Founders, first to the Intendant, and then to Iliana Ghemor.

Once Taran'atar had finally broken free of the mind control that had tied him to Ghemor, Captain Kira had given him a choice—something he had neither asked for nor wanted. He could stay on Deep Space 9 or not. He therefore decided to return to the Dominion to face judgment for his long string of lapses. He anticipated a swift execution that would, at least in his final moments, bring him back to the life of a Jem'Hadar soldier. He deserved to die, and so his death would allow him to serve his gods one final time.

Except that I have no gods, he thought again. With that truth, he could no longer trust the Founders to properly administer justice. On his journey from Deep Space 9, he had begun to fear that, once he reached the Dominion, Odo would send him back to the space station. Taran'atar could accept the legitimacy of a death sentence, but not the pointlessness of another exile.

I am Jem'Hadar, he told himself, seeking meaning from the words. Being Jem'Hadar had always signified obeisance and obedience to the Founders, and living a soldier's existence. He could no longer bring himself to practice the former, but he could still attempt the latter. That was why he had elected to turn the scoutship away from the Dominion and in pursuit of the distress call's source. The equation became simple: somebody required protection, and so he would provide it.

That meant Taran'atar would need arms. He turned his attention to the main console, where he searched for anything that resembled a weapons panel. Kira had told him that the vessel had been disarmed, but he hoped that he could reverse that.

After a few moments, he identified charging, targeting, and firing controls for a single phaser bank. None of them responded to his commands. Using sensors, he found a phaser emitter mounted at the bow of the ship, but the supporting infrastructure—batteries for the charge, conduits, energy-transfer nodes—had all been physically removed. If he had a place to set the ship down, he could replicate the necessary tools and proper components and install them himself, but that would require many days of effort.

Instead, Taran'atar ran through a list of the scoutship's systems: communications, navigational deflectors, defensive shields, warp engines, impulse drive, environmental controls, computer. He considered all of them subpar and of little use to him, but even with their limitations, he saw a means of creating a weapon. Over the next hour, he developed a program to channel all of the scoutship's power, from all systems but the transporter, through the main deflector array. The result would produce a single pulse of energy that he could direct outward from the bow of the ship. The blast would destroy the deflector and render the vessel impossible to safely navigate, and with the shields drained of power, the ship would become defenseless, but the plan would at least provide him with some offensive capability.

Afterward, Taran'atar brought up a schematic of the ship's interior. He found a panel at the aft end of the main cabin that concealed a small weapons locker. When he opened it, he saw slots for four handheld arms, all of them empty. A utility drawer once used to store scanners likewise contained nothing.

Taran'atar absently reached to the side of his hip, to where he normally carried his *rens'takin*, a short-bladed combat knife. The sheath hung from his belt, unfilled. Prior to his return to Deep Space 9 with Commander Vaughn aboard *Defiant*, he had surrendered all of his arms.

Moving to the scoutship's lone replicator, Taran'atar attempted to produce an energy weapon for himself. Design limitations precluded him from doing so, but he did fashion a new blade. He sheathed it on his belt, where it hung with a satisfying weight.

Seated back at the main console, Taran'atar considered what other preparations he might make for the coming battle. He thought again about donning an environmental suit, but doing so would impede his ability to shroud. That would undermine a significant tactical advantage he would have in hand-to-hand combat, should such a situation arise—and Taran'atar hoped that such a situation would. He doubted whether his single deflector-directed energy discharge would alone succeed in fending off the *Even Odds'* attackers, and he had no intention of staying aboard the scoutship once it had become incapacitated.

Taran'atar reached forward to the main console and reactivated the ship's comm system. *"—one within range of this transmission. Our ship is under attack. Repeat, we are under attack. Please, if anyone is receiving this, we request immediate assistance."* After a brief pause, the message began again. *"This is the independent courier* Even Odds, *calling anyone within range of this transmission."* Taran'atar checked the signal strength and saw that the assaulted vessel no longer moved toward the scoutship. That suggested that the pursuit of *Even Odds* had ended. Taran'atar waited to see if another message would replace the first, informing anybody receiving the message that the crew of *Even Odds* had survived the encounter with their attackers.

Instead, the distress call ended in midsentence. No other message replaced it. Unsure whether *Even Odds* had been destroyed, Taran'atar made yet another decision: he continued on, still prepared for battle.

THE TWO VESSELS hung beside each other in space, motionless. As Taran'atar approached them in the Bajoran scoutship, he examined a magnified view of the scene on a screen beside the main console. The larger vessel appeared somewhat boxy, nearly as wide as it was long, and about half as tall. Ports along its visible flank suggested that it contained four decks stacked atop each other. Taran'atar did not recognize the overall design, but portions of the vessel seemed as though they had been appended after its initial construction. The piecemeal architecture included components readily identifiable as Paradan, Trelian, and Cardassian, as well as elements of unfamiliar origin.

As Taran'atar studied the larger ship, he saw one unifying detail across many of its surfaces: numerous parts of the hull had been blackened by weapons fire. The vessel looked wounded. There could be little doubt as to its attacker.

Although he had never before observed one in person, Taran'atar could easily classify the smaller ship. Colored a flat black and barely visible in the void, illuminated only by the running lights of its prey, the blade-shaped, single-passenger vessel had been a design long known to the Founders. Attacks on the Dominion by the Ascendants had been on the rise over the previous decade, bringing Jem'Hadar forces into conflict with them on a number of occasions.

Taran'atar scanned both ships. The Ascendant vessel showed only the mildest hints of damage, its shields still almost wholly intact. Taran'atar read no life-forms aboard.

As he expected, the defensive shields on the larger vessel—presumably *Even Odds*—had been compromised. Power levels fluctuated throughout the ship. He read the existence of some unusual equipment, some of which he recognized, some of which he didn't. Sensors detected only two life signs, neither of which the Bajoran scoutship's database could identify, but which Taran'atar could. One was an Ascendant, the other, a Jeflinic, a humanoid species with gray skin and light eyes. He did not think a physical battle between the two would last long. Assuming that *Even Odds* carried a complement larger than one, it seemed reasonable to assume that the Ascendant had already killed everybody else aboard; even if they had attempted to flee in an evacuation vehicle, the Ascendants, once they decided on a target, rarely allowed anybody to escape.

Taran'atar could think of no better test of his soldier's mettle than the one that lay before him. Even if the Bajoran scoutship's lone phaser bank had not been removed, the Jem'Hadar knew that he could not possibly have hoped to succeed in a battle against an Ascendant's vessel. Depending on the weaponry his impending adversary carried, one-on-one combat could also prove close to impossible. Even unarmed, the Ascendants had earned a reputation among the Jem'Hadar as challenging enemies. Tall and lithe, they moved quickly, possessed lightning-fast reflexes and considerable physical strength, and their exoskeletons provided them natural protection against bodily assaults, even with energy weapons.

Fortunately, I have no such weapons, Taran'atar thought with grim humor.

The Ascendants also had a reputation as instinctive tacticians. Perhaps of even greater import, they fought with the single-mindedness of zealots. They would rather die along with those they considered heretics than allow them to go free.

Taran'atar understood that mind-set. For almost all of his existence, he would gladly have laid down his life in order to defend the Founders. Those days had passed, though. He no longer had anything for which to die.

Maybe that means I need to find a way to live, he thought. The idea made him uncomfortable.

As the scoutship neared the two vessels, Taran'atar quickly adjusted the deflector array not to discharge the buildup of energy within it, but to detonate. He then called up a navigation panel and programmed a new course, which he tied into the ship's sensors and the deflector. Once he completed those preparations, he targeted the transporter, gave himself a thirty-beat countdown, and set his plan in motion. He rose from the main console and strode aft, into the chamber between the cockpit and the passenger compartment. There, he stepped onto one of the pads on the two-position transporter platform.

"I am dead," he said aloud, beginning to recite the soldier's oath that all of his people made before heading into combat. "I go into battle—" He stopped. The words, he realized, no longer carried any meaning for him.

Taran'atar took hold of his substitute rens'takin and drew it from its sheath. He tensed his body and focused his concentration. For the first time in a long time, he felt . . . directed. Not by the Founders, nor by Iliana Ghemor, but by his own sense of duty and purpose. He was a soldier, and he was entering the battlefield. He declaimed the final part of his oath, which he discovered did matter to him after all: "Victory is life."

Moments before the Bajoran scoutship would surge forward, Taran'atar centered his thoughts. He channeled his energy outward and shrouded, rendering himself invisible through the might of his will. In the next instant, the transporter enfolded him in its beams and carried him away.

*   *   *

SHROUDED, TARAN'ATAR MATERIALIZED in flickering light. His mind still focused on his practical camouflage, he unleashed his senses on the ship he expected to become his battleground. He saw several replicators lining the bulkheads, and tables and chairs standing about the spacious but otherwise empty compartment. The almost inaudible buzz of a failing light panel reached his ears, and the various scents that filled his nose identified not only some of the food that had recently been consumed in that space, but the species of at least a few of those who had taken their meals there: the musky canine smell of an Aarruri, the slightly sweet fragrance of a Wadi, and the earthy aroma of a Hissidolan, among others. His coarse flesh logged a crisp temperature—

The ship quaked, coincident with a tremendous din. Taran'atar shifted his balance and easily kept his feet, but his concentration wavered momentarily. His shroud faltered as he visualized the Bajoran scoutship following the instructions he had programmed into its helm and engineering systems, accelerating until it slammed into the much smaller Ascendant vessel and detonating as it did so, the buildup of power in the deflector array sparking an explosion that blew both ships apart. Some piece of the resultant wreckage had obviously crashed into *Even Odds*. Taran'atar didn't know for what reason the Ascendant had boarded the ship—either to extinguish heretical thought or to acquire useful technology, he suspected, or perhaps both—but whatever the case, the trespassing alien would have to make a stand there.

Taran'atar calmed his thoughts and reestablished his shroud. Flexing his fingers to feel the haft of the knife in his grip, he padded toward the side of the compartment's door. There, he waited and listened. He had beamed over to *Even Odds'* second deck, which had read on the scoutship's sensors like the crew's living area. The scans also showed that the Ascendant stalked around the command-and-control center on the deck above, while the Jeflinic life-form—presumably the last surviving member of the *Even Odds* crew—had taken refuge in the cargo and maintenance areas below.

The Jem'Hadar knew that he had already altered the plans of the Ascendant, whose vessel no longer existed. There could be no escape there, and no planets fell within transporter range. The Ascendant would have to commandeer and repair *Even Odds*, and eliminate the remaining crew member.

And have to face me, Taran'atar thought. *Victory is life.*

The Jem'Hadar heard nothing on the other side of the door. He stepped in front of it, but it remained shut—no doubt a consequence of the ship's flagging power, as evidenced by the inconsistent lighting. Taran'atar located and opened a small panel in the bulkhead adjacent to the doorway, then threw the manual release within it. The door jumped partially open, sliding to one side, and he pushed it the rest of the way. Still shrouded, he moved out into a corridor.

The overhead lighting continued to stutter off and on. It did so with a regular rhythm, suggesting that its intermittence had come not as the product of damage to the ship incurred during the Ascendant's attack, but by intention. Taran'atar imagined that the crew, when faced with being boarded, might have sabotaged *Even Odds*, rigging its power distribution to malfunction—perhaps to make it a less attractive prize, or to thwart the Ascendant's ability to use the vessel's internal systems to track and trap the personnel aboard. With the Bajoran scoutship's sensors having shown only one crew member left alive, those efforts had plainly failed. Taran'atar vowed to himself that he would protect the life of the sole survivor.

The Jem'Hadar glided rapidly down the corridor, alert for sound and movement up ahead of him. He would assume that the Ascendant had registered the transporter beam that had deposited him aboard. As long as he remained shrouded, though, Taran'atar could be neither seen nor scanned. He would need to maintain that advantage for as long and as often as possible.

At an intersection, Taran'atar spied a semicylindrical alcove halfway along the connecting corridor, which crossed the width of the ship. Semicircular rungs lined the recess and formed a ladder that reached up and down to the decks above and below. He quickly headed for it. When he reached the ladder, he sheathed his knife and began climbing. At a closed hatch, he stopped and listened again. When he heard nothing, he reached up, twisted the manual locking mechanism, and slid the circular hatch into the overhead.

Once on the top deck, Taran'atar again drew his knife. He found himself in another corridor that spanned the breadth of *Even Odds*. The scans of the vessel that he'd taken aboard the scoutship indicated that the command-and-control center sat forward of his position. Doors in the bulkhead along that side of the corridor likely led there. Taran'atar chose one of them, again listened for any noise, and then manually released it. Beyond lay a short passage, not longer than ten or so paces. It ended at another door which stood open, pushed three-quarters of the way into the bulkhead.

Across the threshold stretched an inert body.

Taran'atar approached cautiously. His senses keenly tuned, he could detect no respiration and no pulse in the motionless humanoid. Though lying supine, the female body looked taller and broader than the Jem'Hadar. Muscular, bald, and colored dark green, the corpse belonged to a member of the Eline-dumayo tribe on Enskith VI. In each flash of light from the overhead, he saw curls of smoke rising from a large black circle that had been burned through the woman's clothing and into her chest, the cause clearly an energy weapon. Taran'atar smelled the fetid, distinctive odor of seared flesh.

At the same time that Taran'atar noticed a disruptor pistol gripped in the dead woman's fingers, he heard movement in the compartment beyond: controls being tapped and the answering feedback tones. Regardless of his ability to shroud, he likely would have only one opportunity to surprise the Ascendant— and perhaps not even that. The sounds Taran'atar heard came from the other side of the semicircular command-and-control center, out of his view to the left, though whether from the sunken interior portion of the compartment or its raised outer section, he could not tell. Either way, he would have to cross the deck in order to engage in hand-to-hand combat. Even invisible, he risked detection by the Ascendant, whose people possessed both formidable martial skills and advanced technologies.

Taran'atar quickly made a tactical choice. He set his course in his mind, then refocused so that he could maintain his shroud. The instant he felt prepared, he raced forward and dived over the fallen *Even Odds* crew member. He reached for the disruptor pistol with his empty hand, adjusting it into a firing grip even as he rolled onto his shoulder and across the deck of the command-and-control center.

The weapons fire began at once—but not by Taran'atar. He heard and felt a coherent beam of energy cut through the air just above him. He had intended to come up onto his haunches, but instead, he continued to roll, staying low until he stopped in a prone position. His gaze swept the compartment and, in the stroboscopic effect of the overhead lighting, augmented by the glow of control panels, he picked out the Ascendant: down on one knee, a weapon held in front of him with both hands, leveled roughly in Taran'atar's direction.

An ambush.

The Jem'Hadar did not hesitate. Where he had come to lie, he squeezed the trigger of the disruptor he'd just taken from the fallen crewwoman. The pistol barked out a high-pitched whine, but it did not fire.

The Ascendant's weapon did.

Another pulse of energy streaked across the command-and-control center, and pain erupted in Taran'atar's shoulder. A grazing shot, the energy bolt exploded against something behind him. As he felt his shroud collapse, the Jem'Hadar pushed himself to the side. He took cover behind a freestanding console just as a blast of energy struck it, sending up a burst of sparks and clouds of thick, acrid smoke.

Taran'atar glanced at his shoulder. His clothing there had been burned away, and his roughly textured hide exposed and singed. He flexed his arm, raised it, rotated it in its socket, testing its function and range of motion.

He had been right to assume that the Ascendant had known he'd transported aboard, but he should have realized that the corpse of the Eline-dumayo had been staged to lure him into revealing himself. The Ascendant, anticipating Taran'atar's shroud, had been waiting for him to take the disruptor pistol from the dead crew member. When the Jem'Hadar had done so, the Ascendant had begun firing his own weapon. The sounds of work at a control panel had clearly been a ruse.

Taran'atar took stock of his situation. He needed to act. The Ascendant would work quickly to eliminate the threat that the Jem'Hadar posed.

Once more, Taran'atar cleared his mind, even as another energy bolt shook the console behind which he crouched. He reinstituted his shroud. Invisible again, he adjusted his grip on the handle of this knife. Then he waited.

When another energy blast rocked the console, Taran'atar dashed back toward the doorway. As he ran, he tracked the energy fire back to its source and brought his arm whipping downward, hurling his blade. His attack caused his shroud to dissolve, but the knife sliced across the compartment and into the Ascendant's weapon. The beam immediately ceased as the pistol flew from the alien's hand. Taran'atar saw it clatter along the deck, the point of his blade buried within it, just before he leaped over the dead *Even Odds* crewwoman and headed back down the short passage.

As he hurried through the second door and back out into the main corridor, Taran'atar glanced behind him. He saw a blur of silvery motion. He evacuated the doorway, moving off to the side, but only a few steps. He attempted to concentrate and wrap himself in his mentally driven shroud, but he did not have enough time: the Ascendant sped through the open door.

Taran'atar drove one leg onto the deck and thrust himself forward and down. He rammed his uninjured shoulder into the Ascendant's midsection. It felt like running squarely into a tritanium bulkhead. The impact sent a painful jolt down through Taran'atar's side and into his hip. Regardless, he pushed ahead, wrapping his arms around the Ascendant's waist and knocking him from his feet. The two of them crashed heavily onto the deck.

Taran'atar quickly scrambled to his knees astride the Ascendant. The Jem'Hadar raised his fist and propelled his knuckles into the alien's face. A gash opened in the flesh beneath one large, golden eye, and cloudy silver blood gushed from it. The Ascendant cried out, the highly melodic nature of his voice unable to mask his surprise and pain.

Taran'atar hammered his other hand—the disruptor still clutched in his grasp—into his adversary's chest. The weapon's handle struck the Ascendant's exoskeletal sheath, sending fresh shudders of agony reverberating through Taran'atar's arm and into his wounded shoulder. He gasped in pain, but only for a moment: the Ascendant's hand shot up and grabbed him by the throat, cutting off his ability to breathe.

The disruptor dropped from Taran'atar's fingers as he instinctively clawed at the Ascendant's hand, attempting to dislodge it from around his neck. Instead, the powerful alien reached up with his other hand and doubled his grip around the Jem'Hadar's throat. Though he had heard about the great strength of the Ascendants, it still startled him to experience such tremendous force firsthand. Taran'atar grabbed his adversary's wrists and tried with all of his might to pull them away. The Ascendant only tightened his hold.

Blackness began to form at the periphery of Taran'atar's vision. Changing tack, the Jem'Hadar jammed his legs down into the deck like pistons, trying to push himself up and away. The action had no effect. The Ascendant held him fast.

Desperate, Taran'atar allowed his eyes to flutter closed and his hands to slacken. He willed himself to relax his muscles even as the Ascendant worked to strangle the life out of him. He expected his adversary to ease his grip, but he didn't; he continued to choke the Jem'Hadar.

With time running out, Taran'atar looked down and jabbed

at the face of the Ascendant, plunging his fingers into one of the alien's eyes. For the second time, the Ascendant yelled out in pain. His fingers loosened about Taran'atar's neck, and the Jem'Hadar used the opportunity to his advantage. He pulled the Ascendant's hands apart and jumped to his feet. Before his adversary could recover, Taran'atar raised one leg and slammed the hard heel of his boot into the alien's chest.

Taran'atar felt his own tibia fracture. He heard the break not only externally, but internally as well, the unmistakable sound translated to his ears not just through the air, but through the bone and blood and tissue of his own body. Agony screamed in his leg, the impact of his foot against the Ascendant's exoskeletal sheath sending shockwaves through him. Not allowing his injury to stop him, he kicked out again, swinging his damaged leg toward his adversary's head. Taran'atar's foot connected, but with only a glancing blow.

The Jem'Hadar staggered sideways as he brought his wounded leg down onto the deck. He fell against the bulkhead and gasped for breath, gulping in great lungfuls of air. Taking his weight off his broken leg, he sought to recover enough to act.

Suddenly, the Ascendant reached for Taran'atar's good leg and swept it out from under him, sending him crashing to the deck. The Jem'Hadar's broken bone howled.

The Ascendant came at him. A punch landed on Taran'atar's face, snapping his head back with great force. A second struck, and then a third. The cartilage in his nose crumbled. He reached up both arms to protect himself, only to have the Ascendant pummel his torso, driving the air from his lungs.

Through the gap between his forearms, in the staccato flashes of light from the overhead panels, Taran'atar saw his adversary's face. One eye looked as though it had deflated, like a gas-filled sac that has ruptured. A mass of viscous golden fluid filled half the socket and spilled down the Ascendant's cheek.

Struggling to breathe, the Jem'Hadar lashed out. The Ascendant moved to protect his face—and obviously his remaining eye. Taran'atar instead leveled his attack at his adversary's chest, where a milky stain had spread around the crack in the exoskeletal sheath. The Jem'Hadar felt something give in his hand as he drove his fist over and over into the Ascendant's breastplate. Taran'atar saw his own little finger extending awkwardly out from his closed hand and realized that he had dislocated it. He ignored the new injury and continued his assault. The alien emitted a music-like squawk that sounded equal parts anger and pain.

Finally, the Ascendant fell backward onto the deck, his hands reaching toward the wound in his chest. Taran'atar started after him, but his adversary swung about wildly, connecting on the side of the Jem'Hadar's head. Waves of dizziness and nausea buffeted him. Taran'atar quickly scuttled away. When he looked back at the Ascendant, he saw the alien starting to rise.

Urgency filled the Jem'Hadar. He needed to regroup. Despite the damage he'd inflicted on the Ascendant, Taran'atar could not mount much more of an attack, given his own injuries. He attempted to clear his mind and shroud, but had no success.

Taran'atar pulled himself back up on his feet, steadying himself against the bulkhead. He thought that perhaps he could find a weapon—surely some must be stored somewhere aboard *Even Odds*. But that meant that if he could locate a firearm, so, too, could the Ascendant.

As Taran'atar began to stumble away, he espied the disruptor that his adversary had left for him in the hand of the dead Eline-dumayo. He doubted that the Ascendant would have provided him a weapon that could be repaired and fired, but he still thought he might make use of it. He considered the nature of *Even Odds* and its multiple cargo holds, and an idea began to germinate in his mind.

Taran'atar rushed forward as best he could, limping on his broken leg, his arms held out straight before him. He reached toward the Ascendant's wounded chest, and the alien moved to block him, as the Jem'Hadar expected him to do. Taran'atar adjusted his aim and struck his adversary's shoulders, causing the alien to overbalance and tumble back to the deck. The

Jem'Hadar's dislocated finger bent further out of position, erupting in a fresh torrent of pain.

Extending his wounded leg out to the side, Taran'atar bent and retrieved the disruptor. He tucked it into his belt, then headed for the ladder that had brought him to *Even Odds'* top deck. Nursing his injuries as best he could, he lowered himself down and through the open hatchway.

As he did, he glanced back along the deck and saw a trail of amber drops marking the course he'd taken. Taran'atar hadn't realized he was bleeding, and he could only conclude that his broken bone had punctured his skin. He peered down past his waist and saw blood seeping through the lower leg of his black coverall and onto his boot. He considered what he would need to do to prevent himself from leaving a trail, then decided against it.

No matter what I do, the Ascendant will find me, he thought. *This ship is not that big, and I'm badly wounded.* Even considering the damage that Taran'atar had inflicted on the Ascendant, the Jem'Hadar realized that he should not be asking himself how he could avoid his adversary, but how he could use their next eventual encounter to his own advantage.

Taran'atar descended clumsily to the second deck, pausing only to close the hatch behind him, and then to open the next one below. He climbed down to the third level, and then to the fourth and lowest deck. There, he threw his back against a bulkhead and held his wounded hand up before his face. He quickly reached up and wrenched his dislocated finger back into place. Although momentarily torturous, the ache in his hand settled down to a dull throb.

The Jem'Hadar then tore at his coverall, ripping both sleeves off. He tied one tightly around his thigh to stem the bleeding of his broken leg, and the other about his tibia in order to keep his fractured bone in place. He once more attempted to shroud, without result.

Taran'atar didn't wait to see how long it would take for the Ascendant to pursue him. He shambled as best he could along the corridor toward the starboard side of the vessel, and then aft when he reached an intersection. Behind him, he saw, his boot left amber smudges on the deck plating.

Lurching down the corridor that traversed the length of *Even Odds*, Taran'atar performed a mental inventory of what little he carried with him, and reckoning what he could expect to find on the bottom deck. He might locate a weapons locker, but considering the sabotage he believed *Even Odds'* crew to have perpetrated on their ship, he suspected that they might have hidden—or even destroyed—whatever armaments they hadn't taken for themselves. If he could locate their bodies, he might find some of their weapons, but he also thought that the Ascendant would have been careful to collect them for his own use.

Then again, Taran'atar's adversary had been carrying only a single firearm. The Jem'Hadar had thrown his knife during the battle, leaving him with only the faulty disruptor. If he could locate some tools, he still might make use of the weapon. Since both of *Even Odds'* two lower decks had profiled on sensors as housing engineering and cargo facilities, Taran'atar believed that he could find what he needed.

As he tottered down the corridor, he pulled the disruptor from where he had tucked it into his belt. He examined the weapon as he worked to solidify the rudiments of his plan into a detailed prescription for survival. He would need to find an engineering compartment and then a cargo bay.

Taran'atar stopped at the first door he reached. He worked to manually open it. In the on-again, off-again overhead lighting, he saw the interior of a turbolift. He moved on.

The second door led into a refresher, but the third revealed an engine room. He went inside and spotted a toolkit almost at once. Within, he found instruments he could use.

As Taran'atar worked to open up the disruptor, he heard a sound from off in the distance: the light ring of something tapping against a metal surface. Then he heard it again . . . and again: footfalls on the rungs of a ladder.

The Ascendant was coming.

*　　　　*　　　　*

BEHIND A LINE of irregularly stacked cargo containers, Taran'atar sat on the deck, his injured leg twisted out in front of him. The pain had not completely subsided, but it had changed, from a sharp, piercing sensation to a deep, abiding ache. His scorched shoulder had gone numb, and his re-set finger pulsed only dully. He thought that he might actually be able to shroud again, but he elected not to try.

From his position, Taran'atar could not see the large hatchway through which he had entered the cargo hold. He had inserted an optronic coupler into the shirtsleeve he'd tied about his thigh, spinning the device to tighten the fabric just above his knee. His makeshift tourniquet had stemmed his bleeding, and so he'd avoided leaving an amber trail leading directly to his location, but he still expected the Ascendant to readily track him down. Taran'atar had taken cover behind the gray, cube-shaped cargo containers not for the purpose of concealment, but for protection. Once his adversary—

A leaden thud resounded through the half-empty hold, a sound Taran'atar recognized as the activation of the inner hatch's manual release. The Jem'Hadar had closed it behind him when he'd entered the expansive compartment. The rasp of metal on metal followed as the Ascendant forced open the hatch, then pushed it closed. The alien had taken seconds longer than Taran'atar had anticipated to reach the hold, and the Jem'Hadar hoped that the inexact work he had performed— quickly and under duress—would not only provide the result he sought, but that it would not do so too early.

Taran'atar waited, but he heard no footsteps. Alert to the amount of time passing, and also to the possibility that somebody other than the Ascendant might have entered the hold— the scoutship's sensors had placed the Jeflinic life-form on the lower decks—the Jem'Hadar scuffled to his feet. He made only a cursory attempt to do so silently. He supported himself against the cargo containers, shifting to one side in order to peer past the edge of the last one in the row. As he moved, he felt the tug of his belt around one of his arms, hindering his movement. He adjusted his stance, then leaned out so that he had a clear line of sight to the hatchway.

The Ascendant stood there, staring with his remaining eye in Taran'atar's direction. The overhead lighting continued to blink off and then on, and then off once more. By the time it illuminated the cargo hold again, the Ascendant had started racing toward the Jem'Hadar.

Concerned only moments before that his adversary would not arrive soon enough, Taran'atar suddenly grew anxious that the Ascendant would reach him too quickly. The alien's long legs devoured the distance across the hold. His chest still wore a cloudy mask around his wound, and cords of muscle and nerve hung from the dark hole where his eye had been.

Taran'atar braced himself as best he could on his intact leg. He prepared to launch a volley of punches, visualizing in his mind how he would meet the Ascendant's attack. In the flashing overhead light, the alien appeared to grow closer in discrete increments, as though bounding across the hold. Over the final stretch of deck, the Ascendant sprang, disappearing into darkness as the lighting panels again switched off. Taran'atar cocked his fist, trying to time his assault.

A brilliant blue-white flare suddenly threw the entire compartment into garish relief. The roar of the explosion reached Taran'atar a fraction of a second later. The concussive force of the blast knocked him to the deck even as a windstorm burgeoned in the cargo hold, capturing both the Jem'Hadar and his adversary in its swift currents. Taran'atar felt himself lifted into the air as he saw the Ascendant's direction change in mid-leap, both of them carried toward the great, ragged hole that had been torn in the compartment's outer hatch, exposing the ship to space.

The flash of the detonating disruptor pistol faded, replaced for a few moments by the orange glow of fire. Before the Jem'Hadar had affixed the weapon to the outer hatch, he had rigged it to overload. The lighting panels in the hold began to flicker, not with the regular off-and-on cadence Taran'atar had so far witnessed aboard *Even Odds*, but sporadically.

The cargo containers shifted, their bulk pushed forward by the atmosphere blowing out into the void. Several toppled from the stacks, one of them breaking apart and loosing heaps of clothing onto the deck. A flurry of garments flew with the rush of air out into space, but the weight of the containers held them in place against the diminishing gusts.

Taran'atar's arm jerked against the belt he had tied around it, the other end secured to a handhold in the bulkhead. He craned his neck to look toward the compromised bulkhead where the outer hatch had been, and he saw the Ascendant tumbling toward it. The alien clawed at the deck, desperately seeking purchase.

He did not find it.

The Ascendant slid across the deck. He grabbed for the outer bulkhead as he slammed into it. His hand clutched at something there, momentarily halting his progress, but then he tumbled toward the jagged hole and through it. Taran'atar saw his adversary's silver fingers holding on to a flap of uneven metal.

As the atmosphere in the hold rushed out into space, its force continued to diminish. Taran'atar felt himself released by the gales, leaving him in an airless calm. He did not hold his breath, but released it very slowly, wanting to avoid damaging his lungs in an environment abruptly robbed of pressure. He kept his attention on the Ascendant's hand, and saw a second set of fingers join the first as the alien attempted to climb back into the ship.

Taran'atar quickly untied his belt from around his arm and staggered as fast as he could toward the hole. Pain shrieked through his leg. Above him, the lighting panels sparked three times in rapid succession, then died totally, plunging the cargo hold into darkness. Only the span of stars visible out in space provided a break in the otherwise-pervasive black.

As Taran'atar neared the hole, he saw a shape blot out some of the stars: the silhouette of the Ascendant working to pull himself back aboard. The Jem'Hadar lengthened his stride as much as possible. He wanted to scream but didn't, understanding the need to continue releasing his breath slowly, as well as the futility of crying out with no medium to carry the sound.

The form of the Ascendant's head and torso became visible against the backdrop of stars as he hauled himself back through the hole in the outer bulkhead. Taran'atar took one more leap across the deck, landing on his intact leg, then adjusted his weight so that he could kick with it. His boot connected with the Ascendant's head, which snapped back.

Taran'atar crashed to the deck, his broken leg taxed beyond its limits. A hand groped for his other foot, and the Jem'Hadar thrust the heel of his boot toward his adversary. It impacted against the Ascendant's shoulder, but did not dislodge the alien's grip on the bulkhead. Taran'atar kicked out again, hitting his adversary in the head. The Jem'Hadar cocked his leg once more, preparing to strike again, but he no longer saw the figure of the Ascendant.

Reaching for the broken edge of the bulkhead, Taran'atar hauled himself forward so that he could look out into space. Even in the dim light provided by the distant stars, he picked out the Ascendant, its silver exoskeleton acutely reflective. The alien had been thrown from the ship, and even as Taran'atar watched, his adversary's body grew smaller the farther he drifted from *Even Odds*.

Taran'atar couldn't breathe. He had emptied his lungs, and the explosion of the overloading disruptor pistol had cleared the cargo hold of its atmosphere. He turned away from the hole and looked toward the location of the inner hatch, the heavy door lost in the darkness. He pushed himself up, but when he tried to walk, he could no longer put any weight at all on his broken leg. He fell back to the deck

Out of habit, Taran'atar refused to surrender. He began to crawl forward across the compartment. He intended to reach the inner hatch and open it, so that he could return to the ship's atmosphere before sealing the cargo hold closed behind him. As he pulled himself along in the darkness, he pictured the hatchway ahead of him, judging its distance from him by memory.

Taran'atar made it only halfway across the deck before he lost consciousness.

"I FOUND HIM that way," said Dez, still seated in the mess hall, across the table from Kira. Taran'atar had remained standing as he'd related the circumstances that had first brought him aboard *Even Odds*. "I was monitoring the Ascendant with passive sensors when Taran'atar showed up on the ship."

"You're a Jeflinic, then?" Kira asked, and Dez nodded. Until Taran'atar had told his story, Kira had never heard of the species. "You were one of the crew members still on board—the only one left alive by the time Taran'atar arrived." Many of those she'd met aboard *Even Odds* claimed to have lived on the ship for years, but the battle with the Ascendant had occurred just nine months earlier. Since Taran'atar's scans had shown only two lifeforms aboard—the Ascendant and a Jeflinic—Kira reasoned that Dezavrim had sent the majority of his crew off of *Even Odds* prior to the attack, perhaps in an auxiliary or emergency vessel.

"Well, I was the only one that Taran'atar and the Ascendant could detect on sensors," Dez said, putting the lie to Kira's conclusion.

"You employed sensor inhibitors?" Kira asked.

"Not exactly," Dez said. "I'll let Taran'atar show you where the rest of the crew hid themselves. I told you that the *Even Odds* is an interesting ship."

"But you didn't go into hiding yourself," Kira said, stating the obvious in order to judge Dezavrim's reaction.

"Somebody had to face the Ascendant," he said, "otherwise he simply would have seized the ship for his own use, or at the very least, he would have stripped it of whatever technology he could utilize and then destroyed what was left. Either way, I didn't like the chances for our survival."

"You defended the ship on your own?" Kira asked.

"No," Dez said, and a pall fell over his features. "Bradahk'la stood with me. She functioned as the ship's security, when necessary."

"She was the Eline-dumayo I found dead at the entrance to the command-and-control center," Taran'atar said. "She had the disruptor pistol in her hand."

"I'm sorry," Kira told Dez. She understood more than she ever wanted to the anguish of losing people under her command.

Dez looked off to the side and slowly shook his head. "I brought her aboard as a gemologist, but when our previous security personnel left the ship, Brad wanted to take over that function as well. She considered that her primary job aboard the *Even Odds*, and she treated it very seriously." He gazed back over at Kira. "On a personal level, it was hard to lose Brad, but it also underscored our need for somebody to assume her responsibilities. Fortunately, once Glessin treated his injuries, Taran'atar agreed to join us."

"I see," Kira said, more sharply than she intended. She could not deny that she felt betrayed by the Jem'Hadar—not because he had nearly killed her, since he had been under Iliana Ghemor's control at the time he'd done that, but because Kira had offered him essentially the same opportunity aboard Deep Space 9 as Dez had aboard *Even Odds*. *I offered him the same opportunity*, Kira thought, *but with people who knew and cared about him*.

The story Taran'atar told had revealed why he hadn't stayed aboard the station: he'd wanted to return to the Dominion, and to the life he had known for most of his existence. Clearly, the distress signal transmitted by the crew of *Even Odds* had altered the Jem'Hadar's personal trajectory. In initially defending them against the Ascendant, and then in subsequently becoming their security officer, he'd found a new purpose—albeit one that strongly resembled his lifelong purpose, and one that he could just as easily have undertaken aboard DS9.

Taran'atar did not react to Kira's blatant discontent with the decision he'd made, but Dez seemed to when he said, "It took some convincing."

"I know how obdurate Taran'atar can be," Kira said.

"No, I didn't mean that I had to convince Taran'atar," Dez said. "I had to convince most of my crew. When I retrieved him from Four Bay, he was unconscious and suffering from all the injuries he mentioned: a badly broken leg, a burned shoulder, and a dislocated finger, not to mention internal bleeding and deep bruising. It took our medic hours to initially treat him, and several more days to fully repair his leg."

Kira recalled the man who had tended to her in sickbay, Allo Glessin—a Cardassian. She remembered her own reaction when she'd first met the medic, an emotional, unthinking response born out of the anger and resentment she'd felt for Cardassians—for *all* Cardassians—during and after the Occupation. Considering the hundreds of millions of Glessin's people who had died at the hands of the Jem'Hadar less than two years prior, at the end of the Dominion War, Kira imagined that it must have been difficult for the medic to minister to Taran'atar's needs, and she said as much.

"No, I don't think it was difficult for him at all," Dez said. "He's a man of medicine, and Taran'atar was his patient, so he treated him with no hesitation that I could see."

Kira scolded herself. For years, she had watched Doctor Bashir work hard to save the lives of countless individuals, including those he considered enemies of the Federation. Indeed, for all her life, she had observed high-minded medical professionals employ their skills, no matter the identities of their patients. She should have known better.

"Now, whether or not Glessin wanted to invite a Jem'Hadar to be a member of our crew, that was a different matter," Dez added. "We generally try to stay clear of the Dominion, and especially the Jem'Hadar. Their martial capabilities are known throughout the Gamma Quadrant."

"*And* throughout the Alpha Quadrant," Kira noted.

"Of course," Dez said. "So you can understand why most of the crew felt nervous about having a Jem'Hadar aboard. We were far from any place where we could safely off-load him, and I didn't want to sacrifice our auxiliary vessel or any of our emergency escape pods. Plus he would need some degree of medical observation and care while he convalesced. Some of the crew suggested keeping him sedated until we made planetfall, but Glessin counseled that doing so for an extended period would hinder his physical recovery."

"So you allowed him to regain consciousness," Kira said.

"We did," Dez confirmed. "At first, fear overshadowed curiosity for most of the crew, and they stayed away. But as the days passed and Taran'atar underwent rehabilitation for his injuries, we all met him, and even began to develop a rapport of sorts with him." Kira stole a glance at Taran'atar, who continued to stand unmoving beside the table, his expression stoic, giving no indication at all that he even listened to the captain's words. "We'd lost Brad during the Ascendant's attack, and so the notion of bringing true muscle aboard the ship arose and began to take hold. Taran'atar concurred with our assessment that he could be of vital assistance to our crew, and so he agreed to join us."

Kira again looked up at the Jem'Hadar. It troubled her that he had chosen to join the crew of *Even Odds* after he had declined to stay aboard DS9; she couldn't help but take his decision personally. She attempted to console herself that it had been a matter of timing and circumstance, and that before he'd left the station, Taran'atar hadn't yet been prepared to alter the nature of his life. Once he had opted not to return to the Dominion and to pursue his own path instead, she supposed that becoming a member of the *Even Odds* crew seemed as likely as anything else a method of restoring purpose to his existence.

"It also helped us to see that Taran'atar is different from other Jem'Hadar," Dez said. "He demonstrated that when he came to our rescue with no more impetus than his receipt of our distress call. We didn't understand just how different he was until after Glessin had fully examined him." Kira understood the reference to Taran'atar's abnormal lack of dependence on ketracel-white.

Dez stood up. "I need to get to the bridge and check on

our status," he said. "We're making a delivery to Vrynax Two, and we often run into problems getting there." When Kira rose from her seat, he added, "It's really been a pleasure to meet you, Captain."

"And you, Captain," Kira replied. "I don't think I've said so, but I'm grateful to you and your crew for recovering me."

"We're happy to have done it," Dez told her. "If it's all right with you, I'd like Taran'atar to take you on a tour of our ship. Perhaps he can also tell you about the time he's spent aboard the *Even Odds*."

"I *would* like to see the rest of the ship," Kira said, "and I'm certainly willing to listen to whatever you and Taran'atar and the others have to say." Although she didn't yet know precisely how she would or even should proceed, Kira doubted that she would remain aboard *Even Odds* for much longer. Before she departed, though, she wanted to learn as much as she could about the ship.

"I will leave you to it, then," Dez said. "Shall we reconvene here for dinner? I'd like to hear your impressions." Kira agreed, and Dezavrim left the mess hall, headed for the bridge.

Once he'd gone, Kira looked to Taran'atar. "We can begin on D deck," he said, "and work our way upward." She followed him through the door and out into the corridor. They walked in silence to the nearest turbolift.

Once they had boarded the cab, Kira said, "You appear to have made quite an impression on Captain Dezavrim."

"The crew of the *Even Odds* were accustomed to avoiding the Jem'Hadar, for fear of having to face them in battle," Taran'atar said. When the door closed, he stated their destination as Aft Engineering Control, and the lift began to descend. "They did not expect a Jem'Hadar soldier to come to their aid."

"It sounded like there was more to it than that," Kira observed. "Dez said that they only realized how different you were once Glessin examined you. They must have determined that you don't require doses of ketracel-white to survive."

"They did," Taran'atar said. The turbolift completed its downward journey and began moving horizontally. "They also discovered that many of the cells in my body have regenerated."

"What does that mean?"

"Glessin believes it means that, even though I am a Jem'Hadar elder, I am not on the verge of dying," Taran'atar explained. His tone remained level despite the apparent momentousness of the information he revealed.

The Founders, Kira knew, had engineered the Jem'Hadar to live limited lifespans, typically little more than two decades in length. By all accounts, Taran'atar should have been nearing the end of his life. "How much longer does Glessin think you'll live?"

"He can't know with certainty," Taran'atar said as the turbolift glided to a halt, "but he estimates that I can survive for at least another decade, and perhaps even two." He delivered the information with no inflection, with no hint that he considered the change to his personal circumstances a positive one. Kira suspected that, as with his time aboard Deep Space 9, he did not know how to process the situation.

She nevertheless told him, "That's wonderful." If Taran'atar could not see the value in his continued existence, perhaps Kira could lead him in that direction.

The Jem'Hadar did not respond. Instead, he exited the turbolift, turned left, and marched down the corridor. Kira followed.

They approached a door marked with symbols that she interpreted as meaning *engineering* and *warp drive*. As Taran'atar keyed in a sequence on a panel in the bulkhead beside the door, Kira realized that she would have to reevaluate the purposes for which the Prophets had sent her back into the past. She had considered that saving the life of Taran'atar might be among Their reasons, but she had discounted that possibility given the likelihood that, had he not died in the *Even Odds* disaster, he would shortly thereafter have faced his own intrinsic mortality anyway. With the revelation of his extended lifespan, though,

Kira would have to factor that in to whatever course of action she chose to take.

10

Fresh from the sonic shower, Ro stepped out of the refresher and into her bedroom. She had pulled on her undergarments and maroon uniform shirt when the comm system sounded its multitoned activation signal. The voice of the operation center's delta-shift duty officer followed.

"*Hub to Captain Ro,*" said Ensign Vigo Melijnek.

"Ro here. Go ahead, Vigo."

"*Captain, you have an incoming transmission from Bajor,*" Melijnek said. "*It's First Minister Asarem.*"

The news surprised Ro. After her meeting the previous day with Commander Desjardins, the captain had followed his advice and contacted the Bajoran minister of justice, Elren Dast. Ro detailed for Elren the arrival on the starbase of the man calling himself Altek Dans, and explaining the ensuing predicament. Because she and her crew had been as yet unable to confirm Altek's identity, or to verify the information he'd given them, the captain sought to transfer custody of the stranger from Federation jurisdiction to that of the authorities on Bajor, thereby creating a legal—if morally hazy—justification for his continued detention. The justice minister promised to take the matter under advisement, and to render a timely decision.

Ro had therefore expected to hear from Elren or one of his deputies that day—the last on which the captain could lawfully hold Altek without charging him with a crime—but she did not doubt that the first minister was contacting her about the situation. "Stand by," she told Melijnek. Ro grabbed her black uniform pants from where she'd laid them on the bed and quickly pulled them on. She didn't bother to put on her gray-shouldered tunic.

Ro walked out into the living area of her quarters and

crossed to the inner bulkhead, where she took a seat behind her desk. "Go ahead, Ensign," she said, knowing that the ship's comm system would relay her words to the Hub. "Put Minister Asarem through." She activated the companel on her desktop with a touch, and the asymmetrical chevron of the Starfleet emblem appeared on the screen.

"Aye, sir."

The Starfleet insignia winked off a moment later, replaced by the image of the Bajoran first minister. Long, straight black hair framed her fetching, sienna-colored features. Though a decade older than Ro, Asarem looked to be of no particular age, having a timeless quality about her. She had a fit, almost athletic build, and she carried herself with a stately grace.

Ro saw that the first minister sat at the desk in her office, which was housed in a government building in Ashalla, Bajor's capital city. She wore an elegant royal-blue blouse made of a shimmery material. Since moving into a political life at the end of the Occupation, Asarem had long served her people. She had initially taken the position of second minister under her predecessor, Shakaar Edon, and had then succeeded him after he had been taken control of by an invading parasitic life-form and eventually killed. She had finished out the final months of his six-year term as the political leader of Bajor, and she'd been reelected twice since then, notably earning more than three-quarters of the vote in her most recent election.

"Good morning, Captain Ro," Asarem said. Ro could see the bright rays of the just-risen B'hava'el slanting across the wall behind the first minister. Deep Space 9's simulated twenty-six-hour day corresponded directly to that of Ashalla.

"Good morning, First Minister."

"I know it's early," Asarem said, acknowledging but not apologizing for the dawn contact. *"I judged it best to speak with you as soon as possible."*

"I presume that you want to discuss Altek Dans."

"I do," Asarem said. *"Minister Elren informed me of your request for Bajor to extradite Mister Altek from Federation cus-*

tody. He considered the issue and reached a decision on his own, but given the nature of recent events, he felt compelled to consult with me before making a final ruling."

"May I ask what conclusion the justice minister reached?" Ro suspected that Elren intended to deny the extradition, and that the first minister needed to understand the reasons that she should overrule him. Even if Elren sided with the captain, though, Asarem likely wanted to hear from Ro directly about the unusual request.

"Minister Elren told me that, under normal circumstances, he would have declined extradition without even seeking my opinion."

"And what *is* your opinion, First Minister?" asked Ro, her tone respectful but firm. She fully anticipated Asarem agreeing with her, even if the Bajoran leader needed some measure of convincing. Since Ro had taken over command of the original Deep Space 9 six and a half years prior, she had enjoyed a solid rapport with Asarem on those infrequent occasions when circumstances had obliged them to work together. After the destruction of the station, the first minister acted quickly and decisively to establish an interim working environment on Bajor for the surviving DS9 crew, and she played an instrumental part in expediting construction of the new starbase. During that time, Asarem and Ro coordinated and collaborated far more often than they had previously, which only strengthened their relationship.

"I agree with Minister Elren," Asarem said.

It took a moment for Ro to realize that she hadn't heard what she'd expected. The first minister's words left her nonplussed. Though she had in some ways softened during her years in power, Asarem still possessed a reputation as a hard-nosed leader, quick to act when it came to ensuring the safety of her people. It made no sense to Ro that the first minister would not do everything she could to detain Altek until they could be sure of his intentions in the Bajoran system.

"But why?" Ro finally asked.

Asarem's jaw clenched, a reaction Ro thought demonstrated

that, while the people around the first minister could debate issues, they rarely challenged her directly. *"I agree with rejecting your request to extradite Mister Altek,"* Asarem said, her voice hardening, *"because there is no legal justification for transferring him to Bajoran custody."* Ro also noted the toughening of the first minister's choice of words, shifting from *declining* the extradition request to *rejecting* it.

"With all due respect, First Minister," Ro said carefully, "the justification is what happened eight days ago on Deep Space Nine." She didn't know for how long President Bacco's assassination would inform thought processes and decision making throughout the UFP and beyond, but she understood that the timeframe would ultimately be measured in years, not in days. "The Federation—and by extension Bajor—was attacked in the most villainous way possible. Until we know with certainty who committed the assassination, and who was behind it, I think we have all the rationale we require to continue holding Altek."

"Captain Ro, I genuinely appreciate your concerns, and I share them myself," Asarem said. *"The difficulty is that yours is not a legal argument."*

"Maybe not, but it *is* an attempt to safeguard the thousands of people under my command, the ten thousand civilians on this starbase, and the billions on Bajor." It actually surprised Ro that the first minister did not subscribe to such an obvious and reasonable point of view.

"I understand the potential threat of which you speak," Asarem said, *"but we are charged with protecting more than simply the lives of those whom we lead: we must protect their values."*

Ro slowly shook her head as she tried to fathom the first minister's reluctance to keep Altek in custody for three additional days. The captain liked Asarem Wadeen, both as a person and as a leader. Ro generally found her straightforward in their dealings, but it would be folly to ignore either the political necessities incumbent upon the first minister's position, or the corresponding skills that she brought to bear. The captain wondered if her refusal to extradite Altek Dans had anything to do with the DS9 crew arresting Asarem's own chief of staff, Enkar Sirsy, as the president's assassin. Although additional evidence later vindicated Enkar, Ro knew that the first minister was still dealing with the political fallout of having a member of her administration even suspected of such an odious crime. Asarem might simply want to avoid the complications sure to arise from transferring Altek from Federation to Bajoran confinement.

"First Minister, it does little good to preserve somebody's values if you can't keep that person alive and healthy," Ro argued. "Altek might or might not pose a threat to Deep Space Nine or to Bajor if we release him, but he definitely won't if we keep holding him."

"*I disagree,*" Asarem said. "*If we illegally detain Altek, the threat we face is to our way of life. We cannot selectively enforce our laws. To do so diminishes us as a civilization, and lowers us to the moral and ethical ranks of those who oppose us.*"

Ro looked away from her companel screen. She understood Asarem's point, but the captain had never allowed rules and regulations—or even laws—to prevent her from doing what she believed needed to be done. She had certainly witnessed and fought against wrongful detention—the Cardassians had essentially imprisoned the entire world of Bajor for decades—but she also remembered, in vivid detail, the sight of President Bacco staggering backward, not once but twice, before crumbling to the floor, the victim of three shots from a sniper's projectile weapon.

And Nanietta Bacco wasn't the only victim, Ro thought angrily. The assassination impacted all the people of the Federation. She didn't know if Altek Dans intended to add to the misery and instability the president's murder had wrought, but she did not wish to take that chance.

"First Minister, your refusal to approve Altek's transfer into Bajoran custody means that I will have no choice but to release him later today," Ro said. "What happens if tomorrow—or even next month or next year—he sets off an explosive on this starbase, or brings down a government building on Bajor, or assassinates the next Federation president?"

"Of course, we must all do what we can to prevent that."

"That's what I'm trying to do," Ro said, her voice rising as she leaned in toward her companel.

"But you're doing it in the wrong way," Asarem snapped back, color rising in her cheeks. She paused, appearing to rein in her emotions. When she spoke again, she did so with intensity, but not anger. *"It would obviously be awful if we release Altek Dans and he commits some terrible act. I will likely pay a steep political price if that happens. But it is not my responsibility to protect my job; it is to lead the people of Bajor, to act in their best interests."*

Ro took a breath and settled back in her chair. "That's what I'm asking you to do," she said.

"It is not leadership to act based on fear," Asarem said. *"We have laws, but more important than that, we have bedrock moral principles underlying our laws. It is not acceptable for us to bring the weight and resources of the Federation or Bajoran governments down upon an individual based solely on suspicions. We cannot restrict the freedom of a man simply because we do not know who he is or where he came from, or even because of what he thinks or says. Actions are punishable by the state, and nothing more. To the best of my knowledge, Altek Dans has not committed any crimes, has he?"*

"No, First Minister," the captain said with reluctance. Ro wanted to point out the unfairness of some laws, and the historical record of states treating people unjustly. How many times had Ro bent Starfleet regulations, or outright violated them—and not always to good effect? How often had she broken Bajoran or Federation laws in favor of doing the right thing?

More times than I can list, she thought. *And I'm trying to get around the law now.* Somehow, though, her attempted actions felt different, particularly in light of what the first minister had said. Where Ro had so often taken justice into her own hands in order to aid an individual or a small group of people, she had lobbied Minister Elren to act *against* a single person.

All at once, Ro felt that she had lost her way.

Very quietly, Asarem said, *"I trust your judgment, Laren."* Juxtaposed with the onset of her self-doubt, the first minister's declaration seemed generous. *"You're plainly worried that this Altek Dans could be a danger to Deep Space Nine or Bajor,"* Asarem continued. *"Can you qualify your concerns? Is there anything at all besides the timing and unexpectedness of Altek's arrival, and your inability to verify his identity, that makes you consider him a threat?"*

"When he came aboard," Ro said, "he was carrying a projectile weapon with him—a firearm similar to the one used to assassinate President Bacco."

"How similar?"

"It was a projectile weapon, but archaic," Ro admitted. "Analysis shows that it was fashioned out of primitive materials by an outmoded manufacturing process. It resembled the weapon that killed the president only in type."

"Is that the primary source of your concern?" Asarem asked.

Ro thought about that. At the time, the possession by Altek of such a firearm had immediately motivated her to take him into custody, although he had not intentionally brought the weapon aboard, since it had been Ro who'd ordered him transported onto the starbase. Regardless, it had been his lack of a confirmable identity or history, along with his claim that he did not know where he was or how he had come to be there, that troubled her the most. She told all of that to the first minister.

"Maybe he's telling the truth," Asarem suggested. *"If he came to the Bajoran system with some nefarious plan, wouldn't he have fabricated a believable identity and backstory for himself?"*

"You'd think so," Ro said.

"The Prophets sent Akorem Laan out of the Celestial Temple, out of the past," Asarem noted. Ro had seldom heard the first minister reference anything in a religious context, either in public or in private. The captain had always assumed that Asarem, as secular leader of the Bajorans, purposefully observed the distinction between her duties and those of the kai, the people's spiritual guide. Ro knew, though, that the first minister

nevertheless counted herself as a believer. *"Perhaps the Prophets have delivered Altek Dans from another time as well."*

"Perhaps," Ro said, "but I've read through the accounts of Akorem's return. There are significant dissimilarities between his story and Altek's. For one thing, Akorem Laan was traveling in a lightship when he entered the wormhole. Altek Dans makes no such claims. Akorem also experienced a form of communication with the—" Ro intended to call them the *wormhole aliens*, but she didn't wish to offend the first minister. "—with the Prophets. He saw them in the guises of people in his own life, but he still understood it to be the Prophets, and that they were responsible for sending him out of the wormhole." She realized that she should have used the term *Celestial Temple*.

Asarem took a deep breath, then exhaled slowly. *"It's a difficult situation."*

Ro had no idea how to respond. An uncomfortable silence fell between the two women. Ro didn't know what else she could say to try to convince the first minister to approve Altek's extradition, nor did she any longer know if she should. Asarem was right: fear was not reason enough to act—and particularly to act unjustly. The captain did not trust the mysterious stranger who had emerged from the wormhole, especially on the heels of the assassination, but that alone did not justify violating his individual rights—not only for his sake, but for that of Bajoran and Federation society.

"Is there anything else I can do for you?" the first minister asked.

You haven't done anything for me yet, Ro immediately thought, but then she reproached herself. Asarem hadn't approved the measure that the captain had requested of her administration, but the first minister had helped Ro recognize that she'd erred in her handling of the Altek situation. She needed to do better.

"Before Minister Elren officially denies my request," Ro said, "I will withdraw it."

"I'm pleased to hear it," Asarem said.

"I'll do that at once. Thank you, First Minister."

"Thank you, Captain," Asarem said, visibly pleased by Ro's decision. *"I appreciate your willingness to come to an agreement on this matter."* She reached to one side on her desk and tapped a control. Her image disappeared from the captain's screen, replaced by the Starfleet crest. Ro deactivated her own companel.

As she rose from her desk and crossed back to her bedroom, she said, "Ro to the Hub." A run of tones indicated the opening of a communications channel.

"This is Ensign Melijnek in the Hub."

"Vigo, contact Justice Minister Elren on Bajor," Ro said. "I need to speak with him immediately."

"Right away, Captain."

Ro hesitated, then reluctantly gave an order she knew she must. "I also want you to contact Admiral Akaar's office on Earth," she said. "I need to speak directly with the admiral, in real time, at his earliest convenience."

"Aye, sir."

"Ro out." She collected her uniform tunic from atop her bed. After pulling it on and fastening it closed, she returned to her desk to await the responding transmission from Minister Elren. Ro knew that she would also have to speak with Lieutenant Commander Blackmer to find out whether security had learned anything new about Altek—or whether they had made any progress at all regarding the mysterious visitor.

Although still nearly an hour before the start of alpha shift, the captain decided that, after she talked with the Bajoran justice minister, she would forgo her morning meal and head directly for the Hub. Ro had much to do and even more to consider before reaching a final determination about what to do with Altek Dans. At that point, she would have to either violate his rights and order his detention continued, charge him with a crime he didn't commit, or release him.

It was going to be a long day.

BLACKMER REGARDED THE DETAINEE through the doorless entryway. The security chief stood close enough to the transparent force field that he could sense the energy coursing through it, and he could hear the soft but threatening sizzle of its operation. Along the far bulkhead, Altek Dans sat in the cell's only chair, facing the large, square shelf in the corner that served as a table. As Blackmer watched, Altek popped a final morsel of food into his mouth, then wiped his hands on a cloth napkin.

"Good morning," the security chief said, though he didn't particularly subscribe to that sentiment. He had slept poorly the night before, and in the week of nights preceding it—mostly because the Federation president had been assassinated on his watch, but not entirely. For the prior two days, he had questioned Altek, but while Blackmer had quickly developed an intuition about the unexpected visitor, he had yet to draw a conclusion firm enough to bring to Captain Ro. He still had time to do so, but it troubled him that it had already taken as long as it had.

"Good morning, Mister Blackmer." Altek spoke without turning around. Although he sat with his back to the entry, he had not started at the sound of Blackmer's voice. Perhaps he had heard footfalls approaching down the corridor, perhaps he had even recognized the cadence of the steps, but the security chief didn't think so; he had trod lightly. Whatever the case, Blackmer judged Altek an especially observant and intelligent man, and one with a composure not easily shaken. After his initial surprise upon being brought on board, and his apparent disorientation, he had settled into a calmness that struck the security chief as suspicious. The man claimed to be a physician, a profession that could at least theoretically explain his cool demeanor, but he gave Blackmer the impression that he utilized the mask of his poise to hide something.

"May I come in?"

Altek rose from the chair and peered over at the security chief. "It's your prison," he said. Though the dirty clothing he'd been wearing when he'd come aboard—thick pants and a long-sleeved sweater, both black, along with heavy hiking boots—had been cleaned, it had also proven too warm. Consequently, one of the starbase's quartermasters had replicated versions of Altek's apparel for him, but in lighter-weight fabrics.

"This is not a prison," Blackmer avowed. He raised a hand to the panel beside the entryway and touched the tip of his finger to it. A horizontal yellow line flashed down the screen, accompanied by a hum. Once the scan completed, he keyed in his access code. A series of touchpads then appeared on the screen, and he lowered the force field to the cell, an action that automatically locked down the entire stockade complex. In addition, Blackmer knew that one of his top deputies, Lieutenant Shul Torem, observed the proceedings remotely, from one of the security offices.

Blackmer walked into the cell, his hands raised and open before him. "I'm unarmed," he said. He had played out the same scene numerous times in the previous two days, ever since the captain had ordered Altek detained. Blackmer had interrogated him multiple times, the security chief's manner firm throughout the first day of questioning, even occasionally tough, and shifting to a gentler, even cajoling tenor on the second.

As the force field reenergized behind him, Blackmer crossed the compartment to the lone bunk. He saw that Altek had straightened the bedclothes. The security chief perched himself on the edge of the sleeping platform. Altek, freshly shaven, turned the seat of the built-in chair toward Blackmer and sat back down. To the left of Blackmer, in the corner, a screen that did not quite reach the overhead protruded from the bulkhead, screening refresher facilities.

"Your assertion that this is not a prison does not change the fact that I have been stripped of my freedom," Altek said. When he had first been delivered into the cell, Altek had tried almost at once to leave it. He received a heavy jolt from the force field, which threw him vigorously backward from the entryway.

After that, over the first two days of his detention, Altek had seemed more or less accepting of his situation. He had also been accommodating in answering questions—although he had been unwilling or unable to provide confirmable information about his identity, where he had come from, or why he had traveled to Deep Space 9. Still, if he'd been concerned or angry about his incarceration, he'd hidden it well to that point, which made his belligerent tone that morning quite noticeable.

"As I've told you, we have no wish to hold you any longer than necessary," Blackmer said. "We only need a few questions answered."

"I have answered *all* of your questions more than once, accurately and to the best of my ability," Altek said. "It seems that you're more interested in hearing *specific* answers, regardless of whether or not they're true."

"That's not the case," Blackmer said. "We only want to know who you are, and how and why you've come here." Because of the possibility that Altek had emerged aboard the Orb not just from the wormhole, but from the past, Captain Ro had ordered the crew, while in the stranger's company, to make no references to the starbase, space travel, or other worlds. Of course, they could not adequately disguise the technology surrounding Altek, nor the alien nature of two of the people with whom he'd come into contact: Blackmer and Chief O'Brien, both of them human.

"I've told you over and over again: I am Altek Dans, a doctor from Joradell." He sounded frustrated, a feeling Blackmer shared. "I don't really know where I am, but I didn't intentionally come here, so I can only deduce that I was subdued somehow, possibly drugged, and then abducted."

It took a beat for Blackmer to realize that Altek had not only offered a possible explanation for his arrival on DS9, but had challenged the integrity of the crew by suggesting their complicity. "We did none of those things to you," the security chief said. "We found you wandering nearby, and because of the assassination that recently took place here, your presence seemed suspect."

"So you've said, but I know nothing about an assassination." It seemed to Blackmer virtually impossible for anybody at all inside the Alpha Quadrant—and especially anybody in the general vicinity of Deep Space 9—not to have heard about the murder of President Bacco, yet Altek steadfastly maintained his ignorance. The assertion made sense only either as a lie, or as a truthful declaration from somebody who hadn't been in the Alpha Quadrant in the days after the assassination—somebody, perhaps, from the past.

"A major event like that," Blackmer said, pushing Altek on the point. "You must understand why it's difficult to believe you know nothing about it."

"Maybe," Altek allowed. "But why should *I* believe *you*?"

"What?" From Blackmer's perspective, the question sounded nonsensical.

Altek rose from his chair, but not in a menacing way. "Why should I believe anything that you have to say, or anything that you imply?" he asked, his voice rising. "You seem intent on having me admit certain things, regardless of whether or not they're true. Why shouldn't I think that all of this—" He raised his hands and gestured at their surroundings. "—is some elaborate deception intended to make me confess to something I didn't do?"

Blackmer smiled without humor. "That sounds like a blatant bit of misdirection," he said. "Accuse the accusers, and by doing so, shift the blame."

"I thought you weren't accusing me of anything," Altek said. "I thought you only wanted answers to a few questions."

"Your refusal to provide verifiable answers does raise our suspicions."

"It's not my fault that you can't—or won't—verify what I've told you," Altek said, growing even louder as he took a stride toward the security chief.

Blackmer tensed, prepared for the man to spring at him. When he didn't, the security chief said, "Please sit down, Mister Altek."

For a moment, Altek didn't move, and Blackmer thought that he might be calculating the possible benefits of attacking him and taking him hostage. If so, then he correctly concluded that such actions would stand him little chance of escape. He returned to his chair.

"Now, then, Mister Altek—"

"It's *Doctor* Altek, as I've told you."

"I'm sorry. Doctor Altek," Blackmer said. "I just wish that we could confirm that."

"I'm not to blame that you haven't." The man seemed to think for a moment, then said, "How have you tried to verify who I am?"

"We . . . have records," Blackmer said vaguely, wanting to avoid mentioning computers, databases, and interstellar communications networks.

"But obviously not records that include me in them," Altek said. "So just go to the hospital in Joradell. Oh, that's right: you've never even heard of Joradell."

"No," Blackmer said.

"I find that difficult to believe," Altek said. He gazed around at the cell. "But then a lot of this is difficult to believe." He paused, then added, "Can you show proof of who *you* are?"

"Yes, I can, actually," Blackmer said. "I can produce numerous records, as well as physical evidence of my identity."

"Yes, I should've known that would be your answer," Altek said, his cynicism evident in his tone. "But can you demonstrate that those records aren't counterfeit, created solely to buttress your claims?" He leaned forward in his chair, his hands on his knees. Quietly, almost under his breath, he asked, "Are you Aleiran?"

Altek's manner made it seem as though he thought the question illicit. Blackmer recalled that, when the man had first been brought aboard, he had described Joradell as an Aleiran city on Bajor. "No, I'm not."

Altek studied the security chief's face, as though searching for some indication of deceit. Blackmer returned the man's steady gaze with his own. Eventually, Altek sat back. "I ask because . . ." He raised a hand to his face and rubbed at the bridge of his nose, along his uniformly spaced rhinal ridges, clearly alluding to the fact that Blackmer had only smooth skin there.

"Aleirans don't have ridges?" the security chief asked.

"You don't know the Aleira," Altek said, his voice filled with disbelief and confusion. "*I* am an Aleiran, and of course we have ridges . . . we *all* have ridges, Aleiran or not. Or at least I thought we did, but I heard talk sometimes at the hospital . . . little more than rumors . . . that some of the Aleiran leaders were considering a eugenics program to eliminate that physical trait."

Blackmer felt his eyes involuntarily narrow at the mention of eugenics. He had been raised to believe selective breeding, as well as genetic engineering, immoral in the extreme. Historical examples abounded of malevolent forces throughout the quadrant employing such procedures for corrupt purposes: both the Nazi Party and the Augments on Earth, the Mentosh Assembly in the Alpha Centauri system, and the Veliki on Regulus III. "Why would they do that?" Blackmer asked.

"For the same reason that they keep Bajoran slaves in Joradell: because they believe that they're superior," Altek said with disgust. "And if only the Aleira had flat noses, that would make it easier to distinguish the people they could subjugate."

"It doesn't sound as though you approve of your own people," Blackmer noted.

"I don't judge all of them as evil," Altek said. "But no, I don't approve of the way my people have enslaved the Bajora." He stood up again and held his arms straight out in front of him, his wrists together, in a recognizable pose of surrender. "So if you're one of the Aleira . . . if all of this—" Again, he looked around to include their surroundings. "—is some sort of feint to ferret out my beliefs . . . to label me as a traitor . . ." He shrugged. "You win. I admit to being anti-slavery. I admit to helping a twelve-year-old girl escape from the hospital so that she wouldn't end up as the sexual plaything of one of the ruling class in Joradell. I accept my punishment."

Blackmer considered the statements, which seemed to him both a confession and a declaration of principles. Altek's appearance matched his words: he stood tall, as though proud of the actions of which he'd spoken, but his extended arms, with his wrists pressed together, demonstrated his capitulation. Blackmer didn't need to know the particulars of Altek's story—the location of Joradell, the identity of the girl, the laws governing the Aleira—to understand the important points of the account.

All of it rang true to the security chief.

For two days, he had met repeatedly with Altek. He had questioned the mysterious stranger, pressed him, inveigled him, promised him fair treatment and an immediate release for the most basic of information. Altek had never deviated from his initial story, which had lacked any meaningful detail.

Blackmer had served in Starfleet security for two decades, and he had observed, participated in, and conducted innumerable interrogations during his career. He knew which techniques worked and which didn't. In similar circumstances, he knew, the Tzenkethi might have tortured Altek, likely extracting all manner of data from him—none of it reliable, and most, if not all of it, false. The establishment of empathy, consistency, and trust provided by far the most effective—not to mention the most ethical—means of obtaining information, and the best way to accomplish that came via conversation. After two days of talking with the security chief, Altek's tongue had been loosened, and although what he'd said had no detectable bearing on Deep Space 9, it did serve to persuade Blackmer that the stranger spoke the truth—not just with respect to his anti-slavery views and actions, but when he'd offered up his identity and place of origin, as well as claimed that he had not come to the starbase of his own free will, or with any purpose.

The security chief stood up, then reached forward and pushed down Altek's hands. "I'm not Aleiran," Blackmer said. "We haven't charged you with a crime, and what you just described to me sounds less like an illegality and more like an act of benevolence." It occurred to Blackmer that it might also have been what he had sensed Altek hiding. "Please, sit back down."

Altek went back to the chair, and Blackmer resumed his position on the edge of the bunk. The two men sat quietly for a few moments. At last, Altek said, "I'm not sure what more I can tell you. I don't know what you want from me." His voice carried no anger, merely a great weariness.

"What we want hasn't changed," Blackmer said softly. "We need to know who you are, and how and why you came here." Altek opened his mouth, clearly to protest the repeated demands, but the security chief held up the flat of his hand to stop him. "I know you've answered my questions many times." Blackmer intended to tell Altek that he believed him, but then he stopped himself from doing so. Instead, he said, "If you don't remember how you got here, what *is* the last thing you remember?"

Blackmer had asked the question before, but Altek's answer, that he'd been out in the woods for a late-night jaunt, hadn't jibed with his appearance when Chief O'Brien had transported him—or the Orb carrying him—aboard. His heavy black clothing and visible flesh had been covered with dirt. Since Altek had divulged his secret, that he had helped a girl escape servitude under an Aleiran official, Blackmer thought that he might reveal more information.

Altek wavered before speaking, as though deciding what he should say. At last, he told Blackmer, "I was on my way to Shavalla."

"Is that another Aleiran city?"

Altek snorted derisively. "It's a Bajoran city," he said. He hesitated again, but then seemed to deflate, as though his will to resist finally deserted him. "I was guiding two Bajora from slavery in Joradell to freedom in Shavalla."

"How did that lead you here?" Blackmer asked.

"I don't . . . I . . ." Altek looked away, but not toward anything in the cell: he gazed off in an unfocused way, as though looking not outward, but inward. "We were making our way through the mountains . . . we were just about to reach the road to Shavalla—" Altek bolted up out of his chair, his eyes growing wide. "I remember . . . I remember that we didn't come upon the road . . . it wasn't there. I was in a field, suddenly alone, and behind me, I didn't see where I had just traveled, but a bridge leading across a gorge to a desolate land. And . . . and—" He looked at Blackmer, his expression one of amazement. "There was an Orb—was it Anora's?—floating there in front of me . . ."

The security chief waited for him to continue. When he didn't, Blackmer asked, "You saw the Orb that brought you here?"

"I don't know," Altek said. Without looking, he slowly sat back down in his chair; if it had been moved, he would have fallen to the deck. "That . . . that's all I remember, until I was standing before you and your captain."

Blackmer considered the account. It sounded suspiciously close to what the security chief had expected to hear all along, and in some sense, what he had *wanted* to hear. Had he unintentionally conveyed that to Altek, and had that prompted Altek to fabricate his tale? Had Altek genuinely recovered his memory of the event, or had he lied about it?

Blackmer stayed in the cell for nearly another hour, continuing to try to extract information from the stranger, and to take his measure. Finally, with time growing short before Captain Ro would either have to release Altek or charge him with a crime, the security chief left the stockade and made his way to the top of the starbase. There, he entered the captain's office to deliver his assessment of DS9's unexpected visitor.

RO SAT AT HER DESK, looking across the width of her office at the large viewscreen affixed to the opposite bulkhead. The outsize figure of Starfleet's commander in chief filled the viewer. Startlingly large—taller than two and a quarter meters, with broad shoulders, a barrel-shaped chest, and tree-trunk–thick legs—the Capellan projected an imposing presence without saying a word. He had dark, almost black eyes, and his long gray hair had been pulled back from his head. When he spoke, his stern countenance and resonant voice only added to his authoritative bearing.

"What have you learned?" Admiral Akaar asked. He stood in front of the desk in his office at Starfleet Headquarters. Behind

him, a wall of windows framed a sweeping vista of San Francisco Bay, with the international-orange span of the Golden Gate Bridge visible off to the left.

Although a simple, straightforward question, it came across to the captain as a challenge. Akaar had never been a supporter of Ro Laren, owing primarily to an incident that had taken place during her service aboard *U.S.S. Wellington* two decades earlier. During an away mission to Garon II, she disobeyed a direct order, an action that subsequently led to the deaths of eight of her crewmates.

Afterward, Ro had stood court-martial. Akaar presided with other officers over the military tribunal, ultimately finding Ro guilty and remanding her to the penal colony on Jaros II. She spent several years there, until Starfleet Command temporarily released her to take part in a special assignment aboard *Enterprise*. On that mission, she played an instrumental role in saving the lives of a group of Bajorans, as well as in uncovering a plot to draw the Federation into the Cardassian-Bajoran conflict on the side of Cardassia. Consequently, Captain Picard secured her permanent discharge from Jaros II so that she could serve aboard his ship.

Less than two years later, Ro had betrayed her Starfleet oath a second time. Ordered to infiltrate the Maquis, she had done so, only to find her loyalties redirecting to their cause. She joined them, never returning to *Enterprise*. She remained with the Maquis essentially for as long as the paramilitary organization endured, until the Dominion, in its new alliance with the Cardassian Union, wiped out almost all of its members.

Eventually, with nowhere else to go, Ro had returned to Bajor, where she had enlisted in the Militia. Ironically, but clearly because of her experience in Starfleet, her superiors posted her to Deep Space 9. When Bajor ultimately entered the United Federation of Planets, Starfleet absorbed the Militia, and Ro faced a choice. She believed neither that the UFP's space service would welcome her back into its ranks, nor that she would find a place for herself there even if it did. Enter Captain

Jean-Luc Picard, who, for the second time in Ro's life, made a difference. He not only smoothed her reentry into Starfleet, but also convinced her that she had a future there.

Staring at the severe aspect of the commander in chief, that future seemed in doubt. The admiral had not laid the responsibility for President Bacco's assassination at her feet—he plainly understood the heinous nature of the crime and the dastardliness of the perpetrators—but she also didn't think that he held her completely blameless. It only added another layer to the distemper he clearly felt when dealing with her.

"We haven't learned much, sir," Ro told the admiral, "but I think it's enough for us to know how to proceed. Altek consented to a medical examination when he first came aboard, and we confirmed that he is Bajoran. My security chief has interrogated the man repeatedly since his arrival, and has concluded that Altek Dans is no threat to Deep Space Nine, Bajor, or the Federation. He believes that the man came here from the past, though he cannot tell from how far back in time."

"Did the medical tests reveal evidence of time travel?" Akaar wanted to know.

"No," the captain said.

"So there is no evidence of Altek traveling in time, other than the perceptions and judgment of your security chief," Akaar said. The statement seemed more than a little confrontational to Ro.

"That's right," she said. "I have confidence in Commander Blackmer."

Akaar shook his head once. *"Blackmer was responsible for security during Deep Space Nine's dedication ceremony,"* he said. Though the statement demanded a response, it sounded less like a question and more like an accusation.

"Yes, sir," Ro said, choosing the discretion of few words as a complex mixture of emotions swirled within her: anger at the admiral's insinuation of fault, protectiveness for a member of her crew, guilt for the terrible event that had taken place on a starbase under her command.

"I want something more definitive than your security chief's

intuition," Akaar said. *"Do you intend to transfer custody of Altek to the Bajoran government?"* Ro had previously briefed the admiral on the possibilities of taking such action in order to legally extend the stranger's detention.

"I withdrew my request to the Bajoran minister of justice because he was going to deny my request," Ro said. "His decision carried the backing of First Minister Asarem."

Akaar looked away and uttered an unambiguous sound of disgust. When he looked back, he said, *"We're trying to protect Bajor, and you can't even secure the assistance of their government."*

"The first minister wishes to protect the people of Bajor, of course, but not if it requires contravention of the law."

"Bajor is within its rights to extradite one of their nationals if he is suspected of having committed a crime in their system," Akaar said pointedly.

"Yes, sir," Ro said, "but as far as we know, Altek has committed no crime, nor do we even have any indication that he intends to do so."

"I'm sure that you can express our concerns in such a manner as to satisfy the letter of the law." The admiral did not offer the observation as a suggestion, Ro thought, but as an order.

"Admiral, the first minister made it clear to me that she will not violate even the spirit of the law," Ro said. "Frankly, I understand her perspective."

"The only perspective I need you to understand, Captain, is mine," Akaar said. He walked around his desk and took a seat behind it before continuing. *"My job as the commander in chief of Starfleet is to allocate our resources as needed. It is the president's job to preserve and protect the Federation, and Starfleet is one of the primary tools he can use to accomplish those objectives. Make no mistake: President Bacco's assassination was an attack on us. We cannot allow another."*

We also cannot allow an attack to divide us from our principles, Ro thought. The more she considered the first minister's point of view, the more she came to agree with it. "I understand your point, Admiral, but—" *But what?* Under the best of circumstances, she found it difficult to persuade Akaar of anything. *But that doesn't mean I shouldn't still try.* "Permission to speak freely, sir," she said.

"This is not a debate," Akaar said. *"President Pro Tem Ishan is adamant about preventing any more attacks on the Federation. I've apprised him of the situation involving Altek Dans, and he insists that we keep him in custody until we can be sure of his identity and his intentions, and that he played no part in the assassination."*

Ishan, Ro thought. The Federation Council had selected him to lead the UFP through the sixty-day period leading up to the special election that would determine Nan Bacco's permanent successor. Ro didn't know much about Ishan Anjar beyond rumors that he had plotted to push Krim Aldos out of his seat on the Council. It concerned her that such a man might be more interested in politics than principles, and so it did not surprise her to learn that he was applying pressure to Akaar to continue detaining Altek Dans.

"Admiral," Ro said, choosing her words carefully, "I can ask to speak again with First Minister Asarem, but I believe it's unlikely that I will be able to change her mind on this matter."

"Then you must find another solution," Akaar said.

"Sir, I don't—"

"Altek arrived at Deep Space Nine through the Bajoran wormhole, is that correct?" Akaar asked.

"Yes, sir."

"Then I suggest you make a show of seeking answers about him from the Gamma Quadrant," the admiral said. *"Since he exited the wormhole in the Alpha Quadrant, it is reasonable to think that he might have entered it at its other terminus."*

Ro understood Akaar's implication. She had suggested such a course to Commander Desjardins: if she sought information about Altek from another location, the law permitted her to hold him for the length of time it would take for a subspace transmission to travel to and from that site, plus an additional day. "The problem is that we have no evidence whatsoever that Altek Dans came from the Gamma Quadrant."

"Then you need to find some," Akaar insisted.

"Admiral—"

"Captain Ro," Akaar interrupted. *"I have my orders, and now you have yours. Let us not argue that which will not change."*

"Yes, sir," Ro said, resigned to the truth of the admiral's observation: she would not convince him to change the order he'd issued.

"Akaar out." He reached forward on his desk, his huge hand extending toward a control panel, but then he stopped. *"Captain Ro,"* he said, *"I know you'll do the right thing."* Then he pressed his finger to a touchpad and the Starfleet Command emblem replaced his image on the screen. A moment later, it too vanished, replaced by the general Starfleet insignia.

Ro stared at the symbol without really seeing it. If she obeyed the commander in chief's orders, she would have to violate the spirit, if not the letter, of the law. If she abided by the Federation's legal system, then she would have to defy Akaar. The situation frustrated her, but as she thought about it, she realized that the admiral's final words confused her.

I know you'll do the right thing.

To begin with, in the more than twenty years since Ro had first disobeyed a Starfleet order, Akaar had never once indicated even the slightest belief in her abilities, much less in her capacity for doing the "right thing." More than that, she had no notion of what he meant by the ill-defined statement. *Does he expect me to follow his orders, or follow the law?* Or was there some other option, some middle ground he wanted her to consider?

As Ro stood up, she saw the Starfleet logo still visible on the screen. "Viewer off," she said, deactivating the display. She circled out from behind her desk and headed for the door to the left of the viewscreen. She paced quickly along the short corridor to its end, where a turbolift opened at her approach. She strode inside as she weighed everything she knew about the circumstances surrounding Altek Dans—from the moment she brought him aboard, to the assessment of the stranger by Lieutenant Commander Blackmer, to the decisions made by First

Minister Asarem and Admiral Akaar. She hadn't received the support she'd wanted from either Bajor or Starfleet Command, so she would have to make her own determination about what next to do.

As the turbolift doors closed, she stated her destination: "Stockade."

11

Lieutenant Commander Wheeler Stinson banked *Tecyr* to starboard. He gazed through the forward viewport as the runabout swooped down toward the surface of Endalla, the largest of Bajor's five natural satellites. The rocky, grayscale terrain looked a great deal like that of Earth's own moon, though with fewer craters. Not that many years ago, Stinson knew, the planetoid had been home to a rudimentary ecosystem, with enough liquid water to support basic plant life, and a thin but breathable atmosphere. That had been before his assignment to Deep Space 9 as its second officer, and before the catastrophic events that had resulted in the deaths of thousands and the transformation of Endalla into a wasteland.

Up ahead, a dark patch appeared on the horizon, an expanse so deeply black that it stood out even against the colorless geography surrounding it. "We've reached Endalla," Stinson announced from the main console. Three passengers traveled with him: Ensign Stig Hallström sat beside him, while Crew-woman Sandra Silverman and Crewman Torvan Pim occupied the two lateral stations on either side of the cockpit. "Approaching the outpost." Calling the small, prefabricated structure an *outpost* always seemed grandiose to the second officer—rather like referring to *Tecyr* as a starship; although technically accurate, in that the runabout could be used for interstellar travel, the auxiliary craft hardly compared to a vessel like *Defiant*.

The dark area grew as *Tecyr* neared it. Stinson verified detection of the outpost's transponder signal, as well as transmission of the runabout's own identification beacon. All appeared normal.

Stinson usually made the weekly run to the outpost in the center seat on *Defiant*'s bridge. The visit typically required only a few minutes in orbit of Endalla, lasting only as long as it required to rotate out the three-person security team stationed there, and for him to receive a status report. The Bajoran moon essentially marked just another stop on *Defiant*'s patrol route. Since the assassination of President Bacco, though, Starfleet Command had ordered the starbase to remain defended at all times by at least one starship. With *Robinson* and *Aventine* having both recently departed DS9, that left only *Defiant*.

On the main console, an indicator began to blink at the same time that an audio signal chirped. Stinson reached forward and activated *Tecyr*'s comm system. A voice immediately filled the cabin.

"Endalla One to Tecyr,*"* said Ensign Ernak gov Ansarg, a member of the Deep Space 9 crew, and one of the security officers assigned that week to the outpost.

Stinson tapped another touchpad on the console, opening a return channel. "Ansarg, this is Stinson. Transmitting our security code now." The second officer worked his controls to send a complex, encrypted password over an ever-changing but prearranged frequency. He waited for Ansarg to verify the cipher.

At last, she said, *"Your identity is confirmed."* Stinson knew that the code also indicated *Tecyr*'s normal operational state. Had there been a problem—if, for example, the runabout had been commandeered by some hostile force and its crew taken captive—he would have sent a different password designed to indicate that. *"You are authorized to land."*

"Acknowledged," Stinson said. He checked the distance to the outpost. "We'll be setting down in less than ten minutes. *Tecyr* out." He closed the channel.

Through the forward viewport, the field of black had spread to port and starboard as far as Stinson could see. As he watched, the runabout flew across its near edge, leaving the vista nothing but an ebony sprawl in all directions. To the second officer, it resembled a deep, tranquil lake, its surface completely smooth, unmoved by any air currents above or any aquatic life below.

Stinson studied the spread of black. He could see an occasional star reflected in the glassy material. In the distance, Bajor's sun, B'hava'el, shined brightly down, and as *Tecyr* sailed toward it, its mirror image grew brighter still. The port automatically polarized as the illumination in the cabin increased.

The vitreous shell on that part of Endalla had been neither a consequence of the disaster that had torn away the moon's atmosphere, nor a part of its natural landscape. It had been created nearly six years earlier, when a group of religious extremists had occupied the site. Members of the Ohalavaru, they followed the teachings of certain ancient texts—writings that many Bajorans believed heretical, and that claimed that the Prophets were not gods, but simply powerful, munificent aliens.

The extremists had occupied Endalla before Stinson's tenure at DS9, but he had since read about the event. The religious zealots apparently interpreted one passage of their apocrypha as indicating that Bajor's largest moon concealed potential evidence of the earthly nature of the Prophets, and they sought to find and expose it. To those ends, they carried a massive amount of explosives to Endalla, intending to essentially strip-mine the planetoid on a large scale, until they uncovered some physical substantiation of their convictions. Both the Bajoran authorities and Starfleet interceded, successfully preventing the extremists' efforts, but not before a mammoth detonation had taken lives and turned a span of the moon's topography into black glass.

Since that episode, Starfleet had provided a security contingent on Endalla. Deep Space 9 personnel initially posted themselves on the surface in a runabout, but the station's engineering crew eventually erected a prefab structure provided by the Corps of Engineers, then installed the necessary equipment to continuously monitor the moon. Three-person security teams spent a week at a time there, keeping watch. To hear them speak about the assignment, few of them found much benefit in protecting the barren moon, though most of the Bajoran members of the crew—many of them believers in the Prophets—fully supported the decision to do so.

A sliver of gray lunar surface finally appeared beyond the lake of glass. A circular edifice stood there, its circumference punctuated by stanchions that supported the outer bulkhead and, reaching up past the radially corrugated roof, ended in spherical conductor nodes for projecting a defensive force field. Officially dubbed Security Outpost Endalla I—a name even more grandiloquent than its designation as an outpost—the simple building contained only a monitor-and-control room and a small living section. Another runabout, for use by the security team, sat beside the outpost.

Stinson looked around at Hallström, Silverman, and Torvan—two humans and a Bajoran, respectively. "We'll be setting down in just a moment," he told them. They each quickly rose from their seats and headed aft, to the storage lockers where they had stowed their travel duffels.

Stinson looked again through the forward port and worked the helm to bring *Tecyr* down on the starboard side of the outpost. He powered up the antigravs and cut the main engines, alighting directly in front of the other runabout, *Elestan*, its bow adorned with the registry NCC-77544—one number down from that of *Tecyr*. Stinson recalled that the two vessels had been delivered to Deep Space 9 at the same time, entering service together.

"We're ready, Commander," said Ensign Hallström, the senior member of the security team, and therefore its leader.

"Acknowledged," Stinson said. After securing the runabout, he reopened the comm channel to the outpost. "*Tecyr* to Endalla One," he said.

"*Ansarg here.*"

Stinson glanced behind him to see that Silverman and Torvan had taken their places in the two-person transporter at the rear of the cabin, their duffels slung over their shoulders. "We're prepared to begin beaming over."

"Aye, sir," Ansarg said. *"Energizing now."*

A familiar hum filled the cockpit, and the two security officers vanished amid a spray of brilliant white specks and streaks. Once transport had completed, Stinson and Hallström mounted the platform. "Stinson to Ansarg. Ready."

When the second officer's vision cleared, he and Hallström had materialized on a small stage at the periphery of Endalla I's semicircular control room. Monitoring and operations consoles lined the curved outer bulkhead and filled the center of the compartment. In the middle of the straight wall that cut the outpost in two, a single-paneled door led to the living area, which included a small lounge, sleeping quarters, and a refresher.

Stinson addressed Ansarg, who stood at a freestanding console in front of the transporter stage. "Permission to come aboard."

"Granted, sir," the Tellarite said.

Silverman and Torvan had already crossed the control room to confer with the crewmen they would be relieving, Ventor Bixx and Barry Herriot. Stinson saw two sets of duffels sitting beside the transporter stage, and as he and Hallström descended the steps to the deck, the ensign added his to a pair sitting together, presumably those belonging to the new security team; the other three, packed and ready to go, no doubt belonged to the departing team. Stinson knew that Ansarg ran a tight ship—not especially punctilious with her subordinates, but exceedingly efficient. The ensign had drawn high marks from Lieutenant Commander Blackmer in the year she'd served with the DS9 crew.

Stinson and Hallström stepped over to the transporter console. Ansarg handed them each a padd. "Status log for the week, as well as the handover report," the ensign said as the second officer skimmed a précis on his display. "We had no incursions into Endalla's perimeter. Sensor sweeps of the surface similarly read clear for the period. We also detected no scans of either the moon or this facility." She paused, then noted, "Basically, it's the same report we always give, but with one exception."

Stinson looked up from his padd, surprised. Rarely did anything interrupt the monotony of observing the empty moon. The security team would intermittently report meteorite strikes on the surface, none of which had ever proven to be anything other than naturally occurring phenomena.

"What happened?" Hallström asked.

"Three days ago, we received an incoming transmission from a spacecraft in orbit around Bajor," Ansarg said. "It was not intended for the outpost, but for a scientist at one of the research labs on Endalla."

"Research labs?" Hallström echoed, clearly confused. Like Ansarg, he had served in the DS9 crew for only a short time.

"Before the incident that wiped out the atmosphere and the plant life here," Stinson explained, "the Bajorans kept several science laboratories on Endalla—mostly to study the moon itself." Of Ansarg, he asked, "Was the message meant for one of those facilities?"

"Aye, sir," she said. "A man calling himself Galdus Mon was attempting to reach a woman named Lenkit Casten. He claimed that she worked at one of the Endalla labs. We checked with the Bajoran Ministry of Science. They confirmed that an ecologist by that name had worked on the moon for several years, but that she was one of those who died when the subspace wave destroyed the labs."

"Galdus Mon," Stinson said. "That's an Yridian name, isn't it?"

"Aye," Ansarg said.

"So many of them are information merchants," Stinson said. "It seems unlikely that he wouldn't have known the fate of Endalla all these years later."

"I questioned him about it," Ansarg said. "He claimed to be a dealer not in information, but in fine arts, mostly plying his trade along the border between the Alpha and Beta Quadrants. He's registered with the Federation Trade Council, and so his movements and dealings are well documented. He said that he met Lenkit a decade ago, on his last visit to Bajor. She purchased a piece of Lorillian sculpture from him, and then they saw each other socially a few times."

"And it all checked out?" Stinson asked.

"It did," Ansarg said. "Mon was very cooperative. He was also visibly disappointed to learn what had happened to Lenkit. It's all in the status log." She pointed to the padd in the second officer's hand.

"All right," Stinson said. He trusted Ansarg's judgment, but when it came to matters of security, it always troubled him when something unexpected happened, no matter how seemingly benign. "Anything else to report?"

"Negative, sir," Ansarg said. "The moon—"

An alert sounded. Across the compartment, Bixx and Herriot raced over to consoles, with Silverman and Torvan right behind them. Stinson and the others started in that direction as well. "Proximity alert," Bixx announced as he examined a display. "A vessel has penetrated the moon's security perimeter."

"Are we under attack?" Stinson wanted to know.

"I'm reading no weapons fire," Herriot said. The crewman worked his controls. "Actually, I'm not reading much of anything inside its hull; there seems to be some sort of interference." Herriot looked over at the second officer. "It appears to be a small vessel, but our ship-recognition routines aren't providing a match. Scans show no other traffic in the vicinity."

"Hail them," Stinson ordered.

Ansarg quickly moved to operate a panel. Stinson noted that the three members of the new security team he had just delivered to the outpost hung back, allowing their counterparts to do their jobs without interference. To himself, he commended them for that; the official handover from the first squad to the second hadn't been completed, meaning that Ansarg and her people remained on duty. It fell to Stinson, as the highest-ranking officer among them, to take charge.

"Hailing frequencies, sir," Ansarg said.

"Security Outpost Endalla One to unidentified vessel," Stinson said. "You are in violation of restricted Bajoran space

without authorization. Identify yourself and withdraw at once."
He waited for a response, but none came. He repeated his message, but still got no reply.

"I can't tell if they're receiving us," Ansarg said.

"Location and course," Stinson said.

"It's almost directly on the opposite side of Endalla from the outpost," Bixx reported. Stinson knew that the satellites in orbit about the moon allowed scans all around it, as well as communications. "Its course is ragged," Bixx continued. "Its crew could be in trouble."

Stinson didn't hesitate. "Ansarg, continue monitoring the vessel and attempting to make contact. Inform Captain Ro of the situation." He hiked a thumb over his shoulder. "Hallström, you're with me," he said, then marched toward the transporter stage.

"TIME TO INTERCEPT?"

"We're coming up on the vessel fast, Commander," Hallström said. "We'll reach it in less than five minutes." The ensign sat beside Stinson at *Tecyr*'s main console, crewing the sensor panel.

The second officer looked up from the helm controls and out through the forward port. He tried to discern the trespassing ship among the backdrop of stars. He glanced over at the sensor display and spied the irregular path the vessel traced above Endalla, but at a lower altitude than the runabout. When he peered back through the viewport, he cast his gaze downward and spotted movement in the distance, not against the bejeweled darkness of space, but over the leaden tones of the lunar surface.

Stinson quickly configured a subpanel so that he could access the imaging controls, then worked to project onto the viewscreen to his left a visual of the ship they pursued. Because of its ash-colored hull, he could barely differentiate it from the ground below it. He magnified the picture until the vessel filled the display. An angular bow roosted at the front of an elongated main body that resembled an elaborate trusswork, and a wide, disc-shaped structure formed the stern. Two cylinders depending from the complex frame could have been warp nacelles. He saw no markings on it.

"It doesn't look familiar," Stinson told Hallström.

"No, not to me either, sir," the ensign said. "But it's not large." He worked his controls and a scale appeared on the display. "It's actually slightly smaller than a runabout."

"Have your scans cleared yet?" Stinson asked.

"Negative, Commander," Hallström said. "Something continues to interfere with our sensors. I think it's some type of radiation."

"Can you tell if its purpose is to block our scans?"

"It's certainly possible," Hallström said, "but it could also be—" He stopped and tapped at a number of controls in rapid succession. "Commander, that ship is emitting delta rays."

"Is it the warp drive?"

Hallström's fingers marched up and down his console. "I'm tuning the sensors to compensate specifically for delta radiation." Stinson watched the ensign work, until at last Hallström said, "A baffle plate on one of the warp nacelles has ruptured . . . there's considerable internal damage in one section."

A baffle plate? Stinson thought. The vessel must have been an old one. "Life signs?"

"I'm trying to isolate them now," Hallström said. "I'm reading one life-form aboard . . . Bajoran . . . their vital signs are still strong, but . . ." His voice trailed off before he finished the sentence.

"But when one baffle plate goes, others are sure to follow," Stinson finished for him.

"I don't remember much from the few engineering courses I took at Starfleet," Hallström said, "but I remember that."

Up ahead, Stinson saw, the vessel had grown in size as *Tecyr* had narrowed the distance to it. "This close, maybe I can punch through the radiation interference," he said. He narrowed the transmission beam, then set it to propagate at multiple offset frequencies. "This is the Starfleet vessel *Tecyr*, to unidentified ship above Endalla. Please respond." Stinson waited several seconds, then repeated his message.

Static suddenly erupted from the comm system, followed by a run of words only intermittently understandable. "*. . . is the* Vellidon *. . . Stoat . . . vigation syst . . . diation leak . . . peat: I require assist . . .*" Despite the paucity of audible and complete words, Stinson had no trouble recognizing the intent of the message.

"This is the *Tecyr*," Stinson said. "We're on our way." He left the channel open, but heard nothing more.

"Can we beam him off the ship?" Hallström asked.

"Listen to the interference in the message," Stinson said, wondering the same thing. He called up transporter control. "It's one thing to get a transmission through," he said, even as he worked to lock on to the Bajoran. "If words are lost, a message might still be understood, but if a transporter beam loses coherence . . ." He stopped speaking as he concentrated on focusing the targeting scanner. Again and again, his attempts failed. "It's no good," he told Hallström. "I can't get a clear lock for transport."

"Sir, I'm reading a surge in delta radiation," Hallström said. "I think another plate may be on the verge of rupturing."

Stinson immediately reached for the helm controls and increased *Tecyr*'s speed beyond safe limits. The runabout jumped forward and rapidly closed the gap with the ship in distress. "Prepare the tractor beam," he ordered.

"Yes, sir," Hallström said. The ensign set to reconfiguring his console.

"As soon as we're in range, I want that ship under tow," Stinson said. "Keep the beam away from the engines. I don't want any additional stresses on the baffle plates."

"Understood."

In just seconds, *Tecyr* reached the troubled vessel. The faltering ship visibly struggled to maintain a steady flight path. Stinson slowed the runabout and modified course, bringing *Tecyr* in above the vessel, providing a clear track for the stern-mounted tractor beam. As the distressed ship passed out of sight through the forward viewport, Stinson watched it on the display.

"Initiating tractor beam," said Hallström. On the monitor, blue rays streaked out and took hold of the troubled vessel. Stinson noticed that the tractor beam connected with the ship across its spine, from bow to stern, but did not touch the nacelles. "We have him under tow, Commander."

"Taking us down," Stinson said. He pointed *Tecyr*'s bow toward the surface of Endalla, pushing the runabout to as great a velocity as he dared with the tractor beam engaged. He continually checked the altitude, until finally he leveled off at twenty-five meters. He then maneuvered both vessels down until he saw dust puff up as he settled the unknown ship onto the ground. "Release the tractor beam."

"Yes, sir," Hallström said. As the ensign worked his controls, the blue rays holding the troubled vessel disappeared. "Tractor beam disengaged—Commander, the delta radiation is spiking. Another baffle plate is sure to rupture soon."

"Retrieve two environmental suits," Stinson said. If necessary, he intended to make his way to the other ship and physically rescue its endangered pilot. While Hallström headed aft to the runabout's storage compartments, Stinson said, "*Tecyr* to unidentified vessel. You must abandon ship immediately. Do you have an environmental suit aboard?"

Again, static spewed from the comm system. "*. . . don . . . land . . . plate . . . critic—*" The transmission cut out, throwing the cabin into silence. Stinson attempted several times to reopen the channel. He did not succeed.

Hallström reappeared carrying a pair of environmental suits. Stinson raced over and took one, with the intent of putting it on, but then, on the viewscreen, he saw a door in the bow of the troubled vessel swing inward. A moment later, a figure clad in a faded, brown environmental suit appeared.

Stinson dropped his own suit to the deck. "Prepare to lift off," he told Hallström. "When I give the order, put as much distance as you can between us and that vessel, as fast as possible." He didn't wait for the ensign to acknowledge the order, but darted through the door at the rear of the cockpit. He headed amidships, to the runabout's airlock. Working its control panel, he depressurized the chamber, then opened the outer hatch. He peered through the port in the inner door, waiting.

Seconds seemed to pass like minutes, and Stinson found himself bracing for the impact on *Tecyr* when the troubled vessel's next baffle plate ruptured and turned the ship into shrapnel. Finally, the pilot of the doomed vessel appeared and rushed to climb into the airlock. Once he had, Stinson brought the side of his fist down hard on the control panel. The outer hatch slid closed, and the airlock began to repressurize.

Stinson slapped at his combadge. "Hallström, the pilot is aboard. Get us out of here!"

"Yes, sir." Stinson felt the runabout begin to move at once.

When the airlock finished its cycle, the second officer activated the door release, and the panel glided into the bulkhead. When the man inside saw that, he reached up, unlatched his helmet, and pulled it off. "Thank you," he said between deep inhalations of breath.

"You're welcome. I'm Lieutenant Commander Wheeler Stinson, second officer aboard Deep Space Nine." He moved aside so that the man could step out of the airlock.

"Nelish Stoat," he said as he did so. A Bajoran, he had dark eyes, and long, dark hair that hung down past his shoulders. Stinson didn't think he could've been much past twenty years of age. "I'm just a civilian."

"What happened out there?"

"I was just leaving Bajor when something happened to the engines," Nelish said. "I think one of the baffle plates might have buckled."

"It did," Stinson confirmed.

"I lost navigational control," Nelish said. "I tried to signal for help, but I think the radiation was interfering with my communications."

"It was," Stinson said.

"I shut down the engines before I left," Nelish said, "but I think it might've been too late."

"Let's see if we can do something to save your ship." He started forward, waving Nelish to follow. As they walked toward the bow, he asked, "Where were you headed?"

"To Pillagra," Nelish said. The Bajoran colony world had been settled more than a century earlier. Located close enough to make civilian travel there a reasonable undertaking, it was also far enough that it had, during the Occupation, provided one of the few refuges for Bajorans fortunate enough to reach it. "I have a friend who moved there last year."

When the two men reached the cockpit, Hallström looked up from the main console. "Commander," he said, and then he read off *Tecyr*'s distance from the troubled vessel. Past him, through the forward viewport, stars shined against the sea of night. To the left, on the display, the troubled vessel sat on the surface of Endalla.

As he crossed to the front of the cabin, Stinson introduced Hallström and Stoat. "What's the status of his ship?"

Before Hallström could respond, and almost as though the second officer's question had invited it, a fireball bloomed on the display. Both Stinson and Nelish snapped their heads in that direction.

"What happened?" the second officer asked. "The baffle plates?"

Hallström was already consulting the sensors. "Yes, sir," he said. "The second baffle plate ruptured, and that started a cascade reaction."

Stinson turned to Nelish, who still carried his helmet in one hand. "I'm sorry," he told the young man.

Nelish staggered over to one of the lateral stations and sat down hard. "I hate to lose my ship, but I guess . . . I guess I was lucky."

"Endalla is a restricted area, so there will have to be an investigation into this incident," Stinson said. "But we can take you back to Bajor." The second officer motioned to Hallström. "Set course for the outpost. Contact Ensign Ansarg and inform her of what's happened. Tell her we'll be there shortly to complete the handover." He would contact Deep Space 9 himself and report the event directly to Captain Ro.

"Yes, sir," Hallström said. "Right away, Commander."

To Nelish, Stinson said, "You'd probably like to remove your environmental suit. Why don't I get you settled in the back of the runabout." With a wave, he indicated the aft door through which they had just entered the cockpit. Nelish rose and headed in that direction. Stinson wanted to speak with him to get more details about his journey and how it had gone so disastrously wrong. He didn't disbelieve the young man, but he also wanted to confirm the veracity of his account.

Nelish answered every question. The young man appeared appropriately distraught at the loss of his vessel, as well as alternately relieved and somewhat traumatized at how close he had come to dying aboard it. Nelish's responses, both verbal and emotional, satisfied the second officer.

Only later would Stinson realize that he had been duped.

12

At last, all of the Ascendants had assembled, Questers and Archquesters alike. Iliana Ghemor stood in the middle of the barren plain, at the base of a small rise that nevertheless rose to the highest point in any direction. She looked upward, to the low summit, where the leader of the Ascendants, Grand Archquester Votiq, turned slowly in place. He gazed down upon the silvery throngs of his people, at the myriad ships that had brought them all—all but Ghemor—to the otherwise empty world that they believed marked the true beginning of the Path to the Final Ascension. Votiq completed a full rotation, then a second, and finally a third, before he spread his arms wide and began speaking in high, rich tones.

Ghemor didn't listen. She didn't need to, nor did she want

to. The words and ideas of a people steeped in superstition meant less than nothing to her: they *offended* her. It amazed and disgusted Ghemor that a species so physically capable could surrender the totality of their lives to the pursuit of something utterly fantastical—to the search for something that, even had it not been so obviously illusory, would have delineated a goal unachievable for most of their kind.

It didn't matter. The faith and rituals of the Ascendants redounded to Ghemor's advantage. They looked upon her as the Fire, as the guiding light in their Quest, and she had not just accepted that mantle, but seized it. She would lead them—not where they wanted to go, but where she needed them to go. They had delivered themselves to her as her army, and she would wield them with dramatic force.

Although Ghemor didn't listen to Votiq's speech, she feigned doing so. As far as she knew, no Ascendant had questioned her appearance or her place among them, but she had been born a Cardassian, raised and taught as a Cardassian, and that meant she nurtured her suspicions, never taking for granted the trust of others—and particularly not that of offworlders. Had she seen uncertainty in the eyes of some Ascendants, doubts about her role as the Fire? Possibly, and so she would provide them no fodder: she pretended to listen to Votiq, playing her part. She locked her gaze upon his form as he orated, her attention seemingly unwavering. When finally he finished speaking, he looked to her, as he'd told her he would, and she climbed the rise to stand by his side. He towered over her, and his powerful body gleamed, but when she faced his people, even with her diminutive form and wearing her dark armor, she knew that she commanded them.

Ghemor did not spin in place, as Votiq had, but walked unhurriedly along the edge of the rise, taking in the sight of her troops. According to the Grand Archquester, the Ascendants had long ago numbered in the billions. Before her massed the last of those remaining, counted only in mere thousands. Still, by virtue of their unceasing zeal and Ghemor's own leadership, she knew that they would prove formidable for her purposes.

On her second circuit around the top of the rise, the Cardassian concentrated on the numerous vessels that had carried the Ascendants there, and that would soon enough deliver them to the wormhole and through it, to Deep Space 9. Many of the ships had been constructed by generations of Questers past, and most of those could accommodate just one or two passengers, though some had room for considerably more. Ghemor also saw other vessels, clearly of alien design and manufacture, their original crews doubtless long since dead, dispatched without remorse by single-minded Ascendants.

As she circled for the third time, Ghemor eyed all the weaponry that the Questers and Archquesters had collected. She spied missiles, mines, and torpedoes; directed-energy generators and emitters; disruptor concentrators and plasma cannon. She had inspected them all as they'd arrived, but to her, one continued to stand out.

In the days since Aniq had appeared, Ghemor had taken pains to thoroughly study the tool that the young Ascendant had brought as tribute, the tribute she had brought as tool. It had initially struck the Cardassian as perfect for her purposes, and her examination of it and all the other weaponry had only solidified her opinion. It had also led her to change her plans. She would not only see her vengeance done, but she would accomplish it in the most satisfying way.

Atop the rise, Ghemor completed her third trip around, then moved to stand side-by-side with the Grand Archquester. She surveyed the eyes raised toward her and Votiq, and saw mostly anticipation and fervor. Ghemor also spotted expressions mixed in among the crowd that bespoke conflicting emotions, including fear and hesitancy. She needed to nourish the former of the pair, and quash the latter.

Ghemor threw her hands into the air. "I am the Fire," she proclaimed loudly. A rush of coordinated movement suffused the multitude of Ascendants as they all dropped to their knees. Votiq did the same beside her. The Grand Archquester had spoken to her of his people's rituals, and especially those that involved the Fire. To start out on the Path to the Final Ascension, she had only to identify herself to the silver horde, select a vessel in which to travel, and then lead them on their way.

"I travel with Votiq, the Grand Archquester," she announced next, her arms still raised, and the Ascendant army rose back to its feet. According to Votiq, the Cardassian could have rightly chosen any ship at all, and it had occurred to her to pick Aniq's older, blade-like vessel, for it hauled the weapon with which she would exact her first great salvo of retribution. Because Ghemor's appearance had been portended by scripture, promising the Ascendants that she would lead them to the Fortress of the True, nobody would have questioned such a choice.

At least, they would not have questioned it publicly, she thought. But Ghemor wanted to minimize any skepticism of her role, whether held openly or privately. To that end, she chose to join the Grand Archquester aboard his vessel, because most of the Ascendants, if not all, would have expected that of the Fire.

Traveling with the Grand Archquester will make no difference to me, she knew. Votiq had informed her that he intended to distribute the Ascendants' weaponry evenly throughout their advancing legion, protecting Aniq's powerful and extraordinary explosive device by placing it at the center of their force. Ghemor had suggested several other schemes, including clustering all the weapons together at the head of their armada. In the end, she had maneuvered him into revisiting his own first plan, but with Aniq and her lethal apparatus prominently arrayed immediately behind the Fire and the Grand Archquester as an important component in the point of their spear. Proximity to Aniq's metaweapon was all Ghemor needed.

"We take our first steps on the Path to the Final Ascension," the Cardassian intoned, her voice carrying loudly over her newfound followers.

En masse, the Questers and Archquesters thrust their fists into the air and bellowed out their excitement, a long, melodic chant that sounded to Ghemor more like a chorus of singers than a battle cry. When the last musical strains of the cheer faded, she called out, "We will not stop until we reach the Fortress of the True—until we *enter* the Fortress and burn in the eyes of the Unnameable." Again, the Ascendants roared out their tuneful endorsement.

"Now," Ghemor cried, "we go!"

One final harmony of approval rose up from the ranks, and then they all moved, boarding their many ships in preparation for the journey to come. Ghemor started down the hill beside Votiq. Together, they approached his knife-shaped vessel, which differed from those of many other Ascendants only in its deep, reddish purple color. Votiq worked a control to open his ship, then stepped aside to allow the Cardassian to climb aboard first. She did so, forgoing entry to the larger compartments belowdecks, and instead taking the rear seat in the narrow cockpit. Votiq followed her inside and sat at the pilot's console. He worked the access mechanism, and the ship's canopy swirled down into place.

The Grand Archquester's vessel hummed to life around Ghemor. She watched as he operated a series of controls. When the canopy became transparent, the glittering array of stars above seemed to reassure her that she would finally find closure and at least some degree of justice among them.

When she had first arrived among the Ascendants, she had imagined returning to the Alpha Quadrant and making only a swift, decisive thrust in order to sate her need for a just reprisal. With Aniq's metaweapon at her disposal, though, she modified her plans for revenge. Rather than attacking Deep Space 9 and quickly ending the miserable, undeserved life of Kira Nerys, Ghemor decided that she would instead launch an offensive on Bajor, exacting her retribution on the people who had set her entire adult life careering wildly out of control—the people whose resistance to Cardassian aid had led to her betrothed's death, which had made her covert mission for the Obsidian Order necessary, and in turn had led directly to her abduction and long, brutal captivity. She knew that laying waste to Bajor would devastate Kira, and would thus provide Ghemor with an appropriate measure of vengeance. Once she had inflicted that incalculable pain, she would make Kira Nerys beg for the release of death—and then, at last, she would deliver a final, killing blow.

As Votiq's ship lifted off, Ghemor felt the thrill of expectation.

13

"I need your help," Ro said. The words twisted a knot in her stomach, a reflex decades in the making. As a girl, and later as a young woman, Ro had loathed asking anybody for any kind of assistance, no matter how insignificant. More than that, it had always troubled her whenever she'd actually *needed* help, whether or not she asked for it. Over time, as she grew into adulthood and eventually—*Finally!*—began to mature, she came to understand and cope with the source of all those feelings.

Ro had been just seven when she'd been lured with a simple piece of sugar candy into the worst hours of her life—either before or since. One of the Cardassian occupiers of Bajor forced her to watch as he brutalized her father, ostensibly questioning him, but more often torturing him in unspeakable ways. It traumatized the young Laren, but the horrific nature of the cruel violence she witnessed shaped only one component of her anguish. Her father supplicated his tormentor, pleaded with him for mercy, and his beseeching tore not only at his daughter's heart, but at the respect she held for him. She felt shamed by his frailty, by the ease with which he allowed a miscreant Cardassian to lay him low. His pathetic cries for help disgraced her, so much so that his death, when it came later that day, brought her not only sadness, but relief.

That terrible incident in Ro's childhood had stayed with her for years—stayed with her *still*. Her experiences aboard *Wellington* and *Enterprise*, then with the Maquis and in the Bajoran Militia, and finally aboard Deep Space 9, had taught her the value of teamwork and friendship. She came to understand the necessity of trusting people, and she eventually learned how to accept, and even to request, the assistance of others. Despite that, doing so still felt to Ro like an improper act—as though surrendering to her own weakness. She always fought the emotion, recognizing its uselessness. She usually succeeded in overcoming it, but the anxiety always returned.

"I don't understand," Altek Dans said. "*You* need *my* help?" He stood just inside the entryway to his cell, peering quizzically at the captain through the force field.

"I do," Ro said. "I want to release you."

"Of course you do," Altek said. He shook his head. "And all you need is my help in answering your questions."

"No," the captain said.

"No?" Altek asked, his voice dripping with disbelief. "Because that's all I've heard for three days now: 'Answer our questions and we'll let you go.'" He glared past Ro, and she didn't need to follow his gaze to know that he intended his look as an indictment of Lieutenant Commander Blackmer. The security chief stood behind the captain, across the corridor, his phaser drawn.

"You needn't be upset with Commander Blackmer," the captain said. "He was acting on my orders. He also believes what you've told him."

Once more, Altek's eyes darted to one side, looking past Ro at the security chief. "That comes as a surprise, but I'm pleased to hear it," he said. "And what about you? Do you also believe me?"

"I trust my security chief," Ro said. "He's very good at his job, and so, yes, I believe you."

Altek waited for a moment, then said, "You believe me, and yet I'm still in this cell."

"That's right," Ro said. "That's because there are people with greater authority than me who aren't persuaded of your innocence in the assassination, or that you haven't come here to commit some other criminal act. Those people don't *dis*believe you, but they want you held until we can verify who you are and why you've come here."

"I keep hearing that, but I've told Mister Blackmer everything I possibly can, and maybe even more than I should have," Altek said. "So if you're here just to repeat his demands of me, don't bother." With an air of general disgust, he waved his hand dismissively toward Ro. His fingers must have come precariously close to the force field, because it emitted a quick warning hum. Altek turned and moved away from the entry.

"Doctor Altek," Ro said. The stranger did not respond, but kept his back to her. She called after him again, then addressed her security chief. "Jeff, I'm going in."

"Captain," Blackmer said, crossing the wide corridor and joining her at the entrance to the cell. "Captain," he said again, dropping his voice to a whisper. "We agreed that as long as we're detaining Altek, nobody but security personnel will be allowed to enter his cell. It's for your own safety, and that of the entire starbase."

"Yes, I agreed with that," Ro said, also speaking softly so that Altek would not hear her. "But I want to talk to that man in there, and I need to establish a rapport with him. I can't effectively do that with a force field between us."

"Captain, letting you in is a violation of the strict protocols we put in place after what happened to President Bacco."

"I understand your concerns," Ro said. She looked back over at Altek, who stood on the other side of the cell, still facing away from her, his hands on his hips. "You told me that you believed him, Jeff. If he didn't have anything to do with the assassination, and if he hasn't come here for some hostile purpose, then I won't be in any danger just by entering his cell."

"But, Captain . . ."

Blackmer's words faded, but the haunted look in his eyes did not. *But, Captain,* Ro felt sure he had started to say, *what if I'm wrong?* Both from knowing Blackmer, and from having served in his position for more than two years, she understood that he blamed himself for the president's murder. *How could he not?* she asked herself. Ro knew that he had spent time in the last few days with Lieutenant Knezo, one of DS9's counselors, but the captain wondered if she should also have another conversation with him about his role in what had happened.

At the moment, though, she needed to concentrate on dealing with Altek Dans. "Jeff, when this force field is deactivated, the entire stockade will lock down. On top of that, the cell is under constant surveillance by your security staff, and you're standing out here with a phaser in your hand."

Blackmer nodded slowly, as though it pained him to lose the argument about protective procedures. "Of course, Captain," he said. He reached up to the panel beside the entry and quickly ran through the process of lowering the force field.

"Thanks, Jeff," Ro said. "For now, leave it down." She did not wait for him to acknowledge—or object to—her order, but paced into the cell. "Doctor Altek," she said, "I'm not here to ask you any more questions, or to tell you again what we require of you."

Over his shoulder, Altek said, "No, you're just here to get my help, is that right?"

"Yes, it is," Ro said. "I told you that I want to release you from custody, but that there are people in higher positions than me who are reluctant to do that. So I'm here to get your help."

Altek finally turned back around. "What is it you think I can do for you?"

Ro inhaled deeply, trying to fashion just what she should tell Altek, and anxious about how he might react. "Our laws about detaining individuals suspected of wrongdoing are very clear," she began. "Because we have no real indication of you committing any crime, I'm supposed to give you your freedom by this afternoon."

Altek said nothing, but the captain saw that she definitely had his attention.

"As is often the case," she went on, "there are different ways to interpret the law. In this case, there are provisions that, when construed from one perspective, would allow me to keep you in custody for a longer time." Ro shifted from one foot to the other, uncomfortable with a concept that would have sounded completely natural if uttered by some smooth-tongued Cardassian leader during the Occupation. It reminded her of the discussion she'd had with her first officer that morning, when Cenn had observed that, of all people, Bajorans should be slow to detain people without due process—and perhaps least of all one of their own.

"I'm not going to do that," Ro said, unsure until just that moment if she would permit Altek to walk out of his cell once they'd finished speaking. "As of right now, you're free to go." She motioned toward the open entryway.

Altek looked in that direction, but he made no move to leave. "And what sort of help must I provide to you in exchange for my freedom?"

"You don't have to do or say anything," Ro told him. "I'm *asking* if you will."

"All right," Altek said. "Ask."

"Because I might have to stand a court-martial for disobeying a direct order to keep you detained, I'd like to ask you not to leave this base for at least a few days." Ro didn't think that Akaar would bring charges against her, primarily because she had a sworn duty—as did all Starfleet personnel—not to obey an illegal or immoral order. Then again, the admiral's continuing disdain for her had begun all those years ago, when she'd served aboard *Wellington* and had defied a superior. "I'd also like to have one of my officers escort you around at all times once you leave this cell. I'll assign you quarters and you can have privacy there, but when you move around the base, I'd like somebody to accompany you."

Altek regarded Ro without saying anything, then sat down in the cell's only chair. "You're in charge of this 'base,' as you call it?"

"I am," Ro said.

"Then can't you simply order your people to follow me?"

"I could, or I could just have you expelled," Ro said, "but I'm not interested in creating an adversarial relationship with you."

Altek glanced around the cell in which he'd been held for nearly three full days, his message clear: they already had an adversarial relationship. He did not address that point directly, but said, "Even if I wanted to leave, I don't have any idea where I am or how to get back home. I imagine that I'd need your help with that."

"I think you would need my help because—" Ro stopped, hesitant to reveal more than she should about Altek's situation. If he had emerged from the wormhole out of Bajor's past, as Blackmer believed, the Temporal Prime Directive prohibited her from saying or doing anything that could potentially alter the timeline. Since Altek's arrival on DS9, though, Ro had studied the incident when Akorem Laan had come forward in time more than two centuries. He had ultimately reentered the wormhole with Captain Sisko, who reported that the Prophets had returned the Bajoran poet to his own time, with no memory of his journey into the future. Ro reasoned that if Altek likewise went back, he also would retain no knowledge of whatever he experienced on Deep Space 9. "You would need assistance to get home because we believe you're a lot farther away than you think, and in a very different way."

"I don't know what you mean by that," Altek said, and again he looked around at his cell. "Although it certainly feels like I'm farther from home than I've ever been."

Ro crossed the compartment and sat down on the edge of the sleeping platform. She hesitated as she tried to find the right words. According to Blackmer's interrogation reports, Altek claimed to be a doctor, and he'd spoken of working at a hospital. That alone told the captain that, whenever he had come from, he had experience and familiarity with some level of technology. He had been disoriented when they'd first brought him aboard the starbase, which could have been the result of being exposed to twenty-fourth-century advancements, but also might have been caused by his transit aboard an Orb of the Prophets and then being beamed to the stockade. Altek certainly hadn't displayed any extreme reactions to what he'd so far seen, although that included only the transporter room and his cell.

"Doctor Altek, during Commander Blackmer's questioning, he asked you what year it was," Ro finally said.

"He did, and I told him: the seventeenth Year of the Petalune."

Ro shrugged. "I don't know when that is," she said. "I've never heard of the Petalune."

"How . . . how can that be?" Altek asked. "A petalune is a flower, and also the name of a constellation, just like the names of all the years in a cycle."

"None of that is familiar to me."

"Where . . . where are you from?" Altek seemed to be grasping for answers.

"I was born in Lyncar, a small village in Hedrikspool Province," Ro said.

"I've never heard of either of those places," Altek said. "Are they on one of the island continents? Or on one of the archipelagos?"

"No," Ro said. "Hedrikspool is on the main landmass, near the equator, on the western coast."

Altek rubbed a hand across his face, clearly frustrated and trying to make sense of what Ro was telling him. "But where you're describing . . . that's not far from Joradell."

"The city where you practiced medicine," Ro said.

"Yes," Altek said, "and you told me when I first got here that you don't know it."

"No."

"But you know something," Altek said. "What is it you're trying to tell me?"

"There's no easy way to say this, Doctor Altek." *It won't be easy either for him or for me,* Ro thought. Telling him risked inviting a visit by the Department of Temporal Investigations. *Not to mention providing Admiral Akaar with another reason to bring court-martial proceedings against me.* "We believe that you have been displaced in time."

"'Displaced in time,'" Altek repeated, as though searching for meaning within the words. "Time travel?" Just the fact that he employed the term suggested that he at least understood the concept.

"Yes, we think you've traveled into what for you would be the future." It suddenly occurred to Ro that, considering the apparent nonlinear existence of the wormhole aliens, Altek might actually have traveled backward in time, rather than forward. She discounted the idea at once, based solely on the way he had behaved while on DS9.

"Travel into the future," Altek said. "That sounds fantastical."

"I'm sure it must."

Altek stood up. He appeared driven more by emotion than the will to take some sort of action. "How far into the future?"

"Right now, we have no way of knowing," Ro admitted. "Based on some of the things you've said, it seems likely that you've traveled centuries, perhaps even millennia."

Altek's legs gave out, and he fell back down into the chair. "Millennia," he said, his voice no more than a whisper. "Everybody I know—Greta, Veralla, the Cawlders . . . Anora—gone." He sat quietly for a few moments, clearly attempting to process what he'd been told. At last, he looked up and said, "I need you to show me—to prove it to me."

"I can do that," the captain said. "But before I do, there are some other things I need to tell you about." *Things I need to prepare you for,* she thought: Space travel. Alien life. The Prophets and the Celestial Temple. She thought it unlikely that any of those things had been a reality for him in his own time. He had dismissed beaming from the transporter room to his cell as a drug-induced experience, and Blackmer and O'Brien as eugenically altered Aleira.

"Tell me what you have to, and then maybe you can answer my questions," Altek said. "I have a lot of them." Ro saw an expression of desperation on his face. "My first question is: can you send me back home?"

Ro thought about what had happened with Akorem Laan,

how he had been escorted back into the wormhole by Captain Sisko and apparently returned to his own time by the Prophets. She wanted to tell Altek that he could expect the same experience, that yes, he could readily go back to where and when he had come from—but she couldn't. Too many uncertainties surrounded the situation, and she didn't want to promise him something that might not be possible. Instead, she told him the only thing she could: the truth.

"I don't know."

14

"**C**aptain, long-range sensors are detecting energy discharges." Lieutenant Commander Uteln crewed the tactical console on the raised aft section of the *Robinson* bridge. The Deltan spoke with an obvious sense of urgency.

Seated in the command chair, Captain Sisko despaired of what the report could mean. The ship had just arrived at the Federation border. Per Admiral Akaar's orders, the president pro tem wanted the *Robinson* crew to respond to the possibility of Tzenkethi involvement in the assassination of President Bacco by making a show of force where the Coalition would observe it. That meant a patrol route clinging to the Federation border closest to Tzenkethi space.

Beside Sisko, sitting in the first officer's position, Commander Anxo Rogeiro asked, "Is it weapons fire?" His thoughts echoed Sisko's own concerns.

"It's impossible to tell at this range," Uteln said. Sisko heard the taps of the tactical officer's fingertips on his panel. "It could be something like a mining operation, or even something naturally occurring."

"Where is it located?" Rogeiro asked.

"Determining now," Uteln said. "It's on the other side of the border."

Sisko exchanged a look with his first officer. "In Tzenkethi space?" Rogeiro asked.

"Negative," Uteln said. "The discharges are in an unaligned region."

"To us, it's unaligned," Sisko noted. "But who knows if the Tzenkethi have arbitrarily decided to annex another volume of space without informing anybody." The Coalition had a long history of belligerence toward the Federation, as well as a propensity for suddenly declaring unclaimed, unexplored territory as their own.

"Commander Plante, are there any other Starfleet vessels in the region?" Rogeiro asked. At the operations console, Gwendolyn Plante worked her controls. Newly promoted to the rank of commander and the position of second officer, she had first served under the captain aboard *U.S.S New York* during the Borg Invasion.

"There are a number of smaller patrol vessels assigned along this portion of the border," Plante said as she studied her display. "The *Endurance* and the *Mjolnir* are due within the next three days, but we're the first heavy to arrive."

"Which patrol vessel is closest to the energy discharges?" Sisko asked.

"Tying the long-range sensors into the assignments database," Plante said, her hands moving expertly across the ops controls. "It looks like it should be the *Argus*. It's a *Vigilant*-class scout."

"Hail them," Sisko ordered.

Several chirps rose from the tactical console. "Channel open, sir," said Uteln.

Sisko stood up and stepped to the center of the bridge. "*Robinson* to *Argus*," he said. "This is Captain Benjamin Sisko. We've arrived at the Federation border and have detected energy surges near your position. Please provide a status." He waited, and when he got no response, he said, "*Robinson* to *Argus*. Please reply." Again, he heard nothing but silence.

"There's no response, sir," Uteln said. "I can't tell whether or not they're receiving our transmission, and I can't pick up the ship on sensors. There could be interference from the energy discharges."

"Keep trying to raise them," Sisko told Uteln, and then he looked to his first officer. "What do you think?" he asked, though the captain knew that Rogeiro would share whatever opinion he'd formed. When Sisko glanced to where the ship's counselor sat on the other side of the command chair from the first officer, he saw Lieutenant Commander Diana Althouse regarding him. *Studying me,* Sisko thought. He genuinely appreciated Althouse's professional acumen, but he thought that, sometimes, she read his emotional state too well—at least, too well for his comfort.

Rogeiro stood up and joined the captain in the center of the bridge. "I think those energy discharges so close to Tzenkethi space make me nervous," the first officer said. "We should avoid crossing out of Federation boundaries so close to the Coalition, but we have to check it out."

"Agreed," Sisko said, forcing himself not to sigh in resignation. He had no interest in any contact with the Tzenkethi. As he'd told Akaar, he wanted to avoid any actions, no matter how well justified or seemingly benign, that could lead to armed conflict. As much as Starfleet had recovered since the Borg had attempted to wipe out the Federation, and as much as alliances with the Cardassians and the Ferengi had bolstered the ranks of qualified starship personnel, the UFP and the other Khitomer Accords nations could not afford war with the Tzenkethi and their Typhon Pact allies.

And yet here we are, he thought. *With a dead president behind us, and unidentified energy surges in front of us.*

Sisko returned to the command chair, and Rogeiro took his post beside him. "Set course in the direction of the discharges, best speed," Sisko said to Lieutenant Commander Sivadeki, who sat at the conn. "Get as close as you can while staying on our side of the border."

"Aye, sir, laying in a course," she said. Sisko watched as she brought up a sensor readout, then matched the ship's route and destination to the appropriate coordinates. "Going to maximum warp."

On the main viewscreen, the starfield canted to one side as *Robinson* raced onto its new heading. The deck vibrated with the increase in power. The great thrum of the warp drive deepened as the faster-than-light engines pushed the ship to greater velocities.

Rogeiro leaned in toward the captain. "I don't like it," the first officer said *sotto voce*. "Starfleet vessels massing along the border for all the Tzenkethi to see. It's almost as though Command wants to provoke them."

Not Starfleet Command, Sisko thought. *Ishan Anjar.* The president pro tem wanted to send ships to warn—or maybe even to intimidate—the Tzenkethi, based on the belief that they might have conspired to murder Nanietta Bacco. But if the Federation could prove Coalition conspiracy, Sisko wondered what next step the interim president intended to take. Raids on Tzenkethi ships? A massive assault against one or more of their worlds as a punitive measure? An all-out war?

"I don't like it either," Sisko told his first officer, "but Starfleet Command emphasized that we should proceed with extreme caution. We're here strictly to patrol this section of the border, not to cross it, and not to engage with the Tzenkethi if we can avoid it."

"A plan that works perfectly well until sensors register energy discharges just on the other side of the border, and attempts to contact one of our scoutships fail," Rogeiro said.

"Right," Sisko said. All at once, it became perfectly clear that they would not find the energy surges to be some natural phenomenon, or even an act as relatively nonthreatening as mining. Nor would the complement of *Robinson* discover that *Argus* had simply experienced a communications breakdown. *No, it's going to be something far worse,* he thought. *It's going to be the Tzenkethi.* And that meant that he might have to take his ship and crew into battle.

Sisko stood up again, induced to take action by a sickening feeling spreading through his gut. "Commander Uteln, send an encrypted message to Captain French at Helaspont Station. See if they've had any recent contact with the *Argus*. Also find out if they've detected the energy surges, and if so, what they know about them."

"Aye, sir."

"Commander," Sisko continued, addressing his first officer, "you have the bridge. I'll be in my ready room. Contact me at once if we hear from the *Argus* or Helaspont Station, or if we learn anything new about the situation."

"Yes, sir."

Sisko crossed the bridge quickly, almost as though he could outrun his overwhelming uneasiness. He entered his ready room, and as the door panels slipped shut behind him, he moved to his desk. Rather than circle around it and sit down, he walked directly over and leaned heavily on it. His breathing accelerated and grew shallow, and he became light-headed. Beads of perspiration broke out on the bald flesh of his head and spilled down his face. He thought that he might pass out.

Sisko closed his eyes, then fumbled for his combadge. He slapped at it, and it activated with a chirp. He thought of the words he should use—*Sisko to sickbay*—but he didn't say them. He let his hand fall back to his side, and he concentrated on his respiration, attempting to bring it under control. By degrees, he slowed and deepened his breathing. He stopped sweating, and when he finally opened his eyes again, his vertigo had passed.

Pushing away from his desk, the captain made his way across the compartment and into his refresher. He ran cold water in the basin and splashed it onto his face and head. He grabbed a towel and dried himself as he headed back out into his ready room.

He walked over to his desk, intending to sit down behind it, but then he glimpsed the holoprint that stood on one corner. Sisko tossed the towel onto the sofa, then picked up the framed image of his family. He peered at Kasidy, with her dark hair and dark eyes, and her lustrous smile; at their beautiful daughter, Rebecca, an impish nine-year-old who nevertheless sometimes demonstrated insight beyond her years; at his son, Jake, who had grown into a fine man; and at Rena, a splendid woman who had married Jake and brought romance into his life, along with a contentment that Sisko had never known him to have.

The holophotograph had been taken just a few months earlier, not long before the end of *Robinson*'s two-year assignment to guard the Bajoran system, including the new Deep Space 9, which at that time had yet to be completed. Sisko's son and daughter-in-law visited from Earth, where they had taken up residence during Jake's writing studies at the Pennington School in New Zealand. Kasidy made herself available by rescheduling her training as a Federation envoy, and Sisko coordinated his leave from the ship. Together again for the first time in almost two years, the five of them vacationed at Glyrshar Canyon, one of Bajor's few natural wonders that had survived the Occupation fully intact.

Sisko stared at the holoprint, at the five beaming faces, including his own. Their location provided a spectacular backdrop: the group stood together on a promontory overlooking the tallest waterfall on the planet as it thundered down into the vast canyon. When seated at his desk, Sisko looked at the print often, and it never failed to bring him a sense of peace. Holding it up before his face, he allowed it to perform its restorative magic on him.

Feeling better, the captain set the holophoto down and moved to the chair behind his desk. He dropped into it, thinking that, at that moment, he wanted nothing more than to go to his quarters and spend some time with his wife and daughter. Although his rank certainly allowed him the privilege, his family's daily life did not. At that hour, Rebecca would be in school, and Kasidy and the rest of *Robinson*'s diplomatic team would be meeting to study the culture and customs of the civilization that the crew had the best chance of next encountering: the Tzenkethi.

Alone in his ready room, Sisko shook his head. He'd already had his share of experiences with the Tzenkethi, from fighting against them in the Federation's last war with the

Coalition, to watching as one of their teardrop-shaped marauders destroyed the freighter *Xhosa* at a time when he'd believed both Kasidy and Rebecca to be aboard. He hoped that his wife would not have to deal with them—that none of the *Robinson* crew would—but on the trip out to Helaspont Sector, he had discussed the possibility with her. Having mourned the crew she'd lost aboard *Xhosa*, some of whom had become her close friends, she admitted to harboring general animosity for the Tzenkethi. Ever broad-minded, though, she refused to accept that she should assess an entire civilization based on the actions of one rogue crew. And while she sympathized with her husband for the terrible experiences he'd endured at the hands of the Tzenkethi, Kasidy declined to judge its present government by actions taken decades in the past.

Tired of thinking about the Coalition—and certain that he would have to contend with some of its forces soon enough—Sisko activated the computer interface on his desk. He quickly navigated to a file that been rendered obsolete, but that he hoped one day in the near future to revive: the itinerary for the *Robinson* crew's extended exploratory mission out beyond Bajor. The captain had assisted Starfleet Operations in the preparation of the schedule, which had subsequently been approved by Admiral Akaar. The assignment had been left open-ended, with an expected duration of two to three years.

Sisko perused the route that he and his crew would have taken. He examined the few known facts about several of the nearer star systems along the way, some gleaned from astronomical observations, others from automated long-range probes. He had just begun to read up on a number of unexplained interstellar phenomena when the door signal chimed.

"Come in," Sisko said, curious why, if his crew had learned something about the energy surges or *Argus*, Rogeiro hadn't called him to the bridge. The answer became apparent when the doors parted to reveal not his first officer, but the ship's counselor. She entered the ready room and stepped up to the desk. "Commander," Sisko said, "what can I do for you?"

"Nothing at all, Captain," Althouse said. In her sixties and petite, with short blond hair, she regularly proclaimed in conversation to have no interest in any particular subject, but that often belied her desire to address a psychological issue with one of the crew. It didn't surprise Sisko to see her; in the four years since he had first taken command of *Robinson*, he had gotten to know the counselor very well, and she, him. He found her perceptive and astute, and he knew that, of all her duties in maintaining the mental and emotional well-being of the crew, she considered keeping her commanding officer healthy the most important.

"If you're concerned about my having to deal with the Tzenkethi, you needn't be," Sisko told her.

"You mean because you fought in the war against them?" Althouse asked. "And because the crew of a Tzenkethi starship destroyed your wife's vessel and killed most of her crew?" She shrugged. "It never occurred to me."

"It didn't?" Sisko said, not believing the counselor. He chalked up her assertion as some form of reverse psychology intended to draw out his feelings of resentment for the Coalition. "Maybe Starfleet placed you in the wrong position, then."

Without being invited to do so, Althouse sat down in one of the two chairs in front of the desk. "So are you telling me that I *should* be concerned about you possibly having to face the Tzenkethi?"

"No, I didn't mean that," Sisko said. "I just thought . . . based on my personal history, it seemed like a natural conclusion for you to make."

"Not at all," Althouse said. "What I'm aware of is your long and successful career in Starfleet, as well as your overall record of inclusiveness, which contains such deeds as sponsoring the first Ferengi for the Academy. I know you've had difficult confrontations with Tzenkethi before, but I wouldn't think that you'd resent their entire species any more than you'd resent, say, all humans or Bajorans or Starfleet admirals." She leaned forward and reached a hand up to the edge of the desk, motioning toward the captain. "I am right in my assessment that you've had difficult confrontations with humans and Bajorans and admirals?"

"Oh, yes," Sisko said. "And with some counselors as well."

Althouse smiled and rapped her knuckles against the desktop. "There you have it," she said, as though she had just received incontrovertible proof of her premise. "I'm delighted not to be drawn with the same harsh brush as some of my less-than-illustrious predecessors."

Sisko smiled, amused, but he did not forget that Althouse had come to pay him a visit during their duty shift. Not somebody to waste time or effort, she must have had something on her mind. "So, if you're not here to discuss my unbridled hatred for all things Tzenkethi, then why are you here, Counselor?"

Althouse leaned back in her chair. "Actually, I was just wondering why you left the bridge," she said. "You usually stay there during alpha shift, especially when the ship might be headed into a dangerous situation."

"No particular reason," the captain said. He could not deny to himself that, on the bridge, he'd experienced a strong reaction to a potential clash with Coalition forces, but he felt sure that the shortness of breath, dizziness, and perspiration he'd exhibited had been unrelated. *I probably just stood up too fast,* he told himself.

Sisko took hold of the computer interface on his desk and spun it around so that Althouse could see it. "I thought I'd take another look at our route out past Bajor," he explained. He knew that if he didn't satisfy the counselor's curiosity, he would be faced with many more questions—questions that regulations obliged him to answer.

Althouse looked at the display. "Our grand mission of exploration," she said with an air of pomp. Then, with a decidedly disappointed air, she added, "If we ever get to go on it."

"We will," Sisko said at once. He felt strongly about it, though he couldn't tell if his fervor arose out of conviction or mere wishful thinking.

"You sound certain. I wish I could be. After what happened to the president . . ."

"It's important for Starfleet to provide stability and security for the Federation at this terrible time," Sisko said. "But as a people, as an amalgam of worlds that share the same lofty values, we're far more than just interstellar diplomats and military enforcers. Sometimes it's necessary for us to play those roles, but that's not who we are: we're explorers and scientists, reaching for the unknown and to expand our knowledge of both the universe and ourselves."

"High-minded words," Althouse said, not without appreciation.

"They're all the more important because they reflect high-minded ideals," Sisko said. "Our mandate is what it says in the Starfleet charter: 'to boldly go where no one has gone before.'"

A glint showed in the counselor's eyes. "I've never liked the split infinitive," she said wryly.

"To go boldly, then."

"That's better." Althouse stood up, and Sisko thought that she intended to return to the bridge. Instead, she walked past the side of his desk and over to the tall, narrow port that looked out on the stars as they sped past. Staring out, she said, "I do find it frustrating, Captain."

"You find what frustrating?"

Without turning around, Althouse said, "One minute, we're poised to embark on a momentous journey into the unknown, and the next, we're headed toward the border in Helaspont Sector, our bow pointed toward the Tzenkethi Coalition. That doesn't exactly sound equitable, does it?"

"It doesn't need to be equitable," Sisko said. "It's all part of the duty we signed on for."

"Still," Althouse said, at last looking around to face the captain again, "I'm sure that Kasidy must be disappointed. And Rebecca, too."

"Kasidy and Rebecca?" He glanced over at the holoprint. "They're not Starfleet. The change doesn't really affect them."

"Oh, good," Althouse said. "I thought it might be hard for them to know that the ship might be heading into combat."

"I don't believe they think about being aboard the *Robinson* in those terms," Sisko said. *They don't think about it in those terms, but I do.*

"I'm glad that's the case, otherwise Kasidy and Rebecca could find their time on the ship very disquieting." She moved away from the port and back over to the chair in front of the desk, though she did not sit. "I realize that when they finally relocated to the *Robinson* on a permanent basis, they expected a mission like that one." Althouse pointed toward the computer interface, which still displayed the ship's prospective path out past Bajor. "And now, for the *Robinson* to suddenly be thrust into a dangerous situation—"

"Exploring the unknown can be dangerous too," Sisko interjected. "Sometimes more so than taking the ship into combat. The *Robinson* has strong defenses and powerful weapons."

"Yes, it does."

Sisko felt an itch on his forehead, and when he rubbed at it, he realized that he'd begun to sweat again—not profusely, as he had a few minutes earlier, but his fingertips came away slick. "Life aboard a starship is dangerous," he went on. "Starfleet vessels have been destroyed in wars, and they've been lost while their crews have been out exploring the universe."

Very quietly, Althouse said, "I think more have been lost in military battles."

"Yes, of course," Sisko said. He rose to his feet and paced over to look through the port out into space. The counselor's insensitivity shocked him. For her to argue that Starfleet Command's reassignment of *Robinson* to the Helaspont Sector put his family in greater danger—

Why would she do that? Sisko asked himself. *Even if she's right*—and he knew that she was—*why would she make that argument?* He certainly understood as well as anybody the risks to civilians living on a starship—he understood *better* than most: he had lost his first wife—

I lost Jennifer, Sisko thought; *and the counselor knows that.*

He put his hands up to the bulkhead on either side of the port. Out in space, the stars passed, ablaze in their reality, but cold in their distance. Sisko refocused his eyes onto the transparent surface of the port, and he saw his ghostly reflection there. He looked at himself, but he realized that Diana Althouse had looked at him more closely, at least in the past few minutes.

Sisko walked back over to the chair behind his desk and sat down again. The counselor looked at him from where she stood, and he knew he would have to acknowledge the reason she had come into his ready room. "Kasidy and I understood the dangers of bringing our family aboard the *Robinson* and making our home here," he said. "We each thought about it, and we discussed it, and in the end, we decided that this was where we wanted to be. There will be dangers to the ship and the people aboard it, but there will also be immeasurable opportunities to learn about the universe."

Althouse said nothing, and her silence confirmed her intentions. Sisko understood that she would wait for him to say the words she had come to hear him say. On the bridge, she had read his distress, and she wanted to ensure that he did not suppress the emotions that the current situation engendered in him, that he recognized and would cope with them.

Sisko looked at the computer interface, at the exploratory route that had been planned for his ship and crew—planned, and then abandoned. With unhurried movements, he reached over and deactivated the device, blanking its screen. "Yes, I thought when Kasidy and Rebecca came aboard that the *Robinson* crew would be out traveling the galaxy in search of its wonders, not headed for a potential clash with Tzenkethi forces. I always knew that engaging in battle would be a possibility, but this is the first time I've been faced with that reality."

He paused. Sisko wanted to tell the counselor that it didn't matter, that he had considered the circumstances and dealt with them on an emotional level. He knew that she would see through the artifice.

"I'm not happy about it," he finally said. "I'm never happy

when I have to take my crew into battle, and I certainly don't like it any better now that my family is aboard. But I wanted Kasidy and Rebecca with me, and I wanted this post. I accept the consequences, even if I don't like them."

Althouse continued to stand quietly for a moment, then nodded her head once. "Oh, the life of a starship captain," she said in an obvious attempt to lighten the mood.

Sisko smiled up at her, although he didn't feel light. "It all comes with the territory," he said. "At least I'm not saddled with all the dreadful responsibilities of a crew counselor."

Althouse rolled her eyes theatrically. "Don't I know it?" she said, and then she started toward the door. "Well, please excuse the interruption, Captain."

"Of course, Counselor." Content to see her go, Sisko also felt appreciation for the care she provided the crew—perhaps grudging appreciation when it came to his own care, but appreciation nevertheless. He watched her go until the doors glided shut after her.

Sisko brought his hands up to his face and steepled his fingers. He thought about the counselor's visit, and the reason she felt it necessary. After a while, he looked back at the computer interface on his desk. He considered returning to the specs of *Robinson*'s erstwhile exploratory mission, but decided against it. Instead, he called up Captain Ro's report about the Tzenkethi genetic material found on the device implanted in Enkar Sirsy, the woman first suspected of assassinating President Bacco. Back at DS9, Ro had briefed him on the matter, and he had read through her report, but he thought that maybe he should do so again. So close to Coalition space, he wanted to make sure he understood the situation as thoroughly as possible.

THE INDIGO STRAND of interstellar dust and ionized gases glowed on the main viewscreen, its diffuse form twisted luminously through space. Sisko stared from the command chair at the beautiful astral structure, just one portion of the massive Helaspont Nebula that meandered across the sector and beyond. It looked to him more like an abstract work of art than some great celestial object.

"Anything?" Rogeiro asked. The first officer stood beside Uteln at the tactical station.

"Negative," the Deltan replied. "No sign of the *Argus*, and no more energy surges, but the static discharge and ionization effects of the nebula are disrupting our sensors."

"Could that have been what our long-range scans picked up?" Sisko asked. "Could those have been the energy surges we detected?"

"No, I don't think so, sir," Uteln said. "The nebula causes havoc with sensors because its effects are widespread. The energy discharges we read earlier were localized and greater in point magnitude."

"Understood," Sisko said. "Uteln, continue trying to raise the *Argus*. In the meantime, I guess we're going to have to do this the old-fashioned way. Commander Sivadeki, plot a search grid into the nebula."

"Aye, sir," said the conn officer.

Just before *Robinson* had arrived along the patrol route assigned to the *Argus* crew, at the scoutship's last confirmed position, Sisko had received a response from Helaspont Station. The starbase floated at the other end of the sector, on the far edge of the nebula. In his transmission, Captain French indicated that he had last received word from the *Argus* crew less than ten hours earlier, at the regular time for the first of their twice-daily reports. Their message had been routine, with no mention of any trouble aboard ship, and no hint of any Tzenkethi presence in the region. French provided the coordinates of *Argus'* last verified location.

"Search pattern laid in, Captain," said Sivadeki. "It will take us up to and along the Federation border, but not past it. Ready to execute on your command."

"Initiate," Sisko said. He listened to the sounds of the ship as *Robinson* moved onto its new path. He mused to himself that he had opposed his crew's assignment to the border in Helaspont Sector—to *any* crew's assignment there—because he had dreaded an escalation of the tensions already present between the Federation and the Tzenkethi Coalition. With the apparent disappearance of *Argus*, he worried that his fears might be realized sooner than even he had anticipated.

Less than an hour later, they were.

"Captain, sensors are picking up energy discharges again," Uteln said. "The readings are sporadic because of the interference, but they're originating outside the nebula."

"Can you identify the source?" Rogeiro asked. He had returned to the first officer's chair.

"Trying," Uteln said as he operated his panel. "I can tell you that there appear to be two sources, but it's impossible to produce a clean sensor description as long as we're within the nebula."

Rogeiro looked to Sisko for confirmation of the next logical order, but the captain stood up and issued it directly. "Sivadeki, take us out of the nebula. Follow the shortest possible route."

"Aye, Captain," she said. "Computing our trajectory." Her hands dashed across the conn, and in just a few moments, Sisko saw the colorful contours of the Helaspont Nebula shift as Sivadeki piloted *Robinson* toward open space. When the image on the main viewer cleared, showing nothing but stars, he looked to the tactical console, where Uteln operated his controls and studied his displays.

"I've isolated the two sources of the discharges," the tactical officer said. "No . . . not two . . . there are three of them." When he lifted his head, Sisko saw the concern on his face. "They're ships, sir . . . firing their weapons."

"At what? At each other?" Rogeiro said as he jumped up from his chair and raced up the curved starboard ramp to the raised section of the bridge.

"No, not at each other," Uteln said. "I don't see a target, though. They seem to be firing *into* the nebula."

"It's got to be the *Argus* in there," Sisko said. "Can you identify the ships that are firing?"

"Scanning them now," Uteln said. "They all have relatively small profiles. Their hull geometry is—" The tactical officer stopped in midsentence, then glanced up knowingly at the captain. "Their hull geometry is helical."

Sisko understood immediately what that meant. As far as he knew, only one class of starship employed a helix-shaped design. "Tzenkethi harriers."

Rogeiro leaned in beside Uteln and examined a readout on the tactical display. "Captain," he said, "the harriers are beyond the Federation border."

"And their target?"

Rogeiro looked around for that information, but Uteln replied. "The section of the nebula they're firing at is also outside of Federation space."

"Is it a gambit?" Plante asked from the operations console. "Are they attempting to lure us out of our territory and into theirs?"

"They're not within their own borders either," Rogeiro said. "They're in unclaimed space."

"We say it's unclaimed," noted Sivadeki. "They may say otherwise."

"In either case, why would they want to draw a *Galaxy*-class starship out of Federation space?" Uteln asked. "Even three harriers can't hope to prevail against the *Robinson*."

"Maybe they're trying to trigger an interstellar incident of some kind," Plante postulated, "as cover for their involvement in the assassination." Sisko had informed his senior staff of the evidence pointing toward the Coalition.

"Or perhaps they're not firing at the *Argus*," Rogeiro speculated. "What if we get out there and discover that a couple of marauders are waiting for us inside the nebula?"

Two years earlier, during the attack on the original Deep Space 9 that had resulted in the station's destruction, the *Robinson* crew had bested one of the powerful, teardrop-shaped battle cruisers, but just barely, and only after suffering numerous casualties and considerable damage to the ship. Sisko did not want to take his crew into another such battle. He felt confident, though, that no marauders lay in wait for them inside the nebula. Not that the Tzenkethi couldn't be devious, but Sisko's intuition told him what had happened.

He knew the capabilities of the harriers. Though maneuverable and fast, they could not outrun a *Vigilant*-class scoutship—but they could outgun it. Built for speed, *Argus* and its sister ships had little in the way of significant armaments or defenses. Sisko didn't know why the *Argus* crew had crossed out of Federation space—they could have been lured there or forced there, their ship could have suffered a malfunction, or they could have found a valid reason to do so, such as responding to a distress call. Regardless, Sisko felt sure that the three Tzenkethi vessels had surrounded *Argus*, and, unable to fight their way back across the border, the Starfleet crew had taken their ship into the nebula to hide.

"No, there are no marauders hiding in the nebula," he told his bridge crew. "That's our ship out there."

"How can you be sure, Captain?" Rogeiro asked, descending from the raised level of the bridge. The first officer rarely disagreed with Sisko's decisions, and he almost never questioned him in front of the crew. The two men worked well together, and on top of that, they'd also become good friends. Because Sisko valued the man's judgment, he not only trusted Rogeiro to speak his mind, he counted on it.

"I don't know," the captain admitted, "but I feel very strongly about it. We need to rescue the *Argus* crew."

Rogeiro did not pursue a more comprehensive answer to his question. Instead, he began implementing Sisko's order. "Shields up, phasers and photon torpedoes at the ready," he said. "Set course for the nearest harrier, maximum warp. You have the captain's authorization to leave Federation space."

As the crew acknowledged and executed their orders, Sisko returned to the command chair, and Rogeiro sat down beside him. "Hail the closest ship," the captain ordered.

"Hailing frequencies open," said Uteln.

"*U.S.S. Robinson* to Coalition ship," Sisko said. He didn't bother to stand, knowing that the recalcitrant Tzenkethi rarely communicated visually. He considered how best to approach the situation, and quickly decided on a course of action. "This is Captain Benjamin Sisko of the United Federation of Planets. We are in search of a lost vessel and request your assistance in locating it."

Sisko did not receive an immediate reply, and Uteln reported that the harriers continued to fire on the nebula. But then a sound like the peal of bells rang out through the comm system, followed a moment later by the universal translator's interpretation of the language. "*Tzenkethi squadron to Federation starship. This is Nenzet Siv Vel-C. You are encroaching on sovereign Coalition territory and are instructed to withdraw at once.*"

"Siv," Sisko said, employing the Tzenkethi's title, which he knew equated to something like squadron leader. "Perhaps I have not made myself clear. My crew are searching for a Federation vessel with which we have lost contact. I don't know what you're firing at—surely it could not be our missing ship—but it is you who are encroaching on our territory. The Federation has claimed this space as its own."

On the main viewer, a shape appeared in the center of the screen amid the stars, a blue and violet patch of the Helaspont Nebula behind it. As the captain watched, the image blinked, and the shape grew in size, magnified by Commander Plante. The characteristic helical construction of the Tzenkethi harrier always appeared dramatic and unusual to Sisko. The ship tapered from bow to stern, its hull shining with a prismatic gleam.

"*This is* not *Federation territory,*" blustered Nenzet. "*That is an outrageous declaration.*"

"It is not a declaration," Sisko said. "It is merely a report of fact. If you like, I can produce the Ferengi Ledger of Galactic Space, which lists all territorial claims."

"*The Ferengi!*" Nenzet barked, though the bell-like sound of his voice made his tone less than threatening. "*Federation lackeys who would sell you the Soaring Cliffs of Villisang if you let them."* Sisko had never head of the Soaring Cliffs of Villisang, but he imagined that the phrase held the same meaning as a human trying to sell the Brooklyn Bridge, a protected Federation historic landmark.

"I think the Ferengi would quibble with your characterization," Sisko said, careful to speak calmly in the wake of the Tzenkethi's indignation. "But I can still produce the document. Are you officially disputing our claim?" Sisko glanced over at his first officer to see him smiling.

Nenzet did not respond right away, and when he finally did, his words seemed uncertain. *"I do dispute your claim,"* he said, *"but I do not have the authority to do so officially."*

On the viewscreen, the stern tip of the harrier began to glow at multiple points. As Sisko watched, the lights increased in intensity, then started to swirl around the coiled hull, speeding forward until they shot out from the bow of the ship. The captain waited to see if Nenzet had fired on *Robinson*, although, if he had, Uteln would have warned the bridge crew.

When no weapons fire landed on his ship, Sisko said, "Siv, I *do* have the authority to enforce the Federation's claim to this space. I suggest that you stop firing your weapons, which could be considered an act of war."

"It is the Federation who has perpetrated an act of war," Nenzet bellowed. *"Your accusation of Tzenkethi involvement in the assassination of your president is not only false, but an insult and cause for reprisal. The Federation has always hated the Coalition, and your dispatching of your own leader is clearly a naked attempt to sow instability and divide us from our allies so that you can launch an all-out attack on the Tzenkethi."*

Sisko thought that only the outward hostility of Nenzet and his people could match their paranoia, particularly when it came to the Federation. Still, his allegation that the Federation had murdered President Bacco unsettled the captain. For the moment, he ignored that, concentrating instead on finding the *Argus* crew. He also noted that the harrier no longer fired its weapons.

"Nenzet Siv," he said, "we can sit here and continue to denounce each other's governments, or we can end this uncomfortable encounter peacefully."

"You may withdraw at any time," Nenzet said, but Sisko did not believe he spoke with confidence.

"May I suggest a compromise?" Sisko said. "We can both withdraw—your three ships and our two." The captain intended his suggestion as a means of allowing Nenzet to save face in retreating from the area. The squadron leader leaped at the opportunity.

"We do not detect two Federation vessels in the area," Nenzet said.

"As I mentioned, Siv, we are searching for a lost ship," Sisko said. "We believe it is in the portion of the nebula that your squadron is surrounding."

"We . . . are searching for a vessel ourselves," Nenzet said.

"And firing on it?"

"It is piloted by an outlaw, and we have been charged with stopping him." The story sounded improvised. Sisko didn't care, as long as he could find and help the crew of *Argus*.

"Would you object to our entering the nebula and searching for our lost ship?" Sisko said. He knew that Nenzet and his three harriers could do nothing to stop the *Robinson* crew from doing so, and the Tzenkethi surely knew that as well. "If we locate your outlaw, we will gladly deliver him to you. If we find our lost ship, we will escort it—or if necessary, tow it—back across our old border, which would at least honor your dispute, official or not, of our claim to this territory."

"That would be acceptable," Nenzet said. *"But we will not wait indefinitely."*

"Then the sooner we begin, the sooner we can conclude our search. We'll keep you informed of our progress. *Robinson* out."

"Channel closed," Uteln said.

"Institute a new search grid for this section of the nebula," Rogeiro ordered, and Sivadeki set about doing so.

Sisko observed his senior bridge crew with appreciation as

they quickly and efficiently went about their jobs. It did not take them long to visually locate a vessel within the nebula—not the obviously nonexistent outlaw Nenzet had mentioned, but *Argus*. In closer proximity to each other, the two crews managed to make communications function well enough, despite the interference.

Captain Aldany Menzies reported that his crew had detected a ship entering the nebula on the Federation side of the border. When their hails went unanswered, they pursued the ship. *Argus* crossed the border in that chase, and when it eventually emerged from the nebula, its crew found themselves surrounded by the Tzenkethi squadron. Unable to make their way safely back into Federation space, they took refuge in another section of the nebula.

When *Robinson* exited back into open space with *Argus* traveling alongside, the Tzenkethi did not interfere. They waited until the two Starfleet vessels had crossed the border back into Federation space before ultimately vacating the area. Sisko considered the encounter a success: there had been no casualties, and no significant increase in the already existing tensions.

As he commended the bridge staff on a job well done, Sisko noticed the counselor regarding him. He acknowledged her attention with a nod, then continued complimenting his crew. He couldn't tell if Althouse had registered unease when he'd spoken with Nenzet Siv Vel-C. The captain knew the Tzenkethi well enough to recognize their tendency toward hyperbolic rhetoric, but the squadron leader had said one thing that troubled Sisko. Although he couldn't precisely say why, the repugnant idea of Federation complicity in the murder of Nan Bacco carried the faint ring of truth to him.

15

Kira followed Taran'atar around a corner and into a short corridor that ended at a turbolift. As they entered the cab, she noticed an alien glyph adorning the bulkhead. "This is the only dedicated lift to the C-D subdeck," Taran'atar told her. "That character—" He pointed to the symbol. "—identifies it as such."

The Jem'Hadar had just taken Kira on a circuit of *Even Odds'* lowest deck, which housed an impressive array of engineering facilities, as well as a number of cargo bays of various sizes and capabilities. In one hold, she saw that a substantial section of the outer bulkhead had been replaced, its bright yellow color, pebbled texture, and hexagonal component plates contrasting considerably with the smooth gray squares around it. Kira assumed that Taran'atar had endured his final confrontation with the Ascendant there, the weapon he had rigged to overload blasting the outer bulkhead apart and out into space.

After the doors closed, Kira said, "I take it that by *subdeck*, you mean an area that does not span the entire ship, but is situated between two decks and is readily accessible to the crew."

"That is correct," Taran'atar said as the cab began its upward journey. The turbolift began to slow almost as soon as it began to ascend. "The C-D subdeck is the location of what the *Even Odds* crew call the *Wa*."

Kira recognized the name from Jake Sisko's description of *Even Odds* after the ship had been destroyed over Bajor—an event that lay in Taran'atar's future, and that would result in his death. She still wondered if she could somehow prevent that from happening, especially since she had learned that the expected remainder of his natural life could now be measured in years, and perhaps even in decades. She wanted to learn more about *Even Odds* and its crew before making a final decision on how to proceed, but she also knew that she mustn't wait too long and miss her opportunity.

"What is the Wa?" she asked. Jake had described it from a sensory perspective—what it looked like to him, what it sounded like, what it felt like—but he had been short on technical and scientific details. He hadn't been able to explain exactly what the Wa was, other than to state that he thought it had something to do with subspace and possibly other dimensions. Although postmortem analyses of the disaster suggested that a contained region of subspace aboard *Even Odds* might have contributed to what happened, perhaps even triggered it, the explanation lacked detail and remained only speculation. Kira looked forward both to experiencing the mysterious area, and to hearing Taran'atar's description of it.

"It is unclear, both to the *Even Odds* crew and to me, what the Wa is," said the Jem'Hadar. "It appears to be an extradimensional realm, possibly in subspace, or it may only be an access point to other dimensions. It has thus far defied my attempts to analyze it, as it had those of the crew before I came aboard. What Captain Dezavrim and the others have told me is that the Wa is usually confined to the subdeck, although it has been known to shift location, unpredictably, for brief periods of time. It has done this once during my time on the ship, encompassing an aft turbolift and a small volume of space off the stern."

The cab eased to a halt, and the doors opened. Despite Jake's vivid description of the Wa, the scene before Kira surprised her. A white passage stretched into the distance for as far as she could see. Circular in cross-section, its diameter varied along its extent. It measured wider, taller, and longer than any corridor she had traversed aboard *Even Odds*—or aboard *any* ship.

"Before we step out, I must warn you not to wander away from me, and not to touch anything, until I have demonstrated the Wa to you," Taran'atar said. "Even once I have, under no circumstances must you ever approach a gray portal."

Jake had not utilized the word *portal*, but he had spoken about patches of color that allowed passage from within the Wa to other places—possibly also within the Wa, possibly elsewhere. As Kira peered out of the turbolift, she distinguished those whorls of pale pigment, situated all around in no discernible pattern. It took her several seconds before she found one that looked gray. "I understand," she told Taran'atar, meaning not that she comprehended the reality of the Wa, but that she would heed his warnings.

Taran'atar paced out of the turbolift, and Kira did as well. She stayed close to his side as they walked. She tried to focus on the walls around them, but she found it difficult even to perceive them. Soft light permeated the space evenly, though she could not determine its source.

As they moved along, the portals, as Taran'atar called them, became more apparent. She saw scores of them, maybe more, in many different shades. Some took the form of spinning balls, while others appeared two-dimensional. Some hung in mid-air, while others adorned the curving walls that she could not quite make out. Some of the colors looked as though they had been swirled on with a brush and left to drip downward. They all seemed most distinct when she caught sight of them in her peripheral vision, but when she looked at them directly, their hues seemed to fade, as though worn down by time.

After just a few strides, Kira glanced back over her shoulder. She stopped in her tracks. She expected to see the closed doors of the turbolift, but her gaze took in an infinite regress of white, broken only by the view of more portals. "What happened to the lift?"

Taran'atar stopped beside her and pointed slightly to the left of where she had been looking. "There," he said. "Do you see the purple cross?" The Jem'Hadar's voice, normally so deep and rich, sounded tinny to her, and Kira wondered if her senses were somehow being manipulated. She realized that she felt chilled, and that the scents reaching her nose smelled like something out of a barn—like dry hay and wet animal hides.

Kira did not see a cross, and so she searched for the color purple. When she found it, she saw that it did indeed resemble a rough *X* shape. It looked to be a meter or so in height, though she did not trust her sense of scale in those surroundings. "I see it."

"That marks the location of the turbolift," Taran'atar said. "The cross can appear in different colors, but the shape doesn't change."

"It looks so far away," she said. "We haven't come that far."

"Regardless of your location within the Wa," Taran'atar said, "that is how the turbolift appears."

"How can that be?"

"I do not know," Taran'atar said. "I initially suspected that a mind-altering substance infused this place, but I now believe that the Wa is a controlled point of spatial interphase between multiple universes or dimensions."

"Controlled how?"

"I do not know," Taran'atar said. "No science of which I am aware would explain how such a thing could be accomplished."

Kira shook her head, then slowly turned in place, examining the Wa. It no longer appeared to be a tunnel, but more like an oversized, vaguely hemispherical chamber, although its walls and ceiling—and even its floor—seemed present only by implication. "What is the purpose of this place?"

"I do not know," Taran'atar said again. "The crew of the *Even Odds* generally treats it as an amusement. It is also where most of them hid when the Ascendant attacked the ship. Its original purpose appears to have been lost with its makers."

"And who were they?" Kira wanted to know, although she correctly anticipated Taran'atar's reply.

"I do not know," he said. "According to Captain Dezavrim, he purchased the ship from a salvage dealer almost twenty years ago. The dealer claimed to have found it derelict in space. As far as I've been told, the location, identity, and even the species of those who constructed the *Even Odds* are unknown. That may or may not be true; I do not necessarily believe everything that the captain says, but it is clear that the rest of the crew subscribe to the mysterious nature of the ship's origins."

Kira had heard similar details about the *Even Odds* from Jake—including the suspect nature of its captain's declarations. He also told Kira about the patches of color in the Wa, but she wanted to learn about them from Taran'atar. "You called the colors *portals*," she said. "Where do they lead?"

"To various environments that essentially resemble rooms," the Jem'Hadar said. "Some contain inscrutable equipment. Others contain what may be artwork, and others, what can probably be best described as entertainment, some of it interactive. Still others appear essentially empty, although each typically retains something unique about it, like a certain color or scent or sound."

Jake had spoken of watching a floating sphere spin itself into a sculptural representation of a star as an example of the environments to which the portals could lead. He also mentioned the empty spaces, as well as those filled by enigmatic machines. Because of what had happened—or what *would* happen—to the *Even Odds* at Bajor, the environments with alien equipment most interested Kira.

"Can we go through some of the portals?" Kira asked.

"You may select one for us."

Kira gazed around to find the closest one, but while she could distinguish those near from those farther away, she had trouble estimating precise distances. Because of that, she chose one at random, an orange ball just off to the right. "How about that one?" She walked with Taran'atar in that direction, but it took longer than she'd anticipated. When they arrived before it, she saw that what she had perceived as being roughly the size of a humanoid head actually measured more than a meter across. "How do we use it?" she asked.

"It varies from portal to portal," Taran'atar said. He reached forward and waved the flat of his hand before the orange surface. Nothing happened. He took a step closer to it, almost touching it, and still nothing happened. Finally, he reached out—

—and with no sense of transition at all, the two of them stood in another place. As with the first chamber of the Wa, she felt the boundaries of the environment more than saw them. The place felt far more confined than where they had been, more like a room, as Taran'atar had suggested, even though there seemed to be nothing at all in the space. She waited for something to happen, or even just to see something. At last, she said, "This place is empty."

"It would appear so," Taran'atar agreed. "It may be that the focal point of this environment is simply the shade of its light."

Kira looked around and realized that Taran'atar was right: the white of the environment radiated a slightly different tint than that in the main chamber of the Wa. She also saw that no colored globes or swatches hung in the air or on the walls—including the orange one through which they had come. "How do we leave?"

"There is a focal point in most of the environments," Taran'atar said. "In the case of empty environments, it is just the center of the space. To exit, just step back from the focus or the center."

Together with Taran'atar, Kira stepped backward and immediately found herself in front of the orange portal. She marveled at the instantaneous nature of the travel. It surprised her that the speed of the shift from one place to another caused her no disorientation. "I'd like to try another," she said. Taran'atar nodded, and she pointed to a green sphere. They started toward it, and Kira prepared to reach out to it, but when they got close, they passed through it without warning.

Again, they stood in an environment far smaller than the main chamber of the Wa, but larger than the one in their previous excursion. The tangy scent of the ocean filled Kira's nose. Before them, a misshapen mass of metal rose three or so meters from the floor, its surface fitted with several triangular pieces of glass, which might have been displays or readouts of some kind. She had seen nothing like it. More than anything, the object's twisting form reminded Kira of melted candle wax. It narrowed about a third of the way up its length, and then again at two-thirds. Where it did, Kira saw cavities in the metal. When she moved closer and bent to examine them, Taran'atar said, "Do not touch the device."

Kira straightened. "I wasn't going to," she said. "I said I would adhere to all of your warnings about the Wa."

Taran'atar stared at her for a moment, then bowed his head. "Forgive me, Captain," he said. "I did not mean to imply that you would act rashly."

Kira smiled at the comment. "Why not?" she asked. "The truth is, I've been acting rashly my entire life."

"Are you making a joke?"

"Only if you think the truth is funny," Kira said.

Taran'atar paused, and then said, "Jem'Hadar do not think *anything* is funny."

Kira laughed. It amazed her to think how right Odo had been about the potential of the Jem'Hadar to be more than they had been bred to be by the Founders. If he lived long enough—if he could survive the destruction of the *Even Odds*, or if that destruction ended up not happening—he could become a living example to the rest of his kind—as well as an object lesson to those who would deny anybody the right of self-determination.

Bending down again, Kira studied the cavities in the device. It looked as though, if she reached out, she could fit three fingers into the grooves there. "What do you suppose this does?"

Taran'atar actually sighed. "I do not know," he said, his continual refrain since they'd entered the Wa. "In my time aboard, I have seen numerous examples of technology within the environments of the Wa. I have neither recognized nor been able to reasonably conjecture about the function of any of them."

"Are they all like this?" she asked, returning to the Jem'Hadar's side.

"No," Taran'atar said. "Nothing that I have seen has looked like this. Each piece of equipment appears drastically different from the next."

"Dez hasn't tried to puzzle them out?" Kira asked. "Or tried to remove them so that he could study them, or even peddle them somewhere?"

"Not that I am aware of," Taran'atar said. "I have been told that Atterace Prees, the chief engineer, spent a great deal of time studying the devices in the Wa when she first came aboard, but she was unable to make sense of any of them. She still visits the Wa, but strictly as a diversion."

"I see."

"Perhaps even more telling, Prees told me that she once brought Srral into the Wa," Taran'atar said, referring to the artificial, liquid life-form that served the crew as an engineer. "She introduced it into one of the devices in the hopes of learning something about the technology. Srral became trapped, unable to leave the equipment. The crew eventually had to employ a vacuum chamber to extract it."

"And Srral didn't learn anything at all?"

"Various crew members have quoted him to me, saying that he described the technological environment as 'extremely alien.' Because of Srral's own peculiar nature, Captain Dezavrim and the others afforded that description considerable weight."

"I can imagine," Kira said, not entirely sure herself about the fluidic being's "peculiar nature." Not only did its life not resemble Odo's in any way, but it apparently spent its existence inside technological equipment.

"Srral also confirmed something Captain Dezavrim had long suspected," Taran'atar said. "A considerable amount of power courses through the Wa and its many environments."

"Power that must be provided by the ship's engines," Kira said. "Why hasn't Dez been able to verify that?"

"Because the power within the Wa is not produced on the ship," Taran'atar said.

"What?" Kira said. "How can that be?"

"Nobody aboard understands the mechanism by which it is accomplished, but the Wa must get its power elsewhere."

"Do you mean . . . from another dimension? Another universe?"

Taran'atar just looked at Kira, but didn't bother to provide what had become his standard response to questions about the Wa: *I do not know.* "Wherever the power comes from, Srral estimated it as enough to destroy a planet."

The statement shocked Kira, but she also thought it explained what had happened when *Even Odds* had reached Bajor. It also made her realize that, no matter what else she did, she had to ensure that the ship made it there by the time it would be needed. *And maybe sooner than that,* she thought, speculating that, if *Even Odds* arrived sooner than it originally had, she might be able to save thousands of lives—including that of Taran'atar.

Or maybe I should simply follow the Temporal Prime Directive and work to maintain the timeline by helping events unfold just as they did when I lived through them.

"Enough power to destroy a planet," she said. "That sounds like a good reason not to try to operate equipment you've never seen and don't understand." She pointed back the way they had entered. "Can we try another?" she asked. "I'd like to see some of the supposedly entertaining environments."

Taran'atar nodded, and the two stepped backward, into the main chamber of the Wa. Kira looked for another portal nearby and saw a small pink ball, floating at the height of her knee. She motioned toward it, and for the third time, she and Taran'atar strolled into another place.

Sky blue, the new environment featured a number of small, dark-blue spheres at its center, stacked in the form of a pyramid. An aroma like that of baking bread wafted past. As Kira wondered if the spheres, each about half the size of her fist, had been arranged as artwork, or perhaps to facilitate meditation, they all shot straight up into the air. They floated at chest height in a frenetic jumble. "What—" she started to ask, but then a pair of quarter-circles lighted up on the floor. The same color as the spheres, one led from beneath her feet and around to one side of the environment, while the other ran in the other direction, from where Taran'atar stood to the opposite side of the space. "Are we supposed to follow the lines?"

"I have never seen this before," Taran'atar said, "but it would appear so." He paced along his line, and Kira followed along hers, until they stood facing each other, with the bobbing cluster of spheres between them. When she looked across at him, she saw a dark-blue circle projected on the wall behind him, its diameter matching his height.

"Now what?" Kira asked, but then a ratcheting sound rose up loudly. At the same time, one of the spheres stopped moving and began to glow red. The ratcheting noise occurred a second time, then a third, and finally a fourth. When the environment faded back into silence, the glowing sphere shot toward Kira. She instinctively ducked, but she needn't have. It darted to her right as it reached her, flew past, and slammed into the wall behind her, where it disappeared with a hollow pop. She saw that a dark-blue circle had also been projected behind her, and where the sphere had impacted within it, a solid red circle had appeared.

Kira heard the ratcheting sound again. In the center of the environment, she saw that another of the spheres had stopped and turned red. After the fourth noise, it sped toward Taran'atar. He didn't move. The sphere dipped down and whisked past him, into the wall, where it left its mark.

"It's a game," Kira said. Taran'atar did not respond, but when the next ball turned red, Kira braced herself. It zoomed toward her, and when it got close enough, she swung her open hand forward in an attempt to bat it out of the air. She just missed it, and it struck the wall behind her, popping and leaving behind another red blot. "See if you can stop the next one," Kira told Taran'atar, even as the next sphere changed color and sounded its warning. He did, and as his hand struck the sphere, it buzzed once and vanished.

They played out the string, which totaled fourteen spheres, with seven launched toward each of them. Taran'atar made five successful stops, and Kira three, their misses reflected in the marks left within the circles on the walls behind them. "Well, it's not exactly springball," Kira said, invoking the name of a Bajoran sport, "but I guess it was entertaining."

"Jem'Hadar are not so easily entertained," Taran'atar said, "but the game requires hand-eye coordination and quick reflexes. I can therefore see its value as a training exercise."

Still a soldier after all, Kira thought. His comment put her in mind of the time she had accepted his invitation to take part in one of his combat simulations. It had been a miserable few hours for her as she worked toward an objective in a holosuite program that Taran'atar had coded. As he observed her, she nearly succeeded, failing only at the very last part of the simulation.

The experience might have helped them bond, but it hadn't. It also could have driven them apart, but it hadn't done that either. *It was just another step in those places where our paths intersected,* Kira thought. Except that she knew that it must have been more than that—more than just shared moments in time. Even after all that had happened, she had not wanted him to leave Deep Space 9. And when she had watched him die, it had hurt her.

So maybe some understanding had come out of that experience with the simulation, she supposed. It must even have meant something to her at the time, she realized. Taran'atar had designed and fashioned a combat knife specifically for her to use in the simulation, and she still had it, back in her quarters at the Vanadwan Monastery.

Well, I still have it if I can get back to my own time.

"Since we entered standing beside each other, do we have to leave in the same way?" Kira asked.

"No. Just step back from the focal point."

Kira did so, and she found herself once more back in the main chamber. The small pink ball floated in front of her knee. She expected Taran'atar to be standing on the other side of it, facing her, but he stood beside her. "It's all very interesting," she said. She didn't know if she liked the experience any more than she did a visit to a holosuite, but the construction and the nature of the Wa fascinated her.

"There is more to see," Taran'atar said. "The crew do not know how many portals there are because the colors change and the Wa frequently shifts its position. They are also unsure if the contents of the environments change, but they claim that nobody who has ever visited the Wa for more than a few minutes has ever failed to find something new."

"I might like to explore the Wa more," Kira said, "but I think I'd like to see the rest of the ship before I do."

"Of course." Taran'atar motioned toward the purple *X*, and they both started in that direction.

Partway there, Kira noticed a gray patch hanging in the air off to her left. It reminded her of the Jem'Hadar's admonition to stay away from them. "Why is it important to avoid the gray portals?" she asked. "Are they dangerous?"

"According to Captain Dezavrim, they are," Taran'atar said. "The man who sold him the ship cautioned him against attempting to enter them, but he would say no more on the subject. Periodically, the captain has tried to send probes into them. They have all been designed, built, and programmed using different methodologies to transmit data back to the crew, and to return to the Wa. In each case, communications failed as soon as the probe entered a gray portal, and none of them ever returned."

"Why do you think that is?" Kira asked. Although they kept walking toward the purple *X*, they didn't appear to be getting any closer to it. "Are they being destroyed?"

"You ask many of the same questions that I have asked, and for which I have few answers," Taran'atar said. "Pif believes that the gray portals lead to another dimension where it is essentially easy to get lost and impossible to retrace your entry path. Itriuma thinks that, wherever they lead, they allow transit in only one direction. Prees is sure that they're simply a type of disposal system."

"And what do you think?" Kira asked. "Do you have a theory?"

"Not a theory, no," Taran'atar said. "I do not have enough data about the gray portals to form even a working hypothesis as to their full nature. But . . ."

"But what?" Kira asked, curious. She also noticed that the purple *X* still appeared no closer to them.

"I have . . . dreamed . . . about the gray portals." The word, isolated in his statement, still clearly troubled Taran'atar. In general, Jem'Hadar did not dream, but during his time on Deep Space 9, he had begun to do so. Doctor Bashir hadn't had enough time to determine why that had happened, but he posited three possible causes: the stresses of being forced to abandon the only life he had ever known in favor of one dramatically different; disruptions to his brain chemistry brought about by the mind-control techniques perpetrated on him; or simply old age. Whatever the case, Taran'atar had viewed his dreaming as a personal weakness.

Kira chose to say nothing, instead waiting to see if he would continue. Suddenly, they stood directly in front of the purple *X*. As they continued toward it, the turbolift doors opened, appearing before them in a way that somehow suggested that Kira had been looking at them all along. They entered, and Taran'atar stated their destination as the *Even Odds* bridge.

Once the lift had begun to ascend, the Jem'Hadar said, "I have dreamed on three occasions of going to the Wa, seeking out a gray portal, and entering it."

Kira felt the inclination to ask what had happened in his dreams after that, as people often did when listening to somebody tell a story, but she feared that if she said anything at all, Taran'atar might stop talking. She wanted to hear what he had to say, not because she believed he would provide insight about the gray portals, but because he just might reveal something important about himself. The turbolift had completed its vertical journey and had begun moving horizontally before Taran'atar finally continued.

"Each time, I confronted an incredible danger," he said. "An *impossible* danger."

Kira didn't know whether he meant that he faced a danger that couldn't possibly have existed, or one that he couldn't possibly overcome.

"And each time, I launched myself into combat," Taran'atar said. "In the first two dreams, I woke before the battles ended. In the third, I woke when I died."

Once more, Taran'atar lapsed into a silence Kira did not wish to break. She knew that some cultures considered dying in a dream a bad omen, while others drew psychological understanding from it. She could not tell if Taran'atar had taken anything away from his experiences.

They traveled the rest of the way with the hum of the turbolift providing the only sound. The cab finally slowed as it neared its destination. Then, to Kira's surprise, Taran'atar spoke up again.

"My dreams were so vivid," he said, "I have actually considered entering one of the gray portals."

Kira took his meaning at once. For most of his existence, he had lived for battle, had relished defending his gods so well that he would rise to do so on another day. After he had effectively been stripped of that life, Kira could understand him wanting to test his mettle in the most extreme way possible.

Before she could say anything to him about it, the turbolift doors opened onto the *Even Odds* bridge. The faces of all the crew there turned toward them. Dez rose from where he sat and welcomed her, eager to show her around the ship's command-and-control center.

Only later, after she had retired to her cabin for the night, did Kira reflect on what Taran'atar had told her. She'd initially thought that he'd considered entering one of the gray portals because he wanted to prove to himself that he still possessed the expert combat skills of a Jem'Hadar soldier. Lying awake in her darkened cabin, she interpreted what he'd said differently. She realized that Taran'atar had not thought about entering a gray portal because he wanted to test himself.

He'd thought about it because he had been contemplating suicide.

AT BREAKFAST THE NEXT MORNING, Kira did what she needed to do. She had been awake for much of the night, reviewing what she knew and deliberating again about what actions she should take. Her insight regarding Taran'atar's emotional state troubled her. She understood that his loss of faith contributed significantly to his misery. No matter her opinions about the Founders, she knew that Taran'atar had looked upon them as gods, and so she sympathized with him. She could not imagine how she could possibly endure if her devotion to the Prophets deserted her. It made her wonder how much Taran'atar's disillusionment had played a part in how his life had ended.

How it would end, she reminded herself.

The Temporal Prime Directive weighed heavily on Kira, not because she felt any residual duty or loyalty to Starfleet—although she did—but because she understood and agreed with the principles underlying the regulation. Having traveled into the past, to a time when the Ascendants crisis and the *Even Odds* disaster lay ahead of her rather than behind, she desperately wanted to find a way to save the thousands who would perish—including Taran'atar—when those events unfolded. She understood, though, that doing so would necessarily alter the timeline, producing unpredictable results. For all those she rescued, others might die in their stead—possibly *many* others.

By that morning, Kira had yet to find a way of reconciling her conflicting impulses. She reasoned that she didn't need to, at least not then. She still had time to figure out precisely what to do, but she also knew that, whatever path she chose, the crew of *Even Odds* needed to head for Bajor soon in order to get there by the time they would be needed. Maybe Kira would end up choosing to tamper with events and maybe she wouldn't, but in either case, it seemed clear to her that *Even Odds* represented a part of the solution to the troubles Bajor would soon face.

"I've thought about your offer," she said to Dez, who sat beside her at one of the tables in the mess hall. About half the crew were present, scattered about the compartment. Taran'atar stood at attention off to the side, at what Kira assumed must be his customary place, and she wondered if the Jem'Hadar took his meals alone. The two Ferengi, Feg and Triv, sat at a table by themselves, perhaps because of what Kira deemed the nauseating nature of their native foods, which consisted in large part of insects, worms, and mollusks. Two of the Wadi, Fajgin and Itriuma, dined with Juno Mellias, the ship's archaeologist and gemologist. The other Wadi aboard, Facity Sleedow, had already been eating with Dez when Kira had arrived.

"You mean you've considered becoming a crew member on

the *Even Odds*?" Dez said. His eyebrows danced above his pastel eyes. Sleedow did not look up from her meal. "I do hope you've decided to join us."

"I am tempted," Kira said. "The *Even Odds* is an impressive ship, well equipped and up to date, and the Wa is a fascinating place—or maybe I should say that it's *many* fascinating places."

"It's certainly like nothing else I've ever seen," Dez said, "and believe me, I've seen a lot of things."

The statement sounded vaguely flirtatious, and Kira glanced over at Sleedow to see if she would react to the captain's potentially suggestive comment. Perhaps just as telling as her attention would have been, the first officer continued to stare down at her breakfast. Kira hoped to win her over, if for no other reason than to make the coming journey easier for everybody aboard. To Dez, she said, "I'm sure that the entire crew have had a wealth of experiences on the *Even Odds*. Jake certainly enjoyed his time here."

"We liked having him with us," Dez said. "I'm pleased to hear that he's doing so well." During her brief time aboard *Even Odds*, several of the crew had asked about Jake, and Kira had told them about his whirlwind romance with Azeni Korena and their subsequent marriage, as well as about the return of his father.

"I've also enjoyed meeting most of the people that Jake talked about when he got back," Kira said.

"You've enjoyed meeting only 'most' of the people?" Dez said, picking up on the subtle emphasis Kira had given the word. "Has a member of the crew mistreated you in some way?"

"She means me," Sleedow said, at last looking up from the plate in front of her. "She hasn't enjoyed meeting *me*."

"No, actually, that's not the case," Kira said. "I just meant that I've met most of the people Jake spoke of, but not two of them. You told me about the death of Brad-ahk'la, but there was somebody else Jake mentioned. Komes? Coemes? Something like that."

"Coamis," Sleedow said.

"I think Jake said he was an archaeologist."

"That's right," Dez said. "If I recall correctly, he hadn't been a member of the crew for very long when Jake joined us."

"He left not long after Jake returned to the Alpha Quadrant," Sleedow said. She uttered the sentence as a simple statement of fact, with no attitude or hidden meaning, which pleased Kira.

"I don't think Coamis' nerves were really cut out for the retrieval business," Dez explained. "We didn't ask him to leave, but none of us were surprised when he made his decision."

"And none of us stood in his way either," Sleedow said, speaking as though revealing an unspoken truth. "If he'd stayed, he might've ended up getting injured or killed."

"Or he might've ended up getting one of us injured or killed," Dez said. "Which is not to say that we undertake excessively dangerous ventures; it's more commentary on poor Coamis' constitution and skill set than on the nature of our business."

"That doesn't matter," Kira said. "I'm not particularly squeamish about risk."

"Confidence is always a valuable trait," Dez said.

"So is loyalty," Kira said.

"I would absolutely agree," Dez said.

"Then I'm sure you'll understand my loyalty to the crew serving under me on Deep Space Nine." Kira tried to parse her words in such a way that she would not technically say anything untrue, but if circumstances warranted it, she would have no compunction about lying. "I'm sorry, but I need to return to the Alpha Quadrant."

Dez looked at her, and Kira thought she could see in his eyes the calculations he made in an attempt to determine how best to change her mind. Either he chose treating her decision with respect as a tactic, or he realized that he would not be able to persuade her to stay. "I'm disappointed, of course," he said. "You would have made a valuable addition to the *Even*'s crew."

"I don't know about that," Kira said. "It seems to me you've already got enough leaders on board. As a friend of mine says, 'Too many cooks spoil the broth.'"

"I like that," Sleedow said, and she actually smiled. "Is that a Bajoran saying?"

"It's human, actually," Kira said. She marveled at the rapid improvement in Sleedow's manner. *Since I'm not staying,* Kira thought, *I no longer pose a threat, even theoretically, to her position in the crew—or to her personal relationship with the captain.*

"Well, we're due in at Vrynax Two the day after tomorrow," Dez said. "There's a spaceport there. I'm sure you'll be able to secure transportation back to the Alpha Quadrant."

"Oh," Kira said. She had anticipated that Dez and his crew would not want to bring her back to the wormhole themselves. Under other circumstances, she would have had no problem arranging transportation for herself, but she didn't actually need to return to the Alpha Quadrant—and for the sake of maintaining the timeline, she probably shouldn't—at least not visibly. It was critically important, though, that she make sure that *Even Odds* arrived at Bajor at the same time or prior to the arrival of the Ascendants. "I was hoping that you could take me back to Deep Space Nine directly."

"What is it with you Alphies?" Sleedow said, her good spirits turning that quickly to annoyance. "You get yourselves lost out in space, and we rescue you, but that's not good enough. You expect our crew to abandon everything we've planned for ourselves just so we can give you a ride home." Kira saw the members of the crew at other tables turn their attentions toward the first officer, whose voice had risen.

"Facity, please," Dez said, settling his hand atop hers. She pulled away from him.

"Don't," she said. "This should infuriate you, too. We're not a transport service."

"Actually," the captain said, "there was the time that we took the Second Margrave of Dionby Four—"

"Stop it, Dez," Sleedow said. "This isn't funny. Hey, I liked Jake, and—" She looked over at Kira. "—I'm sure that the captain here is a fine person, too." The words seemed to cost her an effort, Kira thought, but not a great one. "That's not the point. We have our lives and our livelihood on this ship, and we shouldn't be expected to turn it into a ferry just because somebody from the Alpha Quadrant demands to go home."

"I'm not demanding anything," Kira said quietly.

"Jake didn't make any demands either," Dez said. "He asked us to take him home and we turned him down, just as Captain Kira has asked, and just as we've turned her down, too." According to Jake, the *Even Odds* crew had been unwilling to bring him all the way to the Alpha Quadrant, but later, they had traveled to within three light-years of the wormhole on a search for treasure. While on a world there, they helped trigger the reappearance of the Eav'oq, and the shift of the Idran planetary system to a volume of space where it encompassed the Gamma Quadrant terminus of the wormhole. It then became a relatively short journey for Jake to return to Bajor.

"I am concerned because I don't really have anything with which to barter for transport back to the Alpha Quadrant," Kira said.

"I'm sure the commanding officer of Federation Nine can think of something to promise one of the pilots she finds at the spaceport," Sleedow suggested.

"I'm sure I can, too," Kira said. "I can also make that promise to you: provisions for the *Even Odds* . . . medical supplies . . . tools and parts for the ship . . . assistance with repairs."

"What kind of things could we get from an old Cardassian ore-processing station?" Feg called over from another table. The attention of everybody in the room remained on Kira's conversation with Dez and Sleedow—the attention of everybody except Taran'atar, it seemed, who continued to stand at attention and stare directly ahead.

"It's a Starfleet facility now," Kira said, realizing that, back in her own time, Deep Space 9 could no longer be characterized as Cardassian or Federation, since it had been destroyed.

"It doesn't matter," Sleedow said. "The *Even* is a state-of-the-art vessel. We keep it upgraded ourselves. We don't need any of the things you've offered."

"Something else, then," Kira said. She looked to Dez, hoping that his avarice would drive him to reveal what Kira could promise him in exchange for the *Even Odds* taking her to Bajor.

"I'm sorry," he said, holding his hands open and empty before him. "Facity is right. Your station has nothing we need."

Kira felt defeated. She realized her mistake. She had chosen to include the crew—and especially Sleedow—when making her request because she thought that, if she had approached the captain privately and convinced him to take her back to Bajor, the others—and especially Sleedow—might bristle at not being a part of the decision-making process, thus causing Dez to change his mind. Kira could have continued trying to coax Dez and Sleedow and the others; could have offered them something else she knew they would value, such as Bajoran antiquities; could have offered them anything at all; but she believed that such attempts would have demonstrated her desperation to get *Even Odds* to Bajor, which would have cemented their resolve to stay away. She would have to think of something else.

"There's a moderate level of activity at the Vrynax Two spaceport," Dez said. "You shouldn't have too much trouble finding somebody headed toward the Anomaly—somebody who could use what your station can provide them."

A figure suddenly appeared without warning beside the table, and Kira looked up to see that Taran'atar had crossed the room from where he'd stood guard. "I will also be disembarking the ship at Vrynax Two," he said.

The mess hall erupted. Feg and Triv stood up at their table and vocalized their objections. Fajgin, Itriuma, and Mellias also spoke up, imploring the Jem'Hadar not to leave. Only Dez and Sleedow remained quiet. Kira had no idea why Taran'atar had suddenly elected to exit the ship when she would, but she wondered if she might somehow use his decision to her advantage.

After a few moments, the voices settled, though Kira could hear Feg and Triv still grumbling to each other. Beside Kira, Dez rose and faced the Jem'Hadar across the table. "Taran'atar, you're a member of this crew," he said. "You've been with us for a while now. I thought you liked it here."

"I have been useful here," Taran'atar said. "That has been satisfying."

"Then why would you want to leave?" Dez persisted.

"I do not necessarily want to leave, but I have an obligation."

To me? Kira thought, surprised. She did not feel that Taran'atar owed her anything, nor would she want him to act out of a sense of duty to her—at least, not under normal circumstances. For the moment, she held her tongue.

"An obligation to Captain Kira?" Dez asked. "I thought that you left the Alpha Quadrant of your own accord."

Kira wondered how much of his story Taran'atar had told Dez and his crew. She couldn't imagine the Jem'Hadar sharing very many details of his life, but it seemed reasonable that when Taran'atar had agreed to become a member of the *Even Odds* crew, they would have wanted to know certain specifics. They would want to be sure that nobody—not from the Dominion, nor from the Federation—would show up and either demand that they surrender him, or worse, exact retribution by destroying the ship.

"I left by my own choice," Taran'atar said. "As I will leave here."

"Why?" Sleedow asked, the single word awash in accusation. "What has she promised you?" The first officer pointed at Kira, but didn't look away from Taran'atar.

"Captain Kira has promised me nothing. She did not know that I would do this. *I* did not know that I would do this. I only learned that she would be departing the ship just now, when you told her that you would leave her at Vrynax Two."

"But why would that compel you to want to leave, too?" Dez asked. He seemed to be genuinely trying to understand Taran'atar's reasons.

The Jem'Hadar regarded Kira before continuing. "The captain is an excellent Starfleet officer, and an able soldier," he said.

"But it is a considerable distance from here to the Anomaly, and there are forces in the Gamma Quadrant yet hostile to the Federation. The Alpha Quadrant War did not end that long ago. I do not want Captain Kira to make her journey unescorted."

"Thank you," Kira said.

"We don't want you to go," Dez said. "If you do, would you come back and rejoin us?"

Taran'atar did not answer right away, but looked off to the side, his expression pensive. At last, he said, "Once I depart the *Even Odds*, I do not foresee returning to the ship."

Dez marched away from the table, over to the far corner of the mess hall, where he stuck his hands onto his hips. When he turned back, his tone became imploring. "We need you, Taran'atar. You fit into our crew well, and you provide us with a measure of security that we've never had." He paused, clearly reaching for the argument that would induce the Jem'Hadar to change his mind. "You have made yourself indispensable aboard the *Even*. I think that means you have an obligation to this crew."

"I would not disagree," Taran'atar said. "That leaves me with having to choose between obligations, and I have done so."

"Let him go," Sleedow told Dez.

"Facity," Dez said, walking back over to the table and taking her hand. "Facity, on Lodontus Three, Taran'atar saved your life."

"I know," Sleedow snapped back. "But we don't need somebody who doesn't want to be here."

"He didn't say he didn't want to be here," Dez reminded her. "He said he has to go in order to fulfill his duty to Captain Kira."

Sleedow looked up at Dez, and Kira saw that all of the first officer's suspicions and indignation and bravado had been replaced by something else. *Not fear,* Kira thought, *and not sadness. Resignation, maybe?*

"So what would you have us do?" Sleedow asked Dez. "Take all that time out of our schedule just to carry one person back home?" She spoke as though she knew that Dez had been thinking exactly that.

"Why not?" he said. "After our delivery to Vrynax Two, we don't have that much lined up."

From another table, Triv said, "There's the repatriation of *The Pearls of Descan*."

"We can push that back," Dez said. "The Alvont will be thrilled whenever we deliver the sculpture."

"What about our research on the Mendicum Stone?" Feg asked. "We were going to survey the caves on Batrus."

"The caves aren't going anywhere," Dez said.

"And we also talked about investigating those reports about a lost cache of Drensaar relics on—" Triv began, but Dez cut him off.

"Enough," he said. "I know all this. The question for us to answer is whether it's more important to keep our schedule, but do so without the best security this ship and crew have ever known, or to maintain the level of our protection, but do so by having to delay some of our plans." Dez waited for a moment, as though to allow the starkness of that choice to sink in for those present. Kira could not imagine the crew having a better protector aboard than Taran'atar, and they plainly believed that as well.

When nobody said anything, Dez told Kira, "After we make our delivery to Vrynax Two, we'll take you home."

"Thank you," Kira said.

"I hope this means that we won't have to lose you, Taran'atar," Dez said.

"I told you that I have an obligation to escort Captain Kira back to the Alpha Quadrant," the Jem'Hadar said. "Since she will make that journey aboard the *Even Odds*, there is no need for me leave the ship."

Dez took in a deep breath and sighed loudly. Kira heard similar sounds and general murmurs of agreement around the mess hall. Dez sat back down beside Sleedow. "Fac?" he said. "Is that acceptable to you?"

"Oh, it is, Dez, it is," she said. "But does that really matter?"

"What are you saying?" Dez asked. "Of course, it matters." He tried to take her hand again, but she quickly stood up and headed for the doors. Before she left, she looked back and said, "The next time we find somebody floating out in space, we're leaving them there." Then she turned and bolted from the room.

"I hope this isn't going to cause you any ongoing trouble," Kira told Dez. She truly didn't want to foment any rancor among the crew—particularly between Dez and Sleedow, who clearly had a relationship more complicated than just that of shipmates—but she also cared only so much. The important thing was that *Even Odds* was headed to Bajor.

Kira only hoped that the ship would arrive before the Ascendants blackened the skies of her homeworld.

II

Fire

16

Sisko strolled along the path that wound through the green-sward ringing Deep Space 9's primary residential deck. It had been three months since he had last visited the starbase. The captain and his *Robinson* crew had spent the intervening time patrolling the Helaspont Sector. Fortunately, other than a tense encounter with Tzenkethi harriers immediately upon the ship's arrival at the border, the assignment had proven uneventful.

Above Sisko and down to the horizon, clouds scudded across a picturesque azure sky. The holographically projected scene looked and felt as real as anything he had ever experienced on a holodeck, an impressive feat of engineering considering the scale of the simulation. The imaging surface circled the equator of the starbase's main sphere, a bulbous, semicylindrical bulkhead that curved outward from atop the three levels of the Plaza and then back below the crew's quarters on the deck below. During DS9's nighttime hours, the bulkhead faded to transparency in a reproduction of a sunset, allowing the stars to shine down from their place in the firmament.

The captain felt better—happier, less stressed—than he had in a long time. He knew that the election of the new Federation president a month earlier, and all the consequences that followed from it, had a great deal to do with his improved state of mind. A sense of normality had been restored throughout the quadrant, not just because the population of the UFP had chosen its new leader in a special election, but because President Kellessar zh'Tarash hailed from Andor.

Three years earlier, the Andorians, one of the founding members of the Federation, had caused shockwaves by seceding from the historic interstellar alliance. Mired in their reproductive crisis, their population had fallen victim on their world to a chauvinistic, anti-science movement. Zh'Tarash, at the time the leader of the Andorian Parliament's Progressive Caucus, staunchly opposed secession. She also fought for a scientific solution to her people's procreative woes, and worked tirelessly for reconciliation with the Federation.

In the days prior to the special presidential election, zh'Tarash had seen her unstinting efforts rewarded. With the help of people like Julian Bashir, Ezri Dax, and Thirishar ch'Thane, the reproductive crisis had been solved. On the heels of that momentous achievement, the Andorians voted into power a new, progressive governing coalition, which, with the will of the people, applied for their world's readmission to the Federation—an application quickly approved. After the subsequent revelation of the conspiracy within the Palais de la Concorde, zh'Tarash coasted to her election as UFP president.

As he walked along the sinuous path, Sisko spotted a couple of young Bajoran boys equipped with paddles and what look like the rubberized sphere of a springball, although that sport did not require the use of anything but a player's hands. He watched as one of the boys batted the ball up into the air, and then the other raced beneath it. The receiver attempted to catch the ball on the flat of his paddle, absorbing the energy of the impact with a sweeping downward motion. They seemed to be successful only about a quarter of the time, but that didn't appear to dim their enthusiasm.

Seeing young boys at play always made Sisko think of his own son, even though Jake had celebrated his thirtieth birthday that year. It had been so good to see him and Rena when they'd visited from New Zealand several months previously. He and Jake didn't have paddles and springballs, but they did bring their fielder's gloves and a baseball, and they enjoyed playing catch in the awe-inspiring setting of Glyrshar Canyon.

Sisko beamed as he walked. He could not have been more proud of his son. Jake had married well, falling in love with a charming young woman who helped and supported him, who shared her life with him, and who loved him back. He had also taken definitive steps to follow his dreams, accepting his admission into the Pennington School and studying in their comprehensive, demanding, and well-respected writing program.

As Sisko neared his destination, it pleased him to think that both of his children lived in a society where Ishan Anjar had not been permitted to remain in power. *Not Ishan Anjar*, he corrected himself. *Baras Rodirya*.

The design and construction of his conspiracy to seize control of the Federation government truly astonished Sisko. Beyond the misappropriation of Ishan's identity during the Occupation, Baras had schemed to attain the office of president through a series of calculated deceptions and crimes. He began by setting himself up to be Bajor's next representative on the Federation Council, and then maneuvered Krim Aldos out of the position. With the aid of his chief of staff, Galif jav Velk, Baras then concocted a complex plan not only to assassinate Nanietta Bacco and succeed her as president, but to forward his bellicose, isolationist agenda.

Baras' twisted beliefs had allowed him to align with the True Way, an underground Cardassian organization dedicated to restoring the Union as a military state, as well as to severing all ties with the Federation. While Castellan Rakena Garan visited the new Deep Space 9 so that she could attend its dedication ceremony, one of her aides, a man named Onar Throk, assassinated President Bacco. He did so by covertly implanting a device in Enkar Sirsy, the Bajoran first minister's chief of staff. That device rendered her unconscious, allowing Throk to physically manipulate her into shooting the president, thereby manufacturing evidence of the crime and framing her for the murder.

In the days that had followed, Enkar's apparent guilt had provided Baras enough leverage to influence his colleagues on the Federation Council. He managed to convince many of them that, because a Bajoran had murdered the president, it became politically necessary to demonstrate that the Federation did not hold the Bajoran people in any way responsible for the ignoble act of a lone individual. When it came down to a choice between him and Lenith Agreho, the Federation Council member from Vestios, Baras won handily.

The True Way had also benefited from the setup of Enkar Sirsy. News of the perfidious crime spread rapidly throughout the Cardassian Union, magnified and shaped to highlight the unstable and untrustworthy nature of Federation citizens in general, and of Bajorans in particular. Public calls for Cardassia's withdrawal from the Khitomer Accords increased tenfold overnight.

Once all of that had occurred, the device that had been implanted in Enkar Sirsy had been triggered to perform its final deed. Incapacitating itself in such a way as to appear as a malfunction, it provoked a serious medical reaction in Enkar, ensuring its detection. When Doctor Bashir extracted it, he discovered Tzenkethi DNA on it. Planted there by Throk, it served to point the finger of guilt at the Coalition, which then provided Baras with justification for eventually launching an attack against not only the Tzenkethi, but its allies in the Typhon Pact.

Fortunately, Baras Rodirya had ultimately been unmasked and thwarted before he could instigate such a war. He faced a life sentence at a Federation penal colony. Although that wouldn't bring back Nanietta Bacco, it at least supplied closure for Sisko and, he felt sure, for many other people in the Federation.

The fall of Baras from power and the election of Kellessar zh'Tarash had also allowed the Federation to renew its ties with the Cardassian Union. Similarly, those events eased tensions between the Khitomer Accords nations and those of the Typhon Pact—and especially between the Federation and the Tzenkethi. The release of *Robinson* from patrol duty along the border in the Helaspont Sector relieved Sisko, and the ensuing news from Starfleet Command that his crew would soon embark on a two-year exploratory mission elated him.

Sisko came to a divide in the path, and he turned to his left, away from the outer bulkhead and toward the residential units on that level. Once he reached them, he walked along another path, searching for the right quarters. Before he and his crew could begin their mission of discovery, they had been charged with one last task—an undertaking first set in motion by President Bacco in one of her final acts.

Finding the quarters to which Captain Ro had directed him, Sisko approached the door and activated its chime. He could have done what he had gone there to do via the comm, but once he had boarded the starbase to meet with Ro, he'd decided that he'd prefer to deliver his news in person. He anticipated a positive reaction—though not an ebullient one.

The door slid open to reveal Odo standing beyond it. The Changeling held the humanoid form he had long ago developed, his simulated clothing a brown outfit similar to the uniform of the Bajoran Militia. He stared out at Sisko from features etched by neither genetics nor time, a smooth-surfaced simulacrum of a Bajoran face.

"Captain," he said. "I was unaware that you'd returned to the starbase."

"We brought the *Robinson* in just this morning," Sisko said. "May I speak with you?"

"Yes, of course." Odo stepped awkwardly aside, as though it hadn't occurred to him that the captain might wish to talk with him. The Changeling behaved as though he had never had any experience interacting with people. His continuing social clumsiness after spending so much of his existence living in humanoid society always struck Sisko as strange. Odo had returned to the Dominion for more than seven years, and had doubtless passed a great deal of time submerged in the Great Link, but his ungainliness when in his faux Bajoran form antedated all of that. Despite his decades among so-called *solids* and taking on their shape, Odo still didn't seem entirely comfortable in their presence.

Sisko walked past the Changeling and into a comfortably appointed living area. A large picture window fronted on the grassy area outside, though it had been configured to its privacy setting and rendered opaque. Odo closed the door and followed Sisko into the room.

"May I?" the captain asked, pointing toward a sofa positioned against the inner bulkhead and facing the darkened window.

"Please," Odo said. Even after Sisko sat down, the Changeling remained standing. "Have you returned to Bajor to resume patrolling the system?"

"No," Sisko said. "With the starbase now fully operational and more than capable of defending itself, only the *Defiant* will be needed. The *Robinson* will finally be heading out on its exploratory mission, though not out beyond Bajor, but into the Gamma Quadrant."

"The Gamma Quadrant?" Odo said, obviously surprised. Sisko had spoken to him several times in the prior two years about his crew's long-delayed next assignment, which had always been intended to take the ship into unexplored areas of the Alpha Quadrant. At the time the mission had first been planned, the wormhole had collapsed, with no indication that it hadn't been completely destroyed.

"Yes," Sisko told Odo. "After the success of Captain Vaughn's three-month venture there aboard the *Defiant*, and the *Robinson*'s fruitful six-month journey, Starfleet Command decided that it was finally time for a longer, more involved expedition."

"How long will you be gone?"

"Command has left it open-ended, allowing us some flexibility depending on what we find out there, but we anticipate somewhere between two and three years." Sisko could hear the excitement in his own voice.

Odo put his head down and marched across the room. Sisko had seen him wear such a determined manner many times. He suspected he knew the concerns he had just raised in Odo's mind. When the Changeling stopped and looked up, he said, "Captain, I know that I've been away from the Dominion for more than two years, but I am still interested in the preservation of its peaceful status."

"As I would expect you to be," Sisko said. "As I am, too. But you don't have to worry that the *Robinson* crew will do anything to jeopardize that. While the Federation's long-term goal is an active diplomatic relationship with the Dominion, President zh'Tarash and the Federation Council have made it clear that they will respect its current policy of . . . isolationism." Sisko hesitated on the final word, not wishing to offend Odo, but also not wanting to dissemble.

"I know that you don't approve of the Dominion cutting itself off from the rest of the galaxy, but there are good reasons for it."

"Odo, it's not my place to approve or disapprove of what the Dominion does with respect to its interstellar neighbors," Sisko said. "At least, not as long as they refrain from violating the rights of other people, which, as best I can tell, they are doing."

"Before the Dominion can become a part of the greater galactic population," Odo said, as though the captain hadn't spoken, "it needs to bring cohesion to its own."

"That sounds reasonable," Sisko said. "Is that what's happening?" He realized his error as soon as he asked the question. As far as the captain knew, Odo hadn't had any contact with the Founders or the Dominion since he had returned to the Alpha Quadrant. Even if he had, the Changeling consistently made it clear that he would not discuss his people or their empire. He had said as much not just to Sisko; in a face-to-face meeting before her assassination, he had explicitly stated his reticence to President Bacco.

"I don't know what's going on there anymore," Odo admitted. "I hope the Dominion *is* cohering. It's what I was trying to see accomplished before I left."

"That's laudable," Sisko said. "There's an old human saying: 'In every revolution, there is one man with a vision.'"

"I'm not a revolutionary, Captain," Odo said, his tone defiant. "I was only trying to provide opportunities for the citizens of the Dominion."

"Sometimes, opportunity *is* revolutionary," Sisko said. He

wanted to ask Odo about the details of what he had attempted, and about the results he'd seen. He was also exceedingly curious about the Founders. Not long before Odo had ended up back in the Alpha Quadrant, Sisko had gone to visit him on the world the Changelings called home. Unexpectedly, the planet had appeared completely uninhabited. But, Sisko knew, Odo did not talk about such things.

"I'm not interested in revolution," Odo said. "I just want to make sure that, while the Dominion is dealing with its own internal issues, it doesn't have to meet any external challenges."

"I understand," Sisko said. "I can assure you that your people will not have to confront that with the *Robinson* crew. Our preliminary course within the Gamma Quadrant takes us away from the wormhole in a completely different direction. We will travel nowhere near Dominion space."

Odo nodded. "I am relieved to hear that." When Sisko made no move to leave, the Changeling asked, "Is there something else then, Captain?"

"Actually, I didn't come here to talk about the *Robinson*'s upcoming mission or the Dominion at all," Sisko said. "I came here to talk about you."

"About me?" The character of Odo's voice left no doubt that he did not care for the idea of engaging in a discussion about himself.

"That's right," Sisko said. "I've been authorized by Starfleet Command to transport you aboard the *Robinson* from Deep Space Nine to Newton Outpost."

"Newton Outpost?" Odo said quickly, his interest plainly piqued. "I'm not familiar with it. Is that where the possible shape-shifter is being kept?"

"It is," Sisko said. "It is an isolated and heavily secured scientific facility. If you still wish to help determine if the substance the *Nova* crew found is a shape-shifter, I have a weeklong window in which to take you there. After that, my crew will need to complete our preparations back here at Deep Space Nine before we head out into the Gamma Quadrant."

"We can go now," Odo said at once, and he started toward the door.

Sisko immediately thought to ask if the Changeling needed to pack any personal belongings to take with him, but he stopped himself before blurting out the thoughtless question. The captain had never known Odo to keep many material objects—perhaps a consequence of being able to physically *become* virtually any object. He once possessed a bucket he utilized as a receptacle into which he could revert to his natural gelatinous state and regenerate, but once he encountered the Founders, he no longer used it. He eventually gave it to Kira Nerys before he returned to the Great Link.

For an instant, Sisko's mind wandered, wondering what had become of Odo's bucket. The captain had visited Kira's spare quarters at the Vanadwan Monastery, and he hadn't noticed it—although he had seen several framed photographs, including one of Odo. That reminded Sisko that the Changeling also used to display a photo of Kira in his quarters on the old DS9. He wanted to ask Odo about that picture, about whether or not he still had it, and if so, where he kept it—*Somewhere back in the Dominion,* he thought—but he knew the personal nature of the question would have made the Changeling uncomfortable.

Instead, Sisko stood up and activated his combadge. "Sisko to the *Robinson.*"

"*Robinson, this is Rogeiro,*" replied the first officer, his words carrying the light accent of his native Portuguese tongue. "*Go ahead, Captain.*"

"Commander, make preparations for departure," Sisko said. "We'll be traveling to Newton Outpost within the hour."

"*Understood, Captain.*"

"Very good. I'll be back on the ship and up to the bridge shortly. Sisko out." He looked over at Odo. "Whenever you're ready."

Odo resumed walking to the door, and Sisko followed, but then the Changeling stopped before they reached it. "Thank you, Captain."

"It's my pleasure, Odo."

Together, the two men headed for Deep Space 9's x-ring, to Docking Bay Three, where *Robinson* had moored.

17

The volume of voices continued to increase steadily, driving Quark to distraction. He glanced up from the freestanding companel in his office and over at the room's only entrance— the only entrance, not including the deck plate in the corner. A month after Deep Space 9 had become fully operational, Quark had paid a civilian engineer on a three-day leave from his freighter to fashion an emergency access route—or egress route, if it came to that. The Andorian discovered that an equipment conduit ran beneath the office, and so he modified the corner deck plate to function as a trapdoor, while also configuring a hatch in the conduit. He had charged Quark too much, but it made good sense to plan ahead in case of calamity. As the 243rd Rule of Acquisition cautioned: *Always leave yourself an out.*

"So what do you want me to do?"

Quark looked back down at the display on his companel. The gold-tinged face of the Petarian woman stared back at him, her dark eyes narrowing in an expression that seemed to mix appraisal and impatience. Of course, Quark had hired Mayer-een Viray for those two qualities, among others: he wanted her to assess whatever evidence she could find, but not to take too long about it; she had come highly recommended, but she'd declined a flat rate, meaning that he had to pay her for her time. *And time is money,* he thought. That wasn't a Rule of Acquisition, but it was one of the few pieces of sound business advice that he'd ever heard uttered by a *hew-mon.*

"Do you think it's a worthwhile lead?" Quark asked Viray.

"If I didn't, I wouldn't be talking to you about it," she said. "But you wanted me to check with you before I incurred certain expenses. If you want me to follow this lead before it goes cold, I need to hire a fast ship to get to Ardana."

Quark hesitated, as he always did before authorizing payment for anything. He'd already compensated Viray more in the previous two months than the combined sum he'd paid the two detectives who'd worked for him in the preceding half-year. *But then, she's actually found something,* he thought, trying to talk himself into continuing to disburse funds for his fool's errand.

"Do you really think he's gone to the cloud city?" The famed metropolis of Stratos literally floated in the air high above the surface of Ardana.

"If he hasn't, then somebody using his identity did," Viray said. *"Either way, I should be able to learn something there."* She spoke with a confidence Quark found reassuring, but that he also distrusted; he had heard himself employ the same tone of voice in any number of suspect business deals through the years.

"How long before you'll know anything?" Quark asked.

"Ardana's a long way off," Viray said, *"so the faster the ship I hire and the sooner you get me the funds to do so, the quicker I'll have information for you."*

A burst of noise went up, and Quark once again peered over at the door. He had closed only the outer panel, and not the inner, soundproof one, specifically so that he could hear what went on out in the main room of his establishment. One voice had an annoying nasal quality to it, signaling trouble in the form of a disgruntled customer. Quark much preferred the sound of *gruntled* customers.

Although he had brought with him a number of his staff from his bar on Bajor, he'd necessarily had to leave many workers there, under Treir's management, to continue its operation. He therefore had to hire quite a few employees for his new, much larger establishment on Deep Space 9. While many seemed to be working out, Quark still had some concerns about several of the waitstaff, as well as about the dabo boy, Orcam. He feared that one of those suspect workers had done something to upset the vocally unhappy customer.

"Quark?" Viray said sharply. *"If you're no longer interested*

in pursuing this matter, perhaps it's time for us to sever our business relationship."

Quark returned his attention to the companel. "No, no, I'm still interested," he said quickly, feeling the harsh pull of retaining his profits versus his concerns for his friend. He needed to complete his personal business and get back to his *real* business. The midday rush would not wait, and he much preferred bringing in latinum, rather than spending it.

In his head, Quark estimated the going rates for hiring swift spacecraft to traverse the distance between Micsim IV and Ardana, then compared them against the rate he paid Viray. Once he calculated the most economical solution, he accessed the account he kept open at the Bank of Luria. He verified his balance—it never hurt to randomly check your figures—then authorized a payment.

"I've just initiated a transfer of funds to your account at the Bank of Orion," he told Viray. "The amount will cover your transportation to Ardana, as well as the fees for your time in transit and your first few days in the cloud city."

"What about my return trip?" Viray asked.

"This isn't a vacation I'm paying for," Quark said. "Get to Ardana and show me that there's an actual lead there, and I'll send additional funds to cover your return to Petaria."

Viray appeared to consider Quark's demand. For a tense moment, he thought she would reject it, but then she said, *"All right. That's fair. I should have something for you within ten days. Viray out."*

"Ms. Viray," Quark said quickly, before the detective could end her transmission.

"Yes?"

"Please do your best," Quark said. "Morn was one of my best—" He thought *friends*, but rejected the word. "He was one of my best customers."

"I understand," Viray said, and it irked him to see that she probably *did* understand. *"Viray out."*

Her image vanished, and Quark quickly deactivated the

companel. He sat quietly for a moment and thought about the big, bald Lurian who had spent so many nights perched on a bar stool, first at the establishment Quark had run on Terok Nor, continuing when the Federation had taken over the station, and then finally at the bar in Aljuli after the destruction of the original Deep Space 9. Though Morn appeared to make a place for himself on Bajor, he never seemed quite right to Quark. Perhaps he suffered from the grief of losing so many friends aboard DS9, or perhaps something more afflicted him, such as post-traumatic stress or survivor's guilt. Whatever the case, the barkeep attempted to discuss the matter with him, without result. Not long afterward, Morn vanished, though a courier arrived several days later paying off his bar tab in full. And while Quark appreciated the windfall, it had been more than a year since then, and he missed his . . . customer.

A bevy of voices roared out in the main room, and Quark kicked himself for his inattention. He jumped up from behind the companel and hied toward the door. The single panel opened before him. He sped through it, stopping only long enough to lock his office.

Down the corridor and past the stairs that led up to the second and third levels, Quark emerged into his large, main room, separated from the Plaza walkway by a half wall and the wide entrance in its center. Customers packed the dining tables. A few players sat at the poker tables on the far side of the room, and another few circled the dom-jot table, but it pleased him most to see that a large crowd had formed around the dabo wheel. That typically didn't happen until the evening.

Quark stood and briefly observed the run of a few spins in the native Ferengi casino game. Perhaps the sound of the unhappy customer—which he no longer heard—had come from there; to his delight, Quark saw that most of the chips on the table had been raked over to the house's side. As he watched, he judged Orcam's running of the wheel competent, maybe even a little better than that. Of greater import, he appeared to have the effect on the players for which Quark had hoped.

Though not tall or muscular like Hetik, Orcam exuded a quiet, androgynous confidence that seemed to appeal to just about everybody.

As Quark turned toward the bar, intending to resume his place behind it, a familiar profile caught his eye. He grabbed a circular tray and a towel from the nearest workstation, then hurried across the room. When he reached the small table for two, he leaned in to wipe down the surface, although it looked perfectly clean.

"Quark."

"Oh, Captain," he said, as though he hadn't realized Laren sat at the table. "I guess I didn't recognize you. It's been such a long time." He spoke lightly, but his words carried more than a hint of truth. Since the starbase had become fully operational a little more than three months earlier, Quark and Laren had spent almost no time together. Not particularly unusual, that had happened with some degree of frequency during the almost ten years since Laren had first arrived on the old Deep Space 9. In her various roles since she'd come aboard—chief of security, first officer, captain—Laren had taken on a great deal of responsibility, and as a consequence, she went through periods where she had little opportunity—and in some cases, little desire—to spend personal time with anybody.

I can't blame it all on her, Quark thought. His business interests sometimes crowded his own schedule, and even occasionally took him away on various interstellar jaunts. Blame didn't matter to him, though. He only knew that he missed Laren.

"I know, you're right, it has been too long," she said. "It's just that I've been incredibly busy lately."

"I understand," Quark said, letting go of his wounded feelings at once. "Have you heard anything about Doctor Bashir?"

"Only that he's been remanded into Starfleet custody," Laren said. "It looks like he's going to be court-martialed."

"For saving the people of Andor?" Quark asked, incredulous. "Or because that led directly to the Andorians rejoining the Federation?" He could taste the sarcasm in his mouth. Doctor Bashir had been a fine customer for many years, and Quark didn't appreciate—or understand—him not being permitted to return to DS9. His interim replacement as chief medical officer, Beverly Crusher, had briefly transferred to the starbase from *Enterprise*, but she had spent almost no time in the bar. At least the new CMO, Pascal Boudreaux, had been known to stop by Quark's, though still not with the frequency of Bashir.

"I'm not sure precisely what the charges will be, but I've gotten the impression that they will be significant," Laren said. "At least the charges against Captain Dax and the others were dropped." She didn't specifically mention Lieutenant Commander Douglas, but Quark knew that some people on DS9 accepted as a matter of course that the security officer had abetted Bashir, her paramour, in his efforts, first to access classified Starfleet information, and then to escape his subsequent detention. Regardless of whether she had or not, Douglas had taken a leave of absence from her duties so that she could visit the doctor while he remained in custody.

"If you ask me, it's not right," Quark said. "If the doctor had to break the rules in order to save the Andorians . . . maybe it's the rules that are the problem."

Laren offered a half-smile, seemingly genuine, but Quark could see in the unfinished expression the fatigue she clearly felt. Having to deal on a daily basis with ten thousand civilian residents and a full slate of visiting ships and crews, on top of trying to help her own people—and herself—recover from the assassination, she must have been emotionally drained. But Quark worried about more than simple exhaustion; he feared that Laren might be withdrawing into herself, walling off her feelings, even from him. He didn't really know what to make of their relationship—they had never really defined it— but in all the time they'd known each other, they'd both been able to talk openly, and to provide each other with understanding and support. He hoped that he could provide that again for her.

"So what can I get for you, Captain?" he asked. He did not

call her by her given name in public. He did slip into the chair across from her, though, lean in close, and say, "How about a Ferengi surprise?"

The partial smile did not leave Laren's face as she asked, "And what's in that?"

"It's a surprise," Quark told her playfully. "But I can have it delivered directly to your quarters . . . say, after the start of gamma shift?"

"Oh, Quark," Laren said, that same lopsided smile dressing her lovely features. "I'm tempted. I really could use a little rest and relaxation—"

"And a surprise!"

Laren chuckled. "Yes, and a surprise, too," she said. "But I have so much work to catch up on. It's incredibly time-consuming and effort-intensive to run this starbase in the easiest of times, but with everything that's happened lately . . ." She let her words drift into the obvious implication. "This lunch isn't even a break for me," she added. "I'm meeting with Doctor Altek to figure out how best to deal with his situation."

Quark had heard about Altek Dans. Arriving on DS9 aboard an Orb just after the wormhole had reopened, the Bajoran man defied identification. Though he was initially confined to the stockade, the captain released him shortly thereafter, assigning him quarters and providing him an escort. Conventional wisdom suggested that he had come from some point in the past. Quark had seen and heard him on the Plaza, though Altek's visit to the bar that day would be his first.

The barkeep had taken it upon himself to do his own research on the mysterious stranger. He believed it good business to know about new customers before they ever walked through his door—the 194th Rule—but he also hoped that he could provide Laren some assistance. Unfortunately, his efforts had proven futile.

"Maybe we can have dinner sometime, then," Quark said.

"Soon," Laren said, but while Quark did not doubt her sincerity, he didn't care for the noncommittal response.

"All right." With little else he could do, Quark shrugged

and stood up. "So what can I bring you for lunch?" Out in the Plaza, he heard two voices he recognized.

"I think I'll wait for Doctor Altek to arrive."

"If I'm not mistaken, he's just arriving right now," Quark said. He pointed back over his shoulder, but he didn't look in that direction. Even through the din of the lunchtime press, he knew the voice of Grant Masner, an ensign on Commander Blackmer's security staff, as well as that of Altek Dans. Quark had first heard the potential time traveler's voice when he'd sought information about him. The barkeep had enlisted one of his employees to use a remote sensing device to record data about Altek, including what he both looked and sounded like.

Laren leaned to one side to look where Quark had pointed. "After all this time, I shouldn't be impressed," she said, "but those ears are *really* good."

"A man is nothing without his lobes."

"So you tell me."

Quark smiled, the points of his irregularly set teeth comfortably sharp against his lips. "I'll come back in a little while to take your order."

"Thanks."

As Quark started away, he glanced toward the entrance, catching sight of Altek Dans as Ensign Masner accompanied him into the bar. Altek looked taller in person than he had on the sensor recording, and his dark eyes and dark complexion gave him something of a smoldering appearance. *Handsome,* Quark thought, *if you like that sort of thing.*

Back behind the bar, he took orders and served his customers. He occasionally peered over at Laren and Altek, until he perceived that they were ready to place their lunch orders. He began toward their table, but then he stopped and sent one of his waitstaff over instead. Then Quark made his way back into his office, alone, and closed the door.

He even closed the soundproof panel.

*   *   *

THE CAPTAIN STARED at the bowl of *ratamba* stew sitting before Altek Dans as he ate his lunch. Three months earlier, Ro had released the mysterious Bajoran man—the mysterious *Aleiran* man—from the stockade. She and her security chief still believed that he had been displaced forward in time from Bajor's past, despite that Altek's name could not be found in any history texts—or in any historical documents at all. Moreover, the details he employed to describe his life—the names of cities, like Joradell and Shavalla, and the description of a segment of Bajoran society called the Aleira—had also never been chronicled. It could have been that he had fabricated it all, or even that he had come from an alternate universe, but the more that both Ro and Blackmer had spoken with him, the more they had become convinced that he had traveled in time, from a period for which records no longer existed. That might mean he had come from centuries in the past, or possibly even millennia.

Before the captain had released Altek from the stockade, she'd revealed what she and her crew believed had happened to him. He understood the concept of time travel, but doubted its reality. Ro went on to explain that Bajorans had left their world, and that alien beings existed. She described Deep Space 9 to him, and then she showed him the starbase.

Altek had at first been visibly stunned, his mind gravitating to more mundane explanations than the actual truth of the situation. He theorized to Ro that he'd been drugged, or perhaps hypnotized, or maybe he'd even fallen into a coma. The possibilities he offered rooted everything he saw and heard and experienced in the realm of his imagination. Ro didn't attempt to convince him otherwise, but she and other members of her crew spoke with him often, answering his questions as best they could. The captain also assigned Lieutenant Commander Matthias to counsel him.

Eventually, Altek had had little choice but to accept the reality of his situation. For the six weeks or so after the captain released him from the stockade, he mostly remained in the guest quarters she assigned to him. He requested both Bajoran histories and annals of current events. The crew initially provided him with written texts, and later instructed him on how to use the computer interface so that he could watch recaps of the information he sought, accelerating his education.

Since finally coming to accept his fate, Altek had begun venturing out of his quarters to explore the starbase. As agreed, a member of Ro's crew always attended his excursions, although the captain and every member of her senior staff believed he posed no threat. Lieutenant Commander Blackmer insisted on the precaution, though, citing Altek's own safety as a concern, and Ro agreed. Keeping an officer assigned to him also satisfied Admiral Akaar.

Akaar, Ro thought, absently shaking her head. Since the assassination, the captain had faced mounting criticism from the commander in chief, despite that the DS9 crew had worked hard to put the terrible event behind them, and that operations aboard the starbase had more or less settled into a routine. The admiral had not blamed her outright for the death of President Bacco, but since the resolution of the Baras Rodirya conspiracy, he had asked her more than a few pointed questions about the security procedures she'd implemented on the starbase for the dedication ceremony. Akaar also took her to task for the actions of Doctor Bashir, even going so far as to suggest that he did not have full confidence in either her or her crew. As a result, the admiral initially refused her recommendation that Doctor Boudreaux succeed Bashir as DS9's chief medical officer, although once Doctor Crusher departed for *Enterprise* and submitted her report clearing the medical staff, he relented.

"Captain?"

Ro blinked, and she saw that Altek had completely emptied the bowl in front of him, his spoon sticking out of it and leaning against the rim. She realized that she had drifted into her thoughts as he'd been speaking. She'd heard nothing of what he'd said.

"I'm sorry, Doctor Altek. I was thinking of other things."

"I could see that," he told her, not unkindly. "Not at first, though. I was too caught up in my own situation. I guess not everybody loves the sound of my voice as much as I do."

"No, that's not it at all," Ro said, embarrassed for her lapse. "It's no excuse, but I've just got a great deal on my mind." She chose not to mention that she hadn't slept well during the previous few nights, her mind turning again and again in the darkness of her quarters to Akaar's implications about her crew. She deeply resented the insinuations of incompetency about those serving under her.

"I realize that your head *must* be full," Altek said, waving his hand in an arc before him, a gesture plainly meant to take in the whole of Deep Space 9. "The responsibility for all these people, in this huge, enormously complex place. I'm the one who should be apologizing to you for adding to your burden."

"No, please don't think that, Doctor," Ro said. "This starbase and everybody aboard it are my responsibility, yes, but I feel privileged to hold such a position."

"Spoken like a true leader."

Ro chuckled. "It's certainly the case that I'm not much of a follower."

"I know the feeling."

Ro tilted her head to one side. "The anti-slavery movement you talked about?"

Altek nodded. "There weren't really enough of us for there to be followers," he said.

Ro glanced down at her plate, and it surprised her to see that she'd taken only a single bite of her *argendi* sandwich on *mapa* bread. She knew that she should eat, but she just didn't feel hungry. Instead, she picked up her glass of *pooncheenee* and sipped at the orange-red beverage. "So would you tell me what you were saying when I so rudely got lost in my own thoughts?"

"I was just talking about what I've been learning," he said. "I've been reviewing a great deal of Bajoran history, but I haven't been able to determine when *my* time might have been."

"From the information you provided, Lieutenant Aleco and

his team haven't been able to ascertain a timeframe either," Ro said. A Bajoran, Aleco Vel had studied his homeworld's history at university, and the captain had assigned him to lead three other officers with similar expertise in a research effort to at least narrow down from whence Altek had come. "It's difficult, because even though a great deal is known about the First and Second Bajoran Republics, there are still long periods within them that are poorly documented."

"So I've found out," Altek said. He looked down for a moment and fiddled idly with his spoon, as though reluctant to continue. "I have to say, I am anxiously looking forward to when I can actually visit Bajor."

"I know," Ro said. She remembered the drive she'd felt several times in her own life to return to the world on which she'd been born and raised, even though the Occupation had forever changed Bajor. She could not imagine how much Altek must have wanted to see the civilization to which he had sometime long ago contributed. Ro had been deeply moved at the relief and pride he'd displayed when she'd informed him that slavery had not been practiced in Bajoran culture for a very long time. "I wasn't going to mention this to you just yet, but I finally received a reply from the Ministry of State late yesterday."

When Altek had first indicated a desire to go to Bajor a few weeks earlier, the captain had at that point released him from his promise to remain aboard the starbase, and she sent a message directly to Gandal Traco, the minister of state. Ro had requested that his staff generate official documentation for Altek, and that they arrange for him to visit. She hadn't even mentioned his desire for possible repatriation, but regardless, she had not garnered a response. Her second request had also gone unanswered for longer than it should have, before finally resulting the day before in a terse missive, not from Gandal himself, but from the general office of the ministry. Unsigned, it stated only that Altek's applications for identity and travel credentials would both be taken under advisement.

Ro explained to Altek what had happened, as well as the

next step she'd taken. Putting to good use the solid professional relationship she shared with Asarem Wadeen, the captain contacted her office directly, detailing her correspondence with the Ministry of State and their unacceptable reaction. Ro hoped that the first minister would intervene, at least compelling Gandal and his staff to action. "I have yet to hear back from Minister Asarem," she said, setting down her glass. "I hate to say it, but I think if we do get a response, there's a good chance it won't be what you're hoping for."

"They still believe I might be a threat?" Altek asked.

"Honestly, I don't think it even rises to that level of concern," Ro explained. "After all the political turmoil of the past few months, I think the government is just exceedingly sensitive to the potential risk of any public event involving a Bajoran."

"I don't intend for this to be public," Altek said.

"I know," Ro said, sympathetic to his desire to stay out of the spotlight. "But we're talking about a Bajoran who traveled forward in time and emerged from the Celestial Temple. Your return to the planet will cause a stir."

Altek let go of his spoon, and it briefly rattled in the empty bowl. "The Celestial Temple," he said. "It's hard to believe—maybe because I'm so newly a believer myself."

Altek had described himself as one of the Aleira, and not as one of the Bajora, and then had detailed the distinction between the two. In part a matter of location and parentage—and it had been thought, genetics—the primary difference between the two came in the form of their faith: the Aleira had none, and the Bajora prayed to a cache of gods they called the Prophets, who resided in the Celestial Temple. According to Altek, a powerful experience he'd undergone not long before his arrival on DS9 had changed his mind, making him a believer.

"I know the Celestial Temple hasn't opened since you've been here," Ro told him, "but travel through it is set to resume next week. If you're not on Bajor yet, you'll get to see it then."

Altek shook his head. "I don't know what's more difficult to accept—that I'll actually get to witness the Temple opening, or that people travel through it." Ro had described for Altek the rudimentary principles of wormholes, as well as the fact that most people, including some Bajorans, explained the existence of the Celestial Temple without resorting to the divine.

"Since you do believe in the Prophets," Ro said, "and since we have yet to receive an acceptable response from the Bajoran government, it's occurred to me that perhaps we should involve the clergy."

"In the research I've done, I've seen that they have a great deal more power now than in my time," Altek said.

"They have power, and they are extremely influential in guiding public opinion," Ro said. "Because of how you came to be here, I think that if you ask for their assistance, they'll be inclined to help."

"Won't that upset the first minister and the minister of state?" Altek asked.

Ro nodded. "More than just a little bit."

Altek glanced away, a look of concentration in his dark eyes. When finally he peered back across the table at Ro, he said, "I don't know. Since Bajor will essentially be new to me, I don't want to start my time there by making an enemy out of the first minister or anybody else in the government."

"If you've come here the way I think you have, then you've done nothing wrong," Ro said. "I'm sure Asarem and Gandal will not be happy at first, but if the Vedek Assembly and Kai Pralon embrace you, the ministers will have no choice but to accept you."

"I don't know," Altek said again. "I *do* want to go home . . . whatever *home* means in this context."

"We can at least meet with one of the vedeks on the starbase," Ro suggested. "I've already received a number of queries from them since your arrival—nothing travels faster on a starbase than rumors—but I haven't confirmed for them that you appeared here in an Orb that emerged from the Celestial Temple. We can explain your situation to them, your desire to go to Bajor, tell them about your reluctance and your concerns, and see what they have to say."

Altek distractedly picked up his spoon and tapped it against the bottom of the empty bowl. After a few seconds, he said, "All right. I guess it can't hurt to hear their thoughts on the matter."

"Good," Ro said. "I'll set something up with Brandis Tarn. Unlike some of the other vedeks posted in the field, he at least has a good awareness of political realities." The characterization brought her a sudden rush of sadness. "It's a shame Kira Nerys isn't still alive," she said. "She became a vedek after commanding this station—well, not *this* station, but the one that was here before it. She didn't care much for politics, but she could still get things done when it came to affairs of state."

"It seems to me that you're doing a pretty good job yourself," Altek said. "I want you to know that I truly appreciate all the help you're giving me."

"It's all part of my job."

"I think it's more than that," Altek said, a wide smile decorating his face. "I think you like to lift up the downtrodden."

"I've been known to take in a few strays," Ro admitted. "I've even been known to be one from time to time."

Altek wrinkled his brow and gazed at her in confusion. "Somehow, I have trouble picturing that."

"Believe me, I'm just one more disobeyed order away from being a pilot on a second-class freighter," Ro said. She felt certain that Akaar had overlooked her latest transgression—releasing Altek after the admiral had instructed her to keep him in custody—only because acting on his order would have violated both Federation and Bajoran law.

Still appearing skeptical, Altek started to say something more, but then somebody stepped directly up to their table. Ro looked up to see her first officer. "Good afternoon, Captain, Doctor," Cenn said.

"Desca," Ro said. "Would you care to join us?"

"No, thank you, Captain," Cenn said. "I was just on my way to midday services. I knew that you were meeting Doctor Altek here, so I thought I'd stop to see, if you're done with your meeting, if he'd like to go to the temple with me."

"Oh," Altek said. "I . . . I've never been before."

"I thought you believed in the Prophets," Ro said.

"I do, I do, but . . . my faith is still new to me."

"Then attending a service might answer some of your questions and open your eyes even more," Cenn said. He offered the possibility as a suggestion, with no trace of pressure or judgment. Although her first officer did not flaunt his faith, Ro had known fewer people in her life more devout than he.

"I think I might like that," Altek said. "Would you like to join us, Captain?"

Though he knew better, Cenn did not drop the inviting expression from his face. "You're certainly welcome," he told her, and she could see that he meant it.

"Thank you, no," Ro said.

"Too busy with your duties?" Altek asked.

Ro considered taking the easy route and simply agreeing that she needed to return to her shift in the Hub. *But then, I rarely do things the easy way,* she joked to herself. "No, it's not that," she told Altek. "I'm actually a nonbeliever."

"Oh," Altek said, sounding abashed. "I just assumed . . . virtually every Bajoran I've met has been—" He stopped. "My apologies, Captain. I meant no offense."

"And I didn't take any," Ro assured him.

Altek glanced at her lunch plate. "I don't want to leave you while you're still eating."

"I think that ship has gone to warp," Ro said, immediately realizing that Altek would not understand the idiom, although her tone probably made her meaning clear. "Please, go. I'm sure attending services with Desca will be a positive experience for you."

"All right," Altek said. He set the napkin from his lap on the table beside his empty bowl, then stood up and pushed in his chair. "Thank you again for everything, Captain." He smiled at her, and Ro could not stop herself from smiling back.

"It's my pleasure," she said. "I'll let you know when I've set something up."

The two men started away, and Ro watched Ensign Masner follow as they weaved through the busy main room at Quark's and out onto the bustling Plaza. When they had passed out of sight, the captain began to stand, but then she saw her mostly uneaten sandwich. She decided to sit back down.

Suddenly, she found that she had an appetite.

18

The alert broke the calm that normally draped the outpost. It had been three months since the previous incursion over Endalla, and Ensign Ansarg, on her first rotation back to the Bajoran moon since then, cursed her fortunes. She quickly raced across the monitor-and-control compartment to the sensor station. As she examined the readouts, she silenced the alert.

"What is it?" asked Lieutenant Shul from where he sat at the communications console.

"A vessel has breached Endalla's security perimeter." Ansarg read off the global coordinates, which put the ship about a third of the way around the moon from the outpost. "It is not broadcasting an identification beacon, but it profiles as a small civilian craft. I'm picking up two life signs, both Bajoran."

"Civilian," Shul said. "So it has no weapons?"

"Scanning," Ansarg said as she worked her controls. A quick pass over the hull revealed no emitters and no launch tubes, confirming that the vessel lacked any traditional armaments. The ensign then executed a more detailed examination, searching for other offensive equipment and materials. A warning flag appeared on her display. "The vessel is not armed with energy weapons or torpedoes," she said, "but I am detecting large concentrations of cabrodine and infernite." Both chemical substances saw widespread use as explosives. "I'm also reading smaller but still-significant amounts of bilitrium." The volatility of the rare crystalline element made it effective both as a power source and as an accelerant.

In her peripheral vision, Ansarg saw Shul's hands move

across the communications console, eliciting chirrups from the panel. "Security Outpost Endalla One to Bajoran vessel," the lieutenant said. "You have traveled into restricted space and are carrying illicit materials. Identify yourself at once and remove your ship into a parking orbit."

As Shul awaited a reply, Ansarg heard the compartment's inner door open. When she peered over her shoulder, she saw Crewmen Hava Remaht and Cardok enter from the living area of the outpost. Even though the previous incident on the moon had been the result of failing baffle plates on an old civilian vessel, Lieutenant Commander Blackmer had nevertheless decided to double the detachment on Endalla, to six of DS9's security staff, along with a pair of runabouts. Two officers remained on duty and two off in the outpost proper, while the other two patrolled above the moon in one of the runabouts.

"They appear to be receiving our transmission," Ansarg said, consulting a readout that showed the civilian vessel with a powered and functioning comm system. "They have not changed course. They're on a descent trajectory to the surface."

Shul worked his panel and repeated his message. He did not wait long before he tapped the console again and contacted the runabout crew traversing the dark skies above the Bajoran moon. "Endalla One to *Glyrhond.*"

"*Glyrhond* here. *This is ch'Larn. Go ahead, sir.*" Crewwoman Patrycja Walenista accompanied Lieutenant Junior Grade Shanradeskel ch'Larn aboard the runabout. Anticipating their needs, Ansarg transferred the coordinates, course, and sensor readings of the intruder over to the comm station.

"Lieutenant, we're reading an encroachment on the moon," Shul reported. "It's a Bajoran vessel, civilian. It has no ship-mounted weapons, but it's carrying high explosives. The two people aboard have refused to respond." He must have seen the data Ansarg had provided, because he pointed to his panel and gave her a nod. "I'm transmitting the relevant information to you now."

As Shul worked to do so, Hava and Cardok stepped up beside Ansarg and examined the sensor display. Hava, a Bajoran, looked tired, but Ansarg had difficulty discerning any signs of fatigue in Cardok, a Benzite; with his bluish complexion and deep-set eyes, he *always* looked sleepy to her. The two men tucked and tugged at their uniforms, their disheveled appearances suggesting that they had both been awakened by the alert, and had then dressed hastily.

"*We've received the data,*" ch'Larn said. "*We're redirecting our scans.*"

Ansarg studied her readouts. "The vessel continues to descend toward Endalla's surface with no change in course," she reported.

"The vessel is headed for a landing," Shul told the *Glyrhond* crew.

"*We have it on sensors now,*" ch'Larn said. "*We're roughly the same distance from the vessel as you are. Should we move to intercept?*"

"Affirmative," Shul said. As the highest-ranking officer in the six-member security contingent, Shul commanded outpost operations that week. "Do what you can to prevent that ship from landing on Endalla."

"*I understand, sir,*" ch'Larn said. "*We are changing course and increasing speed.*"

"Keep me informed," Shul said. "Endalla One out." The lieutenant closed the channel with a touch. He sat still for a moment, his hand resting on the communications console, his attention directed inward.

"Sir?" Ansarg asked. "Do you think they're religious extremists?"

Shul looked over at her. "I believe so," he said. "They're Bajorans carrying bilitrium, cabrodine, and infernite down to the surface of Endalla. Considering what happened here less than six years ago, I think that gives them away as Ohalavaru fanatics."

"I don't understand," Hava said. "The followers of Ohalu aren't even believers. What point could they possibly be trying to make?" Although the crewman had served aboard Deep Space 9 for a number of years, he had yet to reach his thirtieth birthday. Ansarg thought that his affronted tone made him sound even younger.

"I don't know," Shul said. "I do know that there's nothing wrong with somebody being a nonbeliever. But the people in the trespassing ship, if they are Ohalavaru, are not *simply* Ohalavaru. They are not well-meaning people who happen to hold a different view of the Prophets than you or I do." Ansarg did not know the level of Shul's convictions, but she had often enough seen him entering or exiting the Bajoran shrine on the Plaza. "These are people who are intending to sow destruction, and perhaps even to kill, to demonstrate the veracity of their beliefs."

"But that's just it," Hava said. "They have no belief in the Prophets."

"That's not accurate," Shul said. "The Ohalavaru very much recognize the existence of the Prophets, but like many non-Bajorans, they see Them as 'wormhole aliens' who watch over our people—as benevolent beings rather than as gods."

"But how do they expect to demonstrate that by blowing up an empty moon?" Hava asked. Although Ansarg thought his question legitimate, she also thought that his tone verged on petulant.

"Endalla's not entirely empty," Cardok pointed out.

Shul stood up from the communications console and walked over to face Hava. The lieutenant's expression did not harden, nor did his voice, but when he spoke, his words carried the weight not only of his authority, but of his years of experience; Ansarg didn't know his exact age, but he had to be at least in his seventies. "Crewman, it is important to understand why people do what they do," Shul said. "But right now, that's not our responsibility. Regardless of the reasoning of the two individuals on that vessel, we've been assigned here specifically to protect this moon, and that's what we're going to do."

"Yes, sir."

"Now, your shifts—" Shul motioned to both Hava and Cardok. "—don't begin for another few hours, so why don't you two go back to the living area and try to get some more sleep."

Both crewmen acknowledged their orders, then started back toward the compartment's inner door. Just before they got there, Shul called after Hava. The ensign stopped and turned. "Sir?"

"We can talk about the Ohalavaru later, if you'd like," Shul said. "It *is* an interesting subject."

"Yes, sir," Hava said. "I'd really—"

A second alert blared through the outpost. In her chair, Ansarg spun back to the sensor panel. She deactivated the alert as she read through what her instruments told her. "Another ship has penetrated Endalla's perimeter."

ANSARG PILOTED *YOLJA* above the barren surface of Bajor's largest moon. She thought it strange that such an empty place should invite such threats of violence—or in the case of what had happened with the Ohalavaru zealots when they had last visited Endalla, actual violence. While Ansarg hadn't appreciated Crewman Hava's attitude, she did want answers to the questions he had posed.

"Can you push this runabout any faster?" Shul asked. The resignation in his voice implied that he already knew that she couldn't.

"No, sir," Ansarg said. "Not unless you want me to go to warp this close to the moon." Though not a pilot, Shul surely understood that engaging the faster-than-light drive so deep inside a gravity well would almost certainly result in their destruction.

The lieutenant nodded. He sat beside Ansarg at the runabout's main console, working sensors and communications. Word had just come in from *Glyrhond* that ch'Larn and Walenista had successfully apprehended the crew of the first vessel before they could detonate, set, or even plant their explosives. Though of a slightly different design, the second ship read almost identically to the first in its other particulars. It held two Bajorans, possessed no ship-mounted weapons, and carried substantial amounts of the three highly explosive materials. As with the first ship, its crew had not responded to repeated hails, nor altered course when instructed to do so.

"I don't know if we'll be able to overtake them before they reach the surface," Shul said.

"We'll get there, sir," Ansarg told the lieutenant. "As you said back at the outpost, this is our responsibility."

When the alert had sounded, Shul had immediately ordered Ansarg to accompany him to the outpost's remaining runabout so that they could pursue the second vessel. The lieutenant assigned Hava and Cardok to crew Endalla One in the interim, to raise its defensive shields, and to contact Deep Space 9. Shul wanted the crewmen to relay his request for additional forces. Ansarg knew that he didn't like leaving the outpost without even a single runabout to protect it.

"You were posted here a couple of months ago when the other civilian vessel purportedly lost control and had to set down, weren't you?" Shul asked.

"Yes, sir."

"Are there any similarities between that event and what's happening today?"

Ansarg had already thought about that. "At least superficially," she said. "It was a small civilian vessel, it carried a Bajoran passenger, and it eventually exploded."

"And blew a brand-new crater into Endalla," Shul said.

"A crater that revealed nothing but the subsurface of Endalla," Ansarg said. "I can tell you from what I saw that this moon's subsurface looks a great deal like its surface."

"You didn't witness the explosion, though?"

"Not in person, no, but I did see a recording of it," Ansarg said. "I was stationed in the outpost at the time. Afterward, I provided security for the engineers who came out from Deep Space Nine to study the debris field, so I saw the crater then."

"I read those reports," Shul said. "They supported the claims of the pilot that the baffle plates on his ship failed, but . . . despite the lack of any explosives, the circumstances surrounding that incident seem remarkably comparable to what we're seeing today."

The same thought had occurred to Ansarg. "It could be

that the baffle plates were intentionally made to fail," she said. "Maybe that was actually a step in the Ohalavaru extremists' campaign to unearth whatever they expect to find on Endalla."

"And today's the next step," Shul said. "It's possible. Attacks like this—made by one civilian vessel here, two there, months and even years apart—are consistent with what we know of the radical Ohalavaru. Their numbers are small and they lack resources, but they are tenacious."

"It will be interesting to see if the pilot whose baffle plates failed is among those attempting the attacks today," Ansarg said.

"I agree," Shul said. "If we—"

"Endalla One to Yolja." Crewman Hava's voice sounded steady enough, but Ansarg nevertheless thought she detected a note of alarm.

The lieutenant opened the return channel. "This is Shul aboard the *Yolja*. What is it, Crewman?"

"Lieutenant, a third vessel has infringed our security perimeter," Hava said. *"It is on a direct heading for the outpost."*

ANSARG KNEW that they wouldn't reach Endalla One before the intruder did.

"How much time?" Shul asked.

"Less than two minutes."

After Hava had reported the third vessel encroaching on the moon—and, as with its predecessors, carrying a mass of dangerous explosive materials—the lieutenant had immediately ordered Ansarg to turn their runabout back toward the outpost. With *Yolja* closer to Endalla One than *Glyrhond*, Shul assigned ch'Larn and Walenista—who had already captured the crew of the first trespassing vessel—to pursue the second. The lieutenant contacted Deep Space 9 to inform Captain Ro of the developments. *Defiant* had already departed the starbase, but it would not arrive in time to protect the outpost.

For most of the journey back, Shul had maintained open communications with the third vessel, warning its crew away.

He received no response, but he continued to transmit his message that the outpost was inhabited, and that the detonation of any explosives in the area could result in the loss of life. When *Yolja* finally neared Endalla One, he ceased his efforts.

Up ahead, a short range of small mountains rose up from the lunar surface. Just beyond it, Ansarg knew, the outpost nestled at the edge of the black, glasslike plane that had been fused in the fire of the first Ohalavaru attack on the moon. She hoped she would not witness another.

"Shields up, phasers armed," Shul said. "The third vessel is almost at the outpost."

"So are we," Ansarg said, determined to protect her crewmates. She had brought up a sensor readout on her navigational display, showing the course of the intruder as it hurtled down from space toward Endalla One. She saw that it would arrive half a minute before *Yolja*—enough time to doom the outpost. *Except*—

"The vessel is not headed toward Endalla One," she said. "It's on course toward the center of the vitrified zone." Ansarg looked through the forward port. Past the pale mountaintops, the vast, dark expanse came into view.

"I'm reading a transporter beam," Shul said. "No . . . multiple transporter beams . . . targeting the surface . . ."

Yolja sliced past the mountain peaks, revealing the outpost below, sitting on the shore of the great glass lake. Out on the sleek, ebon surface, sparks of bright white light twinkled into existence along a line, two and three at a time, then faded back into the shadows. Ansarg realized what she was seeing just before the lieutenant said it aloud.

"They're beaming down the explosives."

The solution rose in Ansarg's mind in an instant. "If they're using the transporter, they must be running with shields down," she said. "We're not in weapons range, but we can beam them aboard, then capture their ship with a tractor beam."

"That's it," Shul said. "Energizing targeting sensors." His hands flew across his control panel.

Ansarg glanced at her display, which showed the intruder

growing closer to the surface. She peered upward through the port, searching the dark skies for any sign of the vessel sending potential destruction down to the moon. At the last second, she saw it: a small gray shape, plummeting downward at a steep angle, a sliver of its hull reflecting the Bajoran sun.

"Transporter lock established," Shul said. "Lowering the shie—"

The surface of Endalla erupted. A massive explosion sent debris streaking into the sky. A wide wall of dust and pulverized glass appeared in front of *Yolja* like plumes of smoke and ash shooting from a volcano.

Ansarg banked the runabout hard to starboard. The panorama of destruction fell away in the opposite direction. Just before it passed out of sight, Ansarg saw the terrorists' vessel plunge into the maelstrom.

19

Ro leaned back in the chair in her office, her feet kicked up on her desk. She read through the following week's duty roster from a padd in her lap. It pleased her to see that her first officer had finally scheduled cross-training for some of the crew. Ro and Cenn had talked often during the construction of the new starbase about expanding Starfleet's program, allowing their people additional opportunities to broaden their skills and pursue duties typically outside the scopes of their positions. Captain and exec had agreed that they should wait to implement their plan for a month or so after Deep Space 9 had become fully operational and life aboard had settled into a routine, but the events surrounding the dedication ceremony had thrown everybody aboard into a morass of tension and uncertainty.

This is another sign that things are returning to normal, Ro thought. The crew had worked hard to overcome not only the assassination and the conspiracy within the Federation government, but also the actions of Doctor Bashir. Although many considered him a hero—the captain among them—he had put

DS9 and its crew at risk when he'd bolted the Bajoran system for Andor. It did not escape Ro that her crewmate and friend had acted in a way that she had in the past: flouting authority in the name of the greater good, avoiding detention, abandoning sworn duty for conscience. It looked different viewed from her position of leadership, rather than from the perspective of the rebel. The captain understood why—she could not underestimate the importance of her responsibility for a crew of twenty-five hundred people and a civilian population of ten thousand—but it still bothered her.

Ro scanned the list of crossover assignments. She found herself surprised by some of the requests: an engineer who wanted medical instruction, a nurse who sought tactical training, a security officer who hoped to learn transporter operation. The captain had fretted that she would end up seeing applications from only a handful of the crew, all of them seeking to take over DS9 as its new commanding officer. Instead, the number and breadth of the requests delighted her.

Just as Ro affixed her initials to the duty roster, a signal indicated somebody calling at her door. She glanced at the time on her padd—23:13—and wondered who would be looking for her in her office during gamma shift. "Come in," she said, setting her feet on the deck and her padd off to the side.

In the bulkhead across from her, to the left, the doors parted to reveal her security chief. He had come directly from the turbolift via the corridor, rather than through the door that led to her office from the Hub. He walked inside and over to the desk. A padd dangled from one of his hands.

"Jeff, you're wandering around here a little late in the day," Ro said.

"I just heard a rumor that I thought I should talk to you about," Blackmer said. "If you're busy, it can wait until morning, but I wanted to get it over with."

Get it over with? Ro thought. That didn't sound like Blackmer would tell her something she wanted to hear. "I've got time," she said. "Have a seat and tell me what's on your mind."

Blackmer sat down in one of the two chairs in front of the captain's desk. "I know that you've invited Kai Pralon to Deep Space Nine."

"I have, through Vedek Novor," Ro said. The longest tenured vedek residing on DS9, Novor Tursk oversaw the Bajoran temple on the Plaza, as well as the other vedeks, ranjens, and prylars that served on DS9. After her lunch meeting a few days earlier with Altek Dans, Ro had arranged a meeting with Vedek Brandis Tarn. The three of them spoke at length about Altek's situation. Brandis wanted to help Altek return to Bajor, and agreed that, given the government's apparent reluctance to make that happen, the best way to accomplish it would be through the Bajoran clergy. Rather than making a request of the Vedek Assembly, which could easily have become public and caused a stir—something Altek hoped to avoid—Brandis suggested that the captain extend an invitation to Pralon Onala, who had yet to visit the new starbase. Once the kai came aboard, the captain could quietly approach her about Altek Dans.

Ro made the offer to Onala through the appropriate channels, which meant Vedek Novor. "That was a few days ago. I haven't heard anything back from the kai's office yet." *Not that that's unusual,* Ro thought. *These days, I can't get anybody on Bajor to respond to me in a timely manner, much less with a satisfying answer.*

"I heard today that the Vedek Assembly learned of the invitation," Blackmer said, "and that they're counseling the kai not to make the journey anytime soon."

"Because of the assassination," Ro said, stating the reason as fact, rather than asking for confirmation.

"Yes," Blackmer said. "They are understandably reluctant to send Bajor's spiritual leader to a dangerous place."

"They may be reluctant, but it's not understandable," Ro said, bristling at the characterization of DS9 as a "dangerous place." "What happened here was terrible, but it's not representative of the security aboard this starbase."

"Isn't it, though?" Blackmer said, surprising the captain.

"Shouldn't the fact that the president of the Federation was murdered when she was under my protection concern people who want to come here? And isn't that indicative of the need for a change on Deep Space Nine?" The security chief reached forward and set his padd down on the desktop in front of the captain. He adjusted the device's position so that it faced her.

Ro did not pick up the padd, which she assumed displayed Blackmer's request for a transfer to another Starfleet facility or starship. "Jeff, I'm not interested in breaking in a new chief of security. You know this place. You watched it being built. You lobbied Starfleet to install the new thoron shield, and you established our security protocols in the stockade and around the rest of the starbase."

"All of which left us with a dead president."

Ro shook her head, unwilling to accept Blackmer's claims of incompetence. She stood up from her chair, scooped up the padd from the desktop, and paced out from behind her desk, marching toward the wide port at the far end of her office. She looked at the padd, intending simply to deny Blackmer's transfer application, but then she saw something else she hadn't expected. "This isn't . . ." she said, and peered back over at the security chief. "This is your resignation from Starfleet."

"Yes, sir," Blackmer said. "I've been thinking about it for a long time, but today, when I heard that Kai Pralon might not come to the starbase because the people around her feared for her life . . ." He shrugged almost imperceptibly and looked away. "I realized that it's time."

"It's time for what?" Ro said, her voice growing angry. "To feel sorry for yourself?" She walked back over to the desk and flipped the padd toward Blackmer. He reached to catch it, juggled it briefly, and then it fell to the gray-carpeted deck. "We've served together for three years. You should know me well enough by now to realize that I don't have much patience for self-indulgence."

Blackmer shot to his feet. "With all due respect, Captain, I'm not being self-indulgent." He bent down and picked up the fallen padd, then held it out to Ro. When she declined to take it from him, he let his arm fall back to his side. "This isn't about me feeling sorry for myself. This isn't about me at all. It's about my concern for all of the people aboard Deep Space Nine—all the crew, all the civilian residents, and all those who will pass through this place in the months and years to come."

"Then stay here and see to their safety," Ro told him.

"Captain . . ." Blackmer lowered his head and rubbed at the back of his neck. "Captain, as your chief of security, I have to take responsibility for the assassination of President Bacco. But it's not just that. Doctor Bashir disobeyed direct orders, and I was unable to keep him in custody."

"If you had, the Andorian people might still be facing extinction, they wouldn't have rejoined the Federation, and we wouldn't have a new president that a large majority of the population are thrilled about."

"None of that is relevant to the central question of whether or not I can adequately discharge my duties," Blackmer said. "Captain, when I was the chief of security aboard the first Deep Space Nine, the station was destroyed."

"It was under attack by Breen and Tzenkethi starships," Ro said.

"But that's not what destroyed it," Blackmer said. "Bombs planted aboard the station did that . . . bombs planted on my watch." He turned and put the padd with his resignation back down on the captain's desk.

Ro stepped forward, took hold of Blackmer by his upper arms, and turned him back to face her. "Jeff, you've got to stop blaming yourself for that."

"More than a thousand people died." His voice quavered.

"Let's talk about that," Ro said. "We could talk about your impressive record of accomplishments since you transferred to my command, but let's talk about all the people who died in the destruction of the station. Let's talk about those thousand people because they lead us to the more than fifty-five hundred who survived. That happened only because we knew about the bombs well in advance of when they detonated, and we knew that because of *you*. And the bombs didn't show up on somebody's sensor panel, nobody contacted us to warn us about them. No, something overheard by another crewman triggered suspicion in you, and based only on that, you managed to locate the bombs. Your intuition as a security chief led directly to the evacuation of the station and the survival of all those people."

Blackmer looked at Ro for a long time. She held his gaze, willing him to find the strength within himself that she knew he possessed. She understood his pain and the weight of the responsibility he felt. Not only had she served as DS9's security chief for two years, she had *commanded* it for more than half a dozen. Blackmer's failures, whatever they might be judged to be, were her failures as well. If she believed him anything less than completely capable of fulfilling his duties, she would not merely have accepted his resignation, she would have *demanded* it.

"But President Bacco . . ." His words came out in a tortured whisper. He turned away from Ro and walked across the width of her office, where he collapsed onto her sofa. She followed and sat down beside him.

"Jeff, Starfleet Command has made inquiries about your performance," she said gently. "Once I saw your abilities for myself, I never doubted you, but when Starfleet asked questions, I had to give them answers, and I had to defend those answers. That means I had to carefully review your time on the original Deep Space Nine, at Bajoran Space Central, and on the new starbase. I concluded that you've done a fine job, and I made the case to Starfleet."

"Thank you, Captain," Blackmer said. "I wish you could make the case to me."

"Haven't I been doing that?" Ro asked. "You feel like it's your fault that President Bacco is dead, but do you know who was responsible? Onar Throk, who fired the weapon, and Baras Rodirya, who conspired with him to do so." She hesitated, wondering if she should reveal the other opinion she'd formed about the assassination. She didn't particularly want to speak ill of the dead, but she also knew that Blackmer needed to hear the truth. "It was also partly Nan Bacco's own fault."

Blackmer's eyes grew wide, his surprise at the statement obvious. "I'm not sure how you can say that, Captain. It was my duty to protect her."

"It was, but you're not a dictator," Ro said. "You couldn't make her do something she didn't want to do. And what she didn't want to do, in a theater filled with Starfleet officers attending a dedication ceremony for their new starbase, was to stand onstage behind a protective screen."

"I should have convinced her."

"You tried to," Ro said. "Should we call up your security plans for the dedication ceremony? You recommended a protective screen be erected onstage for all of the dignitaries. None of them wanted it. *None* of them."

"I thought it was important, especially after the assassination attempt on the president last year on Orion."

"Do you know why President Bacco didn't feel the need for a protective screen?" Ro asked. She'd thought a lot about the assassination in the three-plus months that had followed. "It's because she already felt safe—not invincible, I don't think she felt that, not after her chief of staff was killed on Orion, and I don't believe she had an unconscious desire for her own death. I mean that she felt safe because, while she would naturally expect to need protection from her enemies, she wouldn't expect to need protection from her friends."

Blackmer's brow creased in consideration, and Ro saw a glimmer of understanding in his eyes. The captain pressed on. "The president was assassinated by one of Castellan Garan's own aides, a lifelong civil servant of the Cardassian Union and a man with no known inimical intentions toward the Federation. He was supposed to be a friend. Onar Throk conspired with Baras Rodirya, Bajor's representative on the Federation Council. He was supposed to be a friend. Galif jav Velk drove the entire operation, and he was Baras' chief of staff. He was supposed to be a friend. Why wouldn't the president feel safe?"

"Captain, I appreciate what you're saying, but I don't know if I have the confidence to do this job anymore."

"Confidence is a matter of ability, preparation, and will," Ro said. "I know that you have the first two of those, because I've seen it for myself. As for will . . ." She rose from the sofa and crossed back to her desk, where she retrieved Blackmer's resignation. She returned to the sofa and handed the padd to him. "You're going to have to find the will again to do your duty as security chief, because I am formally refusing your resignation."

"I . . . I don't know what to say." Blackmer seemed paradoxically both relieved and distressed.

"Say, 'Thank you, Captain,' then go to your quarters, get a good night's sleep, and report for your shift in the morning," Ro said.

"Yes, sir," Blackmer said, getting to his feet. "Thank you, Captain." As he started toward the door, Ro reached out and stopped him with a touch to his arm.

"Jeff, have you been seeing one of the counselors?"

"Not recently, no," Blackmer said. "I did go to see Lieutenant Knezo a few times, but that was in the days right after the assassination."

"I'd like you to go again, as often as you need to," Ro said. "Consult with Valeska or one of the other counselors and see what they think is appropriate."

"Yes, sir. Thank you."

Ro offered a tight-lipped smile, and then Blackmer exited the way he had entered. She watched him go, then went back to her desk. She sat down again and collected her padd, intending to move on from approving the duty roster to reviewing the latest proposals for scientific experiments on the starbase. She read through the first one, an astrophysical project involving the examination of galaxies with active galactic nuclei, in search of something called a boson star. Ro had never heard of the theoretical object, and the description in Lieutenant Prekka's request did little to make the concept clear. The captain would have to consult with Lieutenant Commander Candlewood for both an explanation of the experiment and an evaluation of its merits.

Ro flagged Prekka's proposal for follow-up, then moved on to the next. Before she could read through it, her mind drifted back to what she had told her security chief: *Starfleet Command has made inquiries about your performance.* Those inquiries had been made to her by Admiral Los Nelatin Lovat, an Alonis who had served in Starfleet for half a century. Lovat asked a great many questions about Blackmer, and indicated that they had come from multiple individuals within the Starfleet hierarchy.

The admiral had seemed satisfied with her defense of DS9's security chief, but that hadn't been the only reason she'd contacted Ro. Lovat questioned the captain's own leadership abilities. The admiral didn't identify the source of those concerns, but Ro knew that they had to be driven by Akaar.

The captain hadn't enjoyed her grilling by Lovat, and so she'd responded strongly. Afterward, though, she chose not to care about it. She would continue performing her duties aboard Deep Space 9 until they decided to take command away from her.

"Hub to Captain Ro." The voice belonged to that night's gamma shift duty officer, Lieutenant Aleco Vel.

"This is Ro. Go ahead, Vel."

"Captain, we're receiving a transmission from our security team on Endalla," Aleco said. *"Crewman Hava reports that two civilian vessels have breached the security perimeter. Both are carrying high explosives."*

Ro was on her feet and heading for the Hub even before Aleco finished speaking.

20

Cenn arrived in the Hub less than two minutes after receiving the message from the captain. He had been in the Bajoran temple on the Plaza—not his regular visit there, not one he had planned to make, but when his spirits had flagged that evening, for no particular reason he could isolate, he decided to bolster himself with a few minutes of meditation and prayer.

He had just entered the temple when his combadge vibrated; he had temporarily disabled its audio signal, so as not to disturb the other adherents present. He left the temple immediately and reactivated his combadge, which delivered Ro's message.

"Colonel Cenn, report to the Hub. There's been a breach on Endalla."

The first officer dashed from the turbolift between the tactical and primary engineering stations, and down the three steps into the Well. There, Captain Ro stood with the starbase's second officer, chief of security, and tactical officer. Above the situation table, a translucent holographic reproduction of Bajor's largest moon hung in midair. Cenn saw a pair of glowing red dots moving above the globe, at positions far removed from each other. He also spied a green dot in a lower quadrant of Endalla, at the edge of the dark plain, which he knew marked the location of the security outpost that DS9 personnel maintained.

"Take the *Defiant*," the captain said to Stinson as Cenn walked up to the group. When she saw the first officer, she said, "Desca, you're here, good." She motioned toward the hologram. "We've just received word from our outpost on Endalla that there have been two incursions past the security perimeter." She pointed to the two red dots. "They're both civilian craft, carrying two Bajorans each, as well as large quantities of explosives."

"The Ohalavaru," Cenn said, his jaw clenching.

"We think so," Ro said. "They refuse to respond to repeated hails, and there's no indication of any malfunction on either vessel. Lieutenant Shul has sent both runabouts to intercept, but that's left the outpost unprotected. I've ordered Commander Stinson to take the *Defiant* to Endalla, with Dalin Slaine at tactical and a security detachment led by Commander Blackmer. I haven't had much luck speaking to anybody in the Bajoran government lately, so I'd like you to contact the minister of defense and the minister of state. Maybe Ranz or Gandal will talk to you. Let them know what's going on, and tell them we'll keep them apprised of the situation as it develops." Without waiting for a reply, the captain looked over to Slaine and Blackmer. "Zivan, Jeff, our preference is to capture the trespassers alive, but don't take any unnecessary risks to make that happen. Those people are carrying explosives, so we have to assume they intend to use them."

"Understood," Blackmer said, and Slaine nodded.

"Good," Ro said, and then, to all of them, "Go."

As Stinson, Slaine, and Blackmer started for a turbolift, Cenn said, "Captain, before the *Defiant* departs, may I have a word with you?" The trio of officers heard him and stopped at the top of the steps between the communications and operations stations.

Cenn saw confusion on Ro's face, but she hesitated only an instant. "One moment," she told Stinson, Slaine, and Blackmer, and then she quickly climbed the same steps that Cenn had just descended. The first officer followed her around to the right, past the tactical station, and through the door in the outer bulkhead that led into the conference room.

The form of the compartment echoed that of the captain's office. Wedge-shaped, it broadened along the longer, side bulkheads, until it reached the wide, rounded rectangle of an exterior port. Cenn spotted several vessels floating freely in space around that part of the starbase—a Bajoran transport, a Frunalian science vessel, and a Klaestron freighter.

Ro stopped at the near end of the long conference table, which mimicked the shape of the compartment, and then she turned to face Cenn. "What is it, Desca?" she asked. "Time may be critical in sending the *Defiant* to Endalla."

"I know," Cenn said. "I wanted to ask if I could lead this mission aboard the *Defiant*."

"You?" the captain said. Cenn understood her obvious surprise. Before accepting the post of Bajoran liaison aboard Deep Space 9, Cenn had spent virtually his entire life on Bajor, rarely traveling offworld. Similarly, since his assignment to the starbase—and before it, to its predecessor, the erstwhile Terok Nor—he had mostly remained aboard, other than for visits back to Bajor. "Have you ever requested to take command of the *Defiant*?"

"No, I don't think so, Captain."

"Then I have to ask: why now?"

Cenn did not dissemble. "Because I take the Ohalavaru attacks on Endalla personally."

"First of all, we don't know with certainty that it's the Ohalavaru aboard those ships, and secondly, they haven't 'attacked' anything yet." Ro paused for a moment, as though gathering her thoughts. "But even if it is the Ohalavaru, and even if they do intend to attack, why would you take that personally? I know that you're devout, Desca, but I also know you don't take offense just because somebody believes something different than you do."

"I absolutely do not dispute the right of the Ohalavaru—or anybody else—to their own beliefs," Cenn said. "I disagree with those beliefs, and it would end there if all we were talking about were beliefs. But we're not. I resent the violent attempts of the Ohalavaru to prove their doctrine, their willingness to destroy Bajoran property, to put lives at risk, and as we've seen in the past, even to kill."

"Desca, I understand your anger," the captain said. "The violence that some of the Ohalavaru have perpetrated upsets me, too, even if it's not an affront to my faith like it is with you. But because it does offend you, I'm concerned that your emotions could interfere with your command duties, with your ability to make good decisions."

"That won't happen, Captain, I promise you," Cenn said. "I have strong feelings about this, but I don't want to lead the mission in order to exact vengeance on the Ohalavaru. I want to take command of the *Defiant* and participate in the mission because it *means* something to me."

Cenn could see in Ro's eyes the calculations she was making. "I don't want any bloodshed if we can avoid it," she finally said. "Especially when it comes to our crew, but I want to apprehend the intruders with a minimum of violence, if at all possible."

"I understand," Cenn said. "If it helps to know, I'd prefer to capture them, too. In the interests of justice, they should stand trial for their crimes."

"You've been my first officer for more than six years," Ro said, as though making the argument to herself. "I trust you."

"Thank you, Captain."

"You're welcome," Ro said. "Now go."

Cenn raced back into the Hub, and then, with Stinson, Slaine, and Blackmer in tow, headed into the turbolift, on his way to Docking Bay One and *Defiant*.

21

Aboard *Defiant*, Stinson sat at a peripheral station on the port side of the bridge. Moved from the center seat over to crew the communications console because Colonel Cenn had taken command of the ship, the second officer felt out of place. *No, it's not that* I *feel out of place,* Stinson thought. *It's that the mission feels rushed and awkward to me.* Despite Cenn's higher position in DS9's hierarchy, Stinson could not pretend that the Bajoran Militia officer had more experience than he did commanding a starship.

But as *Defiant* settled into a parking orbit above Endalla, all of those thoughts fell away from the second officer's mind, and he stood up from his chair. The scene on the main viewscreen demanded his attention. The magnified vista showed the lunar outpost, its circular roof and the surrounding environs partially buried beneath layers of debris, which continued to rain down. The structure appeared intact, and communications with Crewman Hava during the trip from DS9 confirmed that Endalla One, though battered, had survived the explosion on the moon, as had both Hava and Cardok.

The great plain of dark glass had not. At its center, a long, narrow fissure sliced along the ragged contours of Endalla's surface. The sleek, glassy region—itself created in an inferno unleashed by a destructive attack—had been left in tatters by the latest assault. The jagged outline of the newly formed crevasse stretched across the moon like a gaping wound.

"Reopen the channel to the outpost," said Colonel Cenn

from the command chair. Lieutenant Commander Blackmer stood beside him.

For a moment, Stinson did not react. Although he had worked the communications console during the journey from DS9—contacting not only Hava and Cardok at Endalla One, but Shul and Ansarg aboard *Yolja*, and ch'Larn and Walenista aboard *Glyrhond*—the second officer had grown accustomed to commanding *Defiant* whenever the captain remained on the starbase. With a jolt of realization, as well as more frustration then he knew he should indulge, Stinson jumped back to his station and operated his controls. "Channel open, Colonel."

"*Defiant* to Endalla One," Cenn said.

"*This is Shul at Endalla One,*" came the reply. According to the lieutenant's earlier report, he and Ansarg had been return-ing to the outpost aboard *Yolja* when the explosion had rocked the moon. Afterward, the runabout set down beside Endalla One, and the security officers transported over to the outpost.

When he looked back at the main viewer, Stinson could just distinguish the bow of *Yolja* extending out from behind the outpost. The image of Endalla One and the surrounding lunar surface, usually an inert display, contained a strange, creeping movement. The dark remnants of the explosion fell slowly in the moon's lower gravity, trailing ash behind them.

"Lieutenant, the *Defiant* is now in orbit above the outpost," Cenn said. "What is the status of the ship that triggered the explosion?" Ensign Ansarg had reported seeing the vessel fly into the heart of the destruction.

"*Since the detonation, we've seen no further sign of the ship.*"

"Could flying into the explosion have been an act of sui-cide?" Cenn asked.

"*It could have been, sir,*" Shul said. "*But it also might not have been intentional. Perhaps their helm or engines failed.*"

"Or perhaps they intended to follow the course they did, and they haven't been destroyed," Blackmer suggested. "Have you had an opportunity to scan the chasm that the explosion formed?"

"We have," Shul said. *"There's some sort of interference impeding the sensors. It could be a function of the moon's composition at that depth, but we need to conduct a closer, more detailed examination."*

"Understood," Cenn said, and he gestured toward Slaine, who sat to Stinson's right, at the tactical station. The dalin immediately began operating the ship's sensors. "And what is your status, Lieutenant?"

"We're still running diagnostics on all our systems," Shul said. *"Both the outpost and the* Yolja *were pounded by debris, but neither appears to have suffered anything more than minor damage. Some repairs will be necessary on Endalla One, but we're in no imminent jeopardy."*

"What about injuries to the crew?"

"We had a few falls, some contusions, and I think I might have broken my little finger, but we have no major issues."

"We're going to transport you up to the *Defiant,*" Cenn said. "We have a security team standing by to relieve you, and we'll also be sending down engineers to complete the diagnostics and make repairs."

"Colonel, we can finish our tour here," Shul said. Stinson knew that the security officers stationed at the outpost had three more days remaining on their assignment. *"We've got a medkit, so I can set my finger."*

Stinson saw Blackmer lean in toward the command chair and say something beneath his breath, which drew a smile from the first officer. "I appreciate your dedication to duty, 'Doctor' Shul," Cenn said, delivering the words not as a rebuke, but with a comrades-in-arms feel. "I'll give you a few minutes to pack up your belongings, but in the meantime, lower your shields so we can send you some visitors."

"Yes, sir," Shul said.

"Contact Ensign Clark in the transporter room when you're ready to beam up. Cenn out." Stinson dutifully closed the channel, anticipating the first officer's next order, which the colonel issued at once. "Open a channel to the *Glyrhond.*"

Stinson finished working his controls. "Channel open, sir."

"*Defiant* to *Glyrhond*."

"*Glyrhond here. This is ch'Larn.*" As *Defiant* had approached Endalla, ch'Larn had reported that he and Walenista had taken the crews of the two other invading vessels into custody. In both cases, according to the lieutenant, it required only warning phaser blasts across the bows of each ship. Stinson guessed that, even running with shields up, the crews of such small craft, carrying their cargo of dangerous explosives, would not want to take direct fire from energy weapons. Both pair of Bajorans surrendered quickly and without further incident.

"Lieutenant," Cenn said, "what is your status?"

"*We have disarmed and restrained our prisoners in the rear compartment of the runabout,*" ch'Larn said. "*We have both vessels in tow and are headed to the outpost. We'll be there shortly.*"

Slaine looked up from the tactical station and over at the first officer. "Colonel, the *Glyrhond* is already within transporter range."

"Lieutenant, you are close enough for transport," Cenn told ch'Larn. "Lower your shields so we can beam your prisoners into the *Defiant*'s brig."

"*Yes, sir.*"

"*Defiant* out." Once more, Stinson closed the channel. "Bridge to brig." Stinson knew that Blackmer had already sent a security team to ready and stand guard over the ship's holding cells.

"*Brig. Crewman Bixx here.*"

"Crewman, prepare to receive four prisoners via transporter."

"*Acknowledged,*" Bixx said. "*We're ready, Colonel.*"

Cenn signed off, then contacted the transporter room.

"*This is Clark.*" One amid the wave of new crew members assigned to DS9 upon its becoming fully operational, Marguerite Clark had been assigned to the starbase straight out of the Academy. A human woman born and raised on Earth, according to what Stinson had read in her personnel file, she had an excitable way of talking that often brought out certain inflections in her speech. So far, the second officer had been unable to identify Clark's transitory accent, except to think that it couldn't have originated anywhere in the Sol system.

"Ensign, lock on to the *Glyrhond*," Cenn said. "You'll be receiving coordinates from Dalin Slaine. Beam the four Bajorans on the runabout directly into the brig."

"Right away, sir." Cenn waited a few seconds, and then Clark said, *"I have the coordinates. Locking on . . . and energizing."* Several more seconds passed, and then the ensign said, *"Transport complete."*

"Very good. Thank you, Ensign. Cenn out." The first officer stood up from the command chair. To Blackmer, he said, "Commander, we have some prisoners to interrogate." The security chief nodded, and together, the two men headed for the bridge's portside aft exit. As the doors opened before them, Cenn stopped and pointed to Stinson. "Commander, you have the bridge. When the *Glyrhond* arrives with the two hostile vessels, I want detailed scans of the explosives onboard and a plan for them to be safely removed and detonated. Afterward, the *Defiant* will tow the ships back to Deep Space Nine. And let me know at once if we learn anything about the third vessel."

"Yes, sir." As Cenn and Blackmer exited, the second officer rose and moved to the center of the bridge, where he sat down in the command chair. Before he began issuing orders, Stinson paused to appreciate the moment. Suddenly, the mission no longer felt rushed, or awkward, or held in less-than-experienced hands.

BLACKMER STOOD JUST outside one of the holding cells in *Defiant*'s brig, while Colonel Cenn and a security officer looked on behind him. On the other side of the force field, the prisoner lay on his back atop the small compartment's only sleeping platform, which hung from the far bulkhead. In his late thirties, with a medium build and sandy hair, the man had his knees up and a forearm thrown over his eyes. He wore civilian clothing of no distinction, light-colored work pants and a red plaid, long-sleeved shirt. He gave his name as Tiros Ardell, although a search of Bajoran records identified him as Tiros Remna, a farmer from Rakantha Province with no accounts of criminal activity or violence. According to the language and onomastics databases, *Remna* meant "gift of the Prophets," while *Ardell* appeared to be a name with no historical denotations.

As with the three other prisoners—two men and one woman—Tiros had so far refused to say much in response to Blackmer's questions. All four Bajorans freely labeled themselves as Ohalavaru, but about their intentions, they would only repeat what had become a mantra for the sect—and a denial of responsibility for its radical fringe: "We seek only to bring the truth to Bajor."

"I don't understand why you expect bombing Endalla will reveal some unknown truth to your people," Blackmer said, genuinely curious how the extremists could make the connection between what seemed like random violence and the pursuit of knowledge. To the security chief, the very belief in such an equation hinted at mental illness, or at least a form of mass hysteria.

Tiros lowered his arm from his face and swung himself up to a sitting position on the sleeping platform. "You say you don't understand *why* we do what we do," he said, "but I think that you do understand. I think you speak inexactly, and perhaps that leads you to a sloppiness of thought."

Blackmer listened to what Tiros said, then replayed it in his mind before reacting. The man spoke pedantically, but not as though he intended to insult the security chief. Tiros clearly had a point to make, and Blackmer tried to see it. "You mention sloppy thinking," he finally said. "That's a phrase I've heard before, isn't it?"

"Some Ohalavaru have used it as a description for what has happened to Bajoran society," Tiros said. "We did not always believe in gods."

"Haven't you?" Blackmer asked. "Most of you, anyway?"

"No," Tiros said, and he hopped from the sleeping platform onto the deck.

The quick movement of the prisoner provoked a response

in Crewwoman Olivia Dellasant, who stood just behind Black-mer, to his left. Despite the force field that protected the holding cell's entryway, the security officer took a step forward and drew her phaser. Tiros gave no indication that he even saw Dellasant—or, if he did, then he showed no sign that he cared about her or anybody else's presence there. Blackmer eased the crewwoman back with a measured motion of his hand.

"No, we did not always have gods," Tiros continued. "Yes, we did at first, in the same way that all societies do." He padded forward in the small space, directly up to the force field, until he faced Blackmer at close range. After a moment, he turned and stepped back to the rear of the cell, then paced to and fro in front of the sleeping platform. He gazed down as he spoke, gesticulating. "We had a god of the rains, a god of the fields, a god of the seas . . . we invented mythic figures to stand in for our ignorance of the world. We did not know what made a star burn, or even what stars were, and so we prayed that the light that came on the previous morning would reappear on the next, that the warmth that came in one season and faded in another would return the following year so that we could sow our crops and survive. We prayed to the heavens and populated them with beings we imagined to be in some ways like ourselves, but with abilities we could not imagine."

As Blackmer listened to the man and watched him tread back and forth in the confined space, he thought that the same description of early religion could be applied to the cultures of Earth, or of any number of other planets in the galaxy. The security chief did not see what that had to do with the Prophets, who were more or less demonstrably real. The Ohalavaru did not take exception to Bajor's ancient, unproven gods, long ago shed by a developing society, but to the characterization of the modern-day Prophets as gods.

"Except that, as we advanced, we learned about the world around us," Tiros continued, "and those abilities we once ascribed to gods, we came to understand as functions of the universe. The sun did not rise and set because some god carried it around Bajor from one day to the next, but because gravity bound Bajor to a star. We matured and let go of our primitive superstitions. We learned not to fear the unknown, but to embrace it and to seek understanding. What need had we of gods when we had enlightenment?" He stopped walking and looked up expectantly at Blackmer.

"Are you saying that there was a time that the Bajorans gave up their belief in the Prophets?"

"Not in the Prophets," Tiros said. "In the gods we devised before them—the gods we invented to keep us safe in the darkness, who then faded in the light of our growing knowledge." He sounded less like a farmer to Blackmer, and more like a philosopher. "The Prophets came later, in a time of great turmoil, before we knew of life beyond our world. Civilization faltered and darkness seeped back in until it engulfed us once more, and into that great void came an alien race who we called the Prophets, and who, because we did not understand them, we dubbed gods."

The security chief glanced over his right shoulder at Cenn, who he knew was pious. The first officer's jaw had set, and Blackmer saw him open his mouth to say something—no doubt to object to the idea that Tiros had just expressed. The security chief managed to catch Cenn's eye and, with a quick shake of his head, warn him off. Knowing the strength of the first officer's beliefs, Blackmer had suggested on the way to the brig that Cenn absent himself from the interrogation. When the colonel insisted on being present, Blackmer then requested that he avoid contributing any questions or comments, for fear that his doing so could derail the security chief's efforts to learn something from the Ohalavaru. Cenn agreed.

To Tiros, Blackmer didn't quite know what to say in response to his jeremiad. The security chief didn't want to hear about the supposed failures of Bajoran society and the Ohalavaru's desire to repair their civilization, but about the specific aims of the people who had attacked Endalla that day. He would need to maneuver the conversation, but he knew that he would have to do so with care. "I must admit that my familiarity with Bajoran history is rudimentary at best. I know that your civilization goes back tens of thousand of years, and that it has ebbed and flowed in that time. How is it that the Ohalavaru have this determined view of Bajoran history that the rest of your people do not?"

"Oh, but what I've just told you is not in dispute by anybody," Tiros claimed. He sat down on the edge of the sleeping platform. "Some people may use different words here and there, but that's just quibbling."

"Quibbling," Blackmer asked, "or sloppy thinking?"

"The sloppy thinking I referred to was your own," Tiros said. "You stated that you don't know why we've taken the actions on Endalla that we have. But of course you do. You identified us as Ohalavaru before you even spoke to us, so you know who we are."

"You are believers in the texts of Ohalu."

"Which have as their central tenet the idea that the Prophets are not gods, but merely benevolent aliens," Tiros said. "If that was all there was to it, though, then we would not be doing what we're doing. Knowledge for the sake of knowledge is a laudable goal, but there is far more at stake than that. The principles of Ohalu make the case that Bajoran society cannot and will not advance until it has abandoned its willful ignorance, until it sees the Prophets not as gods, but as moral and spiritual equals."

Blackmer saw an opening to provoke Tiros, which he hoped would urge him to defend the Ohalavaru, and thereby reveal something about their precise intentions. "So you're trying to blow up Endalla in order to help the people of Bajor advance?"

"You leap from our act to our goal as though there is a direct cause and effect, as though there are no intermediate stages," Tiros said. "There are many steps on the path we hope Bajor to follow. Our duty on Endalla is just one of those."

"You must understand why people take exception to that," Blackmer said. "Not so long ago, people were killed on Endalla. Even if the progress you seek were assured from the actions you're taking—a premise I do not grant—would it be worth the murder of even one individual, let alone the murder of thousands?"

"The Ascendants . . ."

"Yes, the Ascendants were responsible," Blackmer said. "But what you seem to be telling me right now, and what you effectively told everybody when the Ohalavaru first attacked Endalla almost six years ago, is that you welcomed the destructive actions of the Ascendants. You wanted the atmosphere ripped away from this moon. You wanted the laboratories and scientists here to be purged from the surface. I know that because you're still trying to blow this place up."

"There is some truth in what you say," Tiros admitted, "but it misses other truths. Although, in the deepest interpretations of his texts, Ohalu foretold the Ascendants crisis, no Bajoran had a hand in bringing about those events. And what happened on Endalla after that . . . I wasn't a part of that, but I understand that one member of the Ohalavaru who participated was unstable . . ."

"You have to know that many people—not just on Bajor, but across the Federation—believe that all Ohalavaru are, by definition, unstable."

"Yes, I know that." The fact did not seem to anger Tiros, but to sadden him.

"And you have nothing to say to defend yourself from such a charge?" Blackmer asked. "You have no detailed explanation of why what you're doing is justified?"

"I've just given you my explanation."

"You've given me generalities," Blackmer said. "You're trying to destroy Endalla in order to improve Bajoran society. Didn't the Cardassians make the same sort of declaration when they occupied Bajor?"

Tiros launched himself from the sleeping platform and across the compact cell at Blackmer. He stopped just short of the force field, which hummed at his proximity. From just centimeters way, he glared at the security chief with fire in his eyes. "How dare you?" he said, his voice pitched low. "Most of my family were killed in the Occupation."

"Then what would you say to the people who lost family members six years ago, when the Ohalavaru first attacked Endalla? And what would you say to the Starfleet officers stationed here during your attack today—people whose lives matter so little to you that you attempted to destroy the moon with them on it?"

"We knew that the outpost and the Starfleet personnel here would not be killed."

"I don't believe you." Blackmer knew that he would get nothing more from Tiros just then. He turned and nodded to Dellasant, who stepped up to assume a sentry position beside the force field. The security chief took one last look at the Ohalavaru. "If you decide that you want to tell me what you're really doing here, I'll be happy to listen. Otherwise, you can keep your new-age delusions and self-important justifications to yourself." Blackmer turned and, with Cenn by his side, he stalked out of the brig.

STINSON STOOD BEHIND SLAINE at the tactical console and peered over her shoulder at the display. Before he could respond to what she had just shown him, the portside aft doors whisked open, and Cenn and Blackmer entered the bridge. "Commander," Stinson said at once, "we've found something." Both the first officer and the security chief walked over to the tactical station. "Dalin?" Stinson said, inviting Slaine to repeat her report.

The tactical officer pointed at a column of numbers on her readout, which were immediately replaced by an image that clearly represented the interior of the new chasm on Endalla's surface. A long, thin strip of ground jagged along between steep, ragged walls. "Deep below the surface of the moon," she said, "something is interfering with our sensors." Slaine touched a control, and a wash of dull blue spread through the walls and floor of the chasm. "It has a diffusing effect and seems to be a naturally occurring consequence of the mineral composition. It's subtle. I don't think we could have even detected the effect at all if the surface above hadn't been excavated away."

"Are you saying that our scans can't detect what's down there?" Cenn asked.

"Not within the moon itself below a certain depth," Slaine said. "But the fissure that's been opened in the surface provides a narrow window for our scans to penetrate. There is still residual interference from the surrounding rock, but I think I can tune the sensors to compensate. I was just about to attempt it."

Stinson choked back the order that rose in his mind, then castigated himself for it. Because of his resentment at not being in command during the *Defiant* crew's mission, he did not want to overstep his authority. Functioning as the ship's exec, though, he would have been within the bounds of the position to order Slaine to proceed. Instead, he waited, and after a moment, Cenn did so.

Slaine deftly operated the tactical controls, and the image on the display shifted. Some elements sharpened, while others fell out of focus. After a minute or so, Stinson said, "This may take some time," but then a recognizable shape appeared between the two walls of the chasm, resting on the ground.

It was a ship.

"Sensors are showing quantities of explosives still aboard," Slaine said.

"Are there life signs?" Stinson asked. The vessel looked as though it had soft-landed, not crashed.

"I'm adjusting the sensors to find out," Slaine said. Portions of the image on her display continued to phase in and out of clarity, and columns of numbers cycled down an adjacent readout. Twice, two red points of light appeared beside the ship, but then faded away. "The sensors are detecting something, but I'm having trouble resolving the contacts . . . unless . . ." Slaine's hands scuttled across her panel, until the two red dots returned to the display and at last stayed there. "I read two life-forms, both Bajoran."

Cenn straightened from where he had leaned in over the tactical console, as though snapping to attention. "Bridge to transporter room."

"Transporter room. This is Clark."

"Commander," Slaine said, looking up at the first officer. "We can't beam them aboard. It's why I had trouble isolating their life signs: they've erected a transporter inhibitor at their landing site."

Cenn held Slaine's gaze for a long moment, then looked at Stinson and Blackmer in turn. Finally, he said, "Then we're going down after them."

BLACKMER PILOTED the type-10 shuttlecraft *Tyson* down toward the surface of Endalla. Colonel Cenn sat beside him at the main console in the cramped cockpit, while two members of the security staff—Crewwomen Fran Draco and Costa Trabor—occupied the only other seats, directly behind Blackmer and Cenn. The first officer had wanted to travel down to the moon in one of the runabouts, with its more powerful armaments and defenses, but Blackmer had dissuaded him. Considerably larger than one of *Defiant*'s shuttles, a runabout would have been far more difficult to maneuver down into the fissure. Should the away team need to make a rapid ascent, Blackmer wanted nothing to impede their avenue of escape.

Something thumped topside. Behind him, Draco crewed sensors on a lateral control panel. "Debris falling from the walls of the chasm," she reported. "The structure is unstable."

Scans aboard *Defiant* had revealed the unsound ramparts, another reason that Blackmer had counseled against taking down a runabout. He even suggested to Cenn that perhaps they should delay before entering the chasm, but the first officer feared what the Ohalavaru might do below the surface of Endalla. Blackmer had to agree that waiting for the extremists to emerge on their own did not seem the wisest course.

The security chief also considered encouraging Cenn to allow Commander Stinson to lead the effort to apprehend the Ohalavaru and prevent them from completing whatever misguided plan they had conceived. Although the first officer had so far contained the strong opinions he held about the actions of the extremists,

Blackmer worried that, if the situation led to a confrontation, Cenn might act rashly, endangering himself and the away team. The security chief also did not want a phaser set to kill leveled at any of the outlaws, and while he did not necessarily think that Cenn would do such a thing, he also could not be sure—not with the beliefs Cenn held so deeply directly challenged by the Ohalavaru. In the end, Blackmer had elected to trust the professionalism of the first officer, rather than confronting him.

The shuttlecraft continued down into the fissure. Blackmer had engaged the automated helm system because of the many adjustments required to negotiate the angular, wildly uneven surfaces of the chasm walls, but he stayed prepared to take control of the auxiliary craft should the need arise. He also programmed *Tyson* to descend slowly, which would more readily allow for quick changes to its course if the earth shifted around the vessel. Several more times, rocks fell onto the shuttle from above.

"We are halfway there," Blackmer announced, consulting the navigational readout.

"The Ohalavaru continue to move around outside their vessel," Draco said.

Blackmer peered through the tall, wide port that angled sharply up from the bow and swept in a convex arc up to the overhead. In the darkness in front of *Tyson*, he could see only those spaces illuminated by the shuttlecraft. He looked at Cenn, whose steady expression could not hide his anxiety. "What do you think they're doing down there?" the security chief asked. In part, Blackmer wanted the first officer's analysis of the situation, but more than that, he hoped to gauge Cenn's emotional state.

"I don't know," Cenn said, staring straight into the darkness in front of the shuttlecraft, and then he shook his head. "I don't understand anything that they're doing or that they've done. None of it makes any sense to me."

Blackmer wanted to know if Cenn's lack of understanding originated with the views that the Ohalavaru held about the Prophets, so drastically different from the first officer's own. He would not ask such a personal question—not of a superior, not in front of other personnel, but also because, though Blackmer had a solid working relationship with the colonel, they were not close.

"Do you think—"

The shuttlecraft crashed into the side of the chasm. The vessel jolted hard, nearly throwing Blackmer from his seat. He grabbed onto the console and steadied himself. He reached to take control of *Tyson*, but then the vessel righted. Blackmer halted the shuttlecraft's descent as he searched the helm and navigational displays for an explanation of what had happened. Draco provided the answer.

"There's been an explosion below us," she said. "Nothing on the scale of what created the fissure, but still of considerable force."

"Is everybody all right?" Cenn asked, and the other three members of the away team all replied in the affirmative.

"The explosion must have shifted part of one of the walls," Blackmer said. "It struck the shuttlecraft on the starboard side, forward of the drive cowling. I see no threat to hull integrity."

"I am reading a large amount of rock that's just fallen to the chasm floor," Draco said. "And . . . I no longer detect any life signs."

Blackmer and Cenn looked at each other. "Were they crushed?" the first officer asked.

"No, I don't think so," Draco said. "Sensors pinpointed their last position a distance from the rockfall."

"Then what happened to them?" Blackmer asked. When nobody had an answer, the security chief asked Cenn if they should continue downward. Cenn nodded.

Blackmer reactivated the automated helm system, and the *Defiant* shuttlecraft resumed its descent into the darkness below.

CENN RAISED HIS PHASER as he followed Lieutenant Commander Blackmer toward the rear of the shuttlecraft. Draco trailed behind the first officer, while Trabor would

remain aboard *Tyson* to safeguard their vessel, to continue scanning the area, and to provide whatever support the away team
required. Clad in environmental suits, the trio disembarked
through the aft hatch, then moved along the shuttlecraft's
portside flank. Cenn peered forward as they walked, toward
the area illuminated by the lights in the shuttlecraft's bow and
those in the helmets of the away team.

To the right and left of *Tyson*, barely visible in the surrounding darkness, the craggy walls of the nascent chasm rose
quickly out of sight. Fallen earth and rock lay strewn about, and
just twenty meters ahead, the Ohalavaru vessel sat facing the
shuttlecraft. Larger than *Tyson*, but smaller than a runabout, it
had a triangular design not uncommon among Bajoran ships.
Interior lights shined outward through several small ports, but
Cenn saw no movement within the vessel. All around, granules
of dirt and ash drifted downward like dark snow.

"*This close to their target, the sensors continue to function clearly,*"
Trabor said across the comm system that linked the shuttlecraft
with the away team's environmental suits. "*I'm detecting only the
three of you. No life signs aboard the Bajoran vessel or anywhere in
the vicinity. The rear hatch of their ship reads open.*"

"*Acknowledged,*" Blackmer said. "*We're going to investigate
the ship.*"

The security chief started forward, his movements looking
slow and clumsy in Endalla's lower gravitation. Cenn followed
him across to the civilian vessel, and then along its starboard
bulkhead, until they reached the stern. There, a wide panel had
dropped from the rear of the vessel to form a ramp, matching
the configuration aboard *Tyson*. Light spilled from the opening
onto the ground.

"*Wait here,*" Blackmer said, holding up one hand, flat. With
his other hand, he raised his phaser and sidled along the aft
bulkhead until he reached the ramp. He bent low and looked
into the ship, then quickly pulled back.

The security chief's movements and his confidence
impressed Cenn. As the ranking officer and commander of the

away team, the first officer had intended to take the lead, but Blackmer had suggested otherwise. While Cenn had served in the Militia for many years, he functioned on Deep Space 9 mostly in an administrative capacity, as much Starfleet liaison to the Bajoran government as Ro's exec. He rarely left the starbase on missions, and he had almost no practical experience in environmental suits. The reality of all that reduced the bruising of his ego, but it did not remove his desire to be first on the scene to capture the Ohalavaru.

"The ship is empty," Blackmer said. *"I'm going inside. Cover me."* Draco acknowledged the order, and Cenn watched as she moved her head to and fro, continuously shining the lights of her helmet across the area and scanning it with her eyes, alert for trouble.

As Blackmer surveyed the interior of the vessel, he maintained a running commentary. He reported finding nothing at all of interest. Several storage compartments had been left open and empty, suggesting that the Ohalavaru had taken equipment with them.

"The explosives," Cenn proposed.

"Evidently," Blackmer agreed. *"That could explain the explosion we detected down here, but . . . to what end?"*

They don't need an end, Cenn thought. He did not think of the Ohalavaru as insane, but as rebels dedicated to a destructive cause, naysayers who found their value in stripping away the peace and love that others nurtured and cherished. Cenn could only speculate as to the cause of such behavior, but it would not surprise him if he learned that it had taken root in the terrible injustice and oppression of the Occupation. *Sixteen years gone,* Cenn thought, *and still we bear the scars.*

"I'm coming out," Blackmer announced. When he appeared at the top of the ramp, he stopped and said, *"Trabor, is there any indication where they might have gone?"*

"No, sir, there's nothing on the sensors."

Draco stepped forward, to the bottom end of the ramp, and squatted down. The lights from her helmet illuminated the surface, and as she turned her head, they chased along the ground. *"Footprints,"* she said. She stood up and activated the beacon on the wrist of her environmental suit.

"Let's go," Blackmer said, turning on his wrist beacon as well. He trotted down the ramp to join the crewwoman. *"Same configuration as we move forward. I'm on point. Draco, you're in the rear."*

Cenn fell in again between the two Starfleet officers, activating his own beacon as the security chief moved out. Blackmer kept his wrist beacon aimed at the ground in front of him and slightly to his right; he plainly did not want to muddle the tracks left by the Ohalavaru. They had walked perhaps twenty-five meters before the footprints swerved to one side, directly up to one wall of the crevasse. Cenn saw that the impressions in the ground continued along the rock wall, but then Blackmer said, *"What the hell is that?"*

The shock in the security chief's voice dismayed Cenn more than the actual question. The first officer followed the beam of Blackmer's beacon, which shined on the wall of rock ahead of them. *Except that's not rock—*

Cenn's mouth dropped open. He gazed at the break in the wall and tried to make sense of what he saw. Where the rock ended—where it had been blown away by explosives, he thought—a smooth surface lay revealed. An unpolished black, it seemed almost to absorb the light that shined on it.

"Do you see this, Trabor?" Blackmer asked. Scanners in the away team's helmets transmitted real-time images of what they saw back to the shuttlecraft.

"Yes, sir, I see it," Trabor said. *"Sensors are reading it as a sophisticated composite of the rocks and minerals around it. It's as though it was crafted to blend in perfectly with the surroundings."*

"It might look like the rock around it," Draco said, *"but if an explosion did this, then it's clearly much stronger."*

"Is this what the Ohalavaru are looking for?" Blackmer asked. *"Is this what they're trying to destroy?"*

"I don't know," Cenn said. "I don't know what this is."

The colonel aimed his beacon to the right. He saw only more of the rock wall. When he swung it in the other direction, the beam revealed an expanse of the smooth, black material. His beacon traced along the surface for one meter, and then two. At three meters, the light exposed an irregularly shaped hole, as though it had been blasted into existence. "Commander."

"I see it," Blackmer said, and he raced over to the side of the breach. Cenn and Draco followed. *"Trabor, still no life signs?"*

"No, sir."

"That material, whatever it is, must be what's interfering with our sensors," Draco noted.

"Stand ready," Blackmer said. He turned off the lights on his helmet and wrist, crouched, and then darted forward. As he passed the breach, he looked into it, then came to a stop on its far side. *"I saw lights inside, in the distance,"* he said. *"It looked like two environmental-suited figures. I can't tell how far, but they don't seem close. They appear to be lower than the level of the ground here."*

"What do we do?" Cenn asked.

"We can't go in there," Blackmer said. *"They probably expected that we would pursue them here, so they may have the opening under surveillance. They also might have rigged weapons inside to prevent us from following them. Even if they haven't, we don't know what we'd be walking into."*

Cenn thought about how they should proceed. He felt an overwhelming impulse to disregard the security chief's caution and simply climb through the breach in pursuit of the Ohalavaru. Instead, he said, "I'm going to hail them."

Blackmer said nothing, and into the silence, Draco asked, *"Is that wise, Colonel?"*

"I don't think it's *un*wise," he said. "Commander Blackmer indicated that they probably expected us to follow them. Maybe they don't know that we're here at this moment, but for all we know, they may have sensors that function here. After all, they seemed to have known about this place."

"Maybe they did," Blackmer said. *"Maybe that's been their goal all along."*

"To find this?" Draco asked. *"But what is this?"*

"I don't know," Cenn said again, but something nagged at him from the back of his mind. He pushed it away. "I don't know what this is or what they're doing, but we're not just going to wait for them to come out—not when we don't know what it is they're attempting." He reached up to the neck of his helmet to toggle his comm system to broadcast over a range of frequencies. Before he did, he said, "Do you have any objections, Commander?"

Blackmer said nothing for a moment, and then, *"No, Colonel, I have no objections."* Cenn didn't know what he would have done had Blackmer opposed him.

"Hailing them," Cenn said. He initiated a transmission across multiple frequencies. "This is Colonel Cenn Desca of the Bajoran Militia and Deep Space Nine," he said. "To the Ohalavaru—" He had been about to say, *To the Ohalavaru extremists*, but he stopped himself. "To the Ohalavaru, we have captured two of your vessels and taken four of your comrades into custody." He listed them by name. "We have pursued your third vessel into the fissure you created when you bombed the surface of Endalla. We have commandeered your ship and followed you to your current location underground. We are offering you the opportunity to surrender yourselves before we are forced to take aggressive action."

Cenn waited. He expected to hear nothing. The security personnel stationed at Endalla One had reported that not a single one of their hails to any of the Ohalavaru vessels had been returned. The four who had been apprehended had also mostly maintained their silence. *Tiros Ardell talked a lot*, Cenn thought, *but he still didn't say much*.

"Colonel Cenn," said an unfamiliar male voice, *"my name is Travil Asand. I am one of the two Ohalavaru you are pursuing. My colleague is called Nelish Stoat."*

Nelish, Cenn recalled, had been the pilot of the civilian vessel that had exploded on Endalla when its baffle plates had ruptured. *No doubt a ploy intended to test Starfleet's defenses and procedures on the moon.* The colonel's disdain for the Ohalavaru grew.

"*He and I surrender ourselves into your custody,*" Travil continued.

Cenn thought for a moment that the Ohalavaru must be mocking him, but he perceived no disdain in the voice. "Are you armed?"

"*We are each carrying a disruptor,*" Travil said. "*We hoped not to have to fire them, but we had to bring them to ensure that we would not be stopped prematurely. You have my word that we will not use them against you. As for our explosives, we have exhausted our supply.*"

"What guarantees can you provide for any of that?" Cenn asked.

"*Only my word,*" Travil said. "*Somehow, I expect that will not be enough for you.*"

"You and I agree at least on that point," Cenn said.

"*We have only one condition for our surrender,*" Travil said.

"You are not in a position to make requests, and I am not in a position to grant them," Cenn said. "I am here explicitly as an officer of the Bajoran Militia, deputized only to capture you."

"*The condition is a simple one, and completely in your power to fulfill,*" Travil said, as though Cenn had not spoken. "*You must come to us.*"

"Why?"

"*We have our reasons, which will become clear,*" Travil said. "*We promise that no harm will come to you, and that you will be able to leave at any time, of your own free will.*"

"Your word notwithstanding, that still seems like a foolish thing for me to agree to."

"*It may seem that way, but it's not foolish,*" Travil said. "*Stoat and I will not hurt you. If you review what's happened so far here on Endalla, Colonel, you will see that my colleagues and I have harmed no one.*"

"You have trespassed on and damaged sovereign Bajoran territory," Cenn said, unable to keep a note of anger from entering his voice.

"*I cannot argue that point,*" Travil admitted. "*But again, we took no lives.*"

"You put lives at risk."

"*True, but we took pains to avoid causing any loss of life or even any injury.*"

Cenn hesitated. The Ohalavaru on the three vessels that had come to Endalla might or might not have endeavored to avoid killing anybody, but the first officer could not deny that no lives had been lost during their attack, and only minor injuries suffered. Perhaps he should take Travil at his word. At that moment, Cenn wanted nothing more than for the entire incident to be over.

Across from him, Blackmer made a cutting motion with his hand across his neck. "Stand by," Cenn told Travil, and then the first officer switched his comm system to transmit only to the away team. "What is it, Commander?"

"*Pardon me, Colonel,*" Blackmer said cautiously, "*but I am concerned that you are considering acquiescing to the Ohalavaru's demand. As chief of security, I strongly recommend against such a course of action. It could be an ambush.*"

"An ambush by whom, Commander?" Cenn asked. "The crews in the outpost and aboard *Yolja* reported reading only two life-forms aboard, and our sensors have confirmed that. Even if those scans weren't accurate, you saw the size of their vessel; with all the explosives they carried with them, how many people could they have brought down here?"

"*Even without personnel, they could have prepared a trap for us,*" Blackmer pointed out.

"I understand your concerns, Commander, but what else would you have us do?" Cenn asked. "You don't want us entering through the breach, but they refuse to leave unless we go get them. Are we supposed to wait here until they change their minds?"

"*We could bring down reinforcements, shuttle in equipment to illuminate the area inside so that we can properly assess the risks,*" Blackmer suggested.

Cenn knew that the security chief was right, even despite the dangers of bringing more of the crew down into the unstable chasm. He also knew that he could not delay the apprehension of the Ohalavaru any longer. He disagreed with their beliefs, but of greater import, he did not condone their actions. He could not allow them to walk free and continue their attempts to undermine and attack the Bajoran people and their faith.

"I'm going in," Cenn decided. "Wait here. If I'm killed or taken captive, proceed with your plan to summon assistance."

"Colonel," Blackmer said, and the tone of that one word signaled his intention to oppose the first officer's plan. But then the security chief paused, and when he spoke again, his tenor had changed. *"Colonel, if you're going in, I'm going with you."*

"Very well," Cenn said. "But this time, *I* go first."

"Yes, sir," Blackmer said. *"Draco, stay here and monitor our communications. You know all of our code words."*

"Yes, sir."

"If something should happen," Blackmer told her, *"do as I've recommended."*

"Yes, sir."

The first officer once more reset his comm system. "This is Colonel Cenn to Travil Asand," he said. "My crewmate and I will come to take you into custody."

"We have set down our arms and will be waiting for you," Travil said. *"There is a drop of nearly two meters immediately inside the hole. Once you have negotiated that, you will find the footing stable."*

Cenn did not respond, but he closed the channel with the Ohalavaru. He then moved to the breach and peered inside. The lights on his helmet illuminated a featureless, flat surface that, as Travil had cautioned, appeared a couple of meters down. Cenn secured his phaser to the belt on his environmental suit, then turned and dropped to his knees so that he could enter the breach feetfirst. Blackmer bent to hold on to his arms, and the first officer scrambled inside.

Grabbing hold of the edge of the broken bulkhead—or whatever it was—Cenn lowered himself down. He waited for a disruptor bolt to slice through him, for the duplicity of the Ohalavaru to be the last thing his brain registered, but that didn't happen. He felt for the surface below him, but it remained out of reach. He imagined letting himself fall to find nothing beneath his feet, his body plummeting endlessly into the darkness.

May the Prophets protect me, he thought, and let go. He dropped only a short distance, but when his feet struck something solid, he breathed a heavy sigh of relief. "I'm down safely," he told the rest of the away team. He looked down, and in his helmet's light, he saw the same flat surface as when he'd peered through the breach. He gazed in every direction, and saw only the same thing. When he looked around, he saw distant shadows far ahead, far to each side, and far above. Directly in front of him, he spotted the lights of the two environmental-suited figures.

"I'm coming in," Blackmer said, and Cenn turned to help him. Once the security chief made it down, both men turned toward the two Ohalavaru.

"Let's go," Cenn said.

"I recommend drawing our weapons," Blackmer said.

"Agreed." Cenn pulled his phaser from where he had tucked it at his waist. Once the two men had rearmed themselves, the first officer said, "Let's go."

They started forward, the darkness all around them barely penetrated by the lights of their environmental suits. The floor beneath them—and Cenn could see and feel that it was a floor, not the ground—stretched smoothly away from them as far he could see. The space felt open to him, as though they moved through a vast hollow.

Up ahead, by degrees, the two Ohalavaru grew closer. Not completely stationary, they made no threatening moves, nor did they stray from where they stood. Once more, Cenn anticipated something happening—an attack by the Ohalavaru, or their sudden retreat—but nothing did. He and Blackmer covered half the distance to the Ohalavaru, and then half of what remained.

Suddenly, a blaze of light exploded in the darkness. Momentarily blinded, Cenn slammed his eyes shut, reflexively raising his hands up before the faceplate of his helmet. He waited for the concussion of the blast to knock him from his feet, or to tear through his environmental suit, or to vaporize his flesh in a burst of flames.

None of that happened.

"Colonel, Commander, are you all right?" Draco asked frantically. She must have seen the dramatic change in illumination through the breach.

"We're fine," Blackmer said. *"Stand by."*

Cenn opened his eyes slowly, allowing them to acclimate to the sudden brightness. He saw that the faceplate of his helmet had polarized against the glare, but it could not fully compensate for the brilliance of the light that suddenly glowed in the open space. All around them, scores of high-lumen lighting panels had been activated.

The two Ohalavaru—Travil and Nelish—started toward them, their arms held to their sides and their hands empty. Again, Cenn braced himself. The Ohalavaru continued toward them, and eventually they reached the collection of lighting panels. They walked directly up to Cenn and Blackmer. *"We surrender,"* Travil said.

Before the first officer could react, Blackmer produced two sets of restraints, which he affixed to the wrists of each man. Once he had, he reached up and adjusted his comm system. *"What is this place?"* he asked.

With the prisoners secured, Cenn gazed around. They were in a vast, cavernous chamber, its dimensions so enormous that, in some directions, the first officer could not make out its farthest reaches. A massive metal framework supported the walls and ceiling that Cenn could see. Within that space, a set of huge, complex structures twisted in various forms, all tangling together in an incredibly complicated series of joints and assemblies. It all looked and felt like a marvel of engineering, and like nothing Cenn had ever seen. In some cases, the shapes not only defied description, they challenged the limits of his ability to make sense of them—maybe even his ability to perceive them. They seemed more real, more defined in his peripheral vision than in his direct line of sight, and when he stared at them for too long, it felt as though something inside his mind distorted.

"*It's a falsework,*" Travil said. He spoke with a self-satisfied confidence that Cenn found repugnant.

"Let's go," Cenn said, and he threw a hand behind Travil and pushed him forward, toward the breach. Although he did not feel physically endangered, the first officer wanted desperately to leave the chamber. Blackmer took hold of Nelish and urged him forward as well.

"*A falsework,*" Travil continued, "*is a temporary construction onto which a main work is partially or completely built. A falsework supports the main work during construction until the main structure can stand on its own.*"

"*What are you saying?*" Blackmer asked as he and Cenn guided the Ohalavaru toward the breach. "*That Endalla was built around this . . . this falsework? That this moon is a construct and not naturally occurring?*"

"*All of that is true,*" Travil said. "*But it is not the only truth.*"

"Shut up," Cenn said. He suddenly knew what Travil would say—what he and all of his Ohalavaru comrades *wanted* to say, what they had for so long *yearned* to say—and he did not want to hear it.

"*Endalla was constructed around this falsework to hide it,*" Travil said. "*The falsework itself was an anchor upon which the Bajoran wormhole was first constructed.*"

"Shut up," Cenn said again, and that time, Travil did.

Blackmer notified Draco that they would be bringing out the Ohalavaru. They walked the rest of the way to the breach in silence. Cenn helped the first officer and Draco send Nelish Stoat out through the breach. As Cenn turned to their other prisoner, Travil stared at him from within his helmet. "*What need would gods have for a falsework?*" he said.

Cenn responded by grabbing Travil and slamming him helmet-first into the wall. The first officer felt a hand on his arm, and he realized that Blackmer had moved to stop him from doing anything more to their prisoner. Cenn took a breath and attempted to calm himself, then helped get Travil through the breach.

Outside, the darkness of the chasm seemed deeper than it had before. Broken only here and there by the lights of the environmental suits and the two vessels, the gloom surrounded the away team and their prisoners. Despite that, emerging from the subterranean chamber made Cenn feel as though he had crawled out from beneath a terrible, oppressive force.

By the time the group reached the shuttlecraft, that feeling had abandoned Cenn Desca.

22

From where Ro sat behind her desk, she regarded Cenn. He stood at the far end of her office, his back to her as he gazed out through the port into the perpetual night of space. The colonel had just returned from Endalla aboard *Defiant*, and he had come to make his report. The six Ohalavaru he'd taken into custody and brought back to the starbase had been transferred to the stockade. The Bajoran Ministry of Justice had already preferred various charges against them, including criminal trespass, illegal possession and transport of explosives, reckless endangerment, and willful destruction of property. Ro imagined that the list of crimes would grow during the extradition process. After all the difficulty she'd recently had in coaxing anybody from the Bajoran government to respond meaningfully to any of her various communications, both the Ministry of State and the Ministry of Justice had been in almost constant contact with her since she'd first informed them of the attack on Endalla. Ro had also spoken directly with First Minister Asarem, briefing her on the potentially controversial discovery and claims of the Ohalavaru.

"The . . . uh . . . security . . ." Cenn said haltingly, and then he stopped and started again. "Commander Blackmer has replaced the officers assigned to the outpost. He wanted to spell them after the incident, but he also wanted them back on Deep

Space Nine so that he could interview them in person about the events. We've also sent the *Holana* to replace the *Yolja*, which needs minor repairs."

"I see that in the preliminary report," Ro said, holding up the padd that Cenn had brought with him. She set it down on her desktop. "What I don't see are any recommendations about deploying additional forces to Endalla."

"That won't be necessary." Cenn spoke definitively. "There won't be any more attacks."

"You sound certain," Ro said. The strong words pleased the captain, not just for their content, but because they reflected the inner strength she knew Cenn to have. The episode on Endalla had clearly impacted him on a spiritual level. She had served with Cenn for nearly a decade, and in that time, she had seen him face down many challenges—and, of course, he had come through the Occupation. Though fundamentally even-tempered, he occasionally loosed stronger reactions, depending on the situation, but never before had Ro witnessed him engaged in such an emotional struggle. He maintained an equable demeanor, but she could see raw turmoil just below his professional veneer.

I should never have let him command the mission, she thought, but she also knew that she hadn't made a mistake. Cenn had convinced her of the importance to him of going to Endalla, and she understood the need to participate professionally in something that also carried personal significance. He had rewarded her trust by accomplishing the mission, despite the toll it had apparently cost him.

Cenn turned from the port and paced over to the captain's desk. "I am certain," he said. "The Ohalavaru won't attack Endalla again because they don't need to: they have succeeded in their endeavor by uncovering the . . . the *falsework*." Cenn spat the word out like a mouthful of poison.

Ro recognized the titanic, unexpected construct beneath the surface of Endalla as the wellspring of her first officer's misery, but she did not entirely understand why that should be the case. "Desca," she said, looking up at him as he stood by the front corner of her desk, "I can see that this discovery is troubling you, but just because the Ohalavaru have made a claim about the nature of the subterranean structure doesn't mean that they're right. They obviously knew, or at least suspected, that something might be there, but they only found it a short time before you arrived. They had no opportunity to study it. Before you grow too concerned about what they've said, why don't you wait for whatever conclusions Bajoran scientists draw *after* they've had a chance to examine and analyze it?"

Cenn chuckled without humor and shook his head. "I doubt that the Bajoran government will make public what we discovered today, much less allow anybody to investigate it."

The contentions surprised Ro. "I'm not sure that either First Minister Asarem or Kai Pralon will want to keep the information quiet, or even if they do, I don't know that they'll be able to."

"We'll see," Cenn said. "You told me that you've spoken only with the first minister about what the Ohalavaru found down there, and about what they assert. I'm not convinced that information will spread very far within the Bajoran government, and I wouldn't be shocked if it never even makes it to Kai Pralon."

"I don't see how that's possible," Ro said. "At this moment, First Minister Asarem might be the only Bajoran official who knows about this, but I know, you know, quite a few of our security officers know. And even if the Federation and Bajor classified the information and succeeded in limiting knowledge of the incident, there are the Ohalavaru to consider. As I understand it, their entire goal on Endalla has been to locate the underground structure and then trumpet both its existence and their interpretation of what it means. That tells me that even criminalizing the release of the information would not prevent them from speaking publicly."

Cenn's head bobbed slowly up and down, but his attention appeared to drift away from the captain. He gazed off to the side, his countenance brooding. "Maybe that will be the case," he said, more to himself than to Ro. "Maybe this can't be contained. If it is, if there is only silence about what has transpired, that in itself will speak volumes and demonstrate that the Bajoran establishment is too scared to admit what the Ohalavaru have found. And if it does come out and the first minister and the kai deny it . . ." His words faded as he spoke, but Ro thought that the monologue continued in his head.

The captain waited, but Cenn remained pensive and added nothing more. Finally, Ro said, "Desca . . . are you all right?"

Cenn's eyes came back into focus and he looked at her. "No, I'm not all right," he said. "My world . . . everything I thought I knew . . ." He didn't finish.

"This may not mean anything," Ro said, trying to console him in some way.

In a flash of motion, Cenn raised his fist and thrust it down hard on the corner of the captain's desktop. "It means *everything!*" he said, his voice rising to a shout on the final word. He struck her desk not with the fleshy side of his fist, but knuckles first. Ro heard an awful crunching noise that could only be one or more of the bones in his hand breaking.

Her shock must have shown on her face, because Cenn backtracked from his anger at once. "I'm sorry, Captain, I'm sorry."

Ro leaped up from her chair and hurried over to Cenn. He held his wounded hand tightly against his body, and she gently tugged at his arm until she could visually inspect his injuries. Cenn had bruised his knuckles badly, bloodying one of them. Two of his fingers bent at unnatural angles. "You're hurt," she said. She did not speak just about his hand. "Ro to Sector General."

"Sector General. Doctor Boudreaux here." The easy, rounded shape of his words made the starbase's chief medical officer sound languid, but Ro had seen him move at speed when the situation warranted.

"Captain," Cenn said. "You don't need to call the doctor up here. I can go to the hospital on my own." His anguish had wilted—or perhaps it had settled in for a long stay.

Ro wondered whether her first officer would actually report to Sector General if she allowed him to walk out of her office on his own, but she saw no reason that he wouldn't. "Pascal, Colonel Cenn has suffered an injury to his hand," she said. "He'll be down shortly for treatment."

"Understood," Boudreaux said. *"Have him bring his hand with him."*

"I'll do that, Doctor," Ro said, unable to keep herself from smiling at Boudreaux's consistently amusing manner. It pleased her to see that Cenn smiled as well. "Ro out."

Cenn tucked his damaged hand beneath his other arm. "I'm sorry," he said again.

"Do you want me to walk down to the hospital with you?" Ro asked.

"No, thank you, Captain," the first officer said. "It'll be embarrassing enough with just Doctor Boudreaux there."

"All right," Ro said. "If you need to talk, Desca . . . I'm here as your commanding officer, but I can also be here as your friend, if you just need somebody to listen. And maybe you should consult with Commander Matthias and have her assign you to a counselor."

"I will," Cenn said. Though declarative, the words seemed to the captain like less than a commitment. She opted to let it go—at least for the moment.

"All right," Ro said. "We'll talk later."

"Yes, Captain. Thank you." With his damaged hand still tucked under his arm, Cenn exited her office to the corridor.

Ro watched her first officer go. She recognized Cenn's distress, but she did not entirely fathom it. *But then, I'm not religious.* She understood that the Ohalavaru claims somehow threatened his faith. She guessed that evidence of the Prophets physically constructing something implied that they possessed corporeality. Or maybe just the idea of their utilizing tools or building materials or familiar techniques detracted from their godhood in Cenn's eyes.

Except that the wormhole is something physical that the Prophets supposedly built, Ro thought. There seemed a distinction to be drawn there, though. The wormhole physically existed, but it possessed a mystical quality to it, something far beyond the capability of the Federation to create. The descriptions Ro had so far read and heard about the construct beneath the surface of Endalla sounded far more prosaic.

Can it be as simple as that? Ro wondered. Could the Ohalavaru, if their claims panned out, have taken away the poetry of Cenn's beliefs? In her empty office, the captain shook her head. For her, the notion that the Prophets had toiled in the orbit of Bajor to connect their realm with that of Ro's people seemed far more befitting a god than merely looking down from on high. *And frankly, it seems far more believable.*

Ro circled around her desk and sat back down. She reactivated the computer interface on her desktop—she'd been using it when Cenn had arrived—and accessed the preliminary security status that Blackmer had filed, as well as a draft after-action report that Stinson had sent her. Since the second officer had neither commanded *Defiant* nor led the mission to Endalla, he needn't have produced any report at all, but once she read through it, she saw why he had: he expressed concern for Cenn Desca. According to Stinson, the colonel had behaved in uncharacteristic and questionable ways during the mission.

Lieutenant Commander Stinson did not hide his ambition to one day command a starship—to hold the position and rank of captain—but Ro didn't see his personal aims driving his report. She read genuine concern in his words. She also found similar sentiments in Blackmer's security status, which detailed Cenn's unwillingness to wait for reinforcements, his recklessness in essentially charging into a potentially lethal situation, and slamming somebody in his custody into a wall. Neither man sought or recommended any sort of reprimand or reprisal, but both worried about the emotional health of their crewmate.

The reports concerned the captain, as did the behavior she had seen Cenn exhibit in their meeting. In the end, he had finally regained control of his emotions, but while Ro did not equate her first officer's actions with those of the Ohalavaru, she did view his conduct as a form of zealotry. She would have to keep a watchful eye on him.

23

For the first time in months, Jefferson Blackmer woke up after having slept straight through the night. He rolled over in his bed and glanced at the chronometer he kept on a nearby shelf. When he read the time as 06:27, he thought the device must have malfunctioned, but a quick query to the computer confirmed the hour. That meant that Blackmer had not only had an uninterrupted night, but that he had slept for nearly nine hours—something he couldn't remember doing in a very long time.

In the days since the assassination of the Federation president, the security chief had been plagued by guilt and feelings of professional inadequacy, which had resulted in high levels of anxiety. He often awoke in the middle of the night to thoughts of his failures, ranging from his earliest days in Starfleet on Starbase 189, all the way up to the escape from custody of Doctor Bashir. No matter the memories that visited him upon waking, though, his mind always eventually turned to the murder of Nanietta Bacco. Blackmer had failed not only the president, not only himself and his crewmates, not even just Starfleet, but the entire Federation. That burden never left him.

Sometimes, especially in the small hours of the morning, dreams would interrupt his sleep—terrible dreams. He would often relive his mistakes, recalling them in painfully elaborate detail. Worse, his slumbering but wounded psyche frequently combined events or embellished the specifics. In the end, it always came down to one of two events: the brutal killing of President Bacco, or the fiery destruction of the original Deep Space 9.

But not last night, Blackmer thought as he rose from his bed, amazed at how rested he felt. He activated the lights, and as he made his way to the refresher, it stunned him to realize that he actually recollected another dream—a dream that had nothing to do with the Federation president or DS9 or Starfleet security. In it, he strolled across the *Ponte di Rialto* in Venezia, a young man walking hand in hand with the first woman he had ever really loved. He and Sharon stood at the apex of the ancient stone bridge, in the central portico, gazing out at the silvery white light of Luna gamboling on the waters of the *Canal Grande*. He saw the view clearly in his mind, and alone in his quarters on DS9, he felt his hand close around imaginary fingers as he envisioned Sharon standing at his side.

There was more to the dream than that, he thought, but already it slipped away from him. It hadn't been born of a memory, not exactly, because he and Sharon had never visited Italia, but during the two years they had been together before it had all gone south, they had spoken of Venezia often. For all of the negative connotations the reminiscence could have held for him—a youth now past, lost opportunities, failed romance—it nevertheless made him smile. He had not thought of Sharon in a very long time, and in the three years since he'd become chief of security on the original DS9, he'd had little opportunity for a love life. It cheered him to discover the desire for romance still firing within him.

As Blackmer showered and prepared for his shift, he thought about what lay ahead for him that day. He would continue to interrogate the Ohalavaru, and also interview the members of his staff who'd been on Endalla when the three explosives-laden vessels had descended upon it. He looked forward to all of it, feeling a renewed sense of purpose.

Nine hours of sleep will do that, he thought. He initially attributed his long, unbroken sleep to the busy day he'd had previously, but as he reflected on it further, he considered a different cause: his conversation with the captain. He not only appreciated the confidence she showed in him, he *believed* it. Ro hadn't simply heaped platitudes on him, or discounted his lost self-assurance as unwarranted. Rather, she commiserated with him, referencing her own tenure in the same position. She also revealed Starfleet Command's concerns about his job performance, and talked about her review of the work he'd done since transferring to the old station from *Perseverance*. In particular, two points she made truly helped him: that he had recommended protective screens to the president and the other dignitaries for their speeches at the dedication ceremony, and that they all rejected his advice at least in part because they expected to need protection from their enemies, not from their friends.

As Blackmer put on his uniform, a connection formed in his mind. One of the things that had recently troubled him had been Doctor Bashir's escape from detention. Blackmer recognized all the good that had come from that event: the doctor had helped solve the reproductive crisis on Andor, and like dominoes falling, that had led to new leadership for the Andorians, their return to the Federation, and then the election of President zh'Tarash. While Blackmer would not have wanted to stand in the way of any of those occurrences, he hadn't known how events would turn out, and so he had followed orders and taken Bashir into custody.

I just didn't keep him in custody.

Fully prepared for the day, Blackmer checked the chronometer and saw that he still had nearly an hour before the start of alpha shift. He thought about heading to one of the many eateries on the Plaza, but he didn't typically partake of a meal at breakfast, usually just having a piece of fruit. He went out into the living area of his quarters and selected a *pooncheen* from the bowl he kept in the center of his dining table. Before peeling the rind from the orange-red fruit, he thought of something else he could do with his spare hour. He tossed the pooncheen into the air and caught it, then exited his quarters and headed for the nearest turbolift.

When the order had come in to arrest Bashir, the doctor had been hosting a planetside medical conference on Bajor. Captain Ro took Blackmer and a security team to apprehend him, which they proceeded to do. On the way to the runabout that would carry Bashir back to DS9, the doctor incapacitated a security officer—suspiciously, his inamorata, Lieutenant Commander Sarina Douglas—and sabotaged both a runabout and *Defiant*, all of which ultimately contributed to his successful escape to Andor.

I didn't want Douglas guarding Bashir, Blackmer thought as he entered the turbolift and stated his destination. At the time, he had intimated as much to the captain, but she had overridden his concern. *And she was right to do so. How could we have a cohesive, functioning crew if we don't trust each other?*

Except that Bashir had gotten away from Douglas, which had made the security chief question, if only in his own mind, not just the loyalty of his subordinate, but also that of his commanding officer. Bashir had knocked Douglas unconscious with a ferocious blow to her face, which could simply have been his way of covering for her. *Or maybe the importance of the doctor's mission of deliverance to Andor superseded the value of his relationship with Douglas.*

Afterward, Blackmer and his staff had examined *Defiant.* Bashir's disabling of a runabout occurred during his flight from custody on Bajor, but it remained a question as to when he could have sabotaged *Defiant.* Blackmer searched for such an opportunity, including any times when the doctor had surreptitiously boarded the starship. When the investigation turned up nothing, he personally checked for any evidence of tampering by Lieutenant Commander Douglas . . . or by Captain Ro. He'd never been happier to uncover nothing.

But that means that we still don't know how Bashir managed to sabotage Defiant. Blackmer's suspicions continued to fall on Douglas, who had subsequently left the starbase. After so much time, and considering all that had happened, it might no longer matter who had actually incapacitated *Defiant,* but it could prove important to learn how they had done so.

The turbolift doors opened on the x-ring, at Docking Bay One. Blackmer passed through the security checkpoint without issue and boarded the starship. He rode a turbolift up to Deck One, then walked to the bridge, entering it through the starboard aft doors. "Good morning, Ensign," he said.

The long-maned, light-haired Caitian stood up from the command chair in the center of the bridge and turned to face Blackmer. "Good morning, sir."

The security chief made it his business to know the people who worked and lived on Deep Space 9—a tall order, given the starbase's total permanent population of thirteen thousand individuals. Blackmer actually recognized the ensign, a young man named Grenner P'Tross, but probably less because of the security chief's ability to recognize faces and more because only two Caitians served in the crew. "What's your status?"

"Standing the delta-shift watch, sir," P'Tross said, the purring quality of his speech a match for his feline-like appearance. "I have nothing to report."

"Which is just the way I like it," Blackmer said with a smile. "I'm here because I'm conducting an investigation and need access to the *Defiant*'s computer records. I'll work at one of the peripheral stations."

"Yes, sir," P'Tross said. "Can I assist in any way?"

"No, I don't think so, thank you, Ensign," Blackmer said. "As you were."

As P'Tross returned to the command chair, the security chief sat down at the nearest station along the starboard arc of the bridge. He started his efforts by bringing up the ship's boarding logs for the month leading up to and including the day of Doctor Bashir's escape. Those logs should have included a record of every individual who had been on the ship during that time period.

Once he had done that, Blackmer sent a signal back to Deep Space 9, requesting an upload of mirror files from the same set of days. While docked at the starbase, *Defiant*'s computer routinely transmitted a real-time backup to a secure data vault on DS9. Blackmer thought that if somebody had gained access to the ship, they might have been smart enough to hide their tracks by altering the logs kept on *Defiant*, but they would have found it almost impossible to do the same with the mirror files on the starbase.

Blackmer waited for the upload to complete, then worked to compare the two sets of boarding logs. He felt reasonably confident that he would turn up a discrepancy, but the records all matched precisely. He shook his head and leaned back in his chair, trying to think of what else he could try.

If nobody had altered the boarding logs, he reasoned, that meant that the records contained an entry for whoever had sabotaged *Defiant*. *We expect to need protection from our enemies, not from our friends,* the captain had said. Perhaps the culprit had authority to board the starship, but perhaps they had conducted their sabotage at a time when they hadn't been scheduled to be on *Defiant*.

Blackmer again linked to Deep Space 9's main computer. He accessed the starbase's duty rosters for the month prior to Bashir's flight from custody. He searched through it hoping to find a time when somebody had boarded *Defiant* when they were either scheduled to be elsewhere or off duty.

By the time alpha shift started that morning and he reported to the Hub, Blackmer had the name for which he'd been searching.

24

Ribbons of color spread in various widths across the great globe, each hued band punctuated by circles and swirls that betrayed the turbulent motion of the atmosphere. The fourth of seven worlds in the Larrisint system, the gas giant came dressed in earth tones—umbers and ochers, grays and whites—though it lacked anything resembling a terrestrial surface. Above the pigmented patterns, a wide, dense set of rings girded its equator.

Benjamin Sisko eyed the view with appreciation. He thought that when artists painted images of planets to convey their beautiful but alien nature, they often produced pictures that resembled Larrisint IV. Seeing the scene through the forward viewport of the shuttlecraft, he also heard the siren song of his crew's upcoming mission to the Gamma Quadrant.

"Are you sure you know where you're going?" Odo asked. The Changeling sat beside Sisko at the primary console of *Comet*, one of *Robinson*'s type-6 shuttlecraft.

"It's a secure facility, maintained in secrecy," Sisko said. "I'm gathering that its unusual location might be a part of that." Up ahead of the shuttlecraft, the rings of Larrisint IV loomed.

Once *Robinson* had arrived at the outer edge of the planetary system, Sisko had established communications with Newton Outpost, following protocols provided him by Starfleet Operations. He spoke with Lieutenant Commander Selten, the facility's chief of security. Selten, a Vulcan of distinguished appearance who looked to be in his middle years, directed Sisko to maintain *Robinson*'s position outside the system, and to bring Odo to the outpost in a shuttlecraft. Subspace scramblers prevented the comm signal from being traced to the facility, and the security chief declined to identify even its general location. Instead, Selten instructed the captain to travel to the fifth planet in the system. Once there, the Vulcan directed him to a point just beyond the rings of the fourth planet.

"Selten to Comet.*"*

Sisko opened communications in the shuttlecraft. "*Comet* here, this is Sisko."

"Captain, I am deploying a navigational beacon," Selten said. *"Please follow it at your present velocity. When a tractor beam takes hold of your shuttlecraft, please shut down your engines. Your vessel will be pulled into our landing bay."*

"Acknowledged," Sisko said. He studied the sensor panel. "We have detected the beacon and are adjusting course to follow it."

"Confirming your course change," Selten said. *"Stand by."* The communications panel emitted a chirp, indicating the channel had been closed on the transmitting end.

"I couldn't just beam over?" Odo asked, his tone even more exasperated than usual.

"As I understand it, the outpost has been permanently shielded in materials that prohibit transport," Sisko said.

"I'm sure that will come in handy if there's ever a fire." Odo's normally gruff manner had graduated to full-throated scorn. After another minute, he said, "Captain, we appear to be headed directly into the planet's rings."

"I see that," Sisko said. "That's where the beacon is emanating from. I don't know if that's another feint to disguise the outpost's true location, or if that's where the outpost actually is."

Odo grunted, whether in appreciation or derision, Sisko could not tell. "I suppose that placing an outpost inside planetary rings as densely packed as those might make it difficult for unwanted visitors to even find it, let alone safely reach it."

As the shuttlecraft neared the rings, Larrisint IV grew to fill the entire port. Sisko activated a display on the bulkhead beside him, then set it to show a magnified view of the rings. Amid the dust, a considerable number of small, rocky objects became visible.

Odo's right, Sisko thought. *That's a hell of a place to put an outpost.*

Five minutes later, as the shuttlecraft closed on the rings, an expanding cone of gray-white rays reached out from their midst. *Comet* shuddered as the tractor beam took hold of it, and the captain powered down the shuttlecraft's drive systems. The low hum that provided an undercurrent of sound throughout the journey vanished, leaving the cabin in eerie silence.

Let's hope it stays that way, Sisko thought. The last thing he wanted to hear was the explosive noise of an errant boulder slamming into the hull.

Sisko watched through the port in fascination as the shuttlecraft drew ever nearer the rings. Eventually, a larger object became visible in a narrow gap within them. "There," he said, pointing. "I think that must be a shepherd moon."

"I don't know what that is," Odo said.

"It's a small moon that orbits a planet outside its rings or in a gap between them," Sisko explained. "Its gravitational field helps to define the edges of the rings."

"And you think that's our destination?" Odo asked.

Sisko checked the navigation panel. "Right now," he said, "that's where we're headed."

Fifteen minutes later, the tractor beam pulled the shuttlecraft into a crater on the surface of the shepherd moon.

*　　　*　　　*

THE TURBOLIFT DESCENDED a considerable distance before slowing. When its doors finally opened, they revealed a long corridor that, unlike the complex above, did not appear to be of Starfleet design. Odo thought it more resembled a medical facility, with its unadorned metal surfaces and tile floors.

Not a medical facility, Odo thought. *A laboratory.* He had certainly spent enough years in such places to know.

As he exited the turbolift, a woman stepped forward. She stood about a meter and five-eighths, and had fiery red hair that tumbled down past her shoulders in waves. She wore a white lab coat, open over civilian clothes—black slacks and an aquamarine blouse. While she appeared human, Odo would not make such a presumption.

The woman smiled and opened her hands in greeting, though she made no move to shake his hand. "Mister Odo, thank you so much for agreeing to meet with us," she said. "I'm Doctor Norsa. Welcome to Newton Outpost."

Norsa, Odo thought. *Not a human name . . . Argelian, maybe.* "Thank you, and please just call me Odo." He didn't care much for being addressed with humanoid honorifics. Depending on the situation, he allowed some people to do so, but when he met somebody for the first time, he often tried to stop them. He'd made the mistake of not objecting when he'd initially been called *constable,* and he'd been encumbered with that title for years.

Norsa peered past Odo and into the turbolift. "Thank you, Commander," she said.

Lieutenant Commander Selten had escorted Odo down from the upper level of the complex. The security chief met the *Robinson* shuttlecraft when it set down on the shepherd moon, inside a hangar concealed beneath the shadows at the bottom of a crater. Selten confirmed Captain Sisko's identity via both fingerprint and retina scans, and he verified Odo's status as a Changeling by drawing a sample of his faux blood.

Despite taking such pains to identify the two visitors to the outpost, Selten had denied Sisko permission to leave the hangar and enter the facility, since he had no business there other than to deliver Odo. The captain took no exception to the rigid security procedures. Indeed, he seemed quite satisfied to depart at once.

Odo had thanked Sisko, and then he'd watched as the hatches that formed the roof of the hangar and the floor of the crater parted to allow *Comet* to return to space. After turning over management of the *Robinson* shuttlecraft's departure to another member of his staff, Selten accompanied Odo into an installation recognizably Starfleet, even beyond the personnel stationed there. They passed through a series of checkpoints in a heavily fortified structure. Along the way, Selten said little and kept a stoic demeanor, though Odo could not tell if he did so because he was a Vulcan or because he was a security chief.

Down inside the facility, Selten said, "You're welcome, Doctor." He touched a control and the turbolift doors closed, leaving Odo alone in the corridor with Norsa.

"I know that you've come a long way from Deep Space Nine, so you must be tired," she said. "I can show you to the quarters we've prepared for you." She glanced down, first at Odo's hands and then at his feet, and he realized that she must be looking for whatever belongings he had brought with him.

"Actually, I regenerated in my cabin onboard the *Robinson* not that long ago," Odo said. "I also did not bring anything with me."

"No, of course, you didn't," Norsa said, flustering. "You're a Changeling; you must have few material needs." When Odo said nothing, the woman pressed on. "Forgive me, Odo. I did not mean to offend you in any way. We get very few visitors here, and so I think my manners may be a bit off. Frankly, as a research scientist, I'm not sure that I'm all that well socialized in the first place." She offered a weak smile that seemed equal parts humor and discomfort. "Also, to my knowledge, I have never before met a shape-shifter."

"You haven't offended me," Odo said. "May I ask: what is your position here?"

Norsa shook her head and rolled her eyes. "See: not properly socialized. My official titles are head of biological research and chief of staff. Technically, I run this place."

"Technically?"

"Yes, because we're all scientists down here, so we primarily operate by consensus," she said. "Also, I think Commander Selten and the rest of the Starfleet personnel up above believe that they're in charge."

"You're not in Starfleet, then?"

"Newton Outpost falls under the jurisdiction of the Federation Department of Science, but this facility is run as a cooperative venture with Starfleet." Norsa looked over her shoulder, down the corridor, and said, "If you don't need to rest, and if there's nothing else I can provide you with right now, would you like to meet some of the other scientists working on this project?"

Norsa's reference to the possible shape-shifter as a function of her research rankled Odo. "If you don't mind, I would be more interested to meet the 'project.'"

Odo's repeating of Norsa's impersonal word seemed to shock her. "I've offended you again," she said, although she did not sound apologetic. "I'm sorry if that's the case, Odo, but I want you to understand some things. First of all, the majority of the scientists here believe that there is virtually no chance that the specimen collected by the *Nova* crew is alive, and only a slightly better chance that it ever was. Secondly, we asked that you be invited to assist us in making that determination because, in the unlikely event that the specimen *is* alive, we do not wish to risk harming it or causing it pain. We are aware of what you endured at the hands of Doctor Mora, and we don't want to make the same mistakes that he did. So while you can take offense at my reference to the possible shape-shifter as our 'project' or as a 'specimen,' doing so contributes nothing to our efforts here, and may even prove counterproductive. I think we all have the same goals, so perhaps it would be helpful if we behaved as though we were on the same side."

"I can assure you that I am on no side but that of justice," Odo said. "And the truth is that I don't know what your goals are, so I can't tell you if they're the same as mine."

Norsa nodded. "That's true," she said. "As a research scientist, my goal is always the pursuit of knowledge. That's all it is here. The *Nova* crew found something out in the universe and we want to know what it is. If we find that it's a life-form, then is it alive? If it's alive, then is it intelligent? Can we communicate with it? If it's no longer alive, then how did it die? How did it live? Are there more of them out there? And if it's not a life-form, what is it?"

"You have more questions than I do," Odo said. "I have been searching for more of my people, and I have come here in the hopes of finding one. Short of that, if it is not a Changeling but it is a shape-shifter of some kind, I am interested in helping communicate with it for the reasons you mentioned: to avoid it coming to harm or experiencing unnecessary pain."

"Then I'd say we have enough of our goals in common to work together," Norsa told him. "And to avoid being offended by each other."

Odo recognized the peace offering. "You are perhaps not the only one not well socialized," he said, and though he'd intended the statement as a droll means of easing the tension, he realized its verity. "I have become accustomed to experiencing a certain . . . casual disregard . . . when I am among humanoids—a point of view centered on their immutable form."

"I think I understand that," Norsa said. "I mean, I can understand why humanoids would behave in such a way—after all, we cannot alter our forms at will—but I also see how such perspectives, when ignorant of your own, would be difficult for you to deal with." She paused, then said, "Shall we begin again?"

"Please."

"May I show you the specimen?" she asked. "And after you've seen it, I will introduce you to the other scientists studying the potential shape-shifter."

"Thank you."

Norsa motioned down the corridor, and the two started away from the turbolift. The soft soles of Norsa's shoes made only a faint sound on the tiles. Odo moved in silence, adjusting the density of his feet as he moved in order to absorb their impact on the floor without generating any noise. He had developed the ability long ago, and had refined it in his dealings with Quark, whose impressively sensitive ears provided the Changeling a challenge.

He walked the length of the corridor with Norsa. He saw no doors, ports, or openings of any kind in either of the lateral bulkheads. The bright lighting panels overhead lent the area a stark, antiseptic quality.

The corridor ended at a large, imposing metal door. Norsa activated a panel beside it, keyed in a code, then underwent fingerprint and retina scans. The door issued a series of metallic clicks and clangs before ultimately withdrawing into the bulkhead. It looked as thick as the hull of a starship.

They entered a square room as uninviting as the corridor they'd just left. As the metal door sealed itself closed behind them, Odo saw two smaller, standard doors in each of the bulkheads to his left and right, and two on either side of another large metal door directly ahead. Atop control panels beside each door, small signs provided only the simplistic labels CORRIDOR 1 through CORRIDOR 7.

"Our offices are down Corridor Six, and our quarters and living areas are down Corridor Seven," Norsa said, pointing to her right. "All of the others lead to laboratories and support facilities. We'll be heading to Corridor Four." She gestured forward, then moved to the center door in the wall ahead of them, where she again went through an identification process to gain access.

Once inside, Odo saw another long corridor, broader than the last. On both sides, doors alternated with wide transparent panels. Lights of various colors and intensities spilled through some of the ports, interrupting the more subdued illumination of the corridor.

"This is where we keep foreign objects brought to the outpost for study," Norsa said. "These first two doors—" She pointed to both sides of the corridor. "—lead to storage rooms for environmental suits and other equipment. The other doors open into decontamination chambers, which can also function as airlocks, in cases where we need to maintain an object in a vacuum. The decon chambers allow access into our specimen compartments, which are visible through the viewports."

They began walking, and as they passed the ports, Odo saw consoles below them, doubtless to control the environment within the compartments. Through the first port, he saw a tall *C*-shaped bracket, with vibrating streaks of white light emanating from each tip and ending at a cubic object hanging suspended between them. In another compartment stood a stone obelisk, its visible fascia covered in faded runes. A third contained a metallic disc, no more than half a meter across. It turned out that most of the compartments sat dark, and even some of the others appeared empty.

Odo kept waiting to see what he hoped to recognize as one of his own kind—whether a Changeling or some other form of shape-shifter. He also realized that he knew very little about it. President Bacco had been sparing with details when she had offered him the opportunity to visit Newton Outpost.

"Where was the possible shape-shifter found?" Odo asked.

"The *Nova* crew were surveying a star system called Capricorn Arday," Norsa said.

"They were on a survey mission and just happened to run across it?"

"They had been led there by evidence of a massive burst of energy within the system," Norsa said. "Once there, the *Nova* crew were unable to determine either the source or the cause of their readings, but they did detect some subspace anomalies, which they traced to an asteroid belt."

"The possible shape-shifter was found on an asteroid?" That seemed suspicious to Odo, though he could not quite say why.

"Yes," Norsa said. "When they were studying the abnormal subspace readings, their sensors had difficulty identifying the material making up a part of the surface of a particular asteroid. They attempted to beam a sample up to the ship for analysis, but were unable to establish a transporter lock."

The information confused Odo. "Shape-shifters are not impervious to transporter beams," he said, although he subsequently wondered if he could recast his own composition in some way to accomplish such a feat. As they passed another port, he saw a crescent-shaped net suspended in midair.

"The *Nova* crew opted to beam two of their scientists over to the asteroid in environmental suits, in the hopes that they could collect a sample," Norsa went on. "They found the material firm but malleable, as though in a state between solid and liquid."

"That certainly doesn't sound like a deceased Changeling," Odo said. When one of his people perished, their physical form essentially turned to dust. Concentrating on his conversation with Norsa, Odo no longer peered through the ports they passed.

"They didn't know what it was, so they attempted to collect a part of it as a sample, but were unable to separate even the smallest portion from the whole."

Odo's hope dimmed. Most of what Norsa had told him did not correspond to the characteristics of his people. "So because they couldn't take a piece of what they found, they took all of it."

"That's right," Norsa said. "They managed to pull it from the surface of the asteroid using several tractor beams."

"*Several* tractor beams?"

"Yes," Norsa said. "They found the specimen curved around the asteroid, almost as though gripping it, and they determined that they needed to draw it away in multiple places in order to remove it. They used the starship and several of its auxiliary craft, and conveyed it into the *Nova*'s hangar bay. There, they performed additional testing. They succeeded in analyzing some cellular material, which they discovered contained encoding very similar to your own morphogenic matrix."

"Then it *is* a shape-shifter," Odo concluded.

"Or was, maybe," Norsa said. "We're not sure. The matrix does not completely match that of the Changelings, and it also appears that it may be incomplete. We think it more likely that, if the specimen was a living being, it marked an evolutionary stage short of your own people's."

"I see," Odo said.

Ahead of them, the corridor ended at an intersection. When they reached it, Odo saw that two other corridors marched away to the left and right, and a set of steps rose directly ahead. Norsa began up the steps.

"This way." As Odo followed, she said, "We are keeping the possible shape-shifter in our largest storage compartment. It was not initially of sufficient size, and it took an urgent, round-the-clock effort by the Corps of Engineers to expand it."

"Not *large* enough?" Odo said, surprised. Perhaps the *Nova* crew had run across not one shape-shifter, but many, locked together in a version of the Great Link. "How big is the potential Changeling?"

"Big," Norsa said as they reached the top of the stairs. She pointed directly ahead.

Odo moved to the viewing port there—just one of many extending away in both directions. He found himself looking down into a compartment at least ten meters in depth. It reached perhaps twice that measure in width, and he could not tell how far into the distance it went—at least fifty meters, he estimated, perhaps more.

Whatever the *Nova* crew had found, it easily filled the footprint of the space it occupied. It resembled a great mass of silvern metal that had been melted, spilled, and then resolidified as it spattered. Perhaps as high as a meter or two, its surface rose and fell in motionless waves, like the surface of a lake that has been flash frozen. Its color did not resemble the golden-orange hues of his own people in their natural state, but it also made no sense to entirely judge a shape-shifter by its appearance. It had rounded but irregular contours, and appeared asymmetric. The main portion of its form held a slight curve to it, and Odo imagined it hugging tightly to the asteroid on which it had been found.

Hugging tightly would imply purpose, he thought, but then realized that, rather than intention, it could have been reflex. Plants bent toward sunlight, but that did not make them sentient. Perhaps Norsa was correct in suggesting an intermediary evolutionary step.

"Have you tried to communicate with it?" Odo wanted to know.

"In various and very rudimentary ways," Norsa said. "Flashing the lights in a mathematical sequence, using notes on a scale, that sort of thing. We've seen no reaction."

"There are a number of more involved techniques we might try," Odo said, thinking that, in the end, nothing would tell him more than attempting to link with the huge mass.

"That's why we asked for you to join us, Odo," Norsa said. "We believed that you could help."

"I'm sure I can," Odo said. One way or another, he would help them identify what the *Nova* crew had brought to Newton Outpost.

"I think the next thing we should do is sit down with the project team," Norsa said, "so that they can detail for you all of our efforts with the specimen—not just in trying to communicate with it, but also in our overall analysis."

"Yes," Odo said. "Yes, that would be a good place to start."

"Excellent," Norsa said. "Knowing that you would be arriving today, all of the scientists involved carved time out of their schedules to meet with you. Let's head back to a conference room and I'll gather them together." Norsa started down the steps.

Odo followed, after taking one long last look into the oversized specimen compartment. He didn't know if he saw a Changeling, or a link of Changelings. He didn't know if it was a shape-shifter of any kind. He only knew that he felt excitement about the prospect of finding out.

He had been looking for more of his people for a long time.

III

Ash

25

"We are here."

Iliana Ghemor transmitted her message to the entirety of the Ascendant armada on the heels of the course correction she had earlier sent. Her simple statement provided an answer to the queries that had come in when one Quester after another had realized that the new heading would take them not past the star system ahead, but into it. They all wanted to know why, their interest clearly more than idle curiosity. They did not at that time need to renew their sustenance or fuel, they never sought rest and relaxation. They had only one reason to enter a star system: to purge the universe of another heretical blight. That is, they had only one reason, unless . . .

Ghemor had been able to hear the Ascendants' emotions even in their musical speech: curiosity, yes, and anxiety, but in most cases, anticipation and excitement. Many interpreted their sacred writings to mean that they would find the entrance to the Fortress of the True within a solar system. The course change therefore raised the question in their minds, and they had posed it to her: *Are we here?*

Ghemor answered them in her role as the Fire: "We are here."

In the narrow cockpit of Grand Archquester Votiq's ship, she watched on the display before her as navigational sensors showed the Ascendant armada approaching the Idran system and, within it, she knew, the Bajoran wormhole. Scores of days had passed since she had begun the final leg of her journey, a mere trice when measured against the years and years of her suffering. She would at last find peace—once she had seen her vengeance realized.

Aboard Votiq's vessel, Ghemor would lead the Ascendant

forces to the threshold of the wormhole. She had already fore-
cast its opening to them as the gates of the Fortress of the True
being thrown wide. When the great subspace bridge unfolded
in its swirling maelstrom of blue and white light, the spectacle
would send the Ascendants into paroxysms of awe. They would
follow her into the wormhole, and then through it, into the
Alpha Quadrant.

Ghemor knew that Bajor's Prophets would not stop her or
her armada. They had spoken to her once, and after recognizing her as the Fire, they had sent her to the gathering of the
Ascendants. They knew that Ghemor had her role to play, and
her destiny to achieve. She would not be denied—and if anybody tried to do so, she would burn them down, be they person
or Prophet. With not just an arsenal, but a metaweapon at her
disposal, she possessed the means.

Once through the wormhole, the Ascendants would find
themselves not before the Unnameable, but in the Bajoran system. During the voyage, Ghemor had already preached to her
followers that they might have one more act to perform for their
gods, one final sacrament before being held in judgment. She
would lead the Ascendants to Bajor and have them unleash fire
upon its surface, laying waste to its populace. Once the annihilation had begun, Ghemor would travel to Deep Space 9 and
confront Kira Nerys with a terrible truth: that the responsibility
for the obliteration of the Bajoran people fell at the captain's
feet. The Fire—once and again a Cardassian, for too long a
Bajoran—would revel in the agony that would burn through
Kira. In the end, the woman to blame for all of Ghemor's misery would plead for her own death.

As the navigational display showed the armada nearing the
star system, a tone rang out, a signal Ghemor had come to know
as indication of an incoming transmission. The Grand Archquester toggled a switch on his control panel, and the voice of
another Ascendant filled the cockpit. Ghemor recognized the
musical speech of an Archquester, Seltiq, even before she identified herself. The Ascendant, the next eldest after Votiq, noted

that the armada had entered a region of the galaxy that had not long ago shifted location, and that the system ahead matched the configuration of the historical home of the blasphemous Eav'oq.

Back before she had fallen into the wormhole, Ghemor had learned about Idran. She saw a report about the entire star system moving more than three light-years in a flash, to encompass the Gamma Quadrant terminus of the Bajoran wormhole. She had utilized that information to navigate for the Ascendant armada.

Ghemor had also read of the Eav'oq and their reemergence. During the gathering of the Ascendants, she had heard talk about them, about how the last few of their number had long ago escaped a crusade and gone into hiding. She also heard rumors that, after millennia, the heretics might have returned.

As the Ascendant armada entered the system, Votiq received a message from one knight reporting that he had just encountered a communications relay floating in space, which he had immediately destroyed. More and more transmissions of a different sort followed, all of them referencing Idran and the Eav'oq. When their ships drew close enough to scan the fourth planet, they detected a single city on its surface, populated by a thousand or so life-forms. It took virtually no time for Ascendants across the armada to conclude that the Eav'oq had indeed returned from their self-imposed exile. Calls rang out in the Grand Archquester's ship for the immediate destruction of the city.

Votiq looked to the Fire for guidance. Ghemor wanted only to go on, to reach the wormhole and then Bajor, and to launch the attack that would avenge her. She considered telling the Grand Archquester to order the armada to bypass Idran IV and the Eav'oq, but how could she? On the brink of the Fortress of the True, the Ascendants wanted to do as she had suggested: to take one last action to demonstrate their worthiness to be judged by the True. In message after message to Votiq, Ghemor could hear the consensus of Questers and Archquesters that they must expunge the blasphemy of the Eav'oq, who poisoned the universe with their contemptible faith. If she tried to stop them, she feared that, even with her status as the Fire, she might jeopardize her control of the zealots before she could use them to exact her retribution on the Bajorans and Kira.

Among the many voices reaching out to the Grand Archquester, Ghemor heard Aniq's join the chorus. *"We must spill Eav'oq blood until all their bodies have been emptied,"* the young knight proclaimed. Her voice contained no anger, but it emerged from the comm system in Votiq's ship tainted by a quality far more dangerous and unpredictable: religious fervor.

Fearing that she could lose the asset she most valued, Ghemor operated the communications console to isolate a channel to Aniq's ship. "Aniq, this is the Fire. You wish to punish the Eav'oq for their vile heresy."

"I do," Aniq said.

"And do you wish to lead the effort?"

"Yes!" To Ghemor, Aniq's passion sounded just shy of madness.

"It is but one city," Ghemor said. "Take ten ships. Leave nothing of the Eav'oq but ashes."

"I will do my duty," Aniq said.

"Do not use the metaweapon," Ghemor told her. "It is not necessary." She concentrated on maintaining the air of command, as well as a sense of pragmatism, in her voice. So close to her goal, it would not do to lose control. "Bring it to the Grand Archquester's ship so that we may keep it safe during the course of your attack."

"So says the Fire," Aniq said, *"and so shall I do."*

Ghemor closed the channel, then checked the sensor readouts. Throughout their journey, she had kept watch on Aniq's ship and the valuable cargo it towed. She observed as Aniq broke formation from the ranks, and as other ships joined it. For a terrible moment, Ghemor thought that the squadron of ten vessels would turn at once for the planet, but then she saw Aniq's ship altering course.

Moments later, the young knight contacted the Grand Archquester to say that her vessel had arrived beside his. Votiq activated a tractor beam and took possession of the metaweapon. Aniq departed, the lead ship of the ten that would assault the lone city on Idran IV.

From what she had learned of the Eav'oq, Ghemor expected that the squadron would not require much time to achieve their goal—and if they did, Ascendants on thousands of other vessels stood prepared to back them up. It would therefore not be long before they continued their journey. Although the Ascendants might be disturbed when they emerged from the wormhole without having been judged by their gods, Ghemor realized that she would be able to utilize their desire to eradicate heretics to her advantage. Ten ships attacking a single city of only a thousand would not fulfill the bloodlust of all the knights in the armada, and she would announce to them that it had not satisfied the True. When she offered them all of Bajor and its four billion heretics, they would descend on the planet in a frenzy of destruction.

In the cockpit of the Grand Archquester's vessel, Ghemor smiled.

26

Lieutenant Prynn Tenmei soared above the rolling green expanses of Nanietta Bacco Park. Below, crewmates and civilians teemed in the beautiful surroundings. Some strolled along the paths that meandered through the grounds, some picnicked, some played. Here and there, Tenmei saw heads turned up in her direction, or somebody pointing toward her. Although some members of the Deep Space 9 crew enjoyed making use of the low-gravity envelopes that crowned the park, nobody spent as much time on the wing as she did. For her, the experience embodied the sort of visceral freedom that she had sought for most of her life. From skydiving to surfing, from BASE jumping to white-water rafting, she craved not just the exhilaration that speed delivered, but the sensation of leaving behind all encumbrances.

As Tenmei neared the circular edge of the park, she threw her left wing down, tipped her right one up, and sent herself into a banking turn. She loved the new wings, a gift that Quark had brought to her cabin the previous evening. At first, when she opened her door to find the barkeep standing there holding a large gift-wrapped box in his arms, she thought that he had come to give her a present himself, which she found not only unexpected, but strange. Her surprise and confusion must have shown on her face, because Quark hastily announced that he had been contracted to oversee the shipment of the package to DS9, and to deliver it to her.

"Who's it from?" Tenmei had asked.

"The services were requested anonymously."

Tenmei had squinted at Quark. "You accept packages from people without knowing their identity?"

"They paid up front, which is all I needed to know," Quark had told her. "The package was inspected by customs when it arrived on the starbase, so you don't have to worry about it being a bomb or anything like that."

Tenmei had not considered that the box might contain something dangerous, and she'd wondered what it said about Quark that the possibility had occurred to him. She took the box from the Ferengi and nearly overbalanced when she did so. The package weighed far less than she'd expected. She set it down in the middle of the deck in the living area of her quarters and unwrapped it. She examined the exterior of the box, which contained no identifying markings and no shipping data. Tenmei supposed that Quark could have removed such information, or even repackaged the gift, but she suspected that it had actually made its way to DS9 through unusual channels.

When she'd opened the box, Tenmei had found a series of long, thin metal rods—some straight, some curved, each extremely light-weight and precision-engineered—as well as two rolls of a beautiful gossamer material. She unspooled the gossamer and saw immediately that they possessed a winglike shape. She searched the bottom of the box for assembly instructions and found them, but she also spotted a small envelope.

Tenmei had eagerly retrieved what she'd hoped would be a card from her unknown gift-giver. She tore the envelope open to find only an unsigned note inside that carried peculiar words of caution: DO NOT USE ABOVE KINGMAN RAPIDS. To anybody else, the warning would have seemed oddly specific, perhaps even cryptic, but Tenmei understood it at once. She recalled that she had been in a holosuite, enjoying a white-water rafting program that reproduced the Kingman River on Izar, when she had been interrupted by a friend asking her for a favor—a *big* favor. The note contained just the warning and nothing else, but the gift could only be a thank-you for what she had done for Sarina Douglas—and, by extension, for Doctor Bashir.

Down below, just to the right, the park's lake rippled lightly in the gentle, manufactured breeze. Several people swam, she saw, while two men sat side by side on the bank, holding hands, their pant legs rolled up and their feet dangling in the water. She also noticed—

Sudden motion to her left startled Tenmei, and she whipped her head around in that direction. To her surprise, another flyer had joined her above the park. It shocked her even more to see that the person who had donned a pair of wings was Ro Laren. In the three months since Deep Space 9 had become fully operational, Tenmei had never known the captain to fly. She wondered if Ro had decided to try it as a means of coping with all that had happened on the starbase, and the tremendous responsibilities heaped upon her by having to oversee such a complex, heavily populated, and heavily visited facility.

Tenmei smiled at the captain. Ro nodded, then lifted her hands behind her back and kicked her legs up, sending her into a dive. She plummeted for only a moment before she contorted her body in a way too quick for Tenmei to make sense of, then swept upward in an arc, until she executed a vertical loop. The lieutenant felt her mouth drop open. She had yet to attempt such a maneuver.

After her impressive aerial display, the captain headed for the nearest of the four designated landing zones, where the low-gravity field above the park reached all the way to the ground. She landed gently. Tenmei followed, alighting just after Ro.

"Wow," Tenmei said as the captain began detaching her wings. "I thought I was the best flyer on Deep Space Nine, Captain, but that was quite something."

"Thank you," Ro said. "I thought that might get your attention."

"You got my attention *and* my admiration," Tenmei said, shrugging out of her own wings. "You moved so quickly, I couldn't even see how you did what you did. When have you had time to practice that?"

"Practice?" Ro said with a smile. "I haven't done that in years, since a visit I made to Izar's Shroud."

As the captain clapped her wings together and hoisted them easily onto one shoulder, Tenmei felt a twinge of anxiety. She had just been thinking of her holosuite program that re-created a setting on Izar. Was it mere coincidence that Ro had just mentioned the planet's perpetually dark moon?

In her mind, Tenmei scoffed at her own paranoia. *That wasn't even that much of a coincidence.*

"Something wrong?" Ro asked.

"No," Tenmei said. "I'm just hoping that I can get you to teach me how to do that."

"I'd be happy to," Ro said. "I guess that'll just depend on our schedules."

Tenmei tilted her head to one side, confused, because both she and the captain worked alpha shift. Ro didn't see her expression, though, because she had already begun walking away. Once more, Tenmei followed her, all the way to the exterior of the park and through the door that led to the officers' lounge. By the time the lieutenant caught up to Ro, the captain had handed her wings over to the attendant, a Bajoran man named Devla Fol. Tenmei did the same, then tagged along after Ro across the lounge.

"Are you by any chance free tomorrow night, Captain?"

"At the moment, I have no plans," Ro said. The statement did not sound entirely inviting.

The captain headed for the turbolift. Tenmei hesitated, thinking she might like to shower before leaving, but she hadn't been flying in the park long enough even to work up a sweat. That made her realize that Ro must have flown for only a couple of minutes, otherwise Tenmei would have seen her. Still fascinated by the aerial feat the captain had accomplished, Tenmei entered the turbolift with her.

"Where are you headed?" Ro asked.

"Actually, that all just happened so quickly, I'm sort of mesmerized by it," Tenmei said. "I was hoping that I could talk to you about your maneuver out there."

"Of course," Ro said, and then, to the turbolift, "Captain's office." The turbolift whirred into motion.

Tenmei had several immediate questions about how Ro had performed her acrobatic move, but before she could give voice to one, the captain asked, "How are your hands?"

"My hands?" Tenmei echoed, confused. "Do you mean from flying?" She held her hands out in front of her, palms up.

"No," Ro said. "I mean from the injuries you sustained aboard the *Defiant*."

Tenmei felt a jolt of anxiety rush through her. The captain had referred to the burns and abrasions to her hands that she'd suffered when the bottom half of her flight control console aboard *Defiant* had exploded. That had been two and a half months earlier, during the DS9 crew's abortive pursuit of Doctor Bashir. It had also been the result of sabotage to the ship that Tenmei herself had perpetrated—the favor that she had done for Sarina Douglas.

"My hands are fine," she said, holding them toward the captain so that she could see. Ro didn't bother to look. "Doctor Boudreaux fixed me up that day."

"That's good," Ro said. "A great deal of good resulted from Doctor Bashir's ability to evade capture—not so much for Julian, but for the Andorians and the Federation."

"I guess that's true," Tenmei said. She tried to mete out her words without betraying her caution. She couldn't quite tell—and perhaps she wasn't supposed to be able to tell—but she thought that Ro might be tacitly approving of what she'd done.

"It would have been a shame if all of that good had depended on you getting seriously hurt," the captain said.

Tenmei shrugged with one shoulder. "Considering what ended up happening with the Andorians, it might have been worth it." Tenmei had rigged the flight control console on *Defiant* in part for the sake of the Andorian people—Sarina had told her that Doctor Bashir had been on the verge of a breakthrough in resolving their reproductive crisis—but she had also done it for her friend. She had intended her sabotage to physically injure nobody but herself, but she had also taken pains to find the middle ground between making it look dangerous and making it genuinely dangerous. She'd expected to come away with wounds, but not untreatable wounds.

"If you'd been seriously injured, it would have impacted this starbase," Ro said. "I could have temporarily or even permanently lost my primary flight controller. If you couldn't continue in Starfleet, or worse, if you'd been killed, I would have lost a friend."

Tenmei wanted to tell the captain that none of that could have happened, that she had carefully planned her alterations to *Defiant*'s conn. But she couldn't. Instead, she said nothing.

The turbolift continued its journey, until it at last slowed as it reached the top of the starbase. The doors opened onto a short corridor. Ro and Tenmei walked to its end, and then turned left, through the doors to the captain's office.

Once inside, Ro spun crisply on her heel to face Tenmei, the action as swift and startling as when the captain had flown into a vertical loop. "I don't care how meticulous you were in your planning, you could've gotten hurt," she said, her voice hard. "Or you could've gotten other members of the crew hurt."

"Captain, I—"

"Don't deny it," Ro warned her.

"No, I wasn't going to," Tenmei said. "I was going to say that some things are worth taking risks for."

Ro turned and stalked toward her desk. When she looked around, she said, "Of course some risks are worth taking. We wouldn't be standing in an artificial environment in the vacuum and absolute zero of space if that weren't the case. It's also not my point." She paced back over to Tenmei. "What you did is a court-martial offense. You could even be extradited to a civilian court. You were never going to be able to get away with it on your own. Frankly, you're fortunate to have made it this long without being caught. If you had been less expert in performing your sabotage, or if you hadn't intimidated Ensign Crosswhite, or if . . . if I didn't trust you so much, you'd probably already be in the stockade."

Tenmei tried to take in everything the captain had said, but mention of a court-martial and the stockade undercut her ability to process much else. As much as she'd told herself that she'd been willing to take a risk for her friend, she had never believed that she would be found out. The thought rose in her mind that she would need her father's help, only to realize in the next terrible moment that he had been dead for years. Even so long after the fact, she still missed him more than she could express.

"Is that where I'm headed next?" she finally managed to say. "To the stockade?"

Ro regarded her for a long moment, as though trying to read something in her face. Finally, the captain moved behind her desk, where she sat down. "You *should* be in the stockade," she said. "But I don't want to put you there."

"Captain—"

"Don't," Ro said, holding up the flat of her hand. "There's nothing you can say to me now to put this right. And there's nothing you will ever be able to say to put it right. But there is something you can do."

Anything, Tenmei thought, but she chose to do as the captain had bidden and not speak.

"You can trust me, Prynn," Ro said. "You can trust me

because, up until now, I've trusted you. I have a crew of twenty-five hundred; I *have* to trust people. And if I can't trust somebody, then I can't have them serving under me."

Tenmei looked down at her own boots. She felt ashamed, but if she had to do it all over again, could she have gone to Ro? Would she have? Forgetting about whether she trusted the captain or the captain trusted her, or even whether or not the captain would have agreed with what she'd wanted to do, would Tenmei have wanted to risk Ro's career by making her complicit in such an endeavor? As she looked back up at the captain, the lieutenant had to admit that she didn't know.

"Prynn, it's not as true of me now, but there was a time in my life when I was no stranger to controversial actions, including disobeying orders when I thought I knew better. It turned out that I didn't always know better, and it cost me, and it cost other people even more." Ro leaned forward and folded her hands atop her desk. "I can't promise that if you'd come to me with your plan to sabotage the *Defiant* that I would have agreed with you. But I would have listened, maybe offered up a different plan. Or maybe I would have stopped you. But whatever we ended up doing or not doing, we would be in it together."

"I'm sorry."

"Good," Ro said. She parted her hands and slapped them onto her desk. "I won't be able to teach you my flying loop tomorrow night because you'll be asleep in your quarters."

"Sir?"

"Starting tomorrow and for the next thirty days, you'll be standing the delta-shift watch aboard the *Defiant*," Ro said. "That's in addition to your normal alpha-shift duties. I assume that you'll take the time between the two to have a meal and get some sleep."

"Yes, sir." The punishment actually made Tenmei feel good, as though paying even such a small price for her transgressions would at least begin to repair her relationship with the captain. It would make the next month less than enjoyable for her, but she felt pleased—and more than a little fortunate—that she wouldn't spend time in the stockade or stand court-martial.

"In my log, I'm entering the cause of your extra duty as insubordination," Ro said.

"Yes, sir."

"Dismissed."

Relief immediately flooded through Tenmei. She headed back the way she had entered, the doors parting before her. As she reached them, though, Ro called after. When Tenmei looked back, she saw that the captain had stood up behind her desk.

"Even if you didn't take the actions you did," she said, "Julian wasn't going to be stopped." Ro stood gazing at Tenmei for a few seconds more, then sat back down and turned her attention to the computer interface on her desk.

Tenmei continued out of the captain's office and down the corridor. On her trip to the residential deck and her cabin, she replayed Ro's last statement in her mind. *Julian wasn't going to be stopped.* Did that mean that the captain thought that Doctor Bashir would have taken other measures to ensure his escape? Or did it mean that Ro herself would not have allowed his capture?

Tenmei didn't know, but over the next month, she would have many quiet hours on *Defiant*'s bridge to ponder those questions.

27

Ro Laren walked along the outer edge of the Plaza with Altek Dans, an occurrence that had become commonplace over the previous weeks. Even three months after he had arrived on Deep Space 9, the captain felt somehow responsible for the temporally displaced doctor—in part, because she had made the decision to transport aboard the Orb carrying him, but also because she had to that point been unable to convince the Bajoran government to allow him to return to the world he called home. Her invitation to the kai to visit DS9 had caused a stir in the Vedek Assembly, and so far had gone unanswered.

Ro thought that, for a man displaced from his own time by hundreds, if not thousands, of years, Altek had adapted remarkably well to his new life. After his initial disorientation, he'd come to be something other than just overwhelmed by the state of technology in the twenty-fourth century. Though still impressed and sometimes daunted by it, he had nevertheless embraced it. He regularly used the companel and replicator in his guest quarters, and he almost always carried a padd with him as he continued his education about both historical and contemporary Bajor.

As they walked along quietly, their conversation fallen into a comfortable lull, Ro watched Altek as he gazed out intently over the residential deck and through the transparent bulkhead that bowed out at the starbase's equator. At that hour, just after the beginning of gamma shift, the holographically projected daytime sky had given way to the enduring night surrounding DS9. Altek's acceptance of the existence of life beyond Bajor— *alien* life—had provided an early hurdle for him, but once he'd achieved it, he had become fascinated by the myriad species represented on the starbase. He also developed an interest in the many different ships that visited DS9.

As well as Altek had acclimated to his new circumstances, Ro believed that he still sometimes battled melancholy, but then how could that not be the case? Although the memories of his life before his emergence from the wormhole had clouded during his time on the starbase, he still retained at least vague recollections of the people he'd left behind. He hadn't had any family left, and he'd renounced his own people, the Aleira, because he would not be a part of a society that practiced slavery, but Altek had forever lost close friends and comrades.

And maybe somebody special, too, Ro thought. She sometimes perceived that type of sadness in him.

Regardless of the number of people to whom Altek had been close, he had to cope with the reality that, however far in time he'd traveled, they had all perished. And not just his friends and comrades, but everybody who'd lived when he had. Fortunately, he had been amenable to meeting with Lieutenant Commander Matthias for regular and frequent counseling sessions, which seemed to help him.

Ro noticed the padd clutched in Altek's hand. "Are you still reading *When the Prophets Cried*?" she asked. In addition to studying the history of the Bajorans, he also wanted to know about how their religion had developed. A major canonical work, *When the Prophets Cried* had been written centuries earlier, but almost assuredly after Altek's own time.

"I am," Altek said, "but I also started reading a history of the United Federation of Planets."

"Really?" Ro asked, both surprised and impressed by Altek's diligence. Though she had been required to take several survey courses about the UFP during her time at Starfleet Academy, most of what the captain knew about the Federation had come from her experiences living in and around it.

Altek shrugged. "I've been trying to learn about Bajor," he said, "and since we're now part of the Federation, it just made sense."

Ro noted Altek's use of the pronoun *we*. Despite not yet having set foot back on Bajor, he clearly considered himself one of its citizens. That pleased her.

"Have you read enough to draw any conclusions?" Ro asked.

"Not conclusions, I wouldn't say, but it's fascinating to me that the political and territorial clashes I saw on Bajor during my lifetime are the same sorts of conflicts that arose between planets. You'd think that, with all the amazing technological advances, cultures would also advance."

Ro chuckled. "I think we have advanced—I *hope* we have— but I know what you mean."

Before Altek could respond, Ro's combadge chirped. *"Hub to Captain Ro."*

Ro stopped walking and tapped her badge. Altek stopped

beside her. "This is Ro. Go ahead, Suyin." Ensign Zhang Suyin worked communications during gamma shift. Like so many of Ro's immense crew, she had been assigned to DS9 only three months prior. The captain had felt an immediate affinity with the young officer, simply because, despite being human, the ensign's cultural tradition resembled that of the Bajorans, placing her surname first and her given name second.

"Captain, the dockmaster reports a Bajoran transport requesting permission to dock immediately," Zhang said. *"It's not on our schedule, but its flight plan shows it coming directly from Bajor. Its master has asked to speak with you on a secure channel."*

"And we don't know what this is about?"

"They're being very tight-lipped, Captain."

"Who's the shipmaster?"

"A man named Beren Togg."

"I don't know him," Ro said. "All right, Suyin, I'll head to my quarters. Tell Master Beren that I'll speak with him shortly."

"Aye, Captain."

"Ro out." Then, to Altek, she said, "I'm sorry to have to cut our walk short."

"That's quite all right, Captain," Altek said. "You've done so much for me already." He held up his padd. "I'm eager to get back to my book anyway. I'm reading about a very interesting human named Jonathan Archer."

"I had to learn about him at Starfleet Academy," Ro said. "He had an interesting life."

"That's certainly true so far."

"Have a good night, Doctor."

"You as well, Captain."

Ro started for the nearest turbolift.

AT THE COMPANEL in her quarters, Ro sat waiting for Ensign Zhang to establish a secure channel with the Bajoran transport. The captain didn't quite know what to make of the urgent request to dock, least of all from a ship that had come to the starbase directly from Bajor. She wondered if somebody might be seeking political asylum. It also occurred to her that perhaps the first minister had sent an envoy, somebody who would at last directly address Altek's request to return to Bajor.

On the companel display, the Starfleet emblem winked off, replaced a moment later by the image of a woman. Ro had expected to see a man—Shipmaster Beren Togg—and so she didn't immediately recognize the face before her.

"Good evening, Captain," the woman said. *"Please forgive my unexpected arrival and the abrupt communication."* The strong voice—which Ro had personally heard soften in other circumstances—snapped the captain out of her momentary confusion.

"Kai Pralon, no apology is necessary," Ro said. "I must admit that I'm surprised to see you, but I'm delighted that you've chosen to visit Deep Space Nine."

"You should perhaps wait until we've spoken before making that determination." Pralon Onala offered the barest hint of a smile. Ro had always appreciated her sense of humor. Just past her sixtieth birthday, the kai looked at least fifteen years younger, with her well-defined features and bright blue-green eyes. Though Pralon typically wore traditional vestments in public, including a headpiece, Ro saw that she currently had on civilian attire, and that her short, layered blond hair had begun to silver.

"Considering that I can't get anybody in the Bajoran government to speak with me these days," Ro said, "I consider your visit a professional victory." *And it's not just me,* the captain thought. As she understood it, even the extradition of the Ohalavaru to Bajor had stalled.

"I trust that means that we have your permission to dock," Pralon said.

"Of course, Your Eminence," Ro said. "I will have our dockmaster find you a bay at once."

"Thank you," Pralon said. *"Is it too late for us to meet tonight? I would like to speak with you privately at your earliest convenience, and certainly before touring the starbase."*

"It's not too late at all," Ro said. Through Vedek Novor,

the captain had extended an invitation to the kai to take a tour of DS9, but Ro intended such a visit to allow her the opportunity to discuss Altek's situation with Pralon. She hoped the kai understood that. Pralon rarely acted out of expedience, and Ro had always found her a keen and thoughtful observer of the political landscape. "I will have quarters prepared for you, and I will meet you at the docking bay myself."

"I look forward to seeing you, Captain." The kai said nothing explicit to signal the end of the communication, but Ro's screen went dark, adorned only by the Starfleet insignia.

Ro deactivated the companel, then tapped her combadge. She contacted the dockmaster to secure a bay for the Bajoran transport, as well as the duty officer to assign VIP quarters for Pralon. Then she headed for the *x*-ring.

"I'M SORRY that I haven't come sooner, Captain."

Ro waited as Pralon took an easy chair in the large living area of her guest quarters, and then the captain sat down on a sofa across from her. Between the time they had first spoken and when Ro had met her at the docking bay, the kai had dressed in a traditional robe of her office—not the more ornate version that Winn Adami had favored, but the simpler one that Opaka Sulan had always worn. Pralon had chosen a forest green fabric that brought out that color in her eyes.

"I've heard that the Vedek Assembly was resistant to you visiting Deep Space Nine at this time," Ro said.

"They cited security concerns to me," Pralon said.

"Because of the assassination." Ro did not phrase it as a question.

"Yes, but that was just a convenient excuse," the kai said. "There's a vein of caution running through the Vedek Assembly these days that I just can't abide, but they're not concerned that I won't be safe aboard Deep Space Nine. It's that, after all that happened with Enkar Sirsy and Baras Rodirya, they're worried about the political turmoil that could arise from dealing with our visitor."

"You've come to help Altek Dans, then?" Ro asked. She heard gratitude in her voice. It did not surprise her that the kai had seen through the guise of her invitation to visit the starbase.

"I've come to look into the situation," Pralon said. "I will speak with him during my visit, and then we can proceed from there. I know that your requests for identity and travel documents for Doctor Altek haven't been approved."

"As far as I know, my requests haven't been approved *or* rejected," Ro said.

"You're right. I'm sure that's the case, and it doesn't surprise me," the kai said. "Nobody in the government—not the Vedek Assembly, not the Chamber of Ministers, and not even the first minister—wants to deal with any difficulties that could arise from allowing Doctor Altek to return to Bajor. At the same time, nobody wants to go on the record denying him that opportunity."

"But what sort of problems are they anticipating if they let him go home?" Ro asked, genuinely perplexed. "It can't only be that they're sensitive to the Bajoran participation—both perceived and real—in the assassination and the ensuing crisis."

"That *is* a significant part of their concern," Pralon said. "The initial belief that the first minister's chief of staff killed President Bacco stirred up an old drumbeat among Cardassian anti-Bajoran extremists, and when it turned out to be a conspiracy perpetrated by Baras, they only screamed louder."

"But the True Way was part of the conspiracy," Ro argued. "If Cardassians are going to vilify all of Bajor for the actions of one man, they also have to blame all of Cardassia for the actions of that terrorist organization."

"I'm afraid you're making logical arguments, Captain," Pralon said, standing up from her chair. "Believe me, reason doesn't apply when we're dealing with extremists." As the kai walked across the compartment, Ro wondered if she'd meant her last statement to include the Ohalavaru radicals. When Pralon reached the table in the dining area, she opened the carryall sitting there, which one of her assistants had brought from the transport. She reached in and pulled out a dark, oblong bottle. "I brought a Sahving Valley port, and I'm going to pour myself a glass," the kai said. "Would you like one?"

"Yes, thank you," Ro said. As Pralon ordered a pair of wineglasses from the replicator, the captain walked over to join her.

"You're right, Captain," the kai said. She set the glasses down on the table and picked up the bottle. "The Bajoran government isn't only concerned about the potential political fallout of allowing or forbidding Doctor Altek to come to Bajor. They're also worried about the real problems he could bring with him." Pralon poured the deep-red liquid into the two glasses, then handed one to Ro. The rich aroma of the fortified wine drifted to the captain at once.

"What real problems?" Ro asked.

Pralon sipped at the port, and the captain followed her lead. The slightly sweet wine had notes of dark fruit and old wood. Rather than returning to the living area, the kai sat down at the dining table. Ro did so as well.

"The last time a Bajoran emerged from the Celestial Temple hundreds of years after his own time, it was Akorem Laan," Pralon said, invoking the name of the famous poet. "When Akorem appeared, he assumed the mantle of Emissary of the Prophets, with Benjamin Sisko stepping aside for him. That resulted in tremendous confusion and distress among the Bajoran people. Akorem also caused additional turmoil by trying to reinstitute the D'jarras." The strict caste system that specified a family's profession had fallen into disuse during the Occupation. Akorem's attempt to reestablish the D'jarras had been unpopular and divisive, and had his efforts proven successful, Bajor would have been disqualified from membership in the Federation.

"Doctor Altek is not Akorem Laan," Ro said. "I've spoken at length with him about his wanting to go back to Bajor. It's a natural and completely understandable desire. Until he arrived here, he'd spent his entire life on the planet. He has no intention of claiming to be anything other than a citizen of Bajor, and he certainly has no interest in promoting a return to backward social practices."

"I'm prepared to believe that, Captain," Pralon said. "The problem is that there will be those who would use Doctor Altek's presence to forward their own agendas. With Benjamin Sisko no longer functioning as the Emissary, and no longer living on Bajor or stationed on Deep Space Nine, the Vedek Assembly has been fearful of some usurper trying to seize the position that he has forsaken. Even if Doctor Altek does not do so, it is possible that others might claim the title in his name, and then rally against any attempts to deny him."

"Begging your pardon, Your Eminence, but that is a great deal of speculation."

"Perhaps, but given that we've been seeing more religious dissent than ever before in modern times, it's not unrealistic speculation," Pralon said. "Under different circumstances, I would have waited to travel here until I had waded through the politics of it all, to put minds at ease with respect to Doctor Altek returning to Bajor, but these are not normal circumstances."

"Are you referring to the Ohalavaru extremists?"

"Yes." Pralon brought her glass up to her lips, paused, then set it back down on the table without drinking. "I came here now because after I leave here, I will not be able to return anytime soon. My presence on Bajor will be required for the foreseeable future."

"Why?" Ro asked, although she thought she knew the answer.

"Because when I return to Bajor," the kai said, "I will be making a public announcement about the discovery on Endalla."

"How does the Vedek Assembly feel about that?"

"They are divided," Pralon said. "There are many—and I include myself in this group—who feel that we should not be afraid of the truth, even if that truth challenges our beliefs. But there are those who point to the publication of Ohalu's writings and the consequences that followed, including the standoff and loss of life on Endalla six years ago, and the abduction of Rebecca Sisko after that."

"And now the discovery of the falsework," Ro said.

"Yes," said the kai. "Even if the Ohalavaru interpretation of the discovery is incorrect, many vedeks are concerned that it will confuse people and raise doubts in their minds about the Prophets."

"They may be right," Ro said, thinking of the anguished reaction of the devout Cenn Desca.

"They *are* right," Pralon said. "No matter whether the Ohalavaru are correct or not, the existence of the falsework will cause tremors in Bajoran religious life."

"And yet you're going to make the announcement anyway," Ro said. "I admire your courage."

Pralon shook her head. "There's nothing courageous about it, Captain," she said. "It is an act of self-preservation. If I lied about facts to the Bajoran faithful, how could I consider myself their leader?"

"What if you're left with nobody to lead?"

"I don't think that will be the case," Pralon said. "In any event, I can always keep my own counsel."

"Does that mean that your faith hasn't been challenged by the Ohalavaru discovery?"

Pralon looked the captain in the eye and held her gaze for a long time. Ro waited as the silence extended. Eventually, the kai raised her glass and finished the last of her port.

She never answered the question.

28

Kira Nerys prepared to die.

She sat on the bridge of *Even Odds*, close enough to where Facity Sleedow crewed the helm that she could monitor the ship's approach to the wormhole. Kira believed that events would soon begin to move very fast, though she still couldn't be certain. She had spent the previous two and a half months trying to determine what she would do—what she *should* do—when *Even Odds* finally reached the Idran system.

Kira recalled well the fleet of ships that had emerged from the wormhole years earlier—reckoning by the timeline of her life—and had set course directly for Bajor, led by the crazed Iliana Ghemor. She also remembered *Even Odds* charging after the Ascendants, and Taran'atar's last, desperate act, which had changed everything. Back then, she had been a Starfleet captain and the commanding officer of Deep Space 9, but what she hadn't known then—and what she had only recently come to realize—was that a future version of herself had been aboard *Even Odds* at the time of its destruction.

And if I don't do anything to change that, Kira thought, *it means that I'm going to die.*

When Kira had first realized that her journey out of the wormhole had taken her backward in time, she'd thought about what she could do to save Taran'atar and the thousands of others who had been lost when the Ascendants had attacked. Since then, she had agonized over the Temporal Prime Directive and the dangers of altering the timeline, but she also puzzled over what the Prophets intended her to do. They had called her Their Hand, and They had set her upon her current path. Had They done that so that she could take action to prevent the loss of all those lives, or for some other purpose?

Kira had been over it again and again, but she'd always come back to the same conclusion. If the crew of *Even Odds* had not retrieved the Orb carrying her, they would not have headed for the wormhole in order to bring her home—which meant that they and Taran'atar would not be at Bajor when the Ascendants attacked. In that case, deaths would likely have been counted, not in thousands, but in millions, and maybe even in billions. Clearly, the Prophets intended for her to redirect *Even Odds* to where it needed to be to save Bajor.

For a while, Kira had hoped that the ship would arrive at the wormhole before the Ascendants did, but then that again posed thorny questions about her taking actions that would ultimately disrupt the timeline—not to mention the potential dilemma if her past self met her future self. As *Even Odds* carried her toward Bajor, though, it became apparent that it would reach it at the same time as the Ascendants originally had. If she continued on that course, it seemed that events would unfold just as they had before, which made a cold sort of sense to her. According to Benjamin, the Prophets existed nonlinearly in time, so from Their perspective, dispatching Kira from the Celestial Temple into the past, and into the course of Taran'atar and *Even Odds*, must have been what had *already* happened.

This is the path that the Prophets have laid out for me, she thought. *Not just for myself, but as Their Hand.* During the Occupation, Kira had become inured to the possibility of her own death. There had been many instances during her years in the Resistance, and even during her tenure on DS9, when she'd believed she would not survive to see another day. Those had been violent times—times she thought she'd left behind, particularly after resigning her captaincy and becoming an acolyte in the Bajoran religion.

It doesn't matter, she thought. She would do what she must, in the service of her gods and to save her people. If that led to her death, she could not think of a better end to her personal story.

Kira had considered telling the crew of *Even Odds*—or at least Dez—about her traveling back in time and about what lay ahead, but she couldn't be sure that they would agree to sacrifice themselves for the greater good. She also thought about informing Taran'atar, who she believed would remain loyal to her no matter the battle she urged him to fight, but she again worried about disrupting the timeline. In the end, she kept all of it to herself, believing that the Prophets had not set her on a path only for her to fail.

"We're entering the Idran system," announced Sleedow. "Dropping to sublight speed." The deep drone of the warp engines eased as the impulse drive took over.

Dez looked over at her from where he sat in the command chair. On the viewscreen, the rush of stars had settled into a static tableau. "Set course for the Anomaly," he said, using the name that Gamma Quadrant residents employed for the Bajoran wormhole. Only two other crew members were present: Pri'ak, the squat Merdosian engineer with transparent teeth, and Pifko Gaber, the gregarious, four-legged Aarruri.

Actually, there's another member of the crew here, Kira reminded herself. Taran'atar worked the sensor console. Even after spending more than two months aboard and watching him function essentially as the ship's security chief and tactical officer, she had difficulty thinking of him as a part of the *Even Odds* crew. *Maybe because I know that it's not going to last.*

"Sensors detect a large number of vessels near the fourth planet," the Jem'Hadar announced.

Kira's heart began to race. *It's beginning.*

"Are they Federation ships?" Sleedow asked. "Maybe we can hand off Captain Kira and finally get back to our own lives."

"Negative," Taran'atar said. "They are Ascendant vessels."

"Ascendant?!" Dez said, his voice rising as he leaped from his chair. "Facity, get us out of here." Sleedow had begun working the helm even before he'd given the order.

Kira saw the field of stars on the viewscreen shift as *Even Odds* altered course. "No!" she said. "I have to get to Bajor!" The heavy thrum of the warp drive rose around them, underscoring the desperation Kira felt.

"We'll bring you back another time," Dez said.

"If there's anything left to bring you back to," Sleedow muttered, not quite under her breath. On the other side of the bridge, Pif raced back and forth, barking that he thought the Ascendants were nothing more than a myth, a scary story parents told their litters to make them behave.

Kira bolted up from her chair and leaned in over the helm console. She opened her mouth to tell the first officer to turn *Even Odds* back around, thinking that she might have to incapacitate Sleedow and take control of the ship herself. Before she could say anything, though, a hum rose on the bridge. Startled, Kira backed up a step and watched as the first officer vanished in the brilliant wash of a transporter beam. When she looked around, she saw that Dez, Pif, and Pri'ak had also disappeared.

Only Taran'atar remained.

"If you will take the helm, Captain," the Jem'Hadar said, "we can take you home."

Kira threw herself into the seat occupied a moment ago by Facity Sleedow. "Bringing us about," she said as she turned *Even Odds* back toward the Idran system. "What did you do with the crew?"

"I transported all of them into Four Bay," Taran'atar said. "All but Srral, who I beamed into a portable sensor array." Kira had been shown the array at some point during her time aboard, and she knew that it functioned completely independently of the ship's systems.

"Where are the Ascendant vessels?" Kira wanted to know as she set course back into the Idran system. *Maybe if I can reach the Ascendants before they enter the wormhole, I can stop them from reaching Bajor.*

"They are keeping station not far from the Anomaly," Taran'atar said. "No . . . there is also a squadron of ten ships headed for the fourth planet."

No! Kira thought. *Am I too late?* She knew that a small contingent of Ascendant vessels had attacked Idran IV, partly because the incident had resulted in a period of isolationism enforced by the Eav'oq, but primarily because, at the time of the assault, Kai Pralon had been visiting their lone city—called Terev'oqu—as part of a cultural exchange. Kira hadn't factored that into her plan to bring *Even Odds* and Taran'atar to where they needed to be to face the Ascendants because she knew that the kai and the Eav'oq had endured the attack.

But how did they do that? Kira asked herself. At the time, an Eav'oq named Itu—who refused to portray himself as the leader of his people, despite serving in the *de facto* position—had been on Bajor. After surviving the arrival of the Ascendants there, he had learned of the zealots' offensive on Idran IV. Itu immediately traveled back through the wormhole to rejoin his people. While he later sent word to Bajor that the Eav'oq would close the borders of their world at least in the near term, he never offered an explanation as to how his people had withstood the Ascendant onslaught. They had virtually no armaments and no defenses. When the Ascendants had attacked them millennia ago, the Eav'oq had faced the threat by flight and concealment. The kai, when she returned to Bajor, had been able to offer up few details about the Ascendants' barrage, and nothing at all about how Terev'oqu had stood against it. Kira only knew that subsequent scans of Idran IV had revealed destruction on the outskirts of the city, but no wreckage of Ascendant ships, meaning that their squadron had somehow been repelled, not destroyed.

Suddenly, Kira understood why Kai Pralon had said so little about the events on Idran IV. *She was protecting me—protecting the integrity of the timeline.* It made sense to Kira. She must have been the one to save the Eav'oq and the kai. *But how—*

"Taran'atar, Kai Pralon is on the fourth planet," she said. "I have to protect her and the Eav'oq from that squadron. The city has no weapons or defenses."

"We can take the *Even Odds* into the atmosphere," Taran'atar said. "The ship has only limited weaponry, but it has advanced shields, is extremely maneuverable, and is larger than the single-passenger vessels headed for the planet."

"With the shields up, we won't be able to transport the kai safely off the planet," Kira said.

"Take the dropship," Taran'atar said. "You can beam up the kai while I defend against the Ascendants' attack."

This is what happened, Kira thought. *I saved Kai Pralon, but she never said anything in order to protect the timeline.* It all felt right to Kira, and at that moment, the only thing she had to go on was instinct. *Instinct . . . and faith.*

"Transport me to the dropship," she told Taran'atar. "Once I've rescued the kai, beam us back aboard."

Taran'atar turned back to his console and began working his controls, then looked back at her one final time. "Victory is life," he said.

An instant later, Kira heard the hum of the transporter beam, and then the *Even Odds* disappeared around her.

29

Odo paced alongside the massive storage compartment, peering in through port after port at the great amorphous form. As best he or anybody could tell, it remained in precisely the same shape as when it had first been collected from the Capricorn Arday system. Sensors detected no movement, either internal or external, no changes in mass or temperature. It looked the same. In the five days Odo had spent at Newton Outpost, he had done nothing to help the potential shape-shifter.

How can I expect to help it if I don't even know if it's alive?

For his first full day at the facility, Odo had met with all of the scientists who had studied the specimen. Some provided only analytical data taken from various types of scans, while others had supplied information about their attempts either to communicate with it or evoke a response from it. It pleased Odo that they had all erred on the side of caution, taking only those actions that seemed unlikely to cause a shape-shifter discomfort. Nothing worked.

Over the next four days, Odo had done everything he had been able to think of to reach the shape-shifter. He adjusted the temperatures around the specimen, repeating patterns that suggested a form to take. He likewise employed sound in the same way, and light. He adjusted the flow of air around it. He used a portable holographic system to project images of various shapes above the specimen, and then of one shape transforming into another. He continually spoke to it, initially over the comm system, and then, just two days earlier, by entering the compartment with it—something that the scientists had not wanted him to do, but that he'd eventually been able to convince Doctor Norsa to allow him to try.

The day before, Odo had touched the specimen. With its metallic coloring, it looked rigid, but its surface gave beneath his touch—malleable, but returning to its original shape after he withdrew pressure. It did not feel inert or dead, but neither did it feel vital or alive.

Odo remembered when, more than a decade prior, a newly formed Changeling had been brought to Deep Space 9. At the time, Odo had been altered by the Founders, made to retain his humanoid form and unable to shape-shift. He attempted to communicate with the "infant," and to teach it how to use its Changeling abilities—all without employing the harsh methods that Doctor Mora had utilized on him. It took time, but his methods eventually worked—though in vain, since the shape-shifter had been too sick to endure. In its dying moments, it integrated itself into Odo's body, restoring his ability to alter his form—one of the greatest gifts he had ever been given.

At the time Odo had worked with the newly formed Changeling, he had wished that he could simply link with it, something the punishment meted out to him by the Founders had made impossible. Linking with the "infant" would have allowed him to pass on his knowledge virtually instantaneously, without the need for language and interpretation. After nearly a week of fruitless endeavors at Newton Outpost, the time had come for such a measure.

Odo completed his circuit of the compartment, and headed down the steps, along Corridor 4, and out of the foreign-objects storage section of the facility. He found Doctor Norsa in her office. She invited him to sit, and he did.

Norsa's office, like most of the others he'd seen during his time at Newton Outpost, felt cluttered, although it really contained little in it. The scientist sat behind a large, sturdy metal desk on which both padds and paper printouts abounded, barely leaving room for a computer interface and a holophoto of her with her two adult sons. A pair of tall gray cabinets stood against one wall, presumably used for storing the padds and printed reports that couldn't find a place on her desktop. Several large graphical displays covered the remaining wall space, themselves covered with images, lists, and formulae.

"Have you made any progress today, Odo?" Norsa asked.

"Only in my thinking," Odo said. "I've tried everything I can possibly do to communicate with the specimen. That comes on the heels of you and the other scientists trying everything that you could do."

"It often takes time to conceive an experiment," Norsa said. "Just because we've exhausted all of the possibilities we've been able to think of to this point doesn't mean that there aren't other things we can try."

"But to what end?" Odo asked. "Is there any procedure we can attempt that is substantively different from those we've already done?"

Norsa sighed. "I can appreciate your frustration—"

"No, I don't think you can," Odo said, interrupting her. "I spent years searching for my people, and when I finally found them, they went to war against the Federation and most of the Alpha Quadrant. I eventually returned to them after peace was established, but I have been separated from them again for years. Since being essentially stranded here in the Alpha Quadrant, I've spent most of my time searching for more of my kind—not just Founders, but members of the Hundred. I believe that this might be one of them."

"I've read about the Hundred," Norsa said.

"Then you might understand that they are unformed Changelings—shape-shifters who have never altered their shape. They need help. They need guidance. I want to provide that. I don't want other Changelings to have to go through what I went through . . . to have so much time pass before they begin their lives."

"I sympathize with your perspective, Odo."

"And I *empathize* with a potential fellow being," Odo said. "Imagine what it would be like if your children had been left on their own as soon as they'd been born. Try to imagine if that had happened to you."

"I understand what you're saying," Norsa told him. "And I understand *why* you're saying it. You want to do more than you've already done. You want to attempt to link with the specimen."

"I do," Odo said. "Whether it's a success or a failure, it will at least tell us definitively if we have a shape-shifter."

"I can see that being true if you make contact with a living shape-shifter," Norsa said, "but if you don't, will we be able to conclude that it is not a shape-shifter?"

"If it is a shape-shifter but no longer alive," Odo said, "I believe I will know that."

Norsa stood up from her chair and stepped out from behind her desk. "Odo, in situations even remotely similar to this one, but involving humanoid scientists, I would probably deny you the permission you seek. But you're a shape-shifter, so I don't really know how to weigh the risks." She sat down on the front edge of her desk and stared down at Odo. "I need to know, if you try this, what is the risk to you, to the specimen, and to this facility?"

Odo grunted. "I should probably lie to you and tell you that there's no risk," he said. "The truth is that I don't know. If it is a living being suffering from a disease, or possibly even a being that died from a disease, I could be at risk of infection. Both of those possibilities seem unlikely to me because sensor scans have shown nothing like that. I am currently in good health and would not be a risk to a shape-shifter, nor would I intentionally inflict harm on it. If the object is not a shape-shifter, then I will not be able to link with it, and so I would be in no more danger than when I touched it yesterday. And I can't imagine any danger at all to the outpost."

Norsa folded her arms across her chest. "I want to say yes," she told Odo, "but my number one concern has to be safety. You've convinced me, but would you be willing to make your case to the rest of the scientists working on the project?"

Odo stood up and faced Norsa. "I won't enjoy it," he said, "but if that's what will get me closer to trying to link with this possible shape-shifter, then I'll do it."

*   *   *

ODO STOOD in one of the decontamination chambers serving the huge specimen compartment. Behind him, wearing hazard suits, stood Bruce Prestridge, one of the scientists on the project and a medical doctor, and T'Pret, a technician. Another technician, Endos Vinik, stood just outside decon, in the corridor.

Odo looked through the port in the inner door to where the great mass of the possible shape-shifter sprawled in its nebulous form. Across the compartment, several other scientists stared down through the viewing ports. Odo saw Doctor Norsa among them. She had not only agreed with him about the need to take the next step, she had also helped him make the case to the other scientists on the project. In the end, only two of the seven-member team objected.

"I'm ready," Odo said, his words picked up and transmitted to the rest of the team via the combadge he had attached to his simulated uniform. In response, he heard feedback tones from a control panel. A moment later, the inner door cycled open.

Odo stepped into the compartment. He glanced back over his shoulder. As instructed and as he'd agreed, he waited until the door slid closed before proceeding.

Two strides forward took Odo to the stationary undulations of the steely form he had so hoped would be a Changeling, or at least a shape-shifter of some kind. His week at Newton Outpost had dimmed that dream—so much so that his secondary goal had become proving just the opposite, that the *Nova* crew had not found a shape-shifter. Not that long before, Odo had decided that he had spent too much of his life waiting, and he had grown tired of it. If a shape-shifter lay before him, then he would try to communicate with it and help it; if not, then the time had come for him to move on. The Bajoran wormhole had reopened more than three months prior, and yet Kira had not reappeared. Odo needed to admit that she was dead, and so the time had come for him to return to the Dominion to see if anything had grown from the seeds that he had planted there.

Odo lowered himself to his knees and leaned forward. He

brought his hands down on the smooth, curved surface of whatever the *Nova* crew had brought to Newton Outpost. Where he touched it, the substance gave beneath his fingers, but not much. He tried to feel a presence, to sense another mind, but as when he had first laid hands on the object, his intuition told him nothing.

Odo did not close his eyes, but his vision faded as he looked inward. In his mind, he envisioned circular motion, fluids whirling into vortices, water oscillating in tides. Within the spinning movements, he summoned his purpose and gave it the form of formlessness. He felt the fabric of his being ripple. His hands softened and then dissolved, losing their pale Bajoran complexion and quivering with a metallic golden-orange hue.

The moment had come. Odo separated the cells in the shimmering shapes that had once been his hands, widened the spaces between his constituent parts. Alive with the anticipation of contact, he pressed forward, urging himself to become one with the form before him.

Nothing happened.

Disappointment threatened to overwhelm Odo. Despite the lack of hard evidence that he would find a shape-shifter on Newton Outpost, he had dared to hope that he would. Worse, he had allowed himself to *expect* that he would.

And I believed that I would discover not just any shape-shifter, but a Changeling, he admitted to himself. *And not just a Founder, but one of the Hundred.*

Odo felt in that moment that he could liquefy into a sea of tears. He reprimanded himself for his sentimentality, to allow what he wished to color his assessment of reality. He wanted to leave as quickly as possible. He pulled his arms back, detaching from the specimen, and visualized his Bajoran hands, saw precisely the contours that they would take—

The substance in front of Odo swirled into motion. It moved with lightning speed, expanding and contracting, twisting and gyrating, forming into various shapes too quickly for his eyes to discern. He reached out as it surged upward against gravity, and then he saw a part of it descending toward him at speed.

Odo reached out, thinking only about connecting with the majestic form before him, linking with it. He waited for the physical contact, and for what would follow. But then the creature struck him, and his mind exploded in a burst of ghostly white.

Then everything went black.

NORSA STOOD in the corridor, peering through the observation port and down into the oversized compartment. It thrilled her to watch Odo set his hands down on the specimen and begin to change his form. She had seen recordings of shapeshifters altering their bodies, but never before had she been an eyewitness to it.

Norsa doubted that anything would come of Odo's attempt to link with the specimen. It seemed almost certain that the *Nova* crew had not found something living. Her best hope came from the possibility that it had once been alive, and that Odo would somehow be able to determine that.

Even as Norsa thought that, though, she saw Odo pull away from the specimen. His outstretched limbs glistened at their ends, at what had once been his hands and presumably soon would be again. He settled back, apparently finished with—

The specimen moved so quickly that it took a moment for Norsa to make sense of what she saw. From the point at which Odo had made contact with it, it glistened with a silvery light, which spread across its surface in an instant. Directly in front of Odo, the specimen climbed upward. Norsa lost sight of Odo behind it, and then a part of it jutted out and formed into a shape consisting of right angles and flat sides, like an appendage that ended not in a hand, but in a humanoid-sized brick. It rushed down and forward, and then Norsa saw Odo flying through the air. He struck the wall with incredible force. His body flattened and splattered, losing its shape and becoming nothing but a mass of morphogenic fluid that slid down to the floor but did not re-form.

Norsa opened her mouth to yell out, even as she lunged for the control surface that connected to the alert system, which allowed scientists to signal an emergency to the entire outpost.

Before she could utter a whole word, she saw a mass of motion headed in her direction. The specimen burst through the observation port—through *all* the observations ports—like a swollen river bursting a dam. Norsa saw her fellow scientists caught in the swift current of the flowing substance, and then she felt herself picked up and thrown backward. She heard a deafening crunch, and as her consciousness faded, she realized it had been the sound of her head striking the wall.

30

Cenn Desca sat alone at a table on the second level of Quark's Public House, Café, Gaming Emporium, Holosuite Arcade, and Ferengi Embassy.

"Ferengi Embassy to Bajor," he murmured to himself. He stared down at the gamblers crowding the poker games, the dabo wheel, and the dom-jot table, at the people drinking, at other patrons heading back to enjoy the holosuites, and he scoffed at it all. The disrespect shown to his people staggered him, though he did not find any of it a surprise. After the Cardassians had run roughshod over Bajor for half a century, after the Federation had moved in and taken over Terok Nor once the Resistance had finally repelled the Union, and after his people had given up their sovereignty to join the UFP, why should he expect something as simple as respect be accorded the Bajorans?

Cenn raised his stemmed glass to his mouth, but nothing reached his lips. He upended the goblet, and the merest trickle of springwine slipped onto his waiting tongue. He grabbed the long neck of the bottle, but he could already see that he had emptied it of its pale-blue contents. Irritated, he brought his hand down a little too hard onto the tabletop, and the glass rang out.

"You want to be careful with that, Colonel," a voice said close to Cenn's ear. "It's Kaladrys Valley crystal."

Cenn looked around to see Quark standing beside the table. He carried a circular tray before him, half-filled with empty glasses. Cenn reached over and set the empty bottle onto it, but he let go of it too soon and it toppled over, clattering among the other glassware.

"I would like another bottle of springwine, please," Cenn told the barkeep.

"How about some Daronan spring water instead?"

"I didn't ask for spring *water*," Cenn said, annoyed by Quark's resistance to his order. "I asked for spring*wine*."

"Yes, I know what I heard, Colonel," Quark said, raising a hand to gesture toward one of his enormous ears. "But I've also heard from the captain that she will hold me personally responsible if any of her senior staff overindulge."

Cenn glared at Quark. "I'm not overindulging," he said, and then he turned away and looked back down at the bar. "Considering everything that's happened, I'm indulging the appropriate amount."

"Right," Quark said. He reached over and plucked the colonel's glass from the table. Cenn grabbed it back from him and set it down hard, his fingers holding it tightly.

"Springwine," he said again.

With a grumble, the barkeep scampered away, toward the stairs that led down to the first level. Cenn gazed out toward the transparent shell that surrounded the Plaza. As always, numerous ships crowded about the starbase, some arriving, some departing, others docked or keeping station for the duration of their crew's stay. He saw a civilian Cardassian vessel and just shook his head.

Out on the Plaza, past the half-wall that separated Quark's from the wide main walkway, a group of ritually attired Bajorans appeared. Cenn didn't recognize the ranjens, prylars, and vedeks he saw, but he could not mistake the simply attired woman in their midst: Kai Pralon. He stood up and leaned on the railing that lined the second level of the bar.

"Liar!" he cried out, and the olio of sounds in Quark's—voices, the whir of the dabo wheel, the chirps of the dom-jot table, the clink of glassware—diminished. Out on the Plaza, people stopped and turned in his direction, scanning the area for the source of the outburst. Cenn felt embarrassed to have drawn so much attention. He said nothing more, and as people resumed speaking again, it seemed that the moment would pass. But then the first officer pushed away from the railing and the glass in his hand—which he hadn't even remembered he'd been carrying—slipped from his grip. Cenn lurched forward to try to catch it, but far too late. It tumbled down and struck the shelf behind the bar. It shattered, toppling several bottles.

The entire place quieted, eyes all around following the path of the glass upward, to where Cenn stood. Everyone stilled—*almost* everyone. The first officer saw one of Quark's bouncers—a thick, broad-shouldered Filian named Aridesh—head for the stairs that led up to the second level. Out on the Plaza, Crewman Torvan moved toward the entrance to the bar, the security officer's hand tapping at his combadge.

Cenn looked at the kai. He saw the people with her trying to hustle her away, even as she peered up at him. The first officer threw his finger out and pointed at her. "Liar!" he bellowed again. "You lied to all of us!"

Cenn felt a hand on his elbow. "Colonel, maybe it's time to call it a night." The first officer spun so quickly that he nearly lost his balance, only steadying himself at the last instant by grabbing on to the railing. Quark stared up at him. The barkeep had set his tray down, and he held the palms of his hands out in front of him in a placatory gesture. "I'd be happy to have somebody escort you to your quarters."

Behind Quark, Aridesh arrived at the top of the stairs. He moved quickly toward Cenn—more quickly than seemed possible for a man so large. As the Filian approached, Quark stopped the bouncer with a wave. "That won't be necessary, Aridesh," the Ferengi said. "I think the first officer would rather walk out of here on his own. Isn't that right, Colonel?"

Cenn's head spun. He wanted to tell the barkeep to keep quiet and mind his own business, but he knew that, if he did, he would indeed find himself escorted out of the bar. He suddenly discovered that he wanted to leave, that he didn't want all those people staring at him, that he just wanted to go back to his cabin.

The first officer turned around and headed not for the stairs, but for the open lift that traveled on a slope between the three levels of the bar. He felt shaky, and so he held on to the railing as he walked, and then to the side of the lift as it descended toward the first floor. Cenn kept his head up, and as he looked past the patrons in Quark's, out to the Plaza walkway, he saw Kai Pralon still there, watching him.

"You lied to us," he said again, probably too softly for the kai to hear. When the lift reached the first level, though, he pointed at her once more and raised his voice. "You lied," he called out, walking toward the bar entrance. "You and all the kais before you . . . and the Vedek Assembly . . . all of you committed a fraud on the Bajoran people." The patrons in Quark's parted to allow Cenn a path through the bar. "You lied . . . or you're too stupid to see the universe for what it really is."

As Cenn reached the entrance and stepped out onto the Plaza walkway, Crewman Torvan took hold of his arm. "Sir, please," he said quietly.

"How could you do that to us?" Cenn asked, once again pointing at Pralon.

"Colonel, please, it's the kai," Torvan said.

The pain and urgency in the young crewman's voice stopped Cenn. He looked at the security officer and saw confusion on his face. Torvan was Bajoran.

"Don't you see?" Cenn said, grabbing hold of the security officer by both arms. "She lied to us . . . they all lied to us. None of it is true."

"Colonel, don't—"

Cenn raised his head and yelled the truth for everyone to hear: "The Prophets are not gods!" He felt tears streaming down his face. "They're just another alien race." He looked again at Torvan and saw him wearing an expression of horror.

Cenn let go of the crewman and dropped to his knees. "They're not gods," he said again, though more to himself than to anybody else. He knew that he had to get used to the words, that he had to become inured to the anguish that the truth caused him. He had lived a devout life, but the discovery of the wormhole *falsework* . . . the word cruelly taunted him for what it revealed about the beings he had for so long considered deities. "They're just aliens." His voice had fallen to a whimper.

"Desca," a voice said by his ear. He felt hands wrap securely around his upper arm and urge him upward. "Desca, let's get you out of here." It was Jefferson Blackmer.

Cenn clambered to his feet, helped up by the security chief on one side and Torvan on the other. He felt dizzy, and so he closed his eyes, but that only intensified the sensation. When he opened them, he saw the kai approaching him.

"Colonel Cenn," she said softly as she stepped up to him, "everything is going to be all right. I haven't lied to you, but it's all right if you can't see that at this difficult time. Anyone can have a crisis of faith. It's important for you to know right now that you can also regain your convictions, and your devotion to the Prophets."

Cenn blew out a burst of air he'd intended as a laugh. "Don't you mean devotion to the wormhole aliens?" He shook his head, which didn't help his vertigo. "I have nothing but disgust for the 'Prophets' . . . and for you, Kai Pralon, and for the Vedek Assembly . . ." He glanced at Torvan. ". . . and for my fellow misguided Bajorans."

"May you find peace, Colonel," Pralon said.

Suddenly, he felt himself being moved, in the direction of the security office on the Plaza. He felt sick to his stomach, and he immediately knew why. As much disgust as he harbored for the Bajoran religious establishment, it paled in comparison to what he thought of himself.

31

"*Even Odds* to Eav'oq," Kira said, only then noticing the similarity between the name of the ship and that of the people she hoped to save from extinction. Strictly speaking, she sent the transmission not from *Even Odds*, but from its auxiliary craft. She did not want to use her own name, though, still hoping to recover the kai and save the Eav'oq while maintaining the integrity of the timeline—something her anonymity would help to achieve.

She received no response, "*Even Odds* to Eav'oq," Kira said again, working the communications panel in the dropship's cockpit to ensure that she sent her message across a broad range of frequencies. She tried a third time.

As the dropship streaked down through the atmosphere of Idran IV toward Terev'oqu, Kira checked the sensors. *Even Odds* raced toward the city ahead of her, and behind, the squadron of ten Ascendant ships approached the planet fast. She and Taran'atar would not have much time.

Kira adjusted the comm controls. She focused a tight-beam signal toward *Even Odds* and hailed the ship. As with her attempt to reach the Eav'oq, her transmission went unanswered.

Communications are being jammed. She could only surmise that the Ascendants were to blame, though it occurred to her that maybe the crew of *Even Odds* had somehow regained control of their vessel, or at least parts of it. In such a case, she doubted that Dez would choose to risk his life and those of his people to protect the Eav'oq against the Ascendants.

Kira turned her attention to the sensors. She scanned Terev'oqu, searching for Bajoran life signs in an attempt to locate the kai and the cultural team she had taken to visit Idran IV. Among little more than a thousand Eav'oq, it wouldn't take her much time to isolate Pralon Onala and the others.

Except that, as Kira studied the sensor display, she saw confused readings. A handful of life signs appeared and then vanished. She understood at once that the Ascendants were jamming more than just communications.

That left Kira with little choice: she would have to search for the kai visually—and because she would not be able to establish a transporter lock, she would have to retrieve her in person.

*   *   *

TARAN'ATAR GLANCED UP at the main screen on the bridge as the Eav'oq city came into view. Tall, curving buildings, some of them with numerous wings, rose luminously into the sky. Stone paths lined with flowers wove between the structures. Though small, the city provided a dramatic contrast to the rocky, lifeless lands that surrounded it. Taran'atar piloted *Even Odds* directly toward the Eav'oq home.

The Jem'Hadar checked the sensors, and saw the dropship speeding down toward the surface behind *Even Odds*. The Ascendant squadron followed not far behind. He and Kira would have to act quickly.

"I am Taran'atar," he said in the empty bridge, "and I am dead. I go into battle to reclaim my life. This, I do gladly . . ." He hesitated as unfamiliar words rose in his mind. He felt inclined to discard them immediately, but then he reconsidered. So much had changed for him since Odo had sent him on his mission as a "cultural observer" to Deep Space 9. His life had been altered in ways he had never conceived: his purpose stripped from him, new and unfamiliar goals assigned, his mind controlled and turned against him, his gods unmasked as less than divine.

And my life extended.

Somehow, that seemed the oddest turn, almost a cruel joke perpetrated at his expense. When his life as an honored elder shoulder have been close to ending, it had instead changed, his world upended, and then the expectations for his natural lifespan increased. He could make sense of it only by doing what he had always charged himself with doing: reclaiming his life. He could no longer do it for his fallen gods, though; he could only do it for himself, and that necessarily meant finding his purpose. Though it still didn't seem quite right to him, his three-hundred-plus days with the crew of *Even Odds* had allowed him to do that. He had redefined his own function, but in a way not as unrecognizable to him as being a cultural observer: he protected and defended Captain Dezavrim and his band of "retrieval specialists."

Until now, Taran'atar thought. He still intended for no harm to come to Dez and his crew, but he had a debt to repay. He hadn't been able to see it as he'd lived through it, but he could not have survived his time on Deep Space 9, and then in the parallel universe to which he'd essentially been abducted, without the actions and intervention of Captain Kira. When the crew of *Even Odds* had recovered her in the Gamma Quadrant, he had come to her aid in seeing that she be returned safely to her home. So close to accomplishing that goal, he could not simply ignore her plea for help in safeguarding the life of somebody as important to her as the kai.

"I am Taran'atar," he said again. "I am dead. I go into battle to reclaim my life. This, I do gladly . . . for my friend, Kira Nerys. Victory is life." The words sounded awkward, perhaps even wrong, but he said them anyway.

As *Even Odds* neared the city, Taran'atar attempted to scan it, but found his sensors impeded. It didn't matter. He could see for himself that the city, with its few buildings, covered only a small area. Taran'atar's original intention had been to interpose *Even Odds* between the attacking squadron and the city, and to utilize the larger size and extreme maneuverability of the ship to drive off the Ascendant vessels, but he suddenly saw another, better way.

Taran'atar brought *Even Odds* in low over the buildings and visually searched for an open area among them. When he saw one, he quickly took the ship down. He spotted a number of Eav'oq—slender, tall beings with tubular bodies and multiple pink limbs—gazing skyward, each with a single eye that spanned their narrow face. As Taran'atar worked to land the ship, they scattered, propelling themselves away in a manner that looked almost like levitation.

When *Even Odds* had set down, the Jem'Hadar operated the ship's powerful shields. He raised them and measured their intensity, estimating their strength against what he had been told of Ascendant weaponry. He then reconfigured the shields, extending them outward in all directions, covering as much of the city as possible, while still keeping them at useful strength.

Three minutes later, the Ascendants attacked.

Their blade-like vessels streaked across the sky, leveling their energy weapons at the city. *Even Odds* quaked with every volley, the shields successfully defending against the assault. Taran'atar watched as blast after blast failed to reach Terev'oqu. He observed the pattern of the attacks and then anticipated them, continually adjusting power levels to different parts of the shields to increase their effectiveness, but he also knew that the effort was unsustainable. Even if the shields worked against ten Ascendant ships, they would not last against the might of the thousands that waited somewhere in space not far from Idran IV.

Taran'atar reached for a control and opened the outer hatch to Four Bay. If they wanted to, Captain Dezavrim and his crew could take cover on the planet. The Jem'Hadar thought it likely that once the shields failed, the Ascendants would destroy *Even Odds* before the rest of the city.

The ship's destruction and his own death would be worth it, he decided, if his actions allowed Kira enough time to rescue her fellow Bajorans. *She is my friend,* he thought again. The concept still did not feel quite right to Taran'atar, but he also admitted to himself that the idea was not as foreign to him as once it had been.

ILIANA GHEMOR MONITORED the squadron's assault on the Eav'oq. She watched as Aniq led the ten Ascendant ships to the city and launched their attack. They soared above the buildings and sent their energy weapons streaking down on the Eav'oq.

And still the city stood.

Whatever defenses the Eav'oq had, they clearly stymied the Ascendant weaponry. Ghemor considered ordering more ships to the planet, but she feared that the bloodlust of the zealots and their generational hatred for the Eav'oq would motivate them to a more extreme measure: launching the metaweapon on Idran IV.

I can't let that happen, she thought. Ghemor had thousands of Ascendant ships to lead to Bajor and attack, but it would take time to destroy the entire planet—so much time that it could allow Starfleet vessels to reach the system before she had completely secured the full measure of retribution she sought. She needed the metaweapon to ensure the total annihilation of Bajor.

Seated behind the Grand Archquester, Ghemor quietly opened the access panel in the bulkhead to her left. She reached in and pulled out an Ascendant disruptor, then leaned forward and leveled it at Votiq's head. She did not wait to pull the trigger.

The brilliant white beam screeched loudly in the enclosed space. The Grand Archquester slammed against the bulkhead, the lethal beam tearing him apart from within. Votiq screamed briefly, the musical tones of his voice unrecognizable in his agony. His body disintegrated from the inside out, until nothing remained but the sickly scent of death.

Ghemor climbed into Votiq's chair and set course for the Bajoran wormhole.

RAIQ WATCHED FROM HER SHIP as the Grand Archquester's vessel broke formation. She thought for a moment that Votiq, or perhaps the Fire, had decided to take part in the decimation of the Eav'oq, but the ship did not head for the planet. It resumed the course the Fire had set for them through the Idran system—which meant toward the Fortress of the True. It also meant that the metaweapon they intended to use to join with the Unnameable was being taken from the Ascendants.

Raiq opened a channel to the Grand Archquester's ship. Her hail went unanswered. She did not try a second time.

Instead, Raiq contacted the entire armada and sounded the alarm.

KIRA WORKED THE CONTROLS to open the hatch of the dropship. She had seen how Taran'atar had chosen to defend Terev'oqu, and she'd followed *Even Odds* into the city. She found a different place to set down, then watched on a viewscreen to see how effective the Jem'Hadar's defense would prove.

The sleek, black Ascendant ships had descended on the

Eav'oq city in groups, firing their energy weapons as they passed overhead. The shields projected by *Even Odds* brightened in shades of blue where they were struck, but they held. Thunderous waves of sound buffeted the surface. Kira continued to observe, trying to gauge the strength and durability of the defenses.

Finally, she had been able to wait no longer. After lowering the dropship's hatch, she raced out of the vessel and into Terev'oqu. She looked around and then raced for the nearest building, perhaps fifty meters distant.

Halfway to the building, she stopped. The great din of the attack had suddenly quieted. She looked to the sky and saw the Ascendant ships soaring upward.

Confused, Kira turned and ran back to the dropship. She activated the sensors and found them no longer jammed. She confirmed the retreat of the squadron that had attacked the city, and then she scanned nearby space.

She saw the Ascendant fleet moving en masse toward the wormhole.

Having lived through the events about to come, Kira knew what would happen next. She also realized that the kai no longer needed her help—but she knew somebody who did. Focused on fulfilling her destiny as the Hand of the Prophets, Kira opened a channel to Taran'atar.

"DROPSHIP TO EVEN ODDS.*"*

The Jem'Hadar operated the communications console. "This is Taran'atar."

"Taran'atar, you've succeeded," Kira said, *"but the Ascendant fleet is now headed through the wormhole to Bajor. We have to stop them. They're being led by Iliana Ghemor, and they have some kind of subspace weapon."*

"Acknowledged," Taran'atar said. He did not know how the captain had come into possession of such information, but he did not question it.

"Beam me aboard," Kira said.

Taran'atar scanned Four Bay and saw that the *Even Odds*

crew had not left the ship. He quickly worked the transporter controls and beamed them all—including the portable sensor array that hosted Srral—into the Eav'oq city. He then closed the hatch to Four Bay.

"Taran'atar, beam me aboard."

The Jem'Hadar lifted off, in pursuit of the Ascendants.

"Taran'atar, do you read me?"

He closed the channel.

KIRA PUSHED THE DROPSHIP to full speed. Slowly, it gained on *Even Odds*, but not quickly enough. She desperately wanted Taran'atar to catch up to the Ascendant fleet, as she had once watched him do, but she also wanted to reach *Even Odds* before he did.

In her mind, Kira relived those moments above Bajor. She recalled well how Taran'atar had so mysteriously saved her people at the cost of his own life. With the knowledge of *Even Odds* she had recently gained, she thought she understood how he had done so.

On sensors, she saw readings indicating that the Gamma Quadrant terminus of the wormhole had opened. She watched her readout as one Ascendant ship disappeared into the great subspace bridge. Not long after, a second followed, and the rest of the fleet. And then *Even Odds*.

Kira increased the velocity of the dropship, ignoring the alarms that sounded as she pushed the vessel beyond its safety limits. All at once, the purpose for which the Prophets had sent her into the past, and into the path of *Even Odds*, seemed absolutely clear. She would help Taran'atar protect Bajor while also saving his life and all of those who had died on Endalla—or she would die in the attempt.

Without hesitation, Kira piloted the dropship into the wormhole.

Epilogue

Final Sacrament

Deep Space 9's first officer, Commander Elias Vaughn, leaned in over the tactical console in Ops. He waited a moment as Sam Bowers tapped at the panel. Finally, Vaughn asked, "Anything?"

"No, sir," the lieutenant said. "I'm not getting anything at all from the relay—not even a return ping."

Vaughn reached up and ran a hand across his beard. Earlier, Bowers had reported losing contact with the communications relay that Starfleet had established in the Gamma Quadrant, just outside the Idran system. Since the wormhole appeared intact, the lieutenant ran a series of diagnostics, which revealed nothing beyond the loss of signal. Deep Space 9's chief of operations, Nog, then ran his own series of tests on the station's comm equipment, reinitializing some of it and having Bowers try to reach the relay again, all of which resulted in the latest round of failures.

"Not even a return ping," Vaughn echoed, understanding that, even if the sophisticated communications equipment on the relay failed, it should have been able to respond to a simple transmitted command to send a sonic pulse back to the station. "That doesn't sound good."

"No, sir," Bowers agreed.

"All right," Vaughn said. "I'd better tell the captain."

"Tell me what?"

Vaughn turned to see Captain Kira exiting her office and descending the stairs into Ops. "We haven't been able to reestablish contact with the communications relay," he told her. "We're not even getting a return ping out of it."

Kira nodded. "Why don't you get Nog and take the *Rio Grande* out there," she said. "See if you can find out what the problem is."

"Aye, sir," Vaughn said. He started toward the lift, but then Bowers spoke up from the tactical console.

"Captain, the wormhole is opening."

"We're not expecting any guests, are we?" Kira said. "Let's see it."

Vaughn looked up at the large viewscreen that hung from the overhead in Ops. The fulgent blue-and-white form of the wormhole swirled into existence. At its center, a single dark shape appeared, too small to visually make out any detail. "Can you identify that ship?" Vaughn asked.

"Negative," Bowers said. "There's nothing in the ship registry database that matches the configuration. It's relatively small, though. It probably has enough room for only a limited number of passengers."

"Assuming they're the size of typical humanoids," Vaughn said as the wormhole folded in on itself, vanishing as quickly as it had appeared.

"Yes, sir," Bowers acknowledged, somewhat sheepishly.

"Open a channel," Kira said.

"Channel open," said Lieutenant Ezri Dax from the communications station.

"This is Captain Kira Nerys of Deep Space Nine," she said. "Please identify yourself."

As they all waited for a response, Vaughn walked over to stand beside the captain. They looked at each other as the silence extended. Vaughn couldn't help but think that the sudden appearance from the Gamma Quadrant of an unknown vessel might have something to do with their suddenly unreachable communications relay.

"No response, Captain," Dax said.

"What's their course?" Vaughn wanted to know.

"Not for the station," Bowers said. "It looks as though they're headed for Bajor."

"This is Captain Kira," she repeated. "Identify yourself and state your business in this system or face the consequences."

"Captain, the wormhole is opening up again," Bowers called. Vaughn gazed back up at the screen to see the wormhole spin back open. He saw another small, dark shape appear in its center. "The second ship has a configuration similar to the first," Bowers said, consulting his readouts. "It is following the same course." Again, the wormhole collapsed down to a point and disappeared.

Vaughn considered the obvious implication. "Is it in pursuit of the first ship?" he asked.

"Possibly," Bowers said. "I'll scan for weapons—" The tactical officer stopped in midsentence as the great whirlpool of the wormhole rotated open once more. Vaughn watched along with the captain and the rest of the crew in Ops as two more ships appeared, and then five more, and then more than he could count.

Vaughn felt Kira's hand on his arm. "Get to the *Defiant*," she said. As he ran toward the lift, he heard the captain's next orders. "Red alert. We're under attack."

The story continues in
Star Trek: Deep Space Nine®
Ascendance

Acknowledgments

When I finally reach the end of a novel, my gratitude always harks back to its beginning, to the people who started it on its way in the first place. My editors, Margaret Clark and Ed Schlesinger, shepherd the entire *Star Trek* literary line, for which I am thankful, both as a writer and as a reader. I am always grateful for the opportunities they afford me. Margaret and Ed know their jobs and do them well, and their fine stewardship of *Trek* in print reflects their professionalism, along with their understanding and affinity for the material. I appreciate their support and assistance.

I also want to thank the many writers who have contributed to the *Deep Space Nine* story line through the years, and in particular to the mythos of the Ascendants. Since S. D. Perry first introduced the formidable silver aliens in *Rising Son*, they have appeared in one form or another in David Mack's *Warpath* and Olivia Woods' *The Soul Key*. Thanks for keeping the tale alive.

Thanks also to my friends and fellow *Star Trek* scribes Kirsten Beyer and David Mack. In recent years, I've gotten to spend time with the two of them, both on a personal and professional basis. They are good friends and good writers, and I am grateful to have them in my life.

For me, writing a novel is an enormous undertaking, one which I could never hope to complete without the love and support of so many people. Colleen Ragan is one of those people, a touchstone for me when it comes to the definition of family. She is smart, talented, and funny, a beautiful woman with a big heart.

I am also fortunate for the presence in my life of Walter Ragan. He is, quite simply, a good man, who sets a fine example by virtue of his honesty and integrity, his caring and support. Many people feel cursed by their in-laws; I hit the jackpot.

Anita Smith is yet another shining example of the wonderful people I have around me. Only newly an in-law, she has long been an "in-reality," but I am delighted that the designation is finally official. Anita has a loving, sharing, supportive spirit. She is quick to smile, to lend a helping hand, or simply to enjoy life. Anita is a lovely woman who improves the lives of everybody around her.

Thanks also to my sister, Jennifer George, for so many things. It would take far too long to list all that Jenn has added to my life. In addition to being the best sister for which a brother could hope, she is also an impressive woman of many accomplishments. Jennifer continually makes me proud, although I long ago ceased to be surprised when she does.

I am also deeply grateful to Patricia Walenista. A fine woman with a keen mind and an insatiable curiosity, she always provides a great example of how to perceive, travel, and investigate the world. After all these years, I still look to her for unparalleled love and guidance.

Finally, as always, there is the Divine Ms. K. For a man as loquacious as me, it is staggering to realize that there are insufficient words to express what Karen Ragan-George means to me. She is a bright light in the darkness, a warm fire in the cold, sweet music in the silence. I could not accomplish whatever I do without Karen by my side, nor would I want to. Her love elevates me. Beautiful, brilliant, hysterically funny, compassionate, forgiving, artistic, and talented, Karen is the shining center of my universe, and I could not be happier for it.

About the Author

Sacraments of Fire marks David R. George III's fifteenth novel set in the *Star Trek* universe. He has most often contributed to the *Deep Space Nine* story line, with *The 34th Rule*, *Twilight*, *Olympus Descending*, *Rough Beasts of Empire*, *Plagues of Night*, *Raise the Dawn*, and *Revelation and Dust*. He also penned the *Crucible* trilogy—*Provenance of Shadows*, *The Fire and the Rose*, and *The Star to Every Wandering*—an original series set of tales that helped celebrate the fortieth anniversary of the television show, as well as *Allegiance in Exile*, which takes place during the final part of *Enterprise*'s five-year mission. Additionally, David has written a pair of *Lost Era* novels, *Serpents Among the Ruins* and *One Constant Star*, as well as an *LE* novella, *Iron and Sacrifice*, which appeared in the *Tales from the Captain's Table* anthology. He also provided an alternate-universe *Next Generation* novel, *The Embrace of Cold Architects*, for the *Myriad Universes*: *Shattered Light* collection.

David first wrote in the *Trek* universe for television, with a *Voyager* episode titled "Prime Factors." He has also written nearly twenty magazine articles about the shows and books. Of his non-*Star Trek* work, his novelette "Moon Over Luna" is available on Amazon.com, and another novelette, "The Dark Arts Come to Hebron," appears in a genre anthology called *Apollo's Daughters*. His work has appeared on both the *New York Times* and *USA Today* bestseller lists, and his television episode was nominated for a *SciFi Universe* award.

An unrepentant (and unrewarded) New York Mets fan,

David loves to play baseball and racquetball. With his wife, he also enjoys traveling, watching movies, and dancing. He and Karen live in Los Angeles, where they expect that some combination of global climate change and California earthquakes will eventually give them oceanfront property.

You can contact David at facebook.com/DRGIII, and you can follow him on Twitter @DavidRGeorgeIII.